TO ROBIN MATHEWS,
SIR. YOU WERE MY ONLY
ADVISOR ON THIS PROJECT.
YOU GAVE ME BOTH GOOD
ADVICE AND A SENSE OF
CREDIBILITY IN MY WRITING
WHICH ALLOWED ME TO
(FINALLY!) FINISH IT. I THANK
YOU. HERE IS THE RESULT.
FOR WHAT IT'S WORTH...

Dale Burkholder

Looking for God

IN THE FOREST

DALE BURKHOLDER

Order this book online at www.trafford.com
or email orders@trafford.com

Most Trafford titles are also available at major online book retailers.

Printed in the United States of America.

ISBN: 978-1-4669-9424-9 (sc)
ISBN: 978-1-4669-9426-3 (hc)
ISBN: 978-1-4669-9425-6 (e)

Library of Congress Control Number: 2013908500

Trafford rev. 06/03/2013

 www.trafford.com

North America & international
toll-free: 1 888 232 4444 (USA & Canada)
phone: 250 383 6864 ♦ fax: 812 355 4082

*C*ivilisation is a stream with banks. The stream is sometimes filled with blood from people killing, stealing, shouting and doing the things historians usually record; while on the banks people build homes, make love, raise children, sing songs, write poetry, and even whittle statues. The story of civilisation is the story of what happened on the banks. Historians are pessimists because they ignore the banks for the stream

WILL DURANT

This book is dedicated to my favourite storyteller, Tom Waits. I hope my story will resonate with my readers in the same way that Tom's songs have always resonated with me. Thanks, Tom.

CONTENTS

1952: TRADITIONAL VALUES 1

1958: PROGRESS 37

1959: CURTAIN CALL FOR THE TRADITIONAL WORLD . .91

1960: PASTOR BILLY WILSON AND THE BOMB 157

1962: JOHN F. KENNEDY AND THE CUBAN MISSILE
      CRISIS 212

1963: TRADITIONAL VALUES REVISITED 280

1952: TRADITIONAL VALUES

One o'clock on a Sunday August summer's day; the city swelters in the stillness and the heat. It is the Lord's day, the day of rest. The streets for the most part are quiet and empty.

At the corner of Main Street and Fourth Avenue, the traffic light which hangs suspended from a heavy cable above the centre of the intersection changes on each of its four separate faces; from green to yellow to red, from red to green. It hangs there changing, unobserved except perhaps for the three fat pigeons that are feeding on something scattered beneath it on the road.

On the north-west corner of the street, behind a lawn the size of a quarter of a city block, a big white building sits quiet in the sunlight. It is an imposing structure, somehow commanding to the ranks of the two storey worn brick houses that fall into line on either side. Once it had been an opera hall, built in an earlier era for some forgotten patron of the arts.

Ten wide stone steps spanning the front of the building lead up to a broad expanse of dark stone flagging, where three tiers of immense marble columns two storeys tall support the classical portico which shelters the entrance from the elements. Between the rows of columns, two sets of heavy brass bound double oak doors stand closed and silent.

This building wears a worn look about it too, the look of time passed by. The lawn stretches away burnt and frowsy with dandelion spores to the street. The hedge which borders it on two sides is straggly and full of dead wood. The line of the hedge is broken and gapped in places with smooth brown passages worn into the earth. A few tired

1

rose bushes bear mute testimony to the beauty which might once have been there, dropping their dried out petals onto otherwise empty beds.

At the edge of the lawn, where the sidewalk leading up to the steps begins, a white wooden display case with a padlocked glass front bears a message in bold black letters to the world passing by.

The message reads,

> SEEK YE FIRST THE KINGDOM OF GOD
> AND ALL THESE OTHER THINGS
> SHALL BE ADDED UNTO YOU.

This verse, taken from the Scriptures, is the text for the Morning Worship Service; the old opera hall is now the House of God, the home of the First Baptist Church.

Inside the church, the Preacher has concluded his sermon. The choir has just now finished singing the closing hymn. The Preacher stands before the congregation, a tall silver-haired man in a plain grey suit. His smile seems to radiate some inner serenity. The last chord from the organ fades away. He raises his hands, palms pressed together in the attitude of prayer, the gesture familiar to one and all.

Then, in the hushed expectant stillness, with every eye closed and every head bowed, the Preacher closes his own eyes and begins to speak to God.

"Father, we thank You for bringing us together once again, and for Your Presence here among us; as it is written, 'Where two or three are gathered in My Name, there I will be also'."

"We thank You for Your infinite love and Your infinite mercy, in which You have given back to Brother Sorenson his wife and to little Nels his mother. We thank You for the joy of a new life, a baby girl, which You have given to this family to bless them. We pray that You will watch over Sister Sorenson and the child and keep them safe from harm."

"Now, as we leave here to return to our homes, we ask of You that Your Presence may go with each and every one of us, to keep us safe and to guide us."

"For Thine is the Kingdom and the Power and the Glory; forever and ever. Amen."

It is a mighty prayer, delivered with the humble eloquence of one who truly believes. The congregation sits in silence, with eyes still closed, feeling the love of God warm and comforting in their hearts. A few quiet and yet passionate 'Amens' drift on the air.

The Preacher stands, head bowed, a moment longer. Four big older men—the deacons of the church—are up and moving on silent feet to open the wooden doors, fingers reaching to loosen collars damp with perspiration in the heat of the day. The organist strikes up the opening notes of a lively Southern spiritual—'Shall We Gather At The River?' A shuffle and the murmur of voices begins, tentative at first and then growing like the sound of the River itself as the Preacher turns away from the simple wooden lectern, Bible in hand, and goes out through a doorway at the side of the stage.

The congregation is up and on its feet. At this very moment it is good to be alive. Men shake hands over the backs of the pews, in the manner of Baptists. Women in flowery print dresses smile shyly at each other and fuss over hungry little girls and boys. The people begin to move out into the aisles and down the wide staircase which leads from the balcony. Parents shield small children in the press, some grasped firmly to keep them from bolting on limbs grown restless from inertia, stomachs craving sustenance.

Teenaged boys in suits and ties lead the advance, to run the gauntlet of bone-crushing handshakes from the deacons at the doors—a slight gesture of disapproval for their haste—and then to take up the best positions at the bottom of the steps to watch for pretty teenaged girls in dresses and stockings with stern-faced fathers looking on.

The elderly linger on in their seats, with the patience of those who are close enough to the end of their days to know no reason to hurry in this world any more. White-haired old men in ancient black suits with white-haired old women who smell faintly of lavender: the old women with their seamed and wrinkled faces creased into smiles, delighting in the passage of a common humanity, perhaps remembering children of their own, long since grown, in the pink scrubbed faces going by them in the aisles. The old men with gnarled and bony hands clutched firmly to the backs of the pews in front of them, oblivious to the throng; heads still bowed and eyes pressed firmly closed; making their peace with Almighty God.

The people flood out through the wide double doors, a torrent of talking gesturing humanity flowing down over the stone steps and forming one swirling pool of colour and sound on the brittle yellow grass of the lawn. The sharp odour of sweat mingles with the subtle fragrances of dusting powders. The pigeons wheel and soar high overhead in the hot bright afternoon sky.

Six red city buses, each bearing the word 'Special' above the windshield approach the intersection; three from the north, three more from the south. The buses form up into lines beside the yellow bus stops.

The crowd on the lawn begins to melt away under the blazing summer sun; some walking to the east or to the west along Main Street, some to the north or the south along Fourth Avenue. The majority board the waiting buses which will carry them home. There are perhaps twenty automobiles in the small parking lot. It is a working class congregation for the most part and this particular version of prosperity has yet to become commonplace in this part of the city.

The music stops. The crowd that was there only moments before has disappeared. The buses close their doors and move away in a shimmering haze of pale blue exhaust. The tires of the last car to leave make a crunching sound on the gravel of the parking lot. Then it is gone. The hot afternoon stillness settles down once more upon the street.

In the high dim quiet of the empty hall, the presence of God lingered on in the air. There were no religious relics to conjure it up; no crucifixes hung from the walls, no suffering Christs, no stained glass portraits with little lambs—no graven images. There was only the plain wooden lectern on the empty stage.

On the wall behind the stage there was a large mural done in soft colours of a familiar scene, a wooded stream, which was as close to seeing the River Jordan as either the congregation or the artist who had painted it had ever been. The stream flowed down through slender pines and white birches to form a secluded sunlit pool in the foreground.

Directly in front of the pool, a concealed rectangular water tank had been set into the stage. There were steps leading down to its flat bottom. Here, twice each year, the Preacher, dressed in a plain white cotton shift and seemingly up to his waist in the clear flowing stream performed the ritual immersion in water after the manner of his predecessor, John the Baptist, of some twenty centuries before, through which the faithful were brought into His church.

This is all.

For the young man sitting in the pew it is enough. His name is John Sorenson and he has seen twenty-nine summers, but the presence of God has never been so real to him as it is on this day. He sits there, gazing up with distant eyes at the mural of the forest and the stream, unmindful for the moment of every other thing, including his son Nels, who sits beside him.

His dark complexion is accentuated by his cheap black suit. The evidence of strong emotion and of the absence of sleep show in the smudges under his eyes and in the patches of stubble that the razor missed along the contour of his jaw. But his brown eyes are clear and his lips and the line of his brow are calm and relaxed. There is an aura of inner peace and of quiet strength about him.

It is this man on whose behalf the Preacher had offered up the special prayer of thanks at the close of this morning's service; this man whose wife and new daughter, only hours old, lay recovering in the critical care ward of the city hospital, battered by a violent and premature delivery.

For this man, on this day, there is no room for either fear or doubt. In the small hours of the morning, John Sorenson had asked the Almighty for a miracle. He made a silent promise in return. The miracle has been performed. Now he sits there lost in wonder of what has been done, secure in the knowledge of what he is about to do.

At his side a child with hair the colour of sun bleached summer straw sits caught by his father's stillness. He glances up at him with bright blue serious eyes, wanting to ask a question yet somehow held back.

The little boy is puzzled by what the Preacher said in the prayer. His father has told him that his Mother and his new baby sister are sick and that they are at some place called the Hospital.

He does not understand what the Preacher meant when he said that God had given his mother back because she is not here. It was the Doctor and his Auntie Sal who had come in the night and taken her away.

So many strange new things to wonder about: the shapes and sounds in his memory of his mother crying out in the night waking him, as if she were hurt and his father's voice on the telephone. The Doctor coming with his big black bag, and then his Auntie Sal, all out of breath. The two big men carrying his mother on the bed with handles, seen through the crack of his bedroom door.

The Doctor and Auntie Sal holding her hands and talking softly to her as they took her away.

Then the knock on the door and the Preacher was there! Watching, willing himself not to sleep while his Daddy and the Preacher sat with together with their heads bowed at the table and the Preacher talked to God, right there, in the kitchen!

Then it was morning. The Preacher was gone. His Daddy was waking him and hugging him so tight it almost hurt. His Daddy's face was wet with tears, the way that Poppy's face had been the day that the car ran over Tiny, Poppy's dog.

The first thing that he asked for was Kitty. His father had gone and gotten the orange cat and put it on the bed and smiled, all unknowing at the relief in his child's blue eyes.

His father stirred and stretched a little beside him, breaking the spell. He reached out and tugged at his sleeve, wanting to ask his question.

"Daddy?"

John Sorenson looked around and down at his son. He smiled self-consciously, aware for the first time that everyone else was gone.

"Yes Nels."

But the thought was gone, vanished into the present. He said instead,

"What were you looking at Daddy?"

"I was looking at the picture of the forest, son."

He pointed to the painting, as if to show the boy what he had seen.

"Daddy?"

"Yes Nels?"

"Will you take me to see the Forest?"

An image came, to John Sorenson, of the forests of his youth. He felt a sudden urgent need to be out among the trees.

"Yes Nels. I'll take you to the forest. Real soon. Okay?"

"Yeah!"

He smiled to see the child's blue eyes light up with anticipation.

"Let's go home now."

Nels Sorenson was instantly up and gone, moving away in the space in front of the pew at as close to a run as a child can walk and disappearing into the aisle where only the top of his blond head showed above the line of wooden benches.

He rose to his feet, shaking his head at his son's speed.

"Wait for me Nels . . ."

He called out to the boy softly, reluctant to disturb the stillness. He took one last lingering glance at the forest and the stream. Then he made his way across and into the aisle.

The boy reached up and took his father's hand, the urge to run disappearing as quickly as it had come in the sudden desire to be very very close to him. He looked down, measuring the steps of his small blue shoes on the worn soft carpet against his father's big black ones. He felt very good.

The Preacher stood waiting for them, framed in the doorway with the sun at his back. The Preacher was a big man, taller than his father. He reminded the boy of Walker, who he called Poppy, the old Army officer who boarded at Auntie Sal's house.

The Preacher was always smiling. The only time the Preacher stopped smiling was when he talked about the Devil. The boy thought the Devil must be very bad, if even the Preacher got angry with him.

The Preacher saw the quiet strength in the young man smiling back at him, albeit a little self-consciously. John Sorenson was a shy man at heart, a man not accustomed to much attention. The Preacher held out his hand to him.

"Hello John. It's good to see you. How are you feeling?"

"Good thank you Pastor."

The two men shook hands warmly, as two men will who have shared the watch through the night when a life hangs in the balance.

The Preacher turned to look down at the boy's face looking expectantly up at him. He bent his knees, his back held straight, squatting on his heels until he was as close to eye level with the child as his height would allow. He held out his hand to the boy.

"Hello Nels."

The boy reached out and wrapped his hand around two big fingers and shook the Preacher's hand, the way his father had taught him to do.

"Hello Sir."

The Preacher smiled at him, taking the boy's small hand in both of his big hands.

"Do you miss your mother Nels?"

He felt a sudden anxiousness. The smile fled from his face.

"Yes Sir. My mommy's sick and so's my new baby sister. They're at the Hos-pi-tal."

He said the new word slowly, wanting to say it right for the Preacher.

"That's all right son. Your mom and your new baby sister will be all better soon. Then they'll come home to be with you."

He looked into the kind grey eyes, his anxiousness turning back to curiosity.

"Did my Daddy tell you?"

"No son. God told me."

The boy's face lit up with pleasure, accepting what the Preacher said without question. God and the Preacher were friends, and God knew everything.

"Why don't you go and play for a minute Nels? I want to talk to your Dad."

He looked around and up to his father for permission.

"Can I Daddy?"

"Sure son. Just take it easy going down the steps."

"Okay Daddy."

The Preacher took his hands away and straightened up to his full height. Nels Sorenson was already gone, out of the doorway and across the stone flagging, heading for the freedom of the lawn. Both men turned to watch him take the steps.

"That's quite a boy you've got there John. You must be proud of him."

A shy smile played across the younger man's face.

"We are Pastor—we are. But I have to admit he's a trial to his mother sometimes. He's always getting hurt because he goes so fast. It's all a person can do to get him to go to sleep at night. I don't know how Marg'll manage with two of them."

The boy crossed the sidewalk and crouched down at the edge of the lawn, staring intently at something on the ground.

"Bright children are always a trial John. But the rewards of watching them grow and learn are greater still."

"Yes Pastor. I guess you're right about that."

He reached up and ran a finger beneath the unaccustomed tightness of his collar. Sweat was beginning to bead on his throat.

"Sure is warm today eh Pastor?"

"Yes. I expect if must be over ninety degrees."

The Preacher turned to look at the young man beside him.

"Have you heard any more from the hospital?"

He saw the look of wonder flash up and grow in the younger man's eyes. The words came tumbling out, his shyness forgotten and the heat.

"They're going to be all right Pastor. I called and talked to the Doctor just before we came for the service. Marg was sleeping and the baby's in an incubator. As far as they can tell the baby's all right . . ."

He paused, aware of the Preacher's eyes watching his, trying to control the feelings that came swelling up inside of him.

"The Doctor said it's a miracle. The baby wasn't due for two months yet. I guess they nearly lost both of them . . . the Doctor said I could come and see them when they wake Marg up at supper time . . ."

"Do you believe in miracles John?"

"Yes Preacher. I do now. I don't know what I'd have done if you hadn't come—"

He felt the tightening in his throat and the pressure of released emotion behind his eyes. He turned his face away, afraid that he was going to cry in front of the Preacher.

"It wasn't me John. I'm only God's servant. I go where He tells me I'm needed. Last night you prayed for a miracle. The Lord answered your prayer. He was there with us and with your wife in her time of need, because He loves us. Do you believe that now?"

John Sorenson looked back into the quiet grey eyes, unmindful of the single tear that coursed down each cheek. He felt a great stillness settle over him.

"Yes Preacher. I believe that now."

The Preacher knew that there was nothing more that needed to be said. He smiled and patted the younger man on the shoulder.

"I wonder where that boy of yours has gotten to?"

He turned away to look. John Sorenson wiped hastily at his cheeks with the back of his hand, grateful for the kindness.

Nels Sorenson was crouched down, watching a column of red ants which were busily dismembering the ragged carcass of a yellow butterfly.

The Preacher turned back to the younger man beside him.

"Will I see you at the service tonight?"

"Yes Pastor. I may be a little late, after the hospital . . ."

"That's fine, John. We have a prayer meeting before the evening service. We'll be praying for your wife and your child tonight. Tell Margaret that our prayers are with her."

"I will Pastor—thank you."

"If you'll excuse me, I should go now. I have some visiting to do this afternoon."

"Sure Pastor."

"Until this evening John."

They shook hands once more. The Preacher waited, watching from the doorway as the young man in the black suit crossed the stone flagging and went down the steps to join his son. Then he began to close the heavy wooden doors.

The boy was still absorbed in the microcosm of the ants. He looked up, sensing his father bending over him.

"What are you looking at Nels?"

"Ants Daddy. See them?"

"Yes Nels. There's sure a lot of them."

"Yes Daddy. Lots and lots."

"Let's go home."

He reached up and took his Daddy's hand, the world of ants already forgotten, drawn once more into the spell of his father's stillness.

They walked away down Fourth Avenue hand in hand, walking downhill into one of the oldest districts of the city. Tiny bubbles of liquid black tar glistened on the surface of the road. The concrete sidewalk smouldered beneath their feet. Past one long searing block and partway down another, they turned left into a narrow strip of road between the walls of two brick houses, the entrance to the street barely wide enough to accommodate the horse-drawn wagon which brought milk to the families who lived there.

John Sorenson paused on the inside of the passage, looking around at the street. There were the familiar rows of single storey grey brick houses pressed close together—five houses on the left, four on the right—which faced each other across the narrow road. The last house on the left looked down an unpaved lane which ran at 90° to the road, emerging into the cross street.

A high steel fence with a wide steel gate separated the street and the lane from the paved and pitted surface of the school yard beyond it. The school itself, an ancient ugly three-storey brick monstrosity with its blackened and rusted fire escapes trailing from its sides stood away across on the far side of the school yard where it fronted onto the next street. Only the line of big maple trees which flanked the lane kept the school from resembling a prison.

There were times when he had felt caged up here. He never mentioned it to Marg, although he knew she sometimes sensed it when the mood was upon him. He would not have known how to explain it to her. She was born here. The city—and especially this part of it—was the only place that she had ever known. He was grateful for the life he had and he was not given to brooding about the things he could not change. It was only a feeling, an uneasiness, something to be warded off on the days that it crept up on him.

John Sorenson was neither city born nor city bred. It was the railroad and the work that it provided that had brought him to the city. It was the Irish woman he had fallen in love with and married who had wanted to make a home for them here.

Margaret Murphy, when he had first met her, was the youngest daughter of a big close-knit Irish family. The house where she and two brothers and three sisters had all been raised was only one more block away on the other side of the school yard. Her mother had passed on, but her father still lived in his house with one son and his wife and their first child. Of all of Harry Murphy's offsprings, only the other son—who had married a farm girl and discovered a talent for farming—lived beyond an eight block radius of the old family home.

The Murphy clan, for its part, had accepted him unquestioningly into the course of its day-to-day life. Especially Sally, the sister who was closest to his wife. He had become very fond of Sally. The woman was a dynamo, an irrepressible source of warmth and good humour.

Sally had married young and had been widowed by the war and left to raise two children. She had not remarried, although she was a fine figure of a woman. She worked afternoon shift as a waitress in a downtown restaurant. As often as not her children, Danny and Sandy, took their evening meal at the Sorenson household.

The closeness between the two sisters was something that was beyond his own experience. He had instinctively dialed Sally's number as soon as he had hung up from calling the Doctor. He was glad that she had been there with Marg the night before. His sense of male helplessness had been overpowering.

He smiled, lost in the thought of the woman he loved and the daughter he had not seen yet. The sun shone down on the ageing silent houses, on the hollyhocks and the lily-of-the-valley which grew up in the narrow spaces between them. The street was home to him as he stood there, seeing it with changed eyes.

"Grampa! Grampa!"

Nels was yanking on his hand and pointing urgently at his grandfather's hump-backed grey Plymouth parked at the curb in front of their house. Harry Murphy always had a pocketful of humbugs for his numerous grandchildren. The boy's eyes pleaded for his release. He smiled and let go of his hand.

"Go get him Nels."

The boy went pelting away up the sidewalk, past the first house, past the second, pounding up the steps of his own house and across the verandah, now pulling in frustration at the handle of the locked front door, now pounding back down the steps and disappearing into the passage between the brick walls of the houses yelling "Grampa!

Grampa!", shattering the Sunday silence as he flung himself into the tiny back yard.

The back door was locked too. There was no one there. He hesitated, confused for a minute, robbed of his momentum. Then he turned and ran again, headlong into his father's legs as he came around the corner of the house. He went sprawling full length on the grass and slid to a stop on his front.

John Sorenson sighed an all too familiar sigh and went to pick up his son. Nels was already scrambling to his feet and brushing heedlessly at the green stain on the front of his white sailor top.

"There's no one here Daddy!"

"You've got to slow down, Nels, and learn to look where you're going."

"Yes Daddy. Why is Grampa's car here? Where's Grampa?"

"I don't know son."

He took out his keys and unlocked the door and held it open for his son.

"Now go in and get out of your good clothes and we'll see what we can do with them. Your mother'll scalp the both of us if she sees that grass stain."

He said, "Yes Daddy" and slipped by him, running again on quick light feet through the length of the house to stand on tiptoe staring out through the window at Grampa's car in the street.

John Sorenson followed his son through the back porch, past the kitchen and into the dining room, the dimmer light soothing his eyes after the glare of the walk home. Nel's bedroom door was open. No signs of activity came from beyond it.

"Are you changing your clothes like I asked you to Nels?"

"Yes Daddy."

The boy went running past him into his room, tugging the white shirt over his head.

"Slow down son . . ."

He sighed again and turned towards the table, seeing the piece of white paper and the silver key that lay there.

It was a note from Sally. She had been there while they were at church. She said that she would be back at four o'clock, to make him some supper and pack a few things to take to Marg. Nels could stay with her until things got settled. The key was for the Plymouth which Harry had said he didn't need for a few days.

He put the note back down and looked at the key, the mural in the church returning in his mind together with the promises he had made.

"Nels!"

The boy came running barefoot, no shirt on and a pair of play pants hanging open.

"Yes Daddy?"

He bent down, reaching automatically to do up the zipper.

"How would you like to go and see the forest?"

"When Daddy?"

"Now Nels! Right now! Today!"

"Yeah!"

The boy turned and bolted for the door.

John Sorenson laughed, a great shout of pleasure.

"Whoa boy!"

Nels stopped in his tracks and looked back to his father.

"I mean as soon as you've finished dressing and you've had some lunch."

He ran back and grabbed his father's hand and tried to pull him to the door.

"Let's go now Daddy! Please? I'm not hungry"

"In a minute, Nels. Now go and get dressed while I make us some lunch."

He pushed the boy gently towards his bedroom door and stripped of his suit coat and tie, leaving them discarded on the back of a chair.

Peanut butter sandwiches were hastily assembled. Nels, for all his protests of not being hungry ate two of them and washed them down with two cold glasses of milk.

At last the back door was closed and locked. John Sorenson eased the big grey Plymouth down the narrow lane and out onto the street with the boy staring excitedly around on the seat beside him. The tires made a sticky hiss on the soft tar in the road.

"Are we going to get Mommy and my new baby sister and take them to see the Forest too?"

"No son. This is just for us boys."

He felt a pang of guilt at the realization that they had slipped from his thoughts in his urgency to be gone. Nels smiled and said, "Okay Daddy," his attention immediately absorbed again in the street going by beside them.

He settled back, concentrating on the infrequent task of driving his father-in-law's car.

They drove through two short blocks and turned left onto Main Street, heading east with the sun behind them. Past the rows of old stores with their faded signs, driving carefully, glancing now and then at his son squirming around on the seat and trying to look at everything.

Past the fairgrounds and the race track; past more small shops scattered in among the houses and over the tracks, where the factories stood abandoned with only trickles of smoke emerging from their chimneys to show that they were alive, waiting for Monday morning. Past the factories, driving uphill past a continuous flow of houses, the lawns becoming broader and the light dappled with shadow from the big shady trees along the boulevards.

Nels turned round, kneeling on the seat to look back the way that they had come. He shut his eyes against the flickering light on the rear window and was caught by the patterns and colours that streamed across his closed eyelids. When he opened his eyes and turned round again the houses were all gone, replaced by fields of tanned wheat and tall green corn. It seemed to him that they had gone a very long way.

He pointed to the stand of trees close by on the horizon,

"Are we there yet Daddy?"

"Almost Nels."

John Sorenson slowed and swung the big car onto the gravel of a side road.

Nels stood up, off the seat altogether now, straining forward against the dash to stare out through the windshield.

"Is it the Forest Daddy?"

The boy's voice was filled with a childish awe. And his father, although he knew that the vast deciduous forests which had once stood here had vanished forever, and that what lay ahead would be a few acres of some farmer's wood lot said,

"Yes Nels. It's the Forest."

They drove slowly down the gravel road with a white dust cloud billowing out behind them, coating the blue bachelor's buttons and the white milkweed and the goldenrod which grew in rich profusion along the edges of the fields. Butterflies in myriad colours swarmed above the flowers. The big brown locusts went whirring away from the hot stones in front of the car, soaring in long curved trajectories of flight into the walls of corn on either side. Ahead of them the Forest grew larger.

They reached the end of the fields where the trees began. They crossed over a wooden bridge above a creek bed hidden in willows and alder. Beyond the bridge a worn track led off the road to a rough wooden gate and beyond that into the trees.

John Sorenson nosed the Plymouth in to the gate and shut the motor off. He sat back listening, breathing the scented air. Somewhere in the silence, a redwing blackbird sang.

He opened the car door and stepped out, beckoning Nels to slide across the seat and out under the steering wheel. The gate was tied shut with a piece of rope. He opened the gate and stepped through with his son, turning back to tie it again. They walked into the Forest hand in hand.

A black squirrel fretted and chattered above their heads, clinging upside down to the smooth grey bark of a beech tree. A blue jay flew out ahead of them, screeching its warning cry. John Sorenson found himself in a familiar element. It came to him that it had been a long long time.

They walked along looking up at the trees, walking slowly, pausing before each one. He knew their names at a single glance, pronouncing them out loud for his son, letting the boy feel the rough bark with his hands. A memory came, of how he had learned the game of naming the different types of wood in a pile of saw logs with his eyes closed and only the tips of his fingers and his sense of smell to guide him.

A startled rabbit burst from its cover and went bounding away into the underbrush. He stopped to show his son the pile of rounded droppings where the cottontail had been feeding. A few feet away a sapling brought back another memory. He took a pocketknife out and cut a twig from it and put the cut end in his mouth. There was a sharp remembered taste of spearmint.

He cut another twig and gave it to Nels, watching his face as he caught the flavour.

"Like it son?"

The boy smiled around the bit of wood.

"Yes Daddy—it's good."

"It's bush candy. That's what I had for candy when I was young."

He began to feel the heaviness of his limbs and the closeness of the heat. He looked and saw the child's tiredness in the way he was dragging his feet.

"Are you getting tired son?"

The boy forced his blue eyes too far open.

"No Daddy—I'm not sleepy."

He smiled at his son and bent to pick him up.

"It's okay Nels. We don't have to go home right away. Maybe we should look for a place and sit down for a bit. What do you say?"

The blond head nodded gravely, tired and grateful.

He looked around and caught the sparkle of light reflecting on water, close by, through the trees. He turned towards it, stepping off the track and then sidestepping to avoid a pile of fresh cow dung beneath a mass of shiny blue flies.

"What's that Daddy?"

"Cow poop."

The little boy giggled at the sound of the word.

"Cow poop!"

"That's enough son."

"Yes Daddy."

He followed the trail the cattle had left into a dense copse of cedar. They came out of the trees onto the edge of a flooded meadow where beavers had dammed the stream. A dozen cows and calves stood cooling their fetlocks in the shallow water at the edge of the pond. The cattle looked around, big brown eyes nervous at the approach of an intruder. One by one the matted beasts waded ashore, to disappear in single file into the bush.

To the boy they were huge, staring at them passing by.

"What are they Daddy?'

"They're cows, son."

"Will they hurt me?"

"No son. Only bulls."

"What are bulls, Daddy?"

"Never mind son. There's none here."

He carried his son to the edge of the pond and sat him down in the grass in the shade of a willow tree. The air above the surface water shimmered with the heat. The jewelled dragonflies were everywhere.

He sat down in the grass beside his son and rested his back against the willow tree. He put his arm around the boy and drew him close.

"Are you comfortable, Nels?"

"Yes, Daddy."

The child's limbs were limp, like a puppy. His eyelids were heavy, but the blue eyes were still alert.

John Sorenson raised his eyes to the pond. All of the knowledge of his youth was revealed to him in the signs. He saw the weathered tangle of branches that formed the dam; saw where the grasses had taken root in patches of old earth on top of it and the gap where the heavy spring runoff had broken through it on one side. This, together with the thick growth of tall poplar trees on the far side of the meadow told him that the beavers had been gone for a long time. The dam and the pond remained, a tribute to their craftsmanship.

There was more—much more. A bittern stood frozen against a clump of bulrushes, the colours of its plumage blending perfectly with its background. The long slender neck and the spear of its beak were thrust upward, with only the bright yellow eye to give the bird away. A trout rose to pluck a struggling insect from the surface, leaving a single round ripple to widen out and disappear. Close by, the trunk of a fallen tree sloped down into the water. There were piles of droppings on it to show him where the painted turtles came to bask in the sun.

"Would you like to see something very special Nels?"

He whispered the words. The boy's eyes widened sensing a secret.

"Please Daddy . . ."

"You'll have to sit still and not talk, like we do in church. Okay?"

Again the whisper. The boy nodded his head.

"Look at the tree where it's laying in the water."

He pointed with his hand to show him where to look.

Four pointed reptilian snouts pierced the surface all at once. The boy sucked in his breath in sudden wonder. One by one the painted turtles swam up the slope of the submerged log, the largest first, necks stretching forward to reveal their beady eyes and their gaudy red and yellow throats, their clawed feet clinging the bark as they climbed out into the hot sun.

John waited until the turtles were all in place. He moved his hand to point to the big green bullfrog that sat sunning itself on the bank. The boy could see the swelling of its pale cream-coloured throat and the bright yellow tympanum on the sides of its head. And its huge eyes!

The bullfrog gave a 'croak!' of alarm and launched itself, landing with a soft plop and burrowing into concealment beneath the lily pads. John looked around to see what had frightened it. Three feet of sinuous brown water snake rippled down the face of the dam and disappeared into the pond.

A bittern emerged from the reeds, reassured by this natural sequence of events. The bird's head came down, the snakelike neck assumed its fishing posture, ready to strike, staring at close range into the water as it waded. John watched, enrapt as the bird took one stiff slow motion step and then looked to see if its movement had disturbed some smaller creature. Another step.

The bird suddenly struck, the sharp bill flashing downward too fast for his eyes to follow. Then the bird was standing still again—except for the pair of webbed green feet protruding from its beak. The bird tossed its head—the feet were gone. The bittern settled into its fishing posture.

He looked down to see the expression on his son's face. The blue eyes were closed, the blond head settled down on the boy's small chest. He smiled and stretched his son out full length on the grass. He settled back against the base of the tree.

For a while he just sat studying the sleeping child's features, lost in thought. He thought about the woman he loved and the miracle that had happened, their new child. He thought about the night before, and of the promise that he had made.

A great quiet joy flooded through him. He knelt on the grass in the forest beside the stream and poured out his heart to God.

When he opened his eyes again a high thin veil of cloud had begun to creep across the sky. There was the sweet smell of rain in the air. He looked around at his son. Nels was watching him with sleepy blue eyes.

"Who were you talking to Daddy?"

"I was talking to God, son."

Nels Sorenson looked around, more asleep than awake but still wanting to know.

"Is this where God lives Daddy?"

"Yes Nels. This is where God lives."

Nels was asleep in his arms by the time he got back to the car. He was still asleep when he turned into the street and parked in front of the house. He lifted his son out of the car, careful not to wake him and carried him up the steps of the verandah. Sally opened the front door and smiled at them.

"Oh—hi Sally! Is it four o'clock already?"

"Just after. Here—let me take him John."

She reached out and lifted Nels from his arms and held him close.

"The hospital called. Marg's awake. She's asking for you."

"I've got to go Sal."

"Wait John. It's all right. They just called a minute ago. There's some things for her in that case beside the door. Do you want me to make you a sandwich before you go?"

He shook his head, bending to reach past her for the case and then straightening up to face her.

"No thanks Sal. I couldn't eat now."

"Off you go then. Give her my love."

"I will. Thanks Sal."

He turned away and was gone, hurrying down the steps towards the car.

The boy came awake to the sound of the car driving away. When he opened his eyes the forest was gone. Aunt Sally was holding him, carrying him into the house.

He smiled up at her.

"Hi Auntie Sal."

"Hi Honey. Did you have a good sleep?"

"Yes. Where's my Daddy?"

"He's gone to the hospital, to see your Mum."

The boy's face fell. He began to cry.

"I wanted to go too."

"I know you did Honey. I know. It's all right . . ."

She held him close and let him cry on her shoulder while she carried him to the couch and sat down with him. After a while he sat back and looked at her, rubbing the tears with his small fists.

"Why didn't Daddy take me?"

She smiled at him, to reassure him.

"The Doctor's don't let little boys come to the hospital unless they're sick Honey. The people in the hospital are all sick. The Doctors don't want little boys to get germs. You wouldn't want to get germs, would you?"

He considered this for a minute.

"What about my new baby sister? Won't she get germs?"

"No Honey. She has a very special bed. It's got windows all around it so the germs can't get in."

"Wow . . ."

He tried to imagine his new baby sister in the bed with windows all around it. Aunt Sally smoothed his hair and tickled him a little bit, just like Mum did. He giggled with pleasure, the hospital forgotten again.

"So where did you boys go today?"

His eyes got wide.

"We went to God's place!"

"Oh? Where is God's place Honey? At church?"

"No. It's far! Auntie Sal! It's at the Forest!"

"What did you see there?"

"We saw trees. Lots and lots. And we saw cows!"

"How would you like to come for supper and sleep over with your cousins? Then you can tell me all about it."

"Can I Auntie Sal?"

"Sure you can Honey. Let's go get you some pajamas."

"Can I get down?"

"Yes< Nels. You're getting heavy anyhow. You're getting to be a big boy."

"Yeah!"

He scrambled down off the couch and ran ahead of her into the bedroom. His pyjamas from the previous night were lying on the floor. He picked them up and brought them to her as she came into the bedroom. There were dogs of all kinds on the wallpaper.

"These ones Auntie Sal?"

"Let's see if there's some clean ones in your dresser. How about these ones, with the bears on them?"

"Yeah! They're my very favourite!"

"I guess that's all we need for now then."

"What about Kitty?"

"Kitty's had his supper. He's gone outside to play."

"Okay."

He waited at the edge of the porch while Aunt Sally locked the door. The wind had begun to rustle in the maple trees. Massive purple thunderheads loomed up into the afternoon sky.

"Will Poppy be there Auntie Sal?"

He turned to look up at her as they started down the steps.

"No Nels. It's Sunday. Walker's gone to visit his friends at the veteran's hospital. You'll be asleep by the time he gets home. You can talk to Poppy tomorrow."

"Are Poppy's friends sick too?"

"Sort of . . ."

He felt the sadness in her voice, although he did not understand it. Then it was gone in a brilliant flash of lighteing. The first clap of thunder blew away the silence of the street.

"It looks like it's going to rain. Do you think that we should run?"

"Yeah!"

"Come on Honey—I'll race you across the school yard!"

Walker awoke before it was light. There was no more sound of the rain. The air through the open window was fresh and sweet.

He lay still, coming back from the place that he had dreamed of to the narrow cot with the army trunk beside it, both long since familiar. He did not question this, any more that he questioned the fact that he woke each day an hour before the dawn. Thirty years of military service left marks which were indelible on a man.

He reached over and switched the lamp on. The worn khaki fatigues and the khaki shirt were folded neatly on top of the trunk. Aside from his boots and his socks on the floor, the only other object in the room was an 8 x 10 photograph in a stand-up frame on the trunk lid in the pool of lamplight.

The photograph was of a big handsome man in his thirties. He wore an army sergeant's uniform. He stood at ease, feet spread apart, his lips curved up into a careless Irish grin. On either side of him a massive king-boned Shepherd—military trained attack dogs—bared its fangs at the camera. His grin had been for the photographer, who had jokingly asked him if he could get the dogs to smile.

He pushed the sheet back and sat up. The right leg felt like it was filled with lead. He swung the left leg out over the edge, turning at the waist and using his big hands to lift the useless leg over the side. He held it beneath his thigh, lowering it slowly and bracing himself for the throb of pain that came when his heel touched the floor. He sat for awhile, supporting the leg and massaging the ache as the circulation began to return.

The photograph mocked him, sitting on the side of the bed holding his leg. He was still proud.

"Get up you old bastard."

He growled at himself, letting the leg look out for itself as he reached around for his trousers. He pulled them on and laced on his boots. Then he switched the lamp off and picked up his shirt, walking through the darkness to the bedroom door.

He opened the door and stepped through into the kitchen, closing it quietly behind him. The coffee pot was where Sally always left it for him, filled and on the front burner of the stove. He lit the flame and went into the bathroom to shave.

By the time Walker had finished shaving the coffee pot was percolating noisily. He switched off the bathroom light. The kitchen was still in darkness. He poured the first cup by the blue glow of the flame, not minding the grounds which had not had a chance to settle.

The pot went over the pilot light to keep it hot. He bent to light the first cigarette of the day and then switched the flame off, carrying his cup to the table in front of the window.

He missed the little terrier most this time of day, missed its quick bright energy. It still seemed strange that the death of the dog had affected him so much after all the dying he had seen. He told himself again, as he had told himself every day for the last two weeks, that he was too old to get another dog.

He put Tiny out of his mind, turning his thoughts to the river. The heavy rain the night before would have washed a lot of feed into the river. The black bass would be biting in the pool below the bridge. There would be a fish for this morning's breakfast.

He sat and smoked, savouring the strong black brew. When he had finished his second cup, a faint line of light had begun to appear behind the rooftops of the houses. The sky was pale blue.

He sensed rather than saw the first stirring of movement in the poultry coop beneath the mulberry tree. He rose and took the pail of vegetable peelings from under the sink. Then he opened the screen door and stepped out into the morning.

The boy awoke to the harsh crowing of the old man's rooster, hurling its challenge against the new day. The cock in the yard three yards down stretched its neck and screeched a reply. He lay still, bright eyes open, tingling with the primitive urgency of their cries.

The warm insistence of his bladder stirred him into motion. He turned his head watching Cousin Danny's face on the pillow. He slid his body backwards, out over the edge of the bed until his toes touched the floor. He straightened his back, barely daring to breathe until he was sure that Danny was still asleep.

The bedroom door was open. He hitched up his pyjamas and snuck towards it, sending his small animal awareness out ahead of him, listening to the house. The house was silent. He stepped out into the living room, frowning in concentration against the tickle of the carpet on the bottoms of his bare feet. Cautious steps carried him across the living room in the early light, on to the cool, white linoleum of the kitchen floor.

He stopped, staring at Poppy's door, his senses filling with the heavy man-smells of coffee and tobacco. Poppy's door was closed. He hesitated, a child's fear inside of him urging him back to the safety of the bedroom. Auntie Sal had told him that he must never bother Poppy when his door was closed. Poppy could turn into a bear!

The fullness of his bladder and his sense of shame at the thought of wetting himself overcame his fear. He crept forward, a study in concentration, balancing on one foot and watching his feet as he lifted the other foot and pressed his bare toes down ahead of him. He didn't dare to raise his eyes towards the forbidden door.

Walker stood outside on the step looking in, watching the boy with vast amusement. He opened the screened door silently and stepped into the kitchen.

"What are you doing up kid?"

Nels froze at the soft growl behind him.

"I have to pee Poppy."

The old man laughed, a low friendly rumble.

"It's okay kid. Go ahead."

Nels looked around shyly, smiling at once when he saw that it was Poppy and not a bear sitting there.

"Hi Poppy!"

"Good morning kid. Go and pee. Then you can come and talk to me."

"Yes Poppy."

He darted into the bathroom, already tugging down the bottoms of his pyjamas. Walker set the brown eggs in his hands into the sink. They were still warm, with bits of straw stuck on the shells.

"Wash your hands and face while you're in there kid."

"I can't reach Poppy."

"Never mind then."

There was one more cup of coffee left in the pot. He got up and filled his cup and carried it to the table. Beyond the window the world was filling rapidly with light.

Nels came out of the bathroom all tousled hair and pink cheeks, beaming with pleasure at being allowed into the old man's company. He crossed the kitchen at a half trot and stood looking up at him. Walker turned his chair to face him, reflecting that small boys and terriers had a lot in common.

"Hi Poppy."

"Hi kid. What are you doing up so early?"

The boy looked grave and thoughtful.

"The birdie woke me Poppy. Then I had to pee."

The old man grinned at the child's sudden seriousness.

"If that birdie wakes you up again, you just tell me, kid. We'll make a stew out of him."

He wrapped one big hand around his throat, tilting his head and rolling his eyes, letting his tongue hang slack out of the corner of his mouth. The little boy giggled at the face he made. He stopped abruptly, the blue eyes painted with dismay.

"Oh no Poppy! We can't eat the birdie!"

The old man's grin got wider.

"Sure we could kid! You like your Auntie's chicken, don't you? All fried and crispy and brown?"

Nels Sorenson smiled, almost tasting it.

"Oh yes Poppy! It's my very favourite!"

"Well kid—chicken is birdies with their feathers off them."

"How do you get their feathers off them Poppy?"

Walker laughed and the boy laughed too, although he did not know why Poppy was laughing.

"I'll teach you some day when your Auntie's not around. Now let's play a game. We'll pretend we're soldiers. Okay?"

"Okay Poppy. What do I do?"

"Well, the first thing is, you have to learn to stand to attention. All soldiers know how to stand at attention. Put your feet together."

Nels pressed the sides of his bare feet together, looking down to see what they looked like that way.

"Now shoulders back, hands at your sides."

He reached and grasped the boy's small shoulders, straightening the line of his spine. Then he sat back.

"All right Nels. Now you're standing to attention.

Nels held himself rigid, memorising the way his body was, wanting to get it right.

"Got it kid?"

"Yes Poppy."

"Good. Now look at me."

He bent forward, his big hands on his knees, his gray eyes almost level with the child's blue ones.

"When I call you Soldier, you call me Sir and stand to attention. Okay Soldier?"

"Yes Poppy—Sir."

"Try it again Soldier."

"Yes Sir."

The boy tried to straighten himself even more.

"That's good Soldier. There's one more rule. When we're soldiers, you have to look me right in the eye when we're talking. Okay Soldier?"

He smiled, holding the boy's eyes with his own. The boy smiled back at him, delighting in this new game.

"Yes Sir."

"Okay kid—that's enough for now. You remember what I taught you. We'll be soldiers again."

He tickled the boy's ribs with his big fingers. The boy giggled and squirmed away, his soldier's stance forgotten, just a small blond boy with smiling bears on his pyjamas.

"Are you still sleepy kid?"

"Oh no Poppy! I'm not sleepy!"

His face changed, pushing his eyes too far open, afraid that Poppy would send him back to bed. The old man reached out and ruffled his hair.

"It's okay kid. How would you like to go fishing with me?"

"Oh yes Poppy!"

Then, "What's fishing Poppy?"

"Ah—kid—fishing is just about the best thing there is! Go get your clothes and your shoes and bring them out here. And be quiet."

"Yes Poppy."

The boy slipped away, a child's mixture of speed and stealth in his movements.

Walker rose and carried his cup and the ashtray over to the counter. The boy came back and began to dress himself while he looked for a pencil to leave a note for Sally. She was fiercely protective towards the boy, as much so as his mother. He wondered how the other woman was this morning. Sally had looked worn out when she came back from the hospital. From the little she'd said, he'd gathered that it had been pretty close. She didn't need anything more to worry about.

"Can you help me with my shoes Poppy?"

"What? Oh—yeah sure kid."

He reached down and caught the boy's hands and swung him up onto the counter. The boy looked at him with big wide eyes.

"Wow! You're strong Poppy!"

"I used to be. Let's get these laces done up."

He tied the boy's shoes, wondering at himself as he did so. Then he swung him back down to the floor.

"Thank you Poppy."

"You're welcome kid. I just have to leave a note for your aunt, so she'll know you're with me."

He wrote a brief note on an empty cigarette package and left it on the table with the boy's pyjamas.

"Ready Soldier?"

Nels Sorenson straightened to attention and smiled up at him.

"Yes Sir."

"That's good Nels—that's real good. Okay, let's go fishing."

They drove through quiet streets in the big black Ford with the early sun warm on their faces. The puddles from the previous night's downpour had already begun to dry. Only the horse-drawn milk wagons were out before them, the horses oblivious behind their blinkers, champing at nosebags filled with oats. Walker stopped once on the way, at a café, to buy the boy the unaccustomed luxury of a sugar doughnut and an icy bottle of sharp fizzing Coca-Cola for his breakfast. The houses and the tree-lined streets yielded to fields and barns while the boy munched happily, watching.

They came to an old steel bridge with the river running pale brown beneath it. Walker parked the Ford on the side of the road. He helped the boy out on the driver's side, reaching behind the seat for an empty tobacco can. They walked out onto the bridge to stand looking down at the river; the boy at a world newly discovered, the old man one long since familiar.

Above the bridge the river ran broad and shallow between banks covered with nettle and willows. White boulders protruded through the surface. On one of them lay an enormous snapping turtle, looking for all the world like the prehistoric monster which it was. For Walker, the snapping turtle was an old acquaintance. He pointed it out to the boy.

"See the snapper kid?"

"Wow! He's big eh Poppy?"

"Yep. He's been around a long time."

Below the bridge, the river narrowed into a bend, the darker colour of the water showing where millenniums of rainfall had cut deep into the land.

"Are we going fishing now Poppy?"

"Not just yet kid. First we have to go upstream and get some bait."

"What's bait Poppy?"

"You'll see. Come on."

He led the boy down from the bridge, past clumps of stinging nettle almost as tall as a man where jewelled dragonflies hunted on laced wings. A hundred feet up the bank was a shallow cut filled with tepid water above a bare mud bottom. He bent down and took off his boots and socks, rolling his pant legs up to his knees.

The boy began to copy him. He laid a restraining hand on his shoulder.

"No kid. You just watch. Okay?"

"What are you going to do Poppy?"

"I'm going to get us some bait. You watch the water."

He waded into the warm shallow water, stirring up the soft bottom with his feet. The boy crouched down on the bank, staring into the surface, curious to see what this new thing called bait was. Dimly, through the slurry of particles, he saw several sinuous black shapes swimming towards where Poppy was standing.

Walker lit a cigarette and smoked it down. Then he waded back out onto the bank.

The boy saw the black wriggling shapes that were hanging from Poppy's legs. His own skin crawled at the sight of them.

"Poppy! There's things on your legs!"

"It's okay kid. They're leeches. They don't hurt. We're going to catch fish with them. Now you just pull them off and put them in that can we brought."

"Oh no Poppy!"

He started to back away. The old man bent towards him and caught him by the shoulders.

"Now Soldier—look me in the eye. Remember?"

"Yes Sir."

"Are you afraid of them Soldier?"

"Yes Sir. They look awful!"

"Soldiers aren't afraid of anything. They might stick to you a bit but they won't hurt you. You can do it Soldier. Go ahead—give it a try."

The gray eyes made him brave. He bent forward and grasped a fat wriggling leech. The creature slid through his fingers and stayed firmly attached.

"Squeeze him with your fingernails and pull. He'll let go."

The boy grasped the leech again. It came away with a soft plop. He dropped it hastily into the can.

"That's good Soldier. Get another one."

He looked up at Poppy grinning down at him.

"It didn't hurt me Poppy."

"Of course not Soldier. I told you it wouldn't."

He bent forward again. The leeches came away one at a time. The skin on Poppy's legs was scarred and wrinkled with dead tissue. No blood came from where the leeches had been.

When the last leech was in the shiny slithering ball in the can, he looked up again.

"Did I do good Poppy?"

"Yeah kid. You did real good".

"Yes Poppy. What happened to your legs?"

"They got burned. In the war."

"What's the war, Poppy?"

"Never mind, kid. If you're lucky you'll never have to find out."

Walker remembered the women then.

"Listen—kid—we won't tell anybody else about being soldiers, or about getting bait. It'll be a secret, just between us. Okay?"

"Okay Poppy."

"Back to the car now. And watch out for those nettles."

The boy was already well out in front, carrying the bait can and staring at everything around him. A shiny green dragonfly hovered before his eyes. A black bird with a red and yellow patch on its wing screeched at him from above his head in a willow tree.

Walker's long strides caught up with him easily. They crossed the road together. He took out his keys and opened the trunk of the car. Inside was a fine spring-steel rod with a chromed reel and a big green metal box filled with what would become treasure to the boy.

"What's in the box Poppy?"

"Come with me and I'll show you."

A well-beaten path led down to the pool where generations of fishermen had come and gone. Walker went first, carrying the tackle, Nels Sorenson at his heels. He set the box on the ground and opened the lid. The boy saw trays filled with magic things; some shiny metal, others brightly painted.

The old man selected a bronze hook and a lead sinker. He closed the lid. Nels looked disappointed.

"You can look at that later kid. Watch what I do now."

He tied the hook to the line and baited it with three of the leeches, taking care to cover the metal of the hook completely.

"Doesn't it hurt them Poppy?"

"No kid—they can't feel it. Besides, they're going to get eaten soon."

"What's going to eat them Poppy?"

"A fish, kid. A great big fish."

"Will we see the fish Poppy?"

"Pretty soon. Watch now."

He fastened the sinker to the line and cast it accurately to sink at the top of the pool. There was a forked stick already stuck into the bank. He rested the rod in it and lit up a fresh cigarette.

"Now you watch that rod tip kid. Watch it real good. If it moves at all—even a little bit—you tell me."

"Yes Poppy."

The boy squatted down on his haunches, his blue eyes fixed on the tip of the metal rod. The old man stood and watched the boy, savouring the morning. The wet grass had begun to steam in the early heat. A marsh hawk soared high overhead. The boy stared, motionless—the world contained for him in a single perception.

"Poppy!"

The rod tip twitched in a series of short nervous taps. Walker reached forward and loosened off the drag on the reel. He tossed the cigarette away, nodding with satisfaction as the bass took the bait and swam with it to the far end of the pool.

"Is it the fish Poppy?"

"Ssh kid. Quiet now. Yes—it's the fish. But we don't want to scare him."

The boy nodded and whispered,

"What's he doing Poppy?"

"He's eating the bait. We'll see him in a minute . . ."

Walker watched as the line paused at the far end of the pool, knowing that beneath the surface the bass was swallowing the ball of leeches. He lifted the rod from its rest and began to retrieve the slack line as the fish swam back to the head of the pool to take up its feeding station.

"See where the line meets the water kid?"

"Yes Poppy?"

"Watch that spot and you'll see the fish. Now!"

He raised the rod tip high and struck, the spring-steel curling into an arc. The bass took one short run and hurled itself out of the water. The boy gaped in awe at the sight of it, smashing through the surface and hanging green and shiny in the sun. The fish fought well, tearing line from the reel, breaking water several times. Each time the boy cried out at the wonder of it.

At length the old man's skill triumphed. He led the spent fish in to the shallow water, reaching down with his free hand to grasp its lower lip in the vice between his thumb and finger. There was a short wooden club in the tackle box. He took it out and dispatched the fish with one sharp blow to the head. Its gill covers flared a last time and then relaxed as the life went out of it.

He worked the hook loose and laid the fish out on the grass to admire it. It was a good bass, close to two feet in length and all of five pounds in weight. He turned to look over at the boy.

The child had backed away. Now he stood staring at the fish, the wonder in his eyes replaced by something other, afraid to come near.

"What's the matter Soldier?"

He spoke gently, knowing that the child was in the presence of the Mystery.

The boy looked up. His eyes were puzzled and hurt.

"Why did you hit him Poppy?"

"I had to kill him Nels. We're going to eat him."

The child's eyes were drawn back down again to the fish.

"Is he dead Poppy?"

"Yes kid. He's dead."

"Like Tiny?"

"Yes kid. Like Tiny."

He saw that the boy was crying, for the fish. He knelt in the grass and took the child's shoulders in his hands, judging the moment.

"Now Soldier—look at me."

Nel Sorenson looked up through his tears into the quiet assurance of the old man's eyes.

"It's all right Soldier. Sometimes you have to kill things. And that's okay. The fish didn't hurt. Some day, when you're bigger, you'll learn how to kill fish too. Bend down and pet him Soldier. It's all right . . ."

The boy knelt beside him, his sense of wonder returning. He reached out and stroked the fishes' glistening side, feeling the cool wetness of its skin, caught by its stillness.

"Poppy?"

"Yes Soldier?"

"Do fish go to Heaven?"

The old man laughed and prodded the child's stomach with one big finger.

"No kid. They go in here."

1958: PROGRESS

$\mathcal{T}$he last Sunday in May was the first real summer day of the year. The walk home from Church seemed to take forever. Nels Sorenson looked down at his little sister beside him.

"Walk faster Elly."

"I don't want to."

"Leave your sister alone Nels. Your mother and I aren't going to hurry either on a day like this."

"Aw Dad—"

He turned around, walking backwards to appeal to his father.

"It's been three whole weeks since we went to the Forest!"

"It wasn't my doing, having to work the last two Sundays son."

"I know Dad—but by the time we have lunch and get out there it'll be 2 o'clock!"

"It only takes fifteen minutes to drive out to the bush Nels."

"But Dad—"

"That's enough son. It'll still be there when we get there."

"Aww . . ."

His mother smiled at him.

"Why don't you run ahead and open the house if you're in such a hurry? Give him the key John."

He took the key and turned away and sprinted the last block. He was a slender boy. He could run like the wind.

By the time the rest of the family got home he was already changed into runners and jeans. He followed his mother into the kitchen.

"Did you hang your suit up on a hanger Nels?"

"Yes Mom."

"Good boy."

She smiled at him.

"I'll get us a dish of soup and a sandwich and then you can get going."

"Soup takes too long Mom."

"It'll only take a minute. Besides, it's not like you to turn down anything to eat. Now is it?"

"I guess not. Can I take a one of the canning jars?"

"What do you need it for?" Look in the cupboard and see if there's a can of tomato soup, would you dear?"

"Sure Mom—I want to try and get a bullfrog tadpole and bring it home—here's the soup."

"Set it on the counter. You could open it for me if you like. What are you going to do with a tadpole?"

"Watch it grow into a frog."

He went rummaging through the utensil drawer.

"It's not here Mom."

"You men can never find anything . . ."

She set the saucepan on the stove and came to stand beside him.

"It's right here, where it always is. You're not here. You're already in the Forest. Aren't you?"

She ruffled his hair. He grinned at her.

"So can I take a couple of jars Mom?"

"What do you need two for?"

"I told Miss Hartley I'd bring one for school too."

He watched her while she opened the can of soup.

"What are you going to feed them?"

"Fish food. Miss Hartley looked it up in her science books. Can I Mom?"

"Yes dear. As long as you don't starve the poor thing."

"Thanks Mom."

He turned away and she called after him,

"Don't you take my good canning sealers. There's a box of old jars behind the furnace. Did you hear me?"

He called back, "Yes Mom," halfway down the basement stairs.

Lunch was on the table when Nels Sorenson came up from the basement. The family sat down together. His father said the blessing. He wolfed his food, watching impatiently while his mother poured the tea. When his father had finished the last of it, his mother smiled at him across the table.

"I think someone wants to get going John."

His father managed to look surprised.

"Well come on boy! What are you waiting for?"

"Yeah!"

Sunday afternoon had been the same for as long as he could remember.

When they were finally in the rusty red Dodge he waved to Ellen and his mother on the verandah. His father let him toot the horn—just once—as they drove away.

"Do you think the turtles will be out today Dad?"

"They should be son. It's warm enough. How do you propose to catch those polliwogs without a net?"

"Easy Dad! I'll just roll my pant legs up and wade in and grab them!"

"There's likely to be bloodsuckers hiding in the mud Nels."

"I'm not scared of bloodsuckers Dad."

His father turned to grin at him.

"You might be—if you knew what they looked like."

He looked out the side window to hide his own grin, watching the familiar street going by. Past the shops and the fairgrounds; past the factories where the chimneys belched smoke now even on Sundays; past the long line of old houses to where rows of new houses had begun to spring up out of the fields.

"Look Dad—they're starting to put the roofs on them already."

His father made no reply.

"Dad?"

He turned away from the side window to look at him. His father's face was creased into a frown.

"What's wrong Dad?"

"I'm not sure Nels."

He felt the surge of acceleration, following his father's eyes. Away across the fields, a column of smoke rose up above the Forest.

"It's a fire! Hurry Dad! Hurry!"

He strained forward against the dash in near panic at the blue smudge rapidly closing on the horizon. His father's face was a tight mask at the edge of his vision. The side road came up fast.

"Sit back Nels! Sit back!"

John Sorenson reached one hand to push him back against the seat, misjudging his speed and slowing too late as he spun the wheel into the turn. Nels went sprawling against the door. The Dodge slewed wildly as the wheels hit the gravel, the rear end fishtailing as he fought it back under control.

"Are you all right?"

"Yes! Hurry Dad! We've got to stop it!"

The boy clawed his way upright again, oblivious to everything but the clatter of stones on the undercarriage and the blue fog of smoke beyond the bridge.

"Hang on son!"

They were onto the bridge when he hit the brakes. The car skidded past it and slid to a stop on the gravel. The passenger door flew open.

"Nels! Wait!"

It was too late. The boy leaped clear and went racing off into the smoke.

"Nels! Come back!"

He banged the lever out of gear and lunged out of the car and went down hard on the loose stones. The taste of fear for his son was like metal in his mouth. He pulled himself upright on the open door, staring wildly towards the direction of the pond where Nels had gone.

The boy had stopped running. He could see him through the drifting smoke, a hundred yards away, standing still. He sagged against the door in relief, seeing that he was safe. Then the hollow shock of loss hit him as he understood what had happened.

John Sorenson stared out at where the Forest had been, the old knowledge coming back to haunt him. It was a clearing operation. There was nothing left standing in a long deep swath from the creek bed to where the fields began again. Only the most valuable hardwoods had been felled for their timber. A small amount of sawlogs had been stacked where the wagon road led in.

Every other living thing had been ripped out of the soil and bulldozed into huge smouldering piles. Tongues of orange flame fed on the tangles of jagged roots and shattered trunks and tree limbs. Bitter smoke poured up where the fire had not reached, shrivelling the new green foliage. The earth itself was torn and scarred from the work of the machine.

The massive bulldozer sat mindless, hulking down on the broken landscape a hundred yards away near the edge of where the pond had been. The beaver dam had been dynamited and the life-sustaining water bled away. All that remained was an expanse of brown mud littered with debris from the blast. The stream had begun to carve twisted tortuous channels across the face of it. Nels was ten feet out from the edge, bent forward, up to his knees in the mud, staring down at it.

"Nels!"

Nels gave no sign of hearing his shout. He watched as the boy struggled to wrench one foot free and stepped forward, bending to stare again, as if he was searching for something.

"Nels!"

His voice carried out again and was lost in a place where no bird sang. He got into the car and put it into gear, sick at heart as he drove it out of the centre of the road.

It was then that he saw the sign up ahead. It was a big sign, freshly painted in bold red letters, bolted to two posts driven into the ground. The incongruity of the wooden posts struck him first, standing upright against a background of devastation.

He let the car roll a few feet further in gear until he was close enough to read the legend. The sign announced that where the forest had been was the future site of a paint manufacturing plant.

"Damn you!"

He brought his fist down hard on the steering wheel, the gesture as futile as the curse that escaped his lips. Then the anger was gone, swept away by an image of the first day that he had been led to this place.

He pressed his hands to his eyes.

"I'm sorry . . .

He spoke out loud, his voice the only sound except for the crackle of burning wood. He got out of the car, forcing his own loss aside to go and comfort his son.

Two days had passed since the dam had been blown apart. Some of the creatures that lived in the pond had been killed outright by the concussion. Others, like the fish and the tadpoles had been stunned and left to suffocate on the mud. The carrion eaters—the crows and the ravens—had been kept away by the clouds of smoke billowing up into the air.

The boy's run to the pond was compelled by some force beyond his comprehension. He waded into the mud intent on only one thing—to find some other living creature in the nightmare universe around him. He searched frantically, struggling in the deep cloying mud that sucked him down with each step.

There were dead things everywhere—bloated frogs, their pale bellies swollen in the sun; fish with mouths agape in the rictus of astonishment; the broken coils of a water snake, all scattered among the litter of ancient branches from the dam.

And then he saw the turtle. It was half buried, the top part of its shell protruding from the mud several feet in front of him. The gaudy colours of its neck showed, its head stretched forward, the front feet clawing feebly as it struggled to free itself.

The turtle had just climbed out onto the dam when the blast had been set off. The force of the explosion had blown the bottom of its shell away, hurling the animal high into the air above the pond. It had landed on the broken edge of its shell, burying itself in the soft silty bottom. The mud had sealed around its entrails. For two days it had struggled, its fierce reptilian brain refusing to yield to death.

The rush of adrenaline took him. He went surging through the mud, fighting his way to the turtle, reaching to grasp its shell around the middle with both hands and pull it free.

The shock of the open air on its entrails was the final blow that killed it. The beady eyes closed. The head and the neck with its brilliant red and yellow pattern sagged down onto its shell. The boy stood horror-struck, holding the turtle out in front of him, unable to tear his eyes away from the shattered body with its intestines dangling obscenely.

John Sorenson found him there.

"Put the turtle down son. Let's go home."

He spoke softly, trying to draw his son away from the face of death. The boy's eyes sought his, twenty feet away across the barren sea of the mud, full of some mute appeal. He shook his head a little, sadly.

"It's dead Nels. There's nothing we can do."

The boy stiffened, his eyes drawn once more to the mutilated thing that he held in his hands. Then he screamed.

"No!!"

Nels Sorenson hurled the shattered creature away from him and went surging towards the bank. His father stared, awed by the power in his son's slender body as he stalked seemingly effortlessly through the deep mud towards him.

The boy radiated violence. His fists were clenched in front of him, his lips drawn back from his bared teeth in a vicious grimace. He felt the beginnings of a fear for his son that grew as the boy closed the distance between them. Then Nels was facing him on the bank. His blue eyes blazed with an unholy light.

"They wrecked it! They wrecked God's Place. They didn't even kill the turtle! They just left it there with its guts hanging out! I'll kill them for this! I'll kill them! I'll kill them!"

"Stop it Nels! Stop it!"

The boy was beyond hearing. He saw the bulldozer standing close by. He snatched up a huge root and ran at it, swinging it like a club above his head and smashing it down uselessly on the massive steel track. He swung it again and again with inhuman strength.

"Kill you! I'll kill you!"

John Sorenson ran after him and snatched the root out of his hands.

"Kill you—"

He grabbed his son's shirt and shook him hard to snap him out of it.

"Stop it Nels! Stop it!"

The boy stopped screaming abruptly, staring up at him. And his father felt a knife-edge of pain at his betrayal in his son's eyes. The boy wrenched free and ran, away from him, across the savaged earth towards the car.

He let the splintered root drop from his hand, helpless in the wave of emotion that swept over him, staring around at what had once been sacred ground. He turned his back on it and followed his son, hearing the car door slam ahead of him.

When he got to the car, Nels was sitting inside. The boy didn't look around when he got in and closed the door. He turned to look at his son.

"Are you all right Nels?"

The boy just stared ahead, refusing to speak to him.

"Nels . . ."

He reached to put his hand on his arm. Nels flinched away, pressing himself against the passenger door. He took his hand away, looking down at the steering wheel, searching for the words to try and make it right again. He waited until he was sure that his voice would not betray him.

"I'm sorry I was rough with you. I feel just as bad as you do. But you mustn't ever say things like that. It's wrong to even think them. The men who did this aren't bad men. It's their job. They probably feel bad about it too. It's just that . . ."

He stopped again, feeling the weight of his son's accusing silence and his own helplessness in the face of it.

"It's just Progress son. It's just . . . Progress."

He started up the motor and turned the car back towards the city. The boy sat silent all the way home, staring straight ahead with hostile eyes. There were no tears.

It wasn't until he parked in front of the house and shut the motor off that Nels looked over at him. The blue eyes were as hard and unyielding as stone.

"You don't even care!"

The car door slammed before he could defend himself. He watched his son go racing off across the school yard.

Margaret Sorenson heard a car door slam and then the tread of heavy footsteps on the verandah.

"I have to go Sal. Someone's here. I'll call you back." She put the phone down on its cradle, hearing the front door open.

"Hi Daddy."

"Hi Ellen."

She looked around, smiling, as John came into the dining room.

"You're home early."

She stopped, feeling a sudden cold fear at what was in his eyes.

"What's wrong? Where's Nels?"

"He took off towards the school yard."

"Is he hurt?"

"No. Not like that anyhow . . ."

He looked away from her, down at the floor.

She went to him and took his hand, sensing his sorrow and struggling to maintain her composure.

"Are you all right John?"

She spoke to him softly, trying to draw his eyes to hers.

"I guess so . . ."

Still he did not look at her.

"Come and sit down John."

She led him to a chair. He sank down onto it, turning to look up at her. His eyes were bleak and lost.

"It's gone Marg. It's gone forever."

"What's gone John?"

"The bush. They bulldozed all the trees and burned everything except a few logs. They blew the dam and drained the pond. There's nothing left."

"Oh no! . . . Why would they do that?"

"They're putting in a factory. A paint plant."

"Why would they put it way out there?"

"I guess it's not that far any more. There's a subdivision half a mile from there now. I guess I should have known that it couldn't last forever."

"But why there John?" Isn't there lots of open land? Why would they cut all the trees down?"

"I don't know Marg. They probably want the stream to get rid of their garbage."

There was bitterness in his voice. He looked away from her, as if to conceal his eyes. She put her hands on his, trying to comfort him.

"I'm sorry John. I know how much it meant to you."

He shook his head, as if to ward off his loss.

"That's not the worst of it Marg. It's Nels . . ."

"Tell me what happened."

He was silent for a long moment while she fought to stay calm.

"We were on our way out there . . . there was all this smoke . . . I could see it from the highway. I guess I panicked—I thought the bush was on fire. I almost put the car off the road. I couldn't see what it was until we were right there. It was my fault Marg. I stopped the car and he was out and gone before I could stop him."

"That's not your fault John. He's always been too fast for either one of us."

"I know. But if I'd just kept going . . ."

"Don't blame yourself John . . . what happened then?"

"It wasn't any more than a couple of minutes—he went running to where the pond was. I could see him from the road. I pulled the car off and went after him. There was nothing left but a mud hole. There were dead things everywhere. By the time I got to him he'd waded out into it up to his knees. He'd found one of the painted turtles. It was dead—the blast must have gone off right under it. Half it's shell was blown away."

"Oh no . . ."

"He was just standing in the mud, holding it by what was left of its shell. He must have been in shock. I don't think he even realized that it was dead."

"My poor baby . . ."

"It was bad Marg. He's always been such a happy kid—I didn't even know he had a temper. I called to him . . . I said, 'The turtle's dead son. Let's go home.' That's all I said."

He stopped, looking up at her, and she saw the shock still mirrored in his eyes.

"You wouldn't have believed him! He was twenty feet away from the bank, in mud up to his knees. He came through that mud like it wasn't even there! He scared me Marg! His eyes—and then he started screaming that they'd wrecked God's place."

"John—he used to call it that when he was just a little boy."

She saw the stab of pain in his eyes before he looked down and away from her.

"I'm sorry John. What happened then?"

He shook his head, not wanting to tell her.

"Please John . . ."

"He went crazy on me. He started screaming that he was going to kill somebody."

"Oh no . . ."

"He picked up a chunk of root about four feet long and attacked this bulldozer before I could stop him. He was so strong—I don't think he could have even lifted it normally. He was swinging it over his head and smashing it against this huge machine like it was a stick."

She shook her head, not wanting to believe it.

"How could he be that strong? He's only nine years old. He's just a little boy."

"I know Marg—I know. He was screaming the whole time. He was so mad—I had to shake him to snap him out of it. And then he looked at me."

He stopped again. She waited in the silence, full of fear for both her husband and her son. When he spoke again his voice was defeated.

"He took off for the car. I went after him. He wouldn't look at me—he wouldn't even let me touch him. I tried to tell him that it was wrong to talk about killing people. I tried to explain to him about the bush. I made a mess of it. He blames me now. He told me just now that I didn't care."

She knelt in front of him and took his hands, looking up into his eyes, trying to comfort him.

"He didn't mean it John."

"No. He meant it."

"But that doesn't make any sense. You didn't have anything to do with cutting down those trees."

"That's just it Marg. There was a time when it might have been me. Talk to him Marg. I can't face him right now . . ."

She forced herself to smile at him, willing herself not to cry.

"You're being too hard on yourself. I know that this hurt you too. But you can't help Nels by blaming yourself."

She rose to her feet and held him close, stroking his hair as if he were a troubled child.

"Go find him Marg . . . talk to him . . ."

"I will John. I think I know where he is. My brothers used to hide under the school steps when they didn't want to go home. I think that's where he'll be. Will you be all right?"

"I guess so. I just feel . . . I don't know how I feel. Marg—he didn't even cry."

"I'll go find him."

She found him huddled in the narrow space beneath the cement steps. He saw her shadow pass across the opening, turning away from her as she bent down to look in at him.

"Nels . . . are you all right?"

There was only the crinkle of paper as he edged deeper into the litter of discarded gum wrappers. She knelt in the opening, drawn in after him.

"Come on home Honey."

"Leave me alone!"

He swung to face her, staring for the first time into his own shocked separateness mirrored in his mother's green eyes. He wanted to reach out to her—wanted desperately to lose himself in her arms. It was too late. He looked away again, unable to bear the broken smile that trembled at the corners of her mouth.

After an endless silence he heard her say,

"Will you come home when you're ready Honey?"

"Yes."

He waited, lost, not looking around again until he knew that she had gone. It was only then that he began to cry.

Ellen came once, to tell him that supper was ready. She went home puzzled without him. When she was gone, he crept out, watching her over the lip of the step until she was out of sight.

At the corner of the school yard a big maple spread its boughs out over the top of the chain link fence. He sprinted flat out across the open space and climbed up into it, using its boughs to clear the fence and drop down into the lane. He vaulted the low board fences of the neighbour's yard and came to a sudden stop, flattened against the back wall of his own house.

The thought of supper tormented him. The sullen rage inside him held him there, refusing to yield. He crouched there, unable to move, until he heard his father's voice from the front porch.

He crept to the corner of the house, listening in the narrow passage.

"Don't you think I should go and try to talk to him Marg?"

"No John. You go ahead and go to church. We know where he is. He's bound to be hungry by now. He'll come home soon."

"Well . . . I guess you're right. But I'm worried about him."

"So am I John. But I think this is best."

He scrambled out of his muddy pants and shoes and left them outside by the back door. He snuck into the house and into his room, fighting the urge to raid the kitchen in case his mother came in and saw him there. He closed the bedroom door silently behind him.

He got into the warm safety of his bed, hiding from the world in the darkness beneath the blankets, pulling his knees up against his chest and trying to ignore the gnawing hunger inside of him.

Margaret didn't know that he was in the house until she went to put her daughter to bed. She saw the closed door on her way to the kitchen to get the little girl a glass of water. Ellen looked up at her from the pillow.

"When's Nels coming home Mummy?"

"He's home Honey. You can go to sleep now. He's in his room."

"Can I go say goodnight to him?"

"No Honey. I think he's already asleep. You can talk to him in the morning."

She smiled at her, to reassure her.

"Go to sleep now."

The little face on the pillow smiled up at her.

"Goodnight Elly."

She bent to kiss her daughter goodnight and waited until her eyes were closed. Then she turned off the light and tiptoed out, to stand listening to the silence beyond the closed door to her son's room.

"Nels?"

She called him softly. The silence went unbroken. She turned the knob as quietly as possible, letting the light from the dining room spill in across the bed. His face was hidden beneath the blankets, turned towards the wall. She sensed rather than saw that he was awake in the tight curl of his body. For a moment she struggled with the urge to go to him and hold him.

Some new awareness of her son held her back. She turned away, leaving the door ajar and went into the kitchen. When she returned she brought a plate of sandwiches and a big glass of milk. He had not moved, still feigning sleep. She set the dishes on the table beside the bed, bending over him and pulling the blankets back just enough to kiss him lightly on the cheek.

"We love you Nels. Both your Dad and I. It's going to be all right."

She whispered the words in his ear. He felt the single teardrop, warm and wet on his face. He lay still, listening until he heard the door close behind her.

When she went in to check on him an hour later, he was asleep on his back in a tangle of sheets and blankets. She carried the empty dishes to the kitchen and then went out onto the verandah to wait for John.

Sometime in the middle of the night, the image of the dying turtle pursued him into his dreams. He woke up the household with his screaming.

The next two days were harder than anything she could remember.

In the morning, she left him to sleep while she got Ellen ready for school. The fact that his door stayed closed was disturbing enough. He was always awake when she got up to get John off to work.

He came out of his room at 10 o'clock and walked past her, into the bathroom. She called good morning to him and went into the kitchen, thinking that he had only had sandwiches for supper. She heard the toilet flush and the bathroom door open.

"Did you sleep all right, Honey? You must be starving."

She looked around, expecting to see him there. The kitchen was empty. She heard the muffled click of the bedroom door, closing behind him. She took a deep breath and followed him into the bedroom. He was in bed again, lying on his back, staring up at the ceiling.

She sat down beside him on the bed. He would not look at her. His aloneness pierced her, reaching to hold him and hug him close.

His body was stiff and resistant against her. After a moment she let him go, leaning above him, trying to draw his eyes.

"Why don't you tell me what happened Nels? It only hurts worse if you keep it all inside . . ."

"I don't want to talk about it."

"All right."

She summoned up the Irish in her, determined not to cry.

"Well you'd better come out to the kitchen and have some breakfast. You don't have to go to school today but you're going to have something to eat. Okay?"

She got up and took his hand and drew him out of bed. He followed her into the kitchen, where she managed to get a bowl of cereal into him. He kept his head down, avoiding her eyes.

"How about some eggs?"

She went to the fridge to get them out. When she turned back, he was gone again.

He spent the rest of the day in bed, staring up at the ceiling. She tried several times to talk to him but he was closed to her. When John came home from work, she rushed to tell him and stopped, seeing the look in his eyes.

She took his lunch pail instead and gave him a hug and a smile at the door.

"You look tired John. Why don't you go and wash up? I'll get you a nice cup of tea and you can have a rest while I get supper."

"How's Nels?"

"I kept him home today. He's tired out."

"Did he say anything to you? About yesterday?"

"No. Not yet. Go and get cleaned up. I'll get your tea."

"Thanks Marg."

He went past her into the bathroom, looking lost. She went into the kitchen and put the kettle on and then went into her son's room with Ellen close behind her.

"I want you to get up now and get dressed. Your father's home. I want you to come to the table when I call you for supper. You haven't eaten a thing all day."

He followed her to the door and closed it behind them.

"What's wrong with Nels Mummy? He won't talk to me."

"He's not feeling good Elly. Why don't you go talk to Daddy when he comes out of the bathroom? I think he needs a hug."

The little girl brightened.

"Okay Mummy."

"I'd better go and put supper on. Why don't you wait for him in the living room."

She went into the kitchen and tried to concentrate on something other than the silence in the house.

The evening meal was a disaster. John's usual quiet strength seemed to have abandoned him. He picked at his food, casting troubled glances to her across the table. Ellen looked on with puzzled eyes. Nels kept his head down over his plate, wolfing his supper down, unable to resist his body's demands any longer. When John tried to talk to him, she saw the blue glare flash in his eyes before he pushed back his chair and slammed into his room. John got up too and went out on the verandah, to stand staring numbly at the street. She turned to look into her daughter's eyes, trying to find a smile for her.

"Would you like to help me with the dishes Honey?"

The little girl nodded and solemnly followed her into the kitchen.

For the rest of the evening, the brooding silence which she knew visited her husband from time to time settled over him. When they were in bed, she lay awake for a long time with it ringing out in the blackness around her.

"Are you awake Marg?"

"Yes John."

"What are we going to do?"

"I don't know."

She reached for him and held him, trying to find some comfort in his arms.

On Tuesday morning she made Nels get up and go to school. He came home for lunch and she had to push him to get him to go back with Ellen. He came home after school with his shirt torn and his eyes blazing. When she tried to question him about it, he ran into his room and refused to come out for supper. She let him eat in his room, knowing that he would not eat otherwise. John spent the evening on the verandah, staring at the street.

That night Margaret Sorenson fell asleep exhausted. Her dreams were cold and bleak and lonely things.

On Wednesday morning Nels was up and dressed, sitting on the bed when she went in to call him. He ate his breakfast and went off to school without having to be told. He seemed to want to go, and she began to feel better. She put a load of laundry through the ancient wringer washer. The sky was bright blue and the sun was warm when she went out into the yard to hang the clothes on the line.

The school yard was alive with the clamour of children when she went on to check the wash. It was still damp. She came back in, thinking that she would make him some cookies, his favourite ones, oatmeal with raisins in them. She heard the bell sound to end recess while she was mixing the batter. The telephone rang just as she was putting the baking sheets into the oven. She smiled and went into the dining room to answer it. Sally always called this time of the morning.

She wiped her hands on her apron and picked up the receiver.

"Hi Sal."

There was a pause.

"Mrs. Sorenson?"

It was a woman's voice, somehow familiar.

"Yes?"

"I'm sorry to disturb you. It's the school calling. Nels is at the nursing station. Could you come and get him?"

She steadied herself with one hand on the telephone table.

"Is he all right?"

"He has a cut over one eye. The nurse says that it's not serious but it should have some stitches."

"I'll be there right away."

"If you could come to the office."

"Yes. Of course."

"Thank you. Goodbye."

She pressed the button down and dialled Sally's number.

"Sal? Are you busy? Could you come and make Elly some lunch and sit with her? The school just called. Nels' cut himself again. He'll have to have stitches. What? No—they didn't say. He was probably running and somebody tripped him. I'll have to take him to Outpatients. You know how slow they are."

She listened for a moment.

"I'm at my wit's end Sal. This was the last thing he needed today. I'd better go. I'll leave the back door open. What? Oh yes. I'll be all right. I'm used to stitches by now. Thanks love. I'll call you later."

She took off her apron and left it on the dining room table. She was out the back door before she remembered that the cookies were in the oven. She hurried back in and took them out and turned the oven off. She thought about the hospital then and hastily changed from her house dress into a flowered print dress which she wore when she went shopping. She paused a second longer to put some colour on her cheeks. There was one last lapse while she looked through her purse. Then she went out of the house and up the street, hurrying across the school yard.

The secretary was waiting for her when she got to the office counter. Nels was nowhere in sight.

"I'm Margaret Sorenson. I'm here to pick up my son."

"Yes, of course. The Principal would like to speak with you first. Nels is still at the nursing station. Won't you come this way?"

The heavy wooden door with the word 'PRINCIPAL' lettered in gold on the opaque glass panel had always intimidated her as a child. She had never had to see what lay beyond it. She hesitated as the other woman opened the door and turned to smile at her.

"Go right in Mrs. Sorenson. Mr. O'Brian is expecting you."

"Yes—thank you . . ."

She stepped past her, seeing the old man with the thin grey hair and the thick bifocals as he stood up behind the oak desk.

"Come in Mrs. Sorenson."

She crossed to the desk, hearing the door click shut, standing before him with her feet together and her purse clutched in front of her with both hands.

The Principal smiled at her in recognition.

"You're one of the Murphy girls, aren't you?"

"Yes. I'm Margaret, Mr. O'Brian."

She remembered that his hair had been grey when he'd taught her in the seventh grade.

"Please—sit down Mrs.—may I call you Margaret?"

"Of course."

She sat down on the edge of a chair, made nervous now by his attempt to put her at ease. There were big brown liver spots on the backs of his hands when he sat down and folded them on the desk.

"Has something happened to my son, Mr. O'Brian?"

"Yes. I thought we might discuss the boy before I send for him."

He was watching her closely now. She felt a shrinking in the pit of her stomach.

"There's more to it than just the stitches then."

"I'm afraid so. Tell me—do you know if anything's been bothering your son the past couple of days?"

"Yes."

She looked away, down at her hands.

"Please . . . Mrs. Sorenson . . . I would appreciate it if you could tell me about it. I'm here to help if I can."

"I don't know how to explain it to you, Mr. O'Brian. I don't understand it myself . . ."

"Perhaps if you could just tell me what happened . . ."

There was a quiet concern in his voice. She looked up at him, suddenly desperate to talk to someone about it.

"It was last Sunday, after the morning service. Nels and his father went out to a place in the country. It's—it was—a special place for them—a bit of bush with a pond on some farmer's land. It's something that they've done together every Sunday since Nels was just a little boy . . ."

"And something happened to him while they were there?"

She hesitated, not knowing what to say.

"Yes. When they got there, it was gone."

"I'm afraid I don't understand. What was gone?"

"The forest was gone. They were getting ready to build a factory. John—my husband—said that they were burning the trees. They'd blown up the pond—Nels ran off before he could stop him. He found a dead turtle—I haven't been able to help him. He's hurt—I know he is—but he won't talk to me about it. Lord knows I've tried. He won't even look at his father. He had a nightmare on Sunday night. That's why I kept him home on Monday—Mr. O'Brian? What's happened to him? Why am I here?"

"Try to calm yourself Mrs. Sorenson. I can see that this hasn't been easy for you."

"I'm all right. Tell me what's happened."

"I haven't had much time to look into it. Although in the light of what you've told me . . . this is going to be difficult for you."

"Please—go ahead."

"Very well. One of my teachers brought your son and another boy to my office during this morning's recess. There had been an incident on the playground. The teacher saw your son pick up a piece of the pavement and try to hit the other boy with it. The other boy hit him with his fist and knocked him down. The teacher broke it up before it could go any further. The other boy is in the seventh grade. He's a very tough boy. The punch split your son's eyebrow."

"I don't believe it! Nels isn't a fighter—"

"Please—Mrs. Sorenson. Let me continue. I've spoken to both Miss Hartley—Nels' teacher—and to the other boy. His name is

Wolfgang. Nels wouldn't talk to me either, but what I've been able to put together is this."

He paused, seeing the expression on her face.

"Are you all right Margaret?"

"Yes. I think so. Please go ahead."

"Miss Hartley said that Nels was completely changed when he came to school on Tuesday morning. He paid no attention to her in class. She said that he spent the morning staring off into space. He wouldn't talk to her. After lunch, she tried to make him do the lesson. He flew into a rage and pushed his books onto the floor."

"She made him stand in the hallway and then kept him in at recess, to try to find out what was bothering him. She's quite fond of him apparently. He refused to talk to her as well. She said that he was sullen and uncommunicative for the rest of the day."

"When I interviewed the other boy—Wolfgang—he said that Nels had tried to fight with him on the playground after school. Wolfgang refused to fight with him. I've had to discipline Wolfgang in the past for fighting. He said that he had never even spoken to your son. He seemed to have no idea what it was about."

"Unfortunately, boys like Wolfgang always seem to have a little band of followers. Apparently they made fun of Nels, which only served to make him angrier. They're all older than he is. I gather he tried to fight with them too. They laughed at him and pushed his around."

"That's why his shirt was torn when he came home."

"Pardon?"

She'd spoken out loud without realizing it.

"His shirt was torn when he came home. He wouldn't tell me what happened."

"I see. Was he angry when he came home?"

"Yes. He wouldn't come out of his room for the rest of the night."

"And then, at recess this morning, he had another try at Wolfgang. It's fortunate for everyone that he didn't succeed."

She looked up, flashing into anger in his defence.

"I don't know what you mean by that Mr. O'Brian. My son's hurt."

"I understand how you feel Mrs. Sorenson. But he could have hurt someone else."

Her anger dissolved into bafflement.

"But he's not like that! He'd never try to hurt anyone! I know him—he's my son."

She began to cry in spite of herself.

"I'm sorry—please excuse me—I'll be all right in a minute."

He waited while she fumbled for a handkerchief in her purse. She dabbed at her cheeks, and when she looked at him again, her eyes were imploring.

"He's not a bad boy."

"Of course he's not. We both know that. I've taught your family now for two generations. He's a fine boy, from what his teacher tells me. But he's a very disturbed boy just now. And unfortunately, he's created a problem over and above the one that he already had. A problem that now I'll have to deal with."

"I don't know what you mean, Mr. O'Brian."

She struggled to get control of herself, sensing some new danger.

"I'll be quite frank with you Mrs. Sorenson. There has always been a problem with boys fighting in this school. Boys are boys. This has always been a predominantly Irish neighbourhood. A lot of it is harmless enough—boys learning the exercise of their wills, mostly on their friends. Your brother Mike was a fair amateur pugilist when I taught him."

"Sometimes, however, we get a boy where it's much more serious than that. Wolfgang is a case in point. The neighbourhood is changing too. The older families—the ones I've taught for years, like yours—are beginning to move out to other areas. The people who are moving in are, in a lot of cases, new to this country. There are Polish families, German families—please don't misunderstand me. The Irish were maligned enough as immigrants when we came here. I'm not about to malign anyone else because they're new here."

"But these are people who have come from a world that we can't begin to imagine. Their countries were destroyed by the war. Some of the parents I've met have suffered a great deal. They've been uprooted, they don't speak the language. They're here because there was nothing left but misery where they came from. In spite of the pride that we take in our country, I'm often left wondering how they see us."

"In any case, their children bear the scars of the old world. I have to deal with Polish boys and German boys who hate each other, simply because of their last names. In Nels' case, he couldn't have made a worse choice in picking Wolfgang as a target for his anger. Wolfgang grew up in the streets of post-war Berlin. His family moved here three years ago. He's a very disturbed boy, and potentially a very violent boy."

"His parents are good people. I've talked to them. It hasn't been easy for them, speaking very little English and moving into an Irish neighbourhood. There are still some rather lasting sentiments towards German speaking people left over from the war. But they have little control over Wolfgang."

"What does all of this have to do with my son?"

"Just this. Wolfgang could have very easily injured Nels today. He's physically capable of it, and, in his mind, I'm certain that the fact that Nels had a weapon would be sufficient provocation. I can't allow it to happen again.

I can't punish Wolfgang. Nels was clearly the aggressor. I can't see how I can punish Nels either, without making the problem you've described to me even worse. And there's the possibility that your son might choose someone who he could hurt next time. Although I suspect he took on Wolfgang because he is the toughest boy on the yard."

"But I'm sure my Nels wouldn't try to hurt anyone again Mr. O'Brian—I'll talk to him."

"I think that we should call the boy in and ask him for himself."

He looked away from her, getting up and going to the door.

"Mrs. Brown—would you call the nurse and ask her to send the Sorenson boy to my office please. Just send him in when he gets here."

He came and sat back down at the desk.

"This may be difficult for you Mrs. Sorenson. But I'm going to ask you not to interfere until I'm done questioning Nels. Will you do that for me?"

"Yes"

She turned in her chair to watch the door. Nothing that had occurred in the past three days could have prepared her for her son's appearance. He marched into the office without even so much as a glance at her. There was a bandage covering his left eyebrow. There were bloodstains on the front of his shirt.

There was nothing in his manner to suggest that he was beaten. His back was straight and his head held high. He came to a full stop in front of the principal's desk and stood rigidly to attention.

The old man measured the shock in her expression, turning back to study the boy in front of him. The boy's blue eyes locked onto his, not giving ground. He held him there in a test of will. The boy's blue eyes glowed with a cold determination.

"I want to ask you a couple of questions Nels. Did you try to hit Wolfgang with something?"

"Yes Sir."

The boy's voice was flat and final.

"Aren't you afraid of Wolfgang?"

"No Sir."

"Do you know why you wanted to hit him Nels?"

There was no answer this time. He let it hang for a minute, feeling the impact of the boy's silence on the woman who sat helpless, two feet away from where her son was standing.

"I see. Will you try to fight with Wolfgang again?"

"Yes Sir."

"That's all Nels. Go outside and wait for your mother in the hall."

Margaret Sorenson stared after him as he wheeled and marched out of the office, closing the door behind him. The principal took his glasses off and passed his hand over his eyes, coming rapidly to a decision.

"Mrs. Sorenson? Margaret?"

"What? Oh yes."

He waited until he had her attention again, weighing the words in his mind.

"Mrs. Sorenson—bear with me for a moment if you can. I'm an old man. I've been in this business for a long time. This is my last year at the school. In another month I'll be put out to pasture."

"What I'm going to say to you now is for your sake and your son's sake. And perhaps for my own. I think that I have developed a certain intuition in my time."

"Whatever happened last Sunday—and I don't pretend to understand it—is of a profound nature. My intuition tells me that if it is not resolved, it will have far-reaching consequences in terms of your son's development. I would not want it on my conscience that I did not do what I could to try to help you through this . . . change."

"I'd like you to take Nels out of school for the rest of the term. Please understand that this is a request. I'm not suspending him. But if it happens again—and it will—I will have to act. Someone could get hurt and then it will be on his record."

"Even if he had a change of heart, he has violated a certain code that boys have when he picked up a weapon. The others will seek him out and want to fight with him. I've seen it before. And, of course, none of this is going to help with the real problem."

"I've looked over his record. His grades are well above average. I will see that he is promoted, and I will put on his record that his absenteeism is due to reasons of health. But there is one condition."

"What is that, Mr. O'Brian?"

"That you get the boy some help. Think it over tonight. If you decide to accept my offer, I can refer you to someone who will help him."

"I'll have to talk to my husband . . ."

"Of course. I expect you'll want to be with Nels. I won't keep you any longer. If your husband wishes to talk to me, he can call me this evening at home. I'm in the book, on English Street."

"Yes—thank you, Mr. O'Brian."

"Thank you for coming in Mrs.—Margaret."

That evening, after Nels and Ellen were in bed, Sally's daughter Sandy came to mind the house for an hour. The elder Sorensons walked the short distance to the house beside the church where the Preacher and his wife lived. They were expected. John had phoned and asked if they could come and speak to him as soon as Margaret had told him about her conversation in the Principal's office.

The Pastor's wife met them at the door. The Preacher was waiting for them in his study. He had aged over the years since the Sorensons had become members of the church. His silver hair had begun to turn white around the temples. But his grey eyes were as quiet and assuring as ever.

He welcomed the younger couple in and made them comfortable. Coffee was offered and politely declined. Then he listened without interrupting while first John and then Margaret described in detail the events of the past four days.

When she had finished, it was Margaret who posed the question.

"What do you think has happened to Nels, Pastor? He's changed so much . . ."

She left it in mid-air. The Preacher waited a moment longer. He gave them a thoughtful smile.

"It's not just Nels who is changing, Margaret. The world around us is changing rapidly. The fact that the woodlot is gone in order to build a paint plant is merely one example of that change. Whether all of these changes will ultimately prove to be as advantageous as we are being led to believe is not for me to say. The Good Lord does not reveal these things ahead of time."

"But in the light of what you have told me this evening, your son's reaction seems to me to be quite an understandable response. I know how much you feel the loss of this place John. You've told me in the past of the importance it held for you in your life, as a Christian."

John Sorenson nodded sadly in assent. The Preacher saw Margaret reach to take his hand, the gesture purely unselfconscious. He smiled a gentle smile.

"Nels is a very intelligent boy. In some ways, like his capacity to learn the Scriptures, he is quite advanced for his years. In other ways, he is very young for his years. He is still a child . . . a very sensitive child. This is the first time in his life that he lost something which he loved. I have seen it happen with my own children."

"To be truthful with you, it has caused me some troubled moments when I wondered how it is that we, as adults, become so inured to loss. I believe that the reason for the gift of Faith was to replace that loss of innocence. The world that men create for themselves is always possessed of a dark side as well as a light side. It is at best a difficult place."

"Children, in their innocence, do not see the world in the way that we, as adults, see it. Nels is both hurt and angry. He wants to punish someone for the destruction of the woodlot. The business about the turtle is most unfortunate. I'm certain that, to him, it represents a deliberate cruelty, an act of savagery which he could not have even imagined. That would explain the level of his rage."

"But the heart of the matter to me lies in his reference to the woodlot as 'God's Place'. I suspect that, as adults, we may not be able to appreciate just how literally he means that. I think the real problem may be that Nels feels that he had lost not only God's place, but God as well. Nels may feel that, like Adam, he has been cast out of the Garden."

He paused to allow them to consider what he had said. They turned to look at each other. He saw the woman nod her head to her husband in silent consensus. It was John who spoke for them, turning back to face him.

"What you have said seems true to us Pastor. But what can we do to get God back for Nels?"

The Preacher's eyes grew serious and thoughtful.

"I don't believe that you or I can do that for him John. I don't believe that any of us can give the presence of God to another person, as though God were a gift between us, no matter how much we might wish to. The history of the Church is filled with unfortunate examples of men who allowed themselves to be deceived by this false pride.

"Nels has proven himself to be strong willed, despite his youth. I think that he will have to find God again for himself. All that we can do for him is support him and try to point the way."

The couple looked crestfallen. But the Preacher's eyes brightened and he smiled.

"The Lord does not abandon His children, my friends. I believe that He may already have given us the means to help young Nels, although I did not know of your trouble when it came to me this afternoon."

"How do you mean Pastor?"

"The Lord moves in mysterious ways John. This afternoon another couple came to visit me. They're an older couple. Bill and Mary Johnston. They live out of town. They come in for the morning service. You may have met them. They're farm people."

"Yes. I think we have."

"Bill and Mary have raised five children. Three sons and two daughters. Their youngest left home a few months ago. Both daughters and one son are married now, to city people. All three of their sons are working in one of the new automobile assembly plants. I gather that they have well paid jobs."

"Bill's getting on in years. He's finding the work on the farm to be a heavy load as he gets older. He had always assumed that one of his sons would take over the farm. I gathered, from what he said, that he has found out that this is not going to happen."

"Bill's great-grandfather homesteaded the land. His grandfather and his father were farmers. Bill's fourth generation. He is wrestling with the knowledge that when the day comes that he is no longer capable of doing the work, the land will pass from his family forever. I believe that, with time and the help of God, he will come to accept this."

"The hardest thing for them right now is having their children grown up and no longer there to share in their lives. They are lonely. The beauty of the land and their way of life has come to have a veil drawn over it for them."

"Bill told me this afternoon that in the past month, he feels that he has lost sight of the hand of God in His creation. He is already anticipating the loss of the farm."

He paused again. Margaret Sorenson said,

"Pastor—how do their difficulties help my son?"

The Preacher smiled at her impatience.

"In a way, Margaret, Bill's problem is not all that different from Nels' problem. They both feel, each in his own way, the loss of the part of Nature that they have known and loved. They both feel set apart from God and neither of them knows the way back."

He paused again, to let the thought settle.

"You mentioned that the Principal had asked you to take Nels out of school for the last month of the year. I confess that, at the time, I questioned the wisdom of that request. It seemed to me that the boy would see it as a punishment and feel more cut off than ever."

"Upon reflection, I believe that the hand of God is at work here, showing us the way to guide your son back to Him. I believe that if I approached Bill and Mary on your behalf and explained Nels' difficulty as you have explained it to me, they would be glad to take him for that time. They are good Christian people. They have raised five children of their own. I believe that they would be glad to help, and that they would understand."

"The Johnston's farm is a beautiful place. Especially at this time of the year, when it is so abundant with new life. In addition to the land under cultivation, they also have a large woodlot. The river runs right below the house, at the bottom of the hill. You can look right out over it from their kitchen window. Bill has told me that there are fish in it. Young Nels has told me on more than one occasion how much he likes to fish."

"It's a busy time of year on the farm. I'm sure that the help Nels could give Bill with the chores would offset any cost of his keep. I know that Mary would be delighted to have a boy around the house."

"Most importantly, I think that Bill and Nels could help each other with their problems. Bill knows all the secrets and the ways of the land with the knowledge of four generations. These are the things that he has lost sight of. There is nothing like the innocence of children to help us adults to rediscover the freshness and the beauty of the world when it grows stale and familiar. With Bill to guide him I think Nels would discover a whole new Creation to replace the one that has been lost."

"As for Bill, I think that one of the hardest things for a man to bear is to find that the knowledge and the beliefs that he has come to cherish will have no new generation to value and to benefit from them. I believe that, in this way, Bill and Nels could help each other to find God again."

The Preacher rose to his feet.

"Perhaps you would like some coffee now? I'll go and see to it. I'm sure you'd like a few moments to yourselves. Please feel at home."

"Thank you Pastor."

Night had fallen when they left the Preacher's house. They walked home in the soft summer darkness, hand in hand. The familiar streets seemed changed somehow, in the whisper of wind that stirred around them and the bright glow of headlights passing by.

"It feels like such a long time since Sunday."

Margaret Sorenson broke the silence which had fallen over them, tentatively, like a swimmer testing the water.

"Yes. I don't know what we'd do without him Marg. He looked old tonight. I wonder what we'll do when he retires."

The silence closed around them again. She looked over at him, studying his expression in the glow of the streetlight as they turned into the narrow passageway.

"What about you John?" Do you wish you could go and spend a month on the farm with Nels?"

He was silent a moment longer.

"I wish we could all go and live in the country Marg."

He said it with such a passion that she stopped walking, turning to stand in front of him, looking up into his eyes.

"You really mean it, don't you?"

"Yes. I guess I do."

"Don't you like it here any more John?"

He looked past her, at the place which had been home for years, torn inside.

"It's not that. It's just—I don't know. I'm not a city man. Sometimes I feel like a cat in a cage here. That's what it meant to me, going out there with him on Sundays. I didn't feel so trapped, just knowing there was a place where we could go."

"I'm sorry John. I thought you were happy here."

He heard the hurt in her voice. He reached to put his arms around her waist and drew her close.

"I have been Honey. More than I've ever been in my life. I know how much your family means to you. They're family to me too now. But your Dad's gone. We don't see that much of anybody any more except Sally. Even her kids don't come around like they used to. They're grown up now."

He stopped, knowing that he was only making it worse.

"It's just—I don't want my son growing up not knowing anything but these city streets."

She put his hands on his chest, looking into his eyes. He felt the change in her, felt her yielding.

"I couldn't live in the country John. I wouldn't know what to do with myself . . ."

"We wouldn't have to Marg. There's a place I've been looking at for a long time. It's out on the outskirts. We go by there once a week with the train. There's a subdivision there, and there's parkland with a creek running through it. There's fields and bits of bush just out past it. He could ride out on his bicycle and be out of the city in ten minutes."

"You never told me any of this before John."

"I didn't want you to be unhappy Honey. It's just—maybe there's a better life for us in the suburbs."

She summoned up the Irish in herself, smiling for him now.

"Maybe you're right John. The family does seem to be going its own ways. And after talking to Mr. O'Brian today—I don't want my son growing up to be a hoodlum. He's got that Irish streak—he won't quit fighting if we let it get started. I guess it's time we put the kids first."

She was silent for a moment.

"I'll tell you what I'll do John. I'll phone the man we bought the house through and see what he has to say."

"Do you mean that Marg?"

"Yes. My mind's made up."

"Oh Honey!"

He picked her up in his arms and swung her through the air and kissed her right there in the street. She pushed him away, laughing in a flood of sheer relief.

"John—what if the neighbours are looking?"

"Let 'em look!"

"Put me down! We're almost home!"

He set her down reluctantly and she caught at his hand.

"Come on John—I'll race you to the house."

In the morning he awoke to the sound of the back door closing. He lay still, listening to his mother softly singing. She tapped on his door and opened it, smiling in at him.

"Hi Mom. I'm awake."

"Breakfast is almost ready."

"Okay."

He climbed out of bed, hearing her talking at Ellen's door. He took off his pyjamas and reached for his pants, remembering about Wolfgang. His mother was all smiles at the table.

"Here's the milk. The eggs will be ready in a minute. There's no school for you two today."

"How come?"

"Ellen's going shopping with Aunt Sally and I. I thought that, since Ellen has to come with us, you might like to go and visit Walker. You haven't seen him for a while."

He let out a long sigh of relief.

"Sure Mom. Maybe he'll take me fishing."

When breakfast was over she bustled them into the car. Aunt Sally was waiting for them in front of her house. He got out and held the door for her. She gave him a kiss on the cheek.

"Thank you Nels. Walker's in the kitchen. I told him you were coming. You boys have a nice time. And help yourself to the cookies."

He waved as the car drove away and walked up the driveway, hesitating at the back door.

"Come on in kid!"

Walker grinned at him, sitting at the kitchen table.

"Hi Poppy."

"Hi kid. Move those sticks and pull up a chair."

There were two canes on the back of the chair, the old dark wood one and a new one made out of light shiny metal. He carried them carefully and propped them up in the corner, wondering if Poppy was okay.

"Sit down kid."

Walker was looking at the stitches above his eye. He grinned at the boy again.

"What happened to you kid? You walk into a door?"

"Wolfgang punched me. At school."

"Why'd he do that?"

He looked down at the table.

"I tried to hit him with the pavement."

"Hmm. You must've been pretty mad, eh? He hit you first? Say something to you?"

"No."

"Look at me kid. Why'd you try to hit him?"

He thought for a moment, not knowing how to explain it. Poppy's eyes seemed to look inside of him.

"He's the best fighter in the school."

The old man nodded, remembering.

"It's like that, is it? Ah—you're Irish all right. Stand up Soldier."

He got up and stood to attention in front of Walker's chair.

"Look at me. Here's how it is. First thing—you don't hit anybody unless there's no way to walk away from it before it starts. You got that Soldier?"

"Yes Sir."

"Good. If you have to hit somebody, you use your fists. No more rocks or anything else. And if you have to fight, you fight to win. You got that too?"

"Yes Sir."

"All right. At ease now. Let's see you make a fist. Both hands. No, not like that—here give me your hands. Like that. Now I'm going to hold my hands up. You punch the palm of my hand. Spread your feet. You need a stance. Now put your shoulder into it."

They were still practising when they heard the Dodge pull into the driveway.

"Okay kid. Your aunt and your mom are here. Sit down and make like we're just talking."

Aunt Sally came in, with Ellen and his mother close behind. She looked around suspiciously.

"What are you two up to?"

"Nothing, Sal. We just been talking fishing. Haven't we kid."

Walker grinned at Aunt Sally and gave him a prodigious wink.

"You're an awful old man."

She smiled at him fondly.

"Hi Elly. Hi Mom."

"Hi Nels. Hello Walker. How are you?"

"Always good Marg. Hi Ellen."

"Mom—can I go to school this afternoon?"

She smiled at him.

"Well—I wasn't going to tell you. It was supposed to be a surprise. Your Dad's getting off at lunch time today. We've been invited by some people from the church to come and see their farm. We'll be going as soon as we've had lunch."

"I don't want to go! I want to go to school!"

"Really? Oh—I thought that you kids would like to see a farm. There'll be cows and sheep and ducks and chickens . . ."

Ellen said, "I want to go Mummy."

"I want to go to school!"

He looked to Poppy for support.

His mother said,

"Oh well . . . if you don't want to go . . . but you've never been to a farm. Mr. Johnston says there's even a place to go fishing. The river's right beside their house. I just thought you'd like it . . ."

Walker grinned at him.

"You're not going to pass up fishing just to go to school are you kid?"

"But I don't have a fishing pole."

"We'll fix that. Go down the basement and bring up the tackle box and the rod you always use. And bring that little knapsack that's hanging up with my net."

"Yes Sir!"

The Johnston's farm was further out of the city than he had ever been. Twice they got lost on the gravel roads and had to turn around. He began to wonder if they would ever get there, casting longing glances into the stands of trees as they passed by.

At last he heard his father say,

"That must be it there."

"Are you sure John?"

"It's got to be Marg. There's the bridge, just past it."

"Where?"

He leaned forward over the back of the seat to stare out through the windshield. The farmhouse stood on a low rise, half-hidden in a screen of tall poplar trees. Beyond it the land dipped gently down and rose up again, stretching away into fields that were furred with soft green. He could see the black top of an iron bridge sticking up out of the hollow where the road went.

"This is it. There's Bill and Mary."

His father turned the Dodge into the lane, driving slowly, the whole family waving at the couple on the lawn waving back as they came to meet them.

"Mom! They've got a dog! Is he ever big!"

Mr. Johnston was dressed in green work pants and a green shirt. He was a big man, with an old straw hat perched on the back of his head. Mrs. Johnston was almost as big as her husband. She had gray hair and pink muscular arms that bulged out of her short-sleeved summer dress. He liked her as soon as she smiled at him.

The adults were all smiling and shaking hands while he stood beside Ellen and waited for his turn.

"We thought you'd gotten lost."

"I think we turned at the wrong red barn with the windmill."

"I told Bill to tell you that there were two of them. But you're here now."

Something bumped him in the small of his back. He whirled around and began to back up against the car as the huge shaggy dog advanced on him.

"Dad . . ."

Mr. Johnston laughed.

"Don't be afraid of him son. That's Fred. He wouldn't hurt a fly. He just hasn't had a boy to play with for a long time. Go ahead and pet him."

"Hi Fred."

He bent forward, putting his face close to look into the luminous brown eyes. He was rewarded by a lick with a pink tongue that covered half his cheek.

"He likes me!"

"He sure does son. Well—what would you like to do first?"

Ellen was beaming up at Mrs. Johnston.

"I want to see the baby animals!"

"Sure you do dear. Bill, why don't you take the children and show them through the barn?"

"Sure Mary. Want to come along John?"

"I believe I will."

"How about you Margaret?"

"Yes. I'd like to see them too."

"Mary?"

Mrs. Johnston jiggled when she laughed.

"Not me. I spend enough time in the barn. I've got things to do. You will stay for dinner, won't you?"

He looked up hopefully at his mother. She smiled at Mrs. Johnston.

"Why, yes, thank you. That would be lovely."

When they came out of the barn he could barely contain himself. He watched Mr. Johnston anxiously, waiting for a sign. Finally the farmer looked at him.

"Did you bring a fishing pole son?"

"Yes Sir. It's in the car."

"Good. I dug some worms. Why don't you go and get your pole?"

"Yes Sir!"

His father handed him the car keys.

"Come on Fred!"

They watched him race across the yard to the car with the old dog bounding happily beside him.

"Why don't you folks go on in the house for a bit? Mary's got some of our June's dolls for your little girl to play with. You can have a talk while me and Nels get acquainted. Maybe you could wander down and join us when you feel like it John. You'll be able to see us from the kitchen."

"Sounds good Bill."

"He sure moves, doesn't he?"

Nels was already closing the trunk lid. He picked up Poppy's fishing pole proudly with one hand. The knapsack slung on his shoulder bulged with hooks and weights and battered pike plugs.

John Sorenson gave the farmer a wry smile.

"He's too fast sometimes Bill."

"Our boys were too—and we had three of them. I think we'll get along just fine."

The boy caught the look in his father's eye and slowed to a respectful walk, coming up to join them.

"I'm ready Sir."

"Why don't you call me Uncle Bill?"

The boy didn't question this at all. Aside from all of his real aunts and uncles, his parent's best friends had the same honorary status. He smiled.

"Sure Uncle Bill."

Ellen said, "Will you be my Uncle Bill too?"

"Sure I will, honey."

The farmer bent down and patted her cheek.

"Aunt Mary's got some dollies for you to play with in the house. Why don't you go in and see her?"

Nels Sorenson turned, looking past the barn and across the fields to where the forest began, seeing it for the first time. The farmer sensed the change in him. He put one big hand on the boy's shoulder, turning him back towards the river.

"Come on son. Let's go fishing."

The rest of the family crossed the yard to the rambling wooden farm house, looking around. There were spring flowers everywhere, growing in rich profusion. To one side of the house there was a fenced area of cultivated earth. The early vegetables—lettuces, onions, spinach—stood up in long green rows. John Sorenson paused to stare in over the fence.

"Look at the garden they've got Marg! I'd love to have a garden . . ."

"Yes. And all the flowers. Maybe some day John . . ."

Mrs. Johnston opened the screened door for them.

"Come right in. Don't be shy."

"That's quite a garden you've got."

"Yes. But it's getting to be a lot of work, now that the kids aren't here to help out. But you don't want to hear about that. Come into the kitchen. I've got some dollies for you to play with Ellen."

"Goody!"

When the little girl was settled into the big armchair in the kitchen with three dolls to keep her company, the Sorensons and the farmer's wife sat down at one end of the long wooden table. They could see the farmer and the boy on the riverbank quite clearly, a hundred feet away down the grassy slope. Mrs. Johnston poured the tea.

"The Pastor told us about the woodlot. It's a shame, the way people are selling out on the farms."

She stopped, looking away.

"Did I turn the kettle off? Oh yes. As I was going to say, we'd love to have him stay with us until school is over. How do you feel we should approach him about it? Does he know yet Margaret?'

"No. But I have an idea."

"My goodness! I'm sorry to interrupt you dear—but I think he's got something already! Look!"

Even at the distance they could see the rod bucking in the boy's hand and the flash of light as the fish broke water. They watched spellbound until the farmer bent down to pull something up into the long grass with the boy dropping to a crouch beside him. Then Nels was running flat out up the slope towards the house with Fred barking joyously beside him and a wriggling green fish clasped tightly by it's lip in his right hand.

"Dad! Dad! I got a bass! Dad!"

"Go to him John."

John was already gone.

At supper that night, there was more food on the table than the boy had ever seen at one time, except for the Christmas feasts when the Murphy clan gathered together. The bass was there too, fried golden brown, in front of his plate. He insisted that it be passed around the table. Everyone agreed that it was the best fish that they had ever tasted.

When supper was over, after his second piece of pie, Uncle Bill looked across the table at him.

"I've still got some chores to do in the barn. Want to give me a hand, son?"

"Sure Uncle Bill."

His father began to get up too. He saw his mother put her hand on his and smile.

"Not so fast, John. You can help clean up in here."

He was feeling sorry for his father when they went out to the barn. Half an hour later, when they came back in, the dishes were all down. Aunt Mary and his parents were sitting in the parlour. Ellen was fast asleep on the sofa. His father rose to his feet.

"I suppose we should be going Bill. I have to work tomorrow."

Uncle Bill bent down to whisper in his ear.

"Go ahead—ask them son."

"Mom—Dad—Uncle Bill wants to know if I can stay over until Sunday and help him do chores. And maybe go fishing."

He said the last bit quickly, hoping nobody would notice.

His mother and father looked at each other.

"I don't know Nels . . . tomorrow's a school day."

"Please Mom? There's only one day left this week."

"What do you think John?"

"Oh, I suppose one day won't hurt. Okay Nels."

"Gee! Thanks Dad."

His smile faded abruptly.

"What's wrong son?"

"I haven't got any pyjamas to wear . . ."

He looked from his father to his mother, seeing sudden triumph slipping away from him. His mother looked thoughtful.

"Do you know . . . I bought you some socks and underwear and a new pair of pyjamas when we were shopping this morning. I don't remember if I took them out of the trunk. John, go out to the car with him and have a look . . ."

He was out of the door in a flash, with his father and Uncle Bill close behind him. The women exchanged knowing smiles.

"We'll come in early Sunday before church, so that he can get dressed. If there's any problems I'll call you. We'll see what happens by Sunday."

"I don't know how to thank you Mary."

"You don't have to thank me Margaret. I haven't seen Bill this happy in a long time."

"I guess we should both thank the Pastor."

"Yes. And Someone Else too."

They heard him pounding up the porch steps.

"I've got them Mom! I've got them!"

On Sunday morning, the Johnstons and the Sorensons sat together during the worship service. After the service was over, the Johnstons accepted the invitation to have lunch with the Sorenson household. The conversation among the adults flowed smoothly through the meal, but no one failed to notice that the boy became quiet and withdrawn. When the tea was poured he asked to be excused and went into his room.

Margaret followed him in, closing the door quietly behind her. He was sitting on the edge of the bed, staring down at the floor. She sat down beside him and put her arm across his shoulders.

"What's the matter Nels?"

He shrugged his shoulders helplessly.

"I don't know Mom . . . it's Sunday . . ."

She hugged him, keeping her tone gentle and light when she spoke.

"Come back out and sit with us for a little bit longer. Uncle Bill and Aunt Mary will have to go home soon. They've been good to you. You don't want to hurt their feelings by being impolite. Do you."

"No. I guess not."

He went back out with her and sat down at the table. His father and Uncle Bill were deep in conversation.

"I've never been so far behind as I am this year. I've still got calves in the barn that should be pasturing. I can't get far enough ahead to get the fences fixed that the snow took down. Although with Nels here . . ."

They both turned to look at him.

"He helped a lot, the last couple of days, feeding the stock and working with Mary in the garden. It's not that the work's that heavy. It's the little things, like feeding the stock and milking the Jersey that take up so much time. He's a good worker, John. Just the help he gave me saved me enough time to finally get the choke fixed on the tractor. He even had time enough to go fishing. Boy, he sure likes that. Don't you son?"

He smiled, remembering.

"I caught a catfish Dad. My first one."

"It's too bad school's still on. We could use a whole month of his help."

"It is, Bill. They don't seem to do much anyhow, this time of year. I bet you'd rather be on the farm than sitting in school eh Nels?"

He thought about Wolfgang again.

"I sure would Dad."

He said it so fervently that all of the adults turned to look at him. There was a thoughtful silence around the table.

"Would you like to go and help Uncle Bill and Aunt Mary if I could arrange it Nels?"

He looked to his mother, suddenly caught between wild hope and vast despair.

"Oh yes!—but I wouldn't pass my year!"

She smiled at him, looking around to Aunt Mary beside her.

"I've known the Principal for years. He taught me when I was a girl. He's a very nice man. Maybe, if I called him and explained that this is a special situation . . ."

"We could sure use the help, dear . . ."

"Get the telephone book Nels. Look up Mr. O'Brian's number. He's on English Street. You can dial it for me."

He got up slowly and dialled the number that he found in the book, handing her the receiver, hovering at the edge of unreality. The room spun around him. He had to close his eyes to listen.

"Hello? Mr. O'Brian? It's Margaret Sorenson calling. I'm sorry to disturb you on Sunday. Something's come up. We have some friends in, from the country. They'd like to have Nels come and stay with them for a while, and help them on the farm. He'd like to go, but he's worried about his year. His marks are quite good, and my husband and I both think the experience would be good for him."

There was a silence for a moment and be began to pray.

"Yes? Just a moment please Mr. O'Brian."

He felt her hand touch his shoulder. He opened his eyes. She held the receiver out to him.

"Mr. O'Brian wants to speak to you."

"Me?"

"Yes. Go ahead Honey."

He held the receiver to his ear. There were butterflies fluttering around inside of him.

"Hello?"

"Hello Nels. This is Mr. O'Brian. I understand that you'd like to go to a farm for a while."

"Yes Sir."

"I think that's a good idea. I wish that I could go with you. I grew up on a farm myself. I want you to have a really good time. I'll see that you pass, so you don't have to worry about school. All right?"

"Yes Sir. Thank you Sir."

"Goodbye Nels."

"Goodbye Sir."

He put the receiver down and stood there, dazed. His mother said,

"Aren't you going to tell us what he said Nels?"

"He said I can go . . ."

He looked from face to face, seeing the smiles that were there. It was Uncle Bill who spoke for them.

"I guess the Good Lord wanted us to have your help son."

"Yes Sir. Should I go and pack?"

He turned to his mother and saw the two single tears, one on each cheek, in spite of her smile.

"What's wrong Mom?"

"Nothing Honey. I'm just being silly. I'm going to miss you."

He reached for her and held her close, forgetting about the fact that there was anyone else there at all.

The memories of the days that followed were ones that he would cherish for the rest of his life.

He was up with the dawn. When he came outside into the sweet summer mornings with Uncle Bill, Fred was waiting on the porch for one first romp around the yard. The barn was a cheerful commotion of animals all clamouring to be fed.

While he and Uncle Bill did the chores, Aunt Mary prepared huge breakfasts of cereal and home cured bacon and fresh brown eggs that were warm in the nests when he gathered them for her. He learned to milk the Jersey cow by hand, how to twist the teat and squeeze it at just the right angle to send a thin white stream at the barn cats that assembled at milking time, mewing plaintively.

When the breakfast was over and the dishes were washed and put away he helped Aunt Mary in the garden for an hour. He learned to plant and thin and weed, savouring the warm loamy feel of the soil beneath his fingers. The garden was home to a multitude of insects. He carried each new specimen to show Aunt Mary, where its fate was decided by whether it was helpful or harmful to the tender young plants. The helpful ones were put back into the garden. The harmful ones went into a jar to be observed and later to be scattered on the surface of the pool, where small fish devoured them eagerly.

When the gardening was finished he went wading in the shallow rapids above the bridge with Fred. There were myriads of creatures in the warm shallow water. The freshly emptied jar now served a new purpose. Beneath the stones on the river bottom dwelled the hellgrammites and the shy blue crayfish, its shell still soft from moulting, that Walker had taught him were a bass' favourite bait. They were both quick and elusive but he was quicker still.

When a sufficient supply of bait for the morning's expedition was safely in his jar, he went back to the house for the rod and the knapsack. He ate bass and catfish for lunch every day. The farmer and his wife marvelled at what an accomplished fisherman he was for a city boy.

In the afternoons he faded across the fields to explore the new Forest, with the old dog padding happily at his side. On the days that it rained, he read in solitude in the fort that Uncle Bill helped him build in the hay loft of the barn. They built it against the south wall, out of bales of clean sweet-smelling hay. The gaps between the weathered pine boards let the soft light in. He could look out, across the fields to the Forest.

The books that he read were their sons' books. He travelled to Treasure Island and went through the looking glass, with Alice. But the best of them all was a fishing story. It was called The Old Man and the Sea. In his mind's eye, the old man in the story had Poppy's face. He cried when the old man came home and there was nothing left of the fish for him to eat.

By supper time he was ravenous again. The farmer's wife's skill in the kitchen was more than a match for his appetite. When the last chores of the day were finished, there was one more romp with Fred.

Then it was bedtime. The sweet smells of clover and lilac drifted in through the open window while he knelt beside the bed to say his prayers.

"God bless Mom and Dad and Ellen, and Poppy and Auntie Sal . . ."

Most nights he was too spent to go through the litany of all of his cousins and aunts and uncles. He climbed in between the cool white sheets, his body sated with living, to drift off into the pastel coloured evenings. Nesting birds and katydids and crickets sang him a lullaby. God returned, to walk once more in the Garden.

He came in from the country on the first Sunday in July, tanned and smiling. The summer sun had bleached his blond hair almost white. There were little knots of muscle on his arms that hadn't been there a month before. Inside of him there was a deep delicious craving for home. Even the thought of Wolfgang could not distract him from that. He clenched his fists furtively in the back seat of Uncle Bill's car, smiling to himself at the way the muscles stood out below the cuffs of his short-sleeved white shirt.

He sat with his family where they always sat, on the right side of the balcony, looking down to wave at Aunt Mary and Uncle Bill before the service began. When the service was over and they all met outside, Aunt Sally was waiting for them at the bottom of the steps.

Nels took her hand and introduced her to Uncle Bill and Aunt Mary. The Preacher and his wife came over to join them. Aunt Sally looked shy—which was something he had never seen—when the Preacher and his wife invited her to come to church the following Sunday.

The crowd on the lawn diminished and then faded away while the adults smiled and talked around him. He fidgeted from one foot to the other, trying to pay polite attention and answering when spoken to while he fought with the almost irresistible urge to leave them there and run as fast as he could, all the way home.

He almost sighed with relief when the Preacher and his wife took their leave. He forced himself to walk to the parking lot, fidgeting some more while his belongings were transferred from Uncle Bill's blue Chevrolet to the trunk of the old red Dodge.

Aunt Mary hugged him so hard it took his breath away. Uncle Bill shook his hand until his fingers tingled from the grip. He held the rear door open for Aunt Sally and got in beside her, with Ellen smiling across the seat at him from the other side. He waved one last time, hanging out the window to holler,

"Say hello to Fred!"

Then the Dodge was moving. He pulled himself in, straining forward against the back of the seat to look out past his mother as they drove downhill along the beckoning street. Past the two long blocks and he swung around to stare in disbelief at the narrow passageway passing by.

"Dad! That was our street!"

"It's okay son. We're going for a drive."

"But—"

He was still staring when his father turned right towards Main Street. The passage to home disappeared behind him. He swung around again, seeking his father's eyes in the rear-view mirror.

"But where are we going?"

His mother turned to smile at him over the back of the seat. Aunt Sally took his hand. He saw the secret look that passed between them.

"It's a surprise Nels. A very special surprise."

He felt the rush of his dismay already changing to sweet mystery. If Mom and Aunt Sally had prepared a surprise for him, he knew that it would be very special indeed.

"Oh boy! Can I have a hint Auntie Sal?"

She laughed and gave his hand a squeeze.

"No hints, Honey. You just sit back and enjoy the ride."

He leaned out past her, to look across the seat at his sister. Ellen gave him a knowing smile.

"I'm not telling Nels."

"Aww . . . just one hint Elly?"

"No."

"Gee—"

He squirmed around on the seat, barely able to contain himself as his father turned left onto Main Street, heading east. Past the shops and past the fairgrounds, past the factories, his excitement tinged with anxiety now as they drove uphill along the line of big houses towards where the forest had been. His father turned right at the top of the hill. He relaxed his grip on Aunt Sally's hand, looking out at a street he had never been on before.

The houses were even bigger here, hidden back behind hedges among evergreen trees. Huge maples grew along the boulevards, their branches reaching up to meet above the street from either side. He tilted his head back to look out and up into the canopy of the leaves. The bright summer sun flickered behind them. He closed his eyes, letting the last of his anxiety wash away in the bright colours and patterns that flowed across his eyelids.

He opened them again at the solid yellow brightness. The tunnel of the trees was gone. His father brought the car to a stop at the red light of an intersection.

"Are we almost there Dad?"

"Just about son."

Ahead of them the street had changed. The houses were smaller and pressed closely together behind shallow lawns. The odd big maple stood out isolated on the boulevard. He leaned to look past Ellen's window. There was a short stretch of more houses that ended at a band of open grass. A small bridge stood on the road above a hollow where the grass dropped away to re-emerge, green again to the top of a rise with a long low yellow building at its summit. Beyond it the land stretched away into open fields.

The light turned green and they drove on through. They hadn't gone far when the car began to slow down. He heard the clicking as his father put the turn signal on. A small street opened on the left hand side. The car turned into it and came to a stop where the street ended abruptly, no more than the distance from the street that they had turned off than the distance from their house to the school gate.

There was a red stop sign and a row of houses facing them beyond the cross street. Beside the stop sign there was a street sign unlike the white metal street signs with their black letters that he was familiar with. This one was green, with white letters.

The name of the street facing them was Partridge Crescent. It struck him as odd, because partridges lived in the forest. He looked around, just in case. Not only weren't there any partridges; there wasn't a single tree as far as he could see in any direction!

The sudden quiet in the car mirrored his amazement at this discovery. The engine idled softly. The clicking of the turn signal was clear and precise. From somewhere close by he heard the yelling and shouting of boys hard at play. It sounded like recess, which it couldn't be on a Sunday. He looked around for the sound. It seemed to be coming from beyond the houses which faced them.

The car began to move again, slowly, turning left into the cross street. He looked out of the window beside him as the shouting grew louder, looking up into the gap between two houses, seeking its source. There was a glimpse of a long empty yard which ended at a high board fence; but no boys.

He turned to look out ahead of them, his curiosity fully aroused now. The street curved away, disappearing around a bend between a double row of tall brick houses. The absence of trees drew his attention to the line of lampposts on the right hand boulevard. There seemed to be one in front of every second house; tall slender cement poles unlike anything he had seen before. There was a metal bracket at the top of each one, and a brass coloured shield to protect the naked bulb that was there beneath it. The shields looked like the Roman helmets that the centurions wore in his old Bible story book. Stranger still, there were no visible electrical wires connecting the poles together.

His father drove on up the street at little more than a walking pace. The clamour of voices accompanied them, sometimes louder, sometimes fading. He turned back to look out the side window, seeking again for the source of the sound. The gap between the next two houses showed him only another empty yard and what looked like the same board fence.

He began to examine the houses. Each house had a paved driveway which led in up one side of it. There was a thin strip of lawn beside that and then a cement sidewalk leading up to concrete steps and a tiny uncovered cement porch. The porches had wrought iron railings but no flower boxes. The doors to the houses were behind the tiny porches. The rest of the front of the houses were taken up by enormous rectangular windows.

The roofs were tall and steep, their front slopes facing the street. On the end of each house there was a small double window, high enough up under the point where the two slopes met to know that each house had an upstairs. On each rooftop there was the many-fingered design of a television aerial protruding into the blue summer sky.

He brought his eyes down to examine the people who lived in this strange new place. For the first time he saw how many people were there. Every lawn and every sidewalk overflowed with small children. There were little boys on tricycles with brightly coloured plastic streamers on the handlebars, and other little boys clutching plastic toys or munching candy bars in little groups around them. There were little girls too, with dolls or stuffed animals and more candy bars, while bigger girls danced through skipping ropes or sprawled at leisure on the lawns.

In each driveway they passed there was a man with a hose, washing a big shiny car. Some of the cars had tail fins like the rocket ship he had seen on the cover of a book in the library. There were women too, one for each house, sitting in folding chairs on the porches or sitting on the steps. Some of them were wearing their housecoats outside! Even more astonishing, some of them were smoking cigarettes! The spray from the hoses was rainbow coloured in the bright summer sun. He waved to one of the men who looked over at him, but the man looked away again without waving back. Then he noticed how the children had all begun to stare and point at their car as they passed by.

He looked over the heads, watching the houses again, feeling suddenly shy. He stared at the houses, seeking some distraction. Ahead of them, the street curved away into yet another bend with no place to turn off at. It was then that it came to him! All of the houses were the same!

He poked his head out of the window to get a better look. They looked the same; they were all the same height, the line of the rooftops stretching uniformly in either direction. There were differences; some of them had red shingles or green shingles where most of them were brown, but—He let his eyes run along the rooftops, scanning the aerials. Some of them were smaller, mounted at the centre of the peaks. Others were bigger. He saw that these were mounted on metal towers which ran up from the ground. They seemed to be attached to the end walls, tucked in against the bulge of the chimney.

The differences made him begin to doubt. He looked down, at the front of the houses again. There were differences here too. In some the bricks were brown while others were yellow. The odd one was red. Still his conviction lingered. The stares of small children went unheeded. The shapes of the houses looked the same. He let his eyes run back along the line of them. The porches were all the same size. And the windows. The driveways and the front doors were all on the same side. Even the upstairs windows—they were the same! And the lamp posts!

And then another thought struck him—there weren't any old people! He searched the lawns and the porches but there weren't any old people there. The yelling of boys surged up again but he ignored it, watching the windows to see if the old people were inside. He couldn't see them if they were.

He remembered the trees that weren't there. He looked ahead, along the side of the car, to see if any trees had appeared. There weren't any, but the road had straightened. Up ahead, he saw another stop sign and a cross street, with more houses facing it. There were more shiny cars and more children and the sound of recess on Sunday, still echoing up from behind the houses beside him. There were streets that curved, and no trees and no old people; and all of the lamp posts and the houses were the same! It had the aura of a mystery in the hot bright summer sunshine.

His father stopped for the stop sign. There was another green sign beside it. This one said Thornberry Drive. They turned right this time. The yelling was louder now than it had ever been. The car rolled to a stop in the middle of the street. Beside him there was a gap between the houses which was large enough for another house to have been set in its place. Beyond it there was a long open field, surrounded by a high board fence.

The roofs of the houses circled around behind it. In the field a mob of running screaming boys surged back and forth in a wheeling chaotic pack. There were boys with baseball gloves and baseball bats, boys with soccer balls, even boys with football pads, their faces hidden in brightly coloured helmets, all running together while other boys on bicycles veered and swerved in a vanguard on the outside.

He felt a sudden distaste for these boys that verged on superiority. They obviously weren't smart enough to know that it was Sunday. He looked back at the street which was much more interesting. The car rolled forward, past one more house. He leaned to look out through the windshield as his father turned the car into an empty driveway.

The sound of the engine died away. He stared out at the house, sensing a new mystery now. It was built of yellow bricks, with red shingles on the roof. On the far end of the roof the tip of a metal tower stuck up. On top of it there was a large television aerial. Mom and Dad were turned around, smiling at him over the back of the seat. Aunt Sally and Ellen turned to smile at him too.

He remembered the surprise, wondering what it could be, and who they knew that lived in such a strange place, the two thoughts still unconnected but both steeped in the same sense of mystery.

"Who lives here Dad?"

His father looked away, to Ellen.

"You tell him Elly."

He felt Aunt Sally take his hand again. Ellen beamed at him across the seat.

"We do Nels! This is our new house!"

The world dropped away beneath him.

"But—I wanted to go see Poppy and take his fishing pole back—"

He looked to Auntie Sal, holding tight to her hand.

"Poppy wanted you to have it Nels. It was a present."

"But—when can I go and see him?"

He turned back, appealing to his mother now.

"It's all right Honey. We'll take the bus downtown to Sally's tomorrow. You and Poppy can have a nice long visit. He missed you too."

She paused, and for a minute he thought that she was going to cry.

"We all missed you Honey."

He reached his other hand over the seat, to take her hand in his. There was only the warmth and safety of his family inside the car now. The strange new world beyond the window was forgotten.

"I missed you too. I'm glad I'm back."

He hovered there for a moment, out of time.

"Well? Don't you want to see your new house?"

He looked around again, knowing he was safe here, his sense of wonder returning to flood away the stillness that was unnatural to him.

"Yeah!"

He was out of the car and gone with their laughter ringing out behind him, racing up the driveway to explore his new back yard.

1959: CURTAIN CALL FOR THE TRADITIONAL WORLD

On the Friday, which was Christmas Eve, the Sorenson family were gathered in the living room. It was the quiet time, the time before bed. Mom and Ellen were cuddled up together on the couch in their housecoats. Dad was still dressed, relaxing in the big green armchair, the Bible that he read at this hour each night now closed on the table beside him. Nels was sitting on the carpet in his pyjamas, staring up at the Christmas tree, lost in thought.

The only lights on in the room were the coloured lights on the Christmas tree. Bing Crosby sang "Silent Night" in a golden tenor. The room was full of some warm familiar magic. It was there, in the coloured shadows on the closed drapes and the bright angel with gold wings, which glowed on the top of the Christmas tree. It was there too in the favoured hymn and the fragrances of pine boughs and freshly baked shortbread, which mingled like incense in the air.

Even the tree was special. He closed his eyes, visualizing again the pine woods where he had gone with his father to look for a tree. There had been one stop on the way, at the farmer's house, to ask permission to take a tree. The farmer, a grizzled old man in faded green coveralls, had refused to take the money that Dad had offered him, in the spirit of the season.

Dad had told him he could pick out the Christmas tree he wanted. He had chosen this tree out of all the other trees because this tree had a partridge sitting on top of it. The partridge flew off in a loud whirring of wings as they got close. Then Dad had given him the sharp axe and taught him how to cut the tree down.

The music ended in a scratchy hiss, drawing him back from the forest. He got up and lifted the needle from the record, watching his father anxiously out of the corner of one eye as he rose from his armchair, yawning.

"Boy! I can hardly keep my eyes open! How 'bout you son?"

He forced himself to smile.

"No Dad. I'm wide awake."

"Well it's bedtime for me I'm afraid."

He turned to look at his mother, waiting for a sign. But she only smiled at him.

"Yes. Me too. Come on Ellen. Let's go upstairs and I'll tuck you into bed."

His sister's eyes were wide with wonder.

"Is Santa coming soon Mummy?"

"Yes Honey. But Santa won't come until you're asleep. Are you coming upstairs Nels?"

"In a minute Mom."

"All right then. Come and kiss your sister goodnight."

He went to the couch and bent to kiss his sister's cheek. Ellen looked up at him with big startled brown eyes.

"Don't stay awake Nels or Santa might not come!"

He pushed down the sick feeling in his stomach, forcing himself to smile again, for his sister's sake.

"I won't Elly. He'll come. Don't worry."

"Merry Christmas Nelsy."

"Merry Christmas Elly."

He kissed her cheek and stood back to watch as Mom and Ellen left the living room, hand in hand. Dad came to stand beside him, one hand resting on his shoulder.

"Goodnight son. I'll see you in the morning."

"Okay Dad."

"Merry Christmas Nels."

"Yeah—Merry Christmas Dad."

He watched him go, his sickness rising to a climax in the click of the bedroom door closing. He crossed the room, crouching down to stare in under the Christmas tree, struggling to bring the magic back which had abruptly fled.

But it wasn't there, the special present that he wanted so much that it was a hollow ache inside him. It wasn't in the house—he had searched it from top to bottom. He had waited all night for a knock on the back door, or for some vague errand to take his father away in the car.

Now it was too late. It was his own fault. Santa Claus was Mom and Dad, although he kept this knowledge inside him for Ellen's sake. Mom and Dad were going to bed. The thing he wanted more than anything else in the whole universe was not going to come this year.

Hope sprang up in the sound of a car approaching outside in the street. He darted to the window, thrusting the drapes apart with his hands and pushing his face into the opening until his nose touched the cold glass.

The car drove on past, turning up into the crescent. He hung there, lost again between the curtains, watching the red tail lights disappear.

Outside the snow was falling. The big flakes seemed to tumble in the cone of light under the street lamps. The thought came to him, as it always did, whether it was true that every snowflake was different.

The snow fell heavily, masking the street, already beginning to erase the fresh tire marks from the road. He could see the zig-zag of the treads on the snow from the window. The battery of street lamps flooded the road now with a yellow radiance, brighter than daylight in some strange way.

He let his eyes range out over the street. There were lines of coloured lights across the front of each of the houses. Shiny cars reflected reds and greens on their dark windows. On every lawn except one there was a smiling Santa, its festive paintwork shouting colour in the glare of a white spotlight shining up out of the snow.

There were Santas in sleighs behind teams of plywood reindeer; Santas with bulging sacks, one leg down flat plywood chimneys, Santas that waved mechanical hands while their heads wagged from side to side in sheer idiot joy.

He hated them now, with a hatred that brought him close to nausea. The thing he wanted most was gone and it wasn't his fault at all! It was all these stupid Santas' fault! He glared at them, clenching his fists, wishing that the power would go out so he wouldn't have to see them there, mocking him in the snow.

He tore his eyes away from them, turning his head to look at the little wooden house on the porch railing which held the manger scene. He would kill David if anything happened to it! Whether it was wrong or not!

The manger scene had been there on Christmas every year for as long as he could remember. Each year Nels watched his mother as she gently removed the delicate china figurines from their soft cotton packing. They were part of Margaret Murphy's inheritance, from her own childhood.

He watched her handle the baby Jesus and the Wise Men with reverence as she put each one in its place. They were as much a part of Christmas as decorating the tree.

The manger was okay. He looked past it, at the snowman he had built that afternoon. His sickness rose up inside of him again, remembering what had happened on the lawn.

He had been building the snowman, absorbed in his work, not deigning to join the mob of running yelling boys who were snowball-fighting on the playing field. He seldom went into the playing field in the daytime. Each time he did, it always seemed to lead to trouble.

Throughout the spring and the summer and fall it hadn't bothered him. He had his bicycle and his fishing rod and the knapsack to carry his collecting jars. There were fields and little stands of bush within easy range. The creek on the edge of the subdivision was dead, polluted with sewage, and he was forbidden to go near it. He had found another creek, a half an hour away on his bicycle, which sometimes yielded bass and toothy pike.

Winter was hard. The bicycle and the fishing pole were put away. Sometimes he ran with the rest of the pack, just from the need to spend his restless energy. Usually it was David who spoiled it, tripping him or singling him out for derision, leading the rest of the pack to call him Churchy and other stupid names.

He wasn't afraid of David, who was the playground bully. He had faced him down several times, praying silently that David would take a swing at him. But David never did.

None of the other boys did either. He could stare down any boy on the playing field. He said nothing to his parents about it. Each time his mother asked him why he didn't go and play with the other boys, he just shrugged his shoulders and said,

"I don't know, Mom."

That afternoon Nels had been building a snowman. He looked up to see David and Billy coming out of the playing field. They had crossed the street, coming to stand beside him on the lawn. It was David who started it.

"Hey Sorenson—how come you've got all that churchy junk on your porch? How come you don't have a Santa Claus like everybody else?"

He turned his back on them, ignoring the taunt, concentrating on putting a face on the snowman. Behind him, he heard David say,

"Hey Billy! Watch me hit Jesus with a snowball!"

Nels whirled around in a rage. David was grinning, bending down to pick up some snow. Nels caught David full in the mouth with the punch that Walker called the uppercut, putting every ounce of his power into it.

David's head snapped back. He went sprawling, spread-eagled on his back in the snow. David lay still, his eyes closed, his mouth a red ruin. A stream of bright red blood flowed across his cheek, staining the clean white snow.

Nels whirled and lunged at Billy. Billy took off like a scared rabbit, running away up the street. David moaned, and opened his eyes. He almost went down again as he struggled to his feet. His hands went to his mouth and he started to cry.

Nels Sorenson backed away from him, in awe of what one punch had done. There was pain in his hand. His leather glove was stained with blood. He watched in fascination as the other boy staggered up the street. Then he turned and ran, feeling suddenly afraid, into the house to tell his mother what had happened.

Margaret Sorenson turned to stare at him when he burst into the kitchen. His eyes were wild. There was blood on one gloved hand.

She struggled to maintain her composure while he blurted out his story. The telephone began to ring. She ignored it, letting him finish. It rang incessantly, like an alarm.

When he was done, she went to answer it. She stood with her back to him.

From across the room he could hear the shrill angry voice on the line, a woman's voice. His mother said nothing, holding the phone out away from her ear.

And then a strange thing had happened. The voice was still ranting when he heard her say, "Then I suggest you keep your son away from my son!"

She slammed the receiver down on its cradle so hard that it made him jump. When she turned to face him her green eyes were flashing. He felt a force of anger emanating from her that he had never even imagined could be there before.

"Go back outside and finish your snowman Nels! David won't bother you any more!"

At supper that night Mom banged the dishes setting them down on the table. He kept his eyes on his plate, waiting in a kind of dread to hear what Dad was going to say. But his father said nothing, his eyes on his own plate. He glanced up once at him and their eyes met across the table. His mother said,

"Pass the peas John!"

He looked back down at his plate. He excused himself from the table after supper and then lingered beside her, helping her with the dishes.

The rest of the evening, the family prepared for Christmas. The presents were set out under the tree. The ritual feast of Christmas baking had been eaten in the living room. His father read them the Christmas story from St. Luke. Until a few moments ago, when his father had gone to bed, he had almost believed that the incident on the lawn had never happened.

He stared across the street into the entrance of the playing field, seeking something to bring the magic back again. The playing field was the only place in the subdivision where the yellow light of the street lamps could not go. The blackness beyond the entrance possessed a special magic of its own for him. He had no fear of it.

After supper, the mob of boys who ruled the playing field during the daylight hours disappeared from the streets. The blue glow of a cathode ray tube appeared on every window. Television held no fascination for him. The black and white images seemed flimsy and unreal compared to the imagery that his mind could conjure up from the books that he carried home each Saturday from the downtown public library. The imprint of the twine handle on the shopping bag was always there, on his hands, when he got to Aunt Sally's house for his Saturday boxing lesson with Walker.

The playground at night was his sole domain. He populated the quiet friendly darkness with dinosaurs and pirates, soldiers and kings and Cheshire cats. Now he stared across the street, straining his eyes into the blackness, visualizing the thing he wanted more than anything else and wishing that the magic which resided there could bring it to him.

"What are you looking at Nels?"

He drew back in and closed the drapes, turning around to face her.

"Oh, nothing Mom . . ."

"Well it's time for bed."

"Aw Mom—it's only ten o'clock."

She smiled at him.

"I know. But your father has to work in the morning. If we're going to get up early and open our presents before he goes to work, we'd better get some sleep."

She came and put her arm around him.

"Let's go upstairs and I'll tuck you in."

"How come Dad has to work on Christmas?"

"He just does, that's all. You know he wouldn't if he didn't have to. Come on. Let's go upstairs."

They climbed the staircase side by side. He got into bed, looking round when she went to turn the bedside light on.

"Don't turn the light on Mom."

"Okay . . ."

Her voice held the question but it didn't come. She sat down beside him on the edge of the bed. He stared up at the ceiling, trying to screw up his courage, the uncertainty worse than the knowledge of his punishment.

"Mom?"

"Yes Honey?"

"Are you and Dad mad at me?"

"You mean for hitting David?"

"Yeah."

He sat up suddenly.

"I had to do it Mom! He was going to smash the Manger! I only hit him once!"

"I know."

She put her hands on his shoulders and pushed him gently down against the pillow again.

"What David was going to do was wrong. We understand that. We don't blame you for stopping him. But you hurt David. His mother said that you knocked one of his teeth out, and two more teeth went through his lip."

"I didn't know I hit him that hard . . ."

"You did. He's not going to have a very nice Christmas. Are you sorry that you hurt him?"

He squirmed around beneath the covers.

"Well . . . I guess so . . ."

"Okay. I want you to call him and say you're sorry tomorrow.

"Aw . . . do I have to?"

"Do you want Santa Claus to come?"

"Oh yes!"

"All right then. And I want you to promise me that you won't ever hit anybody else again."

He crossed his fingers under the blankets.

"I promise."

She bent over him and kissed his cheek. The magic crept into the room again.

"There's just one more thing Nels . . ."

"What is it Mom?"

"Was that just a lucky punch or did someone teach you to hit like that?"

He began to squirm again.

"Well?"

"Somebody taught me."

"Can I ask who that somebody was Honey?"

"I can't tell Mom! It's a secret! I promised!"

"Okay. But you remember what you promised me. Now go to sleep so Santa can come."

She was leaving the room when she turned at the door and saw him getting out of bed.

"What are you doing Nels?"

"I forgot to say my prayers."

She smiled at him, illumined in the doorway.

"You are a good boy. Merry Christmas."

He knelt beside the bed, on knees that were rubbery with relief. He closed his eyes, visualizing the thing he wanted most, knowing it would come now.

"Thank you God. Amen."

Margaret Sorenson drew the door closed quietly behind her. She crossed the narrow hallway to look in to Ellen's room. In the glow of light from the hall she could see her daughter smiling in her sleep. She closed Ellen's door and then went down the stairs.

She stopped at the bottom to turn the hall light out. The house seemed to draw in around her. This house had always felt smaller than the old house, like a new pair of shoes that were tight when you put them on and that never seemed to loosen up. The staircase opened into the centre of the house. To the left was the narrow kitchen with the bathroom behind it. To the right was their bedroom on the back corner of the house. The doorway into the living room was directly in front of her.

It was the dining room that she missed most, with its big oval oak table and chairs and the sewing area set up in the corner. The memory seemed especially poignant tonight, on Christmas Eve. She stepped forward, standing just inside the living room, looking at the brightly lit tree. There was some magic that was missing for her too.

She remembered John, waiting in the bedroom for her. She squared her shoulders and turned toward the bedroom, wondering what had happened to Christmas.

John was sitting on the edge of the bed, still dressed. He looked up intently at her as she came in.

"Well?"

She turned away from his eyes, closing the bedroom door, not wanting to argue—not now—not on Christmas Eve. Then she summoned up the Irish in herself and turned to face him, knowing that it had to be this way.

"Well what John?"

"What did you say to him?"

"It's over John. It's finished. He told me that he was sorry that he hurt David. I know he didn't mean to hit him that hard. I told him that if he agreed to phone David tomorrow and apologise, and if he promised me not to hit anyone ever again, Santa would still come. He was saying his prayers when I came downstairs."

"I don't like it Marg."

She held his eyes as he stood up frowning, knowing that his sense of right and wrong was as much offended by not being consulted as it was by the incident with David.

"What don't you like about it John?"

He spread his hands, appealing to her.

"You know what a temper he's got Marg! He proved that again today. The last time it was Wolfgang. Now it's David. Oh sure—he promised not to hit anyone again. That's fine—until the next time he gets mad at some kid."

"Keep your voice down John. The children are asleep."

She said it softly. She saw his eyes widen.

"How can you take this so calmly? Marg—he knocked that kid's teeth in! And I don't believe it was just a lucky punch. Was it?"

"No John. It wasn't"

He clenched his hands, finding an outlet at last.

"I knew it! That old devil! I'll have a word with him about this!"

"You'll do no such thing! Do you hear me?"

She moved in on him, hands on her hips, a small Irish woman backing him up against the bed with her sudden fury.

"It's over John! It's finished! You'll say nothing more about it! To Nels—or to Walker! Walker's got troubles enough of his own."

"Walker's got troubles? Not like I'd like to give him, he hasn't! Marg—he taught my son to knock somebody's teeth in!"

"Maybe that somebody deserved it!"

He stared at her in shocked disbelief.

"What? You're not going to tell me that what he did was right? Oh—I don't believe this! Marg—we're supposed to be Christians!"

He turned away from her and began to pace up and down the room. She followed him, pressing home with her hushed intense whisper and her flashing green eyes.

"That's right John! We're Christians! Our son is a Christian! So what would you rather have had happen? Have some little savage smash the Manger in front of him and then go home and tell his mother it was an accident and get off scot-free? Or maybe Nels would have tried to stop him. Maybe Nels would have been the one who got the stitches—like he was with Wolfgang! Now there's a nice picture for Christmas, isn't it John! How would you have explained that to him?"

He stopped pacing and turned back to face her.

"I don't know—we could have called the Preacher."

"It's not us that needs the Preacher!"

"Marg—have you forgotten that we moved out here to get him away from fighting?"

Her anger peaked, thrusting her face up close to his.

"That's right, John! And what did we accomplish? Tell me that! These people have no respect for anything! They give their kids anything they want! They don't discipline them—they don't teach them anything! David Jones is no better than that boy Wolfgang— except that in this case it's his parent's fault! The only thing they worship is the all-mighty dollar! Poor little David! You should have heard what that woman said to me! You'll not punish Nels for this and that's final! And if that Jones woman comes over here and starts it with me I'll give her the back of my hand!"

He raised his eyes to the ceiling in some mute appeal for help.

"We're supposed to set an example Marg."

"Good! Fine! We'll set an example! For our kids! But don't think anyone else in this neighbourhood to respect us for it. Do you know why Nels doesn't go to the playground John? He told me today. The other boys call him 'Churchy' and push him around! This business with David's been going on ever since we got here!"

"Why didn't he say something?"

"What would you have done about it if he had? The kids don't know any better. That boy David would have smashed the Manger and it wouldn't have meant a thing to him—except as a way to hurt

Nels. And then that woman has the nerve to call me trash! Me! A Murphy!"

There were hot angry tears now, stinging at her eyes. He reached for her and pulled her close, crying against his chest.

"I'm sorry Marg . . . I didn't know . . . maybe I should call the Preacher."

She pushed him away, angry at herself now, for crying.

"Leave the Pastor alone! They've got a life of their own. It's Christmas Eve. Its their last few days here. You're not going to be able to call him any more. Let's just have an end of it. I can't take any more of this."

She stopped, wiping at the tears, feeling the anger fade into some deeper sadness. She looked across the distance which had come between them, seeing the sadness mirrored in his face as well. She reached for his hands, trying to close the gap.

"John . . . we've done the best we could to bring Nels up to know right from wrong. But we're not going to be able to protect him from the world. The reason he hit that boy was because we brought him up to know the meaning of Christmas. How could we punish him for that?"

"I guess you're right Marg . . ."

"Oh John . . . I've never had a Christmas like this."

She released his hands and sat down on the edge of the bed. He sat down beside her and put his arm around her.

"Are you all right Honey?"

"I feel so strange. It's not just Nels. It's everything. That woman today—I don't feel like I belong here. It's all changed so fast . . . It's Christmas. You're working. It was supposed to have been my turn to have the family Christmas this year. We've got no place to have it. Rose is in Toronto and Sally's working. Helen's had it two years in a row. It's too much for one person. I think this will be the last Christmas we'll all be together. And then the Pastor leaving . . ."

"Yes. We'll never get a man like him again."

"John?"

She turned to look at him; not wanting to tell him; not wanting for there to be anything else between them.

"What is it Honey?"

"There's something I haven't told you. Sally told me. Walker's dying."

"Oh no. Poor Sally. When did she find this out?"

"Just last week. He hates doctors. He's been going downhill so fast—she made him go. It's cancer John. He's full of shrapnel. The cancer's spread all through him from the metal. There's nothing they can do for him except to give him drugs for the pain."

"How long has he got Marg?"

She looked away from him, down at the floor.

"He's going to the Veteran's hospital on Monday. The doctor told Sally he didn't think he'd last a month."

"Poor old Walker . . ."

"That's what he doesn't want John."

She turned looking back at him.

"He's a proud old man. He doesn't want anybody feeling sorry for him. The only way he'd agree to come for Christmas at Helen's was that nobody else in the family was to know."

"How are we going to tell Nels?"

"I think that's the reason he's coming. Sally said he wanted to say goodbye to Nels. John—you mustn't let on I told you. Nels loves that old man. I know Walker's rough, but he's got a heart of gold where Nels is concerned. If he taught him to fight, it's only because he thought he was doing the best for him. He's Irish John. And so's my son."

"Yes. I know. I guess I was all wrong on this one."

She reached for him then and put her arms around his neck.

"No. You weren't wrong. It's just that it's all changing so fast. I get scared sometimes . . . Just hold me . . ."

After a time she leaned back in his arms.

"You'd better go. I told them at the kennel that you'd be there around eleven. All I'd need now would be for them to have gone to bed."

Still he held her, looking deep into her eyes.

"Do you feel better now Honey?"

"Yes. I'll be all right. I just hate it when anything comes between us."

"Yes. I do too. But it's over."

"It is Christmas, isn't it John?"

He smiled at her then, that special smile that made her all warm inside.

"Yes. It's Christmas. I love you Margaret Murphy."

She smiled back at him with her eyes, putting his hands against his chest in mock disapproval.

"Now don't you start. You have to pick up Nels' present."

"Can I have a kiss first?"

"All right. But just one."

When he had gone she took the three wrapped presents from the back of the bedroom closet. They had waited there all week for this moment, complete except for their name tags, a disguise against her son's constantly exploring eyes. She took her fountain pen, printing the names and the words "FROM SANTA CLAUS" on the tags with smiling Santas on them. Then she placed the tags and bright bows on each present with loving care.

She carried the presents into the living room, pausing for a moment in front of the brightly lit tree. An image came, of a Christmas tree from her own childhood. There had been far fewer presents then, even though there were six eager children around the tree on Christmas morning. For a moment, she tried to remember if the joy of Christmas had been diminished by the fact that her only present that year had been the red woollen hat that her mother had knitted for her. But the thought escaped her, drifting instead into the happy image of her mother and father, presiding over a noisy mob of six Irish children.

She smiled to herself, the magic of her own childhood returning to her as she knelt to place the presents beneath the tree. Two of the three presents she placed at the front, arranging them until their position seemed just right. The third present—a long narrow box wrapped in paper coloured with bright red poinsettias—she placed at the very back, concealing it behind the other gifts. She straightened up, humming a Christmas song softly to herself as she took the children's stockings and carried them into the bedroom, to fill them with small toys and oranges and candy canes.

There was only one thing left to do. From the dresser drawer she took a third stocking, identical in colour and shape to the others but much smaller. Into this she placed a thin strip of rawhide in its cellophane and cardboard packaging. The label on the package read 'Puppy Chew.'

She had just finished placing the stockings in front of the tree when she heard the high-pitched engine of the Vauxhall pulling into the driveway. She took one more look, wanting it to be perfect before she hurried to the back door to meet John as he came in.

She stopped, her heart leaping up in anxious tempo as she saw that there was nothing in either of his hands.

"Oh John—don't tell me you didn't get her!"

He grinned like a boy, one hand pressed against the small bulge beneath his heavy coat. With his free hand he reached up and undid the top two buttons. A tiny blond head popped out, a head with sharp pointed ears flattened back and a long delicate muzzle, brown shoe button eyes peering nervously around. She drew in her breath in sudden wonder.

"John! She's beautiful! Let me hold her."

He unbuttoned his coat the rest of the way and passed her the squirming puppy. The pup keened in fright, disturbed for the second time that night by its passage from the warmth and safety of its nest.

John Sorenson watched her, caught in the spell of her tenderness as she pressed the trembling animal to her breast, crooning to it softly as if it were a child. The puppy relaxed and was quiet, staring up at her with adoring eyes.

"She's so lovely . . ."

He felt the lump in his throat, heard it in his voice when he said, "Not as lovely as you are . . ."

She smiled at him, seeing that he had not moved, feeling the love that was there, in his eyes.

"Take your coat off John."

"Oh yes—I forgot."

He left his coat on the rail at the top of the basement stairs, bending down to unbuckle his galoshes.

"Wait until you see how nice everything looks . . ."

"Let's have a look."

He followed her into the living room, the tree and the gifts barely seen in the magic of her presence.

"It looks great Honey."

She turned, seeing that his eyes were only for her.

"John . . . you're not even looking at the tree."

"Give me a kiss . . ."

"Oh you . . . turn the lights out. It's time for bed."

He bent to switch the lights off. When he straightened up, the pup was wriggling around in her arms, trying to chew on the bottom of her soft brown hair.

"What are we going to do with her tonight Marg?"

"She'll have to come into the bedroom with us."

He sighed, regarding the pup which by now was wide awake.

"I guess I'm not going to get much sleep tonight."

Margaret Sorenson pressed the blond bundle firmly but gently to her breast with one hand, reaching with her free hand to let her fingertips play lightly across his cheek.

"I hope you weren't expecting to, on Christmas Eve . . ."

The boy awoke in darkness, instantly aware, knowing beyond a shadow of a doubt that it was Christmas. He turned his head on the pillow, looking to the window for a sign of morning. Delicate etchings of hoar frost grew across the glass, silhouetted by the glow of the street lamps against the blackness of the night sky.

He slipped out of bed in one fluid motion and went gliding across the warm wooden floor, to stand looking down at the street. The snow had stopped falling. The fresh fall of it filled the road, spreading over the curbs, masking sidewalks and lawns into one smooth glistening surface. The houses slept under soft white blankets, window eyes closed. Nothing moved in the street.

He felt a thrill of secret pleasure, knowing that it was Christmas and that he was the only one awake. Then he turned away from the window, drawn to the magic which sang to him from the living room.

Beyond the bedroom door the house was in blackness. He crept along the hallway on silent feet, reaching Ellen's door now, finding the doorframe with his fingertips and turning, measuring his steps until he felt his bare toes suspended in space above the fall of the first stair. He hovered there for a moment, listening to the magic in the sighing of the furnace through the hot air register and the humming of the refrigerator from the bottom of the stairs.

The sound of soft laughter came to him, muffled by his parent's bedroom door. He smiled to himself and began his descent, balancing on one foot at a time, counting each step and hugging the wall to avoid the creaks in numbers four and seven. By the time he reached the bottom he was breathless with anticipation.

There was no light yet beneath his parent's bedroom door. He hesitated, caught, the magic that called to him from the living room so near in the dark that it was almost irresistible. Ahead of him, his vision waited. But Mom had said that they wouldn't get up to open their presents until 6:30.

He forced himself to turn away from the living room, measuring his steps into the kitchen and feeling with his fingertips until he found the light switch on the wall. He paused again, aiming his eyes to where he knew the clock would appear. Then he flicked the switch on and off again in one rapid motion.

It was only 12:30! He froze, dazzled by the light, racked on an agony of impatience by the idea of six whole hours!

Margaret Sorenson saw the flash of light across the bottom of the bedroom door. She slipped out of John's embrace, raising herself on one elbow and pressing a finger to his lips.

"Ssh . . . he's up . . ."

"Already?"

They whispered, listening. But the house was silent.

"I think I can solve both problems . . ."

She whispered to him again, sitting up naked and reaching down to lift the puppy from where it had burrowed in between them seeking warmth. The pup began to struggle. She held down the urge to laugh at the tickle of silken fur on her breast.

John felt her slip away, sensing her presence moving in the darkness although she made no sound. He barely heard the two faint clicks as the bedroom door opened and then closed again. Then the pup began to keen piteously, alone outside in the hall.

He smiled as he understood. A second passed, and then another. The keening stopped as the pup gave voice to a frightened yip. Then he heard his son's voice, coaxing and filled with wonder.

"It's all right dog . . . ssh . . . it's okay . . ."

The door clicked softly open. He heard her whisper into the blackness.

"Merry Christmas Nels. Take your friend upstairs to bed with you now. And don't play all night. She's just a baby. She needs her sleep."

"Oh thanks Mom! Oh wow!"

He called out softly,

"Merry Christmas son."

"Merry Christmas Dad! Merry Christmas Mom!"

He sensed rather than heard his son's rush up the stairs with the puppy clutched tightly to his chest. Then the bedroom door clicked shut one last time. The house was silent except for the rustle of the sheets as she came back to bed. He reached for her and she came into his arms, pressing her body against him.

"Is this better John?"

"You're wonderful . . ."

"Merry Christmas. I love you . . ."

His answer was lost in their kiss.

When the alarm went off at 6:15 it was far too soon. She reached out and silenced it and sank back again, drifting on the surface of warm voluptuous sleep. The sound of a winter gale intruded on her; the sound of the wind, shrilling and moaning around the corner of the house. She shivered at the sound although the room was warm, turning on her side and snuggling into John's back. All that she wanted was to lay there with him and drift away from the sound of the wind.

The new day came flooding in on her. She remembered that it was Christmas. Margaret Sorenson lay still a moment longer, savouring the awareness and the afterglow of love which still held her in its spell. The temptation was strong, to waken him gently and hold him inside her again.

But it was a working day for him, and the day held its own demands. She sat up reluctantly and turned on the bedside lamp. John was fast asleep, his hair all tousled on the pillow. She rose and put on her flannelette nightgown and then her housecoat, listening for the presence of her son's bright energy in the living room.

There was only the muted howl of the wind. She crossed the bedroom, careful not to wake John, and stepped out into the hall. The living room was black and silent; strangely so. She couldn't remember a Christmas for years when Nels had not been eagerly waiting for her in front of the brightly lit tree. She listened again at the bottom of the stairs. The house slept on, oblivious.

She moved into the living room, turning on the lights to banish the blackness. The stockings were undisturbed; the presents were exactly as she had left them. The strangeness of it followed her as she bent down to turn on the lights on the tree, Christmas somehow suspended in the stillness of the house.

She pushed the feeling away from her, straightening now and moving to the window to part the drapes and look out at the new day.

The wind was racing and pouncing in the street, whipping sheets of snow in front of it, whirling them high up under the yellow lights. The sky above the rooftops was as black as pitch. The neighbouring houses were half obscured by the screen of flying crystals.

She shivered again, knowing that John would be outside in the cold all day. She closed the drapes, the time for Christmas already shortened by the storm, moving into the bedroom to waken him.

"John . . ."

He opened his eyes, smiling sleepily up at her standing beside the bed.

"Morning Honey . . ."

She watched him sit up slowly, yawning and rubbing at the light on his eyes with the heels of his hands.

"Is it time to get up already? I feel like I just fell asleep."

"We stayed up too late last night."

He took his hands away from his eyes and reached for her.

"You were wonderful."

She bent forward to kiss him.

"Merry Christmas John. But you have to get up now."

"I guess I'd better. Nels must be waiting."

The strangeness returned to her.

"No. He's still asleep."

John's eyebrows same up.

"Really? He must have kept that poor dog awake all night."

"Perhaps. But you'd better get up. It's storming."

"Is it still snowing?"

"No, but it's blowing hard, and it's starting to drift in across the road. You'll have to leave early to get to work on time. And we have to open the presents. It's already six-thirty."

"Yes. It's going to be a long day."

"I'll go and get your breakfast on. Maybe the kids'll sleep until you're ready for work. Then I'll wake them up."

He pushed back the blankets, looking up at her as he swung his feet to the floor.

"He's going to be awfully disappointed if I'm up and dressed before you call him."

"I know John. But it can't be helped. You'll have to leave by 7:30."

"Is it that bad out there?"

"Yes. It's a miserable day. Come on. We've only got an hour."

"All right Honey. I'll be out in a minute."

She went out to the kitchen and began the day's work, her mind a whirl of thoughts while her hands moved with an efficiency of their own, stirring oats and making sandwiches, layering thick slices of bacon in the pan. She turned once, to smile at the sight of him crossing the kitchen in his long woollen underwear, arms filled with clothes to protect him from the cold. From time to time, she turned to look, expecting at any minute to see her son's smiling face. There was no one there.

Everything was ready when John came out of the bathroom. He looked like a bear, padded up with layers of clothes under the thick grey melton pants and the old red Mackinaw, faded and soft from years of washings. Outside the wind rose to a furious pitch, shrilling through the gap between the houses.

"Are you going to be warm enough John?"

"I'll be okay Marg. I'll put my coveralls on over this, and then the parka. They'll block the wind. If I get too cold I can get up in the cab of the yard engine and thaw out."

She set the cup of coffee and a bowl of steaming porridge in front of him as he sat down. He paused, to bow his head and close his eyes in a moment of silent prayer. The stitches under the arm of his shirt had pulled out. She made a mental note to mend it again. He opened his eyes and began to fix his porridge, measuring out the spoonfuls of brown sugar and then stirring in the milk with that same preoccupied look that Nels frequently had. She watched him, wondering at how similar they were. He frowned at his porridge.

"It doesn't feel like Christmas Marg—no kids running around and me sitting here dressed, getting ready for work."

She sighed.

"I know. It's going to be hard to keep smiling for the kids. And for Sally. She's taking it hard John. Walker's been there for such a long time. And now she's going to be alone again. It's bringing back Frank, I think, and the war."

"I feel bad now, for what I said about him."

"You were angry John, and so was I. Walker didn't really have anything to do with it."

"No. You're right."

"Just be nice to him at Helen's. That's all I ask."

"Of course I will."

She turned away, to stir the bacon in the pan.

"Should I put your eggs in yet?"

"I guess you'd better. There isn't much time left. I'm surprised Nels hasn't heard us yet."

"I wonder . . ."

She turned back to face him.

"You know, he always sleeps late after he's been upset. He really was upset yesterday John. I guess I didn't tell you all of it. He said the David just laid there bleeding after he hit him, and that David's eyes were closed."

He stared at her.

"He knocked the kid out? Where does he get this strength from?"

"I don't know. But he was really shaken up. I think he must have thought he'd killed him—until David got up and ran away. I don't think he'll hit anyone else again."

"Oh boy . . . I sure hope not. We're going to have to do something about that temper of his Marg."

"Let's not talk about it now. It's Christmas. I've got enough to deal with for one day. Finish your porridge John. The bacon and eggs are done. How's your coffee.

"I could use some more, please."

She set the plate on the table, pouring the coffee with her other hand.

"Thanks Marg. Where's the pepper?"

"It's behind the milk pitcher. You're lunch is all made, and your thermos is full of tea. I put in lots of sugar. I know you like it sweet when it's cold."

"Thanks Honey. Are you going to take the kids to the Christmas service?"

She turned away to pour a cup of coffee for herself, avoiding his eyes.

"I don't see how I can. Between this storm and it being Christmas, who knows when the buses will run? The last time we got caught in that rainstorm, Ellen was sick for a week. It would be different if we could just walk over, like we used to . . .

"You could call the Hurleys and see if they're going."

"I am not going to call the Hurleys!"

She swung back to face him, trying to keep her temper down.

"He drove right by us at the bus stop that day, with nobody else in the car, while we were all half frozen and getting drenched to the skin—and then he had the gall to tell me 'Good Morning Sister' when we got there. I wouldn't ask that man for the time of day!"

"Maybe he didn't see you."

"Oh, he saw us all right! He looked right at us. And then he turned the corner and drove away. Nels saw it too. He was hurt."

"What did you say to Nels?"

"The same thing you just said to me. He's a little too bright for that one too."

He waved his fork despondently at his plate.

"I don't know what's wrong with that man. It's just too bad that I have to work and we all have to miss the Pastor's Christmas sermon."

"Yes. I don't remember the last time that we missed church. I'm not looking forward to telling Nels. He loves to go to church. He's been waiting all week to see his friend Tommy. And then there's his award . . . he's all excited about that. He's worked really hard."

"Well, there's Sunday yet, and his award, before the Pastor leaves. I don't know how he remembers all those verses."

"He's a good boy John. Oh, I know he's got a temper. But we should be proud of him. After all, he's still just a boy."

"Yes. I guess the move out here hasn't been as easy as I thought it was for him. Or for you either."

"I'm all right. How's your coffee?"

"I could use a little more. Listen to that wind! I was sure hoping we'd get a decent day. We've only got one train to put together. Bob said we could all go home as soon as she was ready. But if the spurs are drifted in and the switches are frozen . . . well, we'll get her done."

"I wish you didn't have to go out in this storm."

"Not much I can do about it. None of the boys are going to be too happy."

"Good heavens—look at the time! It's after seven all ready! Hurry up and finish your breakfast. I'd better go upstairs and wake the children."

She paused, bending down to kiss his cheek on her way to the stairs.

"We'll have to be cheerful. For the children. It's Christmas."

"Yes. Maybe I'd better slip out and start the car while you're upstairs."

She left him devouring the remains of his meal and went quietly up the stairs. She paused at the top to open her daughter's door and look in. Ellen was still fast asleep. She smiled in at her, studying the sleeping child's features for a moment before she moved across the hall to her son's room. When she opened the door and turned on the light the bed was empty, stripped even of its blankets.

There was a sudden unreasoning second of panic. Then she heard his sleepy "Good morning Mom" from behind the half-open door.

She stepped into the room, smiling at her fear in the sight of two faces on the pillow behind the door. Boy and dog were curled up together in the blankets on the floor beside the register.

"What are you doing on the floor Nels?"

He looked up at her, all sleepy and serious.

"The puppy had an accident Mom. She didn't mean to."

"Of course she didn't Honey. But you'll have to teach her when to go to the bathroom. And feed her and look after her too."

"I will Mom. I promise. She's beautiful!"

"Merry Christmas Nels."

"Is Dad up yet?"

"Yes. He's finished his breakfast. He's gone out to warm up the car."

He came scrambling up out of the blankets clutching the puppy, blue eyes wide with dismay.

"I slept in! On Christmas! Why didn't you call me Mom?"

"It's all right Nels. We've only been up for a bit. Your father had to get ready to go to work. It's really stormy outside. We'll just have time to open our presents before he had to leave."

"It's not fair! Dad shouldn't have to work on Christmas!"

"I know Honey . . ."

She slipped her arm across his shoulders, speaking softly to him, trying to draw him away from the unfairness of it all.

"Things are different when you're an adult Nels. Sometimes you have to do things whether you want to or not. Your Dad's feeling pretty badly about it too. So let's be cheerful. For your Dad. Okay? Come on—it's Christmas. Haven't you got a smile for me?"

He couldn't resist her, looking up, smiling, the magic returning with the pup beginning to wriggle in his arms.

"That's better. I love you Honey."

"I love you too Mom."

"Why don't you go downstairs and say Merry Christmas to your father while I go wake your sister up? Then we can open our presents."

"Yeah!"

He was gone, down the stairs, through the living room in one swift pass and out to the back door just as his father was coming in. The frozen blast of wind gave him goosebumps before the door closed.

"Merry Christmas Dad!"

"Hey! Merry Christmas Nels! What have you got there?"

"A dog Dad! Look at her!"

He thrust the pup into his father's hands, beaming with pleasure as his father held her up, examining her as if he had never seen her before.

"She's a beauty son!"

"She's a Corgi Dad—just like in the book! Doesn't she look like the baby fox we saw that time in the forest?"

"Yes. She sure does. Here—you take her while I pull my boots off. Is your sister awake yet?"

"Mom just went to wake her. Come on Dad—hurry! It's time to open our presents!"

John Sorenson laughed, the cares of the day forgotten for the moment.

"I'm coming son—I'm coming!"

Ellen came running across the kitchen just as he got his boots off. He scooped her up in his arms and she gave him a kiss.

"How's my girl this morning?"

"I'm still sleepy. Did Santa come?"

"Yes. And look what he brought for you and Nels."

"Yeah! Look Elly!"

"A puppy! Oh—let me see!"

He held the puppy out to her. Then Mom was there, with one arm around him and her other arm around Dad.

"Did the car start all right John?"

"Just barely. It's really cold out there. The driveway's drifting in too."

"We'd better hurry then. Now children—we've only got a few minutes. We'll just open our presents before Dad goes to work. You'll have lots of time to look at them later. Nels, you can pass them out. Okay?"

"Sure Mom. What about the puppy?"

"I think she'd probably like to get down for a while. Don't you?"

"Oh yeah."

"Let's go into the living room then. Ellen, you sit on the couch with Dad and I. Put the puppy down Nels. Why don't you children start with your presents from Santa?"

"Yeah!"

He dropped to his knees before the tree and set the pup down on the carpet. There was a big green box right in front with Ellen's name on it. He passed it across the coffee table, watching his sister's face, thumb in her mouth, doe-eyed and still half asleep.

"Open yours too Nels. We don't have very much time."

"I am Mom."

He looked around, reaching for the red box with his name on it. But it was all wrong somehow. They always opened their presents one at a time, with the rest of the family watching to help admire them.

The pup went bouncing past him, nosing in under the tree. She caught the corner of one wrapped gift in her mouth and began to worry at the paper. He set his present down and reached for her, stalling for time.

"No girl!"

"Leave the puppy alone Nels."

"But Mom! She's eating the presents!"

"She can't hurt anything. Open your present Honey. Do you want some help with the paper on yours Elly?"

"Yes please Mummy."

"I wonder what Santa brought for you? Oh look."

"My dolly!"

He turned to look, still holding the unwrapped present in his hands.

"Let's see Elly."

Ellen held the big pink doll with its bright yellow hair out for him to admire.

"She's real pretty Elly."

"What did you get from Santa Nelsy?"

"Oh yeah."

He tore the paper away in one ragged strip.

"A chess game! Oh wow! How did Santa know I wanted a chess game?"

Everyone was smiling at him. Mom said,

"I guess he must have heard you Nels. You didn't talk about anything else for a week after you stayed overnight at Tommy's house."

"Wait 'till I tell Tommy!"

He caught the look that passed between Mom and Dad, not understanding it, already starting to pull the lid open to marvel at the intricate plastic pieces.

"Leave it for now Nels. You can play with it later. See if you can find presents for your Dad and I, and another one for your sister."

"Oh—sure Mom."

He set the game on the coffee table, out of reach of the puppy. Then he went rummaging through the presents until he found the blue box for Dad and the small crudely wrapped gift with Mom's name on it.

"Here's one for you Dad. From Elly and me. And this is for you Mom. From me."

"Find one for your sister too son."

"I am Dad. What did you get?"

"I don't know yet son. I haven't got all the paper off it. It looks like a new shirt."

"Do you like it Dad?"

"Yes. It's a real nice one. Thank you Nels. Thank you Elly."

"You're welcome Daddy."

"What did you get from Nels, Marg?"

"My goodness! It's dusting powder. It's just what I needed."

He turned away from the tree, both elbows on the coffee table to face her.

"I bought it myself Mom! With my money from my job! I wrapped it too!"

David and Billy had bragged to him that they each got a dollar a week in allowance. But when he had asked for an allowance, Dad had said that he would help him find a job instead. They had found a job for him, selling subscriptions and delivering Liberty magazine once a week in the subdivision. The people whose doors he knocked on were all friendly to him—except for weird Mr. Hurley. Mr. Hurley pretended not to know who he was. But already he had 20 customers. He felt important, going out in the evening to make his deliveries and collect the money.

"Do you like it Mom?"

"Yes Nels. It smells lovely."

He beamed at her proudly.

"Did you find another present for yourself and your sister? And find another one for Dad and I too."

"Sure Mom."

"What time is it Marg?"

"I'll look . . . It's twenty after seven."

"Already?"

He hurried to find presents for all of them. The pup clambered over his hands, trying to lick his face and tearing discarded paper in ferocious puppy attacks. A pile of presents grew, tantalizing, on the coffee table beside him.

There was a watch like the one that the man on TV wore when he jumped into the swimming pool, to replace the old one of his grandfather's which had finally succumbed to one too many dunkings in the creek. There was the chess game, a new jackknife with numerous gadgets and blades, a box of plastic Army men, the stocking—still unexamined!—all stacked together with the inevitable socks and shirts and underwear, waiting to be looked at later. But the best of them all was the little blond beast creating mayhem beside him on the floor.

And then it was over. The carpet was littered with sheets of coloured paper. All that remained under the tree were the presents at the very back for Aunt Sally and Danny and Sandy. He cast a disbelieving glance under the tree, not wanting it to end so soon.

"That's all Mom."

"Are you sure Nels? I don't remember seeing that long red box—right at the very back. Bring it out and see who it's for."

He fended the pup off with one hand, stretching full length under the tree to reach it.

"It's to Dad. From Santa."

His father's look of surprise was genuine.

"For me? From Santa?"

Mom smiled, her secret smile.

"Why not John? Santa can bring presents for big people too you know."

"Let's see Daddy!"

They all turned to look as Dad opened the last present.

"What on earth?"

"It's a fishing pole Dad! Oh wow!"

"I guess you'll have to teach your Dad how to fish Nels."

"Oh gee—sure Dad! But there's no reel!"

"Well, we'll just have to get one for your Dad's birthday. Then you boys will be able to go fishing together. Do you like it John?"

"It's wonderful Marg. And so are you."

"Oh I didn't have anything to do with it. It's from Santa Claus."

Ellen looked up, suddenly serious.

"Santa didn't bring you anything Mummy."

Mom put her arms around Elly and gave her a kiss.

"He didn't have to Honey. I've got all of you. Well—did everyone have a good Christmas?"

"Yeah! The puppy's the best!"

"What are you going to call her Nels?"

"Gee—I don't know."

"I have an idea. Would you like to hear it?"

"Sure Mom."

"Well, the puppy's a Welsh Corgi. When I was just a little girl, your grandmother taught me a rhyme and it went like this: 'Taffy was a Welshman, Taffy was a thief; Taffy went to market town and stole a side of beef.' We could call her Taffy. What do you think?"

"Yeah, sure Mom! C'mere Taffy!"

"Let me hold her Nelsy."

"Sure Elly."

Dad stood up. Dad looked sad.

"I have to go kids. I'll have to shovel out the driveway yet."

"I'll help you Dad!"

He leaped to his feet and raced up the stairs to his room, pulling his pants and a sweater on over his pyjamas and racing back down, almost colliding with his father on the basement stairs in his haste to get his coat and gloves and boots on.

"Slow down Nels."

"Sure Dad!"

Mom and Dad were kissing at the back door when he went flying past them, out into the storm.

The first gust staggered him as he came around the corner of the house and into the driveway. A ridge of snow had begun to build between the car and the street. He attacked it with the small shovel, exhilarated by the icy air, the drift of white powder a tangible foe to be conquered and scattered on the wind. Then Dad was beside him, his big shovel flinging clouds of crystals into the air above his head. He doubled his efforts, working at a furious pace to keep up until he felt his father's hand on his shoulder.

"I think that'll do her Nels!"

Dad's face was close to his, shouting to be heard above the wind and the whine of the engine.

"I wish you didn't have to go Dad."

"Me too son. You be good today and do what your Mom asks you. She's got a lot on her mind. Okay?"

"Sure Dad."

"Okay. I'll see you when I get home. Stand clear now. I'll have to take a run at her to get out. Merry Christmas Nels."

"Merry Christmas Dad!"

He moved around to the front of the car, leaning his shovel against the house and watching anxiously to see if the Vauxhall would make it. The squatty grey car reversed a few feet, losing speed until it came to a stop. The rear tires made a whirring sound. He didn't hesitate, rushing in to grab the bumper and press his shoulder against the grill. He pitted his full strength against it, straining in time to the whirring of the wheels, feeling as though his muscles would burst before the weight of it yielded.

He felt the car begin to move. He sucked in a great lungful of charged oxygen, heaving against the bumper and moving his feet to stay with it until it accelerated away and he went sprawling in the snow. He was back up in an instant, laughing and panting as Dad swung the car out into the road.

Dad waved to him and blew the horn. The tires began to slip as the car inched forward. He caught his breath and ran out onto the road to push again. But the wheels found their grip just as he got there. He dropped behind in the Vauxhall's wake, facing full into the gale, waving and shouting as it slithered off up the street.

"'Bye Dad!' Bye! Merry Christmas!"

He stood in the road waving until the grey car slid around the corner and disappeared. His cheeks burned with the spray of stinging particles. He looked away, towards the house. Mom and Ellen were waving to him in the front window. He waved back in triumph, nodding his acknowledgement as Mom gestured for him to come inside. The drapes slid shut but he lingered, warmed by his efforts, exulting in the power of the storm.

He turned his back to the brunt of it, looking to the east for a sign of morning. The sky was still dark, the streetlights still on. The storm raged around him, the gusts rocking him, the wind sweeping draughts of snow from the roofs of the houses and lashing them horizontally. The metal shields on the concrete lamp posts shuddered in the onslaught.

There were lights on now behind most of the curtained windows. The thought came, as it often did, of how much the houses looked the same with their snow-clad roofs, the colours of the brick blending to one shade of grey in the uniform light.

There was only one outstanding feature in the howling arctic landscape that stretched before him. On the fourth pole up the street, a huge light bulb bulged beneath its metal shield, bathing the blowing snow with an intense bluish-white radiance. That pole stood on the boulevard in front of Mr. Hurley's house. Mr. Hurley was a supervisor for the Public Utilities people. That was how he got to have a special light in front of his house.

The thought of Mr. Hurley made him think of David somehow. He remembered that he had promised to phone David, to apologise for hurting him.

There was a tug of reluctance, but he squared his shoulders against it, striding up the street and up around the crescent to see if the lights at David's house were on. The curtains glowed with a pale morning light. He turned away and strode briskly home, determined to get it over with.

Ellen was sitting on the kitchen floor when he came in. She had her new dolly propped up beside her, both of them watching Taffy eat breakfast. He stooped beside her to stroke the puppy's back.

"Where's Mom Elly?"

"She's in the bathroom."

Ellen looked solemn.

"I wish Daddy was here."

"Yeah. Me too."

He straightened up again, looking around at the phone.

"Where are you going Nelsy?"

"Nowhere Elly. I have to call David."

"Then will you come and sit with me?"

"Sure Elly."

He found the Jones' number in the phone book and dialled it, fighting down the urge to hang up while he listened to it ring. It was David's mom who answered it.

"Hello?"

"Hello Mrs. Jones. May I speak to David please?"

"I don't know if he'll come to the phone. Who shall I tell him is calling?"

"It's Nels Sorenson."

There was a sharp intake of breath and then a venomous whisper that made his skin prickle.

"You little bastard! If I could get my hands on you—you leave my son alone!"

The line went dead with a crash of metal on metal. He was standing there, stunned, still holding the receiver when Mom came out of the bathroom. She caught the look in his eyes and came to stand beside him.

"What are you doing Nels?"

"I tried to phone David to say I was sorry."

"What happened?"

"His mom yelled at me, sort of. Then she hung up on me."

Mom put one arm around him. He realized that he had forgotten the receiver when she took it from his hand and replaced it gently on its cradle.

"Never mind Honey. You tried to do what's right. Goodness—look at you! Your hair's all full of snow . . ."

She gave him a little smile, running her fingers through his hair.

"Mom?"

He looked at her, seeking her eyes.

"Yes Honey?"

"What's a bastard?"

He caught the flash of green anger before it faded into something closer to sadness.

"You mustn't ever say that word Nels. It's swearing."

He stared at her, appalled.

"She swore at me? But Mom! She's a grown up!"

"I know Honey. I guess she doesn't know any better. I think you'd better just stay away from David from now on. Okay?"

"Yeah."

Mom tried to smile again; but he knew that Mom's feelings were hurt. He stared down at the floor, not wanting her to see what was in his eyes, glad now that he had punched David in the mouth! Elly said,

"She's a bad lady, isn't she Mummy?"

"That's enough Ellen. She was just angry. I'm sure she didn't mean it. Well—did you children like your Christmas presents?"

"Yes Mummy. But I wish Daddy was here."

"I do too Honey. You look sleepy. Would you like to come back to bed with me for awhile?"

"Yes please Mummy. Can the puppy come and lay down with us too?"

"You'd better ask your brother."

"Can she Nelsy?"

"Yeah . . . I guess so . . ."

"Goody. Come on Taffy. Can you bring my dolly Mummy?"

"Yes Honey. I'll bring your dolly. You go and get into bed. I'll be there in a minute."

He looked out under hooded lids, standing there watching his sister carry the puppy into Mom's room. Mom reached out to smooth his hair, trying to draw his eyes.

"I guess you're not sleepy are you Nels?"

"No."

He kept his eyes down on the floor.

"Are you all right Honey?"

"It's not fair!"

"No. I know it isn't. But there's nothing more that you can do about it. You tried to do the right thing. The best thing now is to just forget about it. It's Christmas."

"Boy—some Christmas!"

"That's not fair either Honey. To me."

He heard the hurt in her voice, felt it inside of him.

"I'm sorry Mom. I didn't mean it."

He reached for her then and she held him close. After a time she let him go and smiled for him.

"Do you feel better now?"

"Yes Mom. Thanks for getting me a dog."

"Do you like her?"

"Yes. She's the best."

You're a good boy to let your sister have her for a while. What are you going to do while we have a sleep?"

"I don't know . . ."

"Why don't you go and play with your new game?"

"You have to have two people to play it."

He remembered Tommy then.

"What time do we have to get dressed for church?"

"I'm afraid we won't be able to go to the service this morning Nels."

He stepped back, away from her, eyes widening in disbelief.

"What? But Mom! We always go to church!"

"I'm sorry Nels. I can't help it. It's storming outside. I don't even know if there'll be any buses running. You can call Tommy and talk to him later."

"But Mom! It's not just Tommy! I mean—it's Christmas!"

"I'm sorry Nels. I really am. I guess this is going to be a different kind of Christmas. There just isn't anything I can do about it."

"It's not fair! Any of it!"

"Please Nels."

He looked up and saw that she was close to tears. He gave it one last try, almost pleading.

"Couldn't we phone Mr. Hurley and ask him to give us a ride?"

And then he saw the change in her eyes, heard the Irish in her voice when she said,

"No Nels. We wouldn't want to bother Mr. Hurley on Christmas. I have to go and lay down for a while. I've got lots of things to do this morning to get ready to go to Aunt Helen's. Now I want you to be a good boy and go and find something to do for an hour. Okay?"

"Yeah . . . sure . . ."

"Why don't you get yourself some cereal?"

"I'm not hungry."

He looked down at the floor again.

"All right. I'm going to lay down for a while. And I want you to be cheerful when we get up. You wouldn't want to spoil Christmas for your sister. Would you."

"No."

"Okay. I'll see you in a little while."

He turned away from her and went into the living room, pushing the curtains apart to stare out into the storm.

The first grey light of morning had begun to creep into the day. The snow had come again, making the gale that lashed the street more violent than even before. The houses across the street were invisible now.

He let his eyes sweep up the street, the bleakness of the day matching the mood that grew over him, looking for anything that would break the spell. Through the driving snow he caught a flicker of blue-white radiance, the bright star on its pole in front of Mr. Hurley's house.

And then it struck him with the force of a revelation. Mom had known about Mr. Hurley all along! But it couldn't be true—

He drew a Sunday from his memory, trying to fix it in time. It had been in November, just after the new Pastor had come to the church, one of the Sundays that Dad had to go to work.

The day appeared with a photographic clarity. He and Mom and Ellen hurrying to the bus stop with the cold wind chasing them up the street, big black clouds filling the sky and the smell of rain already heavy in the air. The storm broke just as they got there, rain bouncing off the pavement in a grey deluge that stripped away every bit of colour except for the red stop sign. Mom and Elly, trying to huddle beneath Mom's umbrella. The wind yanking it inside out, too late now to turn and run for home. The icy water streaming down his sodden hair and running inside his collar.

And then Mr. Hurley pulled up to the stop sign, twenty feet away, all alone in the warm dry car. He looked across the distance into Mr. Hurley's eyes, smiling his relief and already raising his hand to wave.

Mr. Hurley looked away from him. His car turned the corner and accelerated up the street, leaving them standing in the fury of a November gale.

"That was Mr. Hurley Mom! Why didn't he give us a ride?"

Mom said,

"I guess he didn't see us Nels."

He knew that Mr. Hurley had seen them. But he said nothing more, not wanting Mom and Elly to feel what he felt inside. Elly started to cry.

The bus was late that day. By the time it came they were all soaking wet. His teeth were chattering with the cold. When they got to the church, there was Mr. Hurley, standing beside Deacon Brown, shaking hands with the people coming in! He had never been there before.

Mr. Hurley tried to look past him. He stood his ground, refusing to move until Mr. Hurley shook his outstretched hand. The man had smiled at him but when he sought his eyes, they came to rest somewhere above his head. His handshake was as limp as a fish that had been out of the creek too long.

He thought about it all through the service, unable to pay attention to the sermon, cold and wet with his little sister shivering in the pew beside him. Walker had taught him to watch anyone who couldn't meet his eye. But he was sure that Walker meant only boys like David. It was inconceivable that he had meant adults too.

Ellen was sick all week and couldn't go to school. Mom was sick too, for three whole days. He began to watch Mr. Hurley.

Every Sunday morning, Mr. Hurley's car drove past, up the street, long before Mom and Dad were ready to go to church. Usually he as alone although sometimes Mrs. Hurley and their two small daughters were with him. Every Sunday since that day, Mr. Hurley was there, shaking hands beside Deacon Brown when they came in. And Mr. Hurley still pretended not to know who he was if he said hello to him on the street. But if Mom knew that Mr. Hurley was like that—

The flicker of blue-white light caught his eye again through the driving snow. A new image came, of Mr. Hurley standing in the door of the church, shaking hands with the people coming in for the Christmas service. Uncle Bill and Aunt Mary were there, and Tommy's family—

The image was too much to bear. He let it go, staring into the storm, merging with it in some way that he did not try to understand.

Mom and Ellen were asleep when he looked into the bedroom. He moved silently to the back door and put on his coat and boots and his gloves. The wind tried to snatch the door out of his hands when he stepped outside. He stood for a moment, head back, facing into the wind savouring the sting of icy particles on his forehead.

The world was invisible in the wan grey light. He moved into the driveway, searching with his feet until he found the big lump of ice that Dad had kicked loose from the wheel-well of the Vauxhall. He began to kick it apart, using his strength to shatter it with several blows of his heel.

Three of the pieces were the right size. He moulded them carefully, grinding the edges against each other until each piece fit comfortably in the grip of his throwing hand.

Then he let the wind take him, sweeping him up in the blizzard that raged along the street until he found himself staring up at the bright star on its pole in front of Mr. Hurley's house.

The storm peaked around him. The house itself was unseen. The wind was already filling his tracks when he stopped to look behind him, his bush sense warning him to leave no trace.

The light that blazed above his head was visible in all but the heaviest gusts. He began to pace himself backwards in the road, measuring the angle and the range with a rifleman's eye. He stopped, fitting one of the chunks of ice into the grip of his right hand.

The enormity of what he was about to do struck home to him then. It was all wrong! Mr. Hurley was an adult! The bright star above him belonged to the adult world!

The image came, of David, grinning, bending down to make a snow ball to throw at the Manger. David's mom had sworn at him for it.

He drew back his arm and fired the first missile as hard as he could. It flashed harmlessly above the glow of light and disappeared. He stalked in closer, adjusting his aim, hot anger chilling down into cold determination.

The second missile struck the metal shield with a solid clang, but the glare of light still taunted him. He checked his stance, made nervous by the sound, knowing that it was dangerous to stay where he was much longer.

He fitted the last chunk of ice into his hand, turning it around until it felt exactly right. There was a gap between the gusts. The bulb appeared above him with a shining clarity. He drew back his arm and fired his last missile.

The light exploded in a brilliant flash of blue fire. He fled, feet flying, running blind into the driving wall of snow. Some inner guide sent him racing into his unseen driveway, flattening against the brick wall of the house. It took all of his courage to look back, around the corner.

There was no one there. He stayed there, chest heaving, seeing the flash of blue fire over and over while he worked to slow the hammering of his heart. When it was finally quiet he turned and slipped silently in through the back door.

The house was alive with some strange new energy. He went to the bedroom door and peeked in, seeking its source. Mom and Ellen were still asleep, Ellen's back curled into Mom's front, Taffy and Elly's new doll cuddled up under Elly's outstretched arm. The living room looked the same. The Christmas tree glowed with bright colour, the carpet cleared of bows and paper, their presents neatly arranged under the tree. But something was changed. The angel watched him as he moved restlessly to the window.

He pushed the drapes together until they were open just a crack, staring through it, suddenly afraid that Mr. Hurley would appear on the lawn. There was no one there that he could see. But the storm mocked him now, as though it had eyes and a voice to tell on him.

He pressed his face in further, looking for the Manger, trying to bring the old magic back. Then the terrible certainty leaped out at him—that it was all smashed!—that David had snuck out at the same time that he had and wrecked it with a sneak attack! He panicked, darting to the front door and out into the deep snow on the porch in his sock feet.

They were all right—Mary and Joseph and the baby Jesus, the three Wise Men in their exotic gowns. He reached in with one hand gathering them gently in the crook of his other arm. He carried them inside and laid them on the couch and went back to close the door. He dried each one on his shirt and placed them carefully on the table where Dad kept his Bible.

"You guys'll be safe here. David can't get you."

He whispered to them while they watched him, putting them in their places. But they didn't look right. Especially the baby Jesus, lying there on the bare wooden table.

He turned away and went to close the curtains, trying to shut out this strange new magic that swirled up into the morning. But it didn't help.

Then he did something else that he had never done before. He turned the television on and sat down on the floor close up to the screen, trying to lose himself in the shallow stream of cartoon raccoons and reindeer.

He was still there when Mom came in to open the curtains.

"Are you watching television Nels? That's not like you. You must be bored."

"Yeah. It's dumb."

He slipped to his feet and shut the set off, turning to face her.

"Where's Taffy and Elly?"

"They're still asleep."

Her eyes looked past him, widening as she saw the Manger people on the table.

"What are the figurines from the Manger doing in here?"

"I brought them in Mom. I was afraid that David might try a sneak attack with a snowball!"

"Oh Nels—were you outside in your sock feet? You go and put some dry socks on right now, before you catch your death of cold. And after breakfast, you can put your boots on and put them back outside where they belong."

"But Mom!"

"They'll be all right. After all, it's Christmas. Besides, I don't think even David would be that sneaky."

He hung his head, suddenly sick inside.

"I don't want any breakfast. My stomach hurts."

She came to stand in front of him and put her hands on his shoulders.

"You had a bit of a bad start this morning Honey. I think what you need is a hug."

"Yeah . . ."

She held him then and smoothed his hair.

"I want you to forget all about people breaking things. After you've got some dry socks on and you've had some breakfast, you'll feel a lot better."

Sure enough, he did.

The morning stretched on forever. By noon he couldn't stand it any longer. He went up to his room and put on his suit and tie.

When he came back downstairs, Mom said they weren't leaving until two o'clock. He picked at his lunch, trying to starve himself for the feast. He fidgeted around the kitchen in an agony of impatience until Mom told him to go upstairs and find something to do for an hour. He took his dog and retreated to his room, wondering why Mom was so grumpy.

Dad got home at one-thirty. When Mom called Nels to come downstairs, the front of his suit was coated with dog fur. He fussed and fumed until Mom yelled at him to "Stand Still!" while she brushed every last bit of if off.

The final departure tested his nerves to the breaking point. Mom made three tries at pasting his cowlick down. Dad was running around searching for his hat, which was on his head. Even Ellen had a minor tantrum on the front porch because they couldn't take Taffy, crying piteously on the other side of the locked door. When they were finally in the car he clenched his fists in the back seat, vowing silent revenge if anything happened to the Manger.

He forgot about David as soon as they drove out of the subdivision. The change inside the car was like sudden sunshine. Mom moved over close to Dad and kissed his cheek while he was driving. He reached to put his arm around Ellen, to cheer her up. Mom turned to smile at them in the back seat.

"Are you children excited?"

"Yeah!"

"Me too Mummy!"

"Good. I want you both to be on your best behaviour today. That means no running in Aunt Helen's house Nels. And be sure that you have a visit with everybody. We may not have another chance to all be together for a long time. Okay?"

"Sure Mom."

He settled back to watch contentedly as they drove into the tunnel beneath the big bare trees. Left onto Main Street, driving downhill along the familiar road to childhood. Past the factories; past the fairgrounds and the race track; past the weathered shops and turning right into the old neighbourhood, every detail of every house known to him as they passed by.

"Can we drive by our old house Dad?"

Dad hesitated, slowing for the stop sign.

"What do you think Marg?"

"Oh . . . I guess it wouldn't hurt . . ."

Turning left, and then right again, into the narrow passage between the high brick walls; Dad slowing right down as they passed their old house and the whole family staring out at it going by. And it did hurt—just a little bit—before they turned again into the lane and drove along the school fence, back out into the street.

Then he forgot about it, straining forward against the back of the seat for the first sight of Aunt Helen's big red brick house with its high steps and its wide front porch.

They were all there that day: the family. The afternoon slipped by for the boy on stockinged feet, gliding constantly across the carpets and over the polished wooden floors. Up the stairs, past Cousin Molly's room, the sounds of his girl cousins, giggling behind the closed door; into Cousin Jack's room with Danny and Gord and Jack and Pete—all older than he was—sprawled on the bed and the floor talking hockey and girls while he admired the intricate detail of Cousin Jack's model airplanes on the desk.

Down the stairs again, restless, and happy, drawn like a moth to the adult realm. Through the living room and into the dining room, hovering at the respectful perimeter of his uncle's conversations, gathered by the sideboard; all but Dad with the tiny glasses of amber liquid which Uncle Mike poured from the cut glass decanter, the air wreathed with rich blue clouds of smoke from fat cigars. Uncle Pat and Uncle Ernie, telling hunting stories, and then the talk turning to people he had never met, with names like King and Diefenbaker.

Slipping away again unnoticed; sneaking into the kitchen and trying to be invisible, enchanted in the laughter of his aunts and the fragrances of their perfumes all mingled with the aroma of roasting meats and hot mince pies. Auntie Rose and Aunt Helen, teasing Mom who was the youngest, and Auntie Sal, slipping him shortbread to fend off his ravenous hunger before Mom spotted him and chased him out, grinning, cookies in hand.

The only one who wasn't there was Walker. Aunt Sally said that he'd had some things to do, and that Danny was going to get him when dinner was ready.

By six o'clock, he was sure he would die from hunger. And then the magic moment arrived, just in time. The uncles began unfolding the card tables and setting them up at the end of the dining room table. Mom and his aunts were a flurry of laughing purposeful activity, spreading table cloths, laying plates and silverware. The cousins came down the stairs and into the dining room in a cheerful teasing turmoil When he looked around for Danny, he was already gone.

He moved away from the pack to the front window, watching until the old black Ford pulled up and parked in front of the house. Dad was beside him in the hall when he put on his galoshes. The sky was dark and the wind was up. They went outside together. Dad and Danny helped Walker out of the passenger side and up the stairs, one on each arm. He ran ahead to hold the door open, carrying Walker's canes.

There were twenty-eight people at dinner that night. He counted them, arranged down each side with Mom and Dad and the aunts and uncles at one end and him and Elly and the cousins at the other. Walker, being the eldest, was given the place of honour at the head of the table. When the food was all brought in, the platters and serving bowls covered the table—the colour of the table cloth could barely be seen at all.

There was a giant turkey, golden brown, and a fat roasted goose from Uncle Pat's farm. There was a huge ham, glazed with pineapple rings around it, and steaming tureens of potatoes and vegetables, dressing and gravy. Spread amidst all of this were bowls of bright red cranberry and plates of orange carrots and green celery and more platters mounded up with carefully sculpted jell-o salads.

Uncle Ernie stood up to say the blessing. He closed his eyes, intoxicated by the fragrances of the food, adding his own heart-felt 'Amen' of gratitude at the end. When he opened his eyes and looked up to the head of the table he got a grin and a wink from Walker that was just for him.

He filled his plate three times, looking up the table between bites and straining his ears to hear the adult conversation above the chatter of his cousins and the clatter of silverware. A high good humour prevailed over the table; the adults laughing and joking, the aunts turning frequently to smile at the children, the uncles calling out encouragement each time he or one of the cousins refilled his plate. Walker grinned and joked with them but it seemed strange that all he took on his plate was a small piece of goose and a tiny bit of potato.

When the main course was finished everyone helped to clear the plates and the food away. There were cheers from the cousins and groans from his uncles when the table was laid all over again for dessert.

There were apple pies and cherry pies with criss-crossed strips of golden pastry; pumpkin pies with frosted glaciers of whipped cream on top and mince pies that steamed with spicy fragrance. There was tray after tray of tarts, and fancy shortbreads beaded with green Christmas trees and red bells. At the very centre of the table, the Christmas pudding blazed with festive blue fire.

He stared in a delicious quandary as to which kind of pie to try first. Somehow, among all the turkey and goose that he had eaten, there was room for a piece of apple pie and a piece of cherry pie with ice cream as well. He was entertaining fantasies of butter tarts when Aunt Sally came to stand behind his chair and put her hands on his shoulders. She bent down close, her hair brushing his cheek when he turned to smile at her.

"Did you get enough to eat Nels?"

"Oh yes Auntie Sal. It was delicious. I couldn't eat another bite."

"We'll be going home soon. Walker's tired. He's going into the living room now, to have a cigarette. Why don't you go in with him and find him an ashtray. You can have a visit, just the two of you?"

"Sure Auntie Sal."

She gave his shoulders a little squeeze and turned away and went out into the kitchen. He excused himself from the table, looking up, seeing that Walker had already started to make his way towards the living room, moving slowly, leaning heavily on both canes.

Walker chose an armchair in the corner. He scouted around for an ashtray and carried it over, to stand smiling down as Walker lit a cigarette.

"Well kid—did you have a good Christmas?"

"Kind of. I got a dog Poppy. She's beautiful. She's a Welsh Corgi. We named her Taffy."

The old man grinned back up at him, watching him closely now.

"That's great kid. But what do you mean, kind of?"

"Well . . . I punched David in the mouth, the day before Christmas."

"Did you now? Did he start it?"

He scuffed his feet on the carpet, feeling a bit uneasy all of a sudden.

"Sort of. He was going to smash the Manger. I only hit him once . . ."

"He hit you back?"

"No. I hit him with an uppercut and knocked him down. He got up and ran away. Mom said I knocked one of his teeth out."

"One punch eh? Did you catch Hell for it?"

"Well . . . no. Not really. Mom said I'm not supposed to hit anybody any more. But I think she knows—I mean—about boxing lessons. She asked me . . . I didn't tell her Poppy."

"It's okay kid. Your Mom's Irish. I don't think you need any more boxing lessons anyhow. One punch? You sure?"

"Yes Sir."

"Oh boy . . . it's a wonder she didn't give me Hell."

Walker grinned at him. Nels grinned back, feeling vastly better.

"Sit down here on the arm of my chair kid. I've got something to tell you."

He saw how the old man's grin softened into a smile, the grey eyes serious now.

"Sure Poppy. What is it?"

"Listen Soldier . . . we've been pals for a long time. Right?"

"Yes Sir."

"I taught you lots of good things, didn't I?"

"Yes Sir."

"Well, there's one more thing I have to teach you. Do you remember the first time I took you fishing with me?"

He tried to remember, sensing something important in the question.

"Sort of . . ."

"We caught a bass, and when I killed it, you got real scared, because you didn't understand. And then, after we talked about it, you weren't afraid any more. Remember?"

"Yeah."

He smiled at the vague image of his fear. Walker smiled too.

"Well you see Soldier, it's like that with everything. Fish, dogs, people . . . we all die sometime. It's a part of life. It's important, not to be afraid of it."

He felt a hollow tingling begin inside of him, not wanting to know what was coming.

The old man held his eyes.

"I wanted to tell you this myself Nels. So that you'll understand. I'm going into the Veteran's hospital on Monday."

"But when are you coming back Poppy?"

"I'm not coming back Nels. I'm going to die."

"Oh no!"

Nels wanted to shut it out—wanted to run from it—to make it not happen! Walker's hand closed around his arm, holding him there with a gentle strength that he could not escape. He turned his face away, unable to bear the calm grey eyes.

"Look at me Soldier."

The power of the old man's will was irresistible. It drew him back, turning slowly until the grey eyes were looking inside of him.

"Aren't you scared Poppy?"

"No Nels. I'm not afraid of dying. I've faced it too many times to be afraid of it any more. Now I'm an old man. I've had a good life. I'm just tired. For me it's no different from going to sleep."

"But you—you've got your whole life ahead of you. You see Nels, dying isn't important. It's living that's important. You're not really alive if you're afraid all the time."

"You're very lucky Nels. You're a Canadian. You don't have to live your life with fear hanging over your head every day. You're free. A lot of good men gave their lives so that you could have that freedom."

"You mustn't ever take that freedom for granted. We fought Hitler and the Nazis so that young people like you wouldn't have to grow up being afraid. Maybe you'll be lucky and you'll never have to fight for that freedom again."

"But if you do, I want you to remember this—I taught you to be a soldier. If the time ever comes where you have to risk your life for your freedom, then don't be afraid of it. And don't feel bad for me. We're soldiers. More than that—we're Canadians. You got that Soldier?"

"Yes Sir."

"All right. I've got a present for you. It's outside in the back seat of my car. I want you to go and get it and put it under the seat of your Dad's car. Don't tell your folks, and don't open it until you get home. And Nels—one more thing. Nobody else knows I'm leaving except Sally and your cousins. And likely your Mom. It's just between us, this little talk. Okay?"

"Yes Sir."

"Good."

Walker released his arm.

"Let's see you stand to attention Soldier."

"Yes Sir."

He stood to attention in front of Walker's chair, feeling the quiet approving power of the old soldier's eyes.

"At ease Soldier. Go outside now and do what I told you. Get a little cold air while you're out there. It'll make you feel better. When you come back in, we'll talk a little fishing before I have to go home. Off you go now."

He turned away and crossed the room, back straight and head held high, feeling his mother's eyes on him from the dining room. He held it inside him, pulling on his galoshes, in control until he stepped outside and closed the door.

The Mystery loomed around him in the black winter night, not understanding it at all, just knowing that he would be brave for Poppy. The cold wind stung his eyes, going down the stairs. The outlines of the flat cardboard box were all blurry under the dome light when he opened the car door.

"I'm not going to cry. I won't!"

He said it out loud through clenched teeth, lifting the precious parcel out and carrying it to its hiding place in the back seat of his father's car.

The spasm hit him then. He leaned against the car, letting himself go in its release, part of him detached, watching the last tears of his childhood falling in the snow. He stayed there until the tears stopped, rubbing the traces of them away from his eyes with the heels of his hands.

The cold came to him, icy sharp needles through the thin cloth of his suit coat. He took one deep breath, steadying himself on his feet. He turned away and went up the steps, into the warmth of Aunt Helen's house.

Walker smiled as he came and stood in front of him. The grey eyes measured him.

"Are you all right Soldier?"

"Yes Sir. It was just the wind."

"Oh—you're a good kid Here . . . come and sit on the arm of the chair. You know—I was thinking while you were outside . . . do you remember that pike we hooked that time? The one that broke the line?"

The image came, of a great fish lashing the shallow water into a frenzy with its powerful body.

"Yeah! He was huge!"

"Biggest one I ever saw."

He lost himself in visions of his childhood, and the river. All too soon Auntie Sal was there, smiling down at them.

"Are you tired Walker?"

"Yes Sal. I guess it's time to go home."

"I'll go and get your coat then."

"Thanks Sal."

He turned to look once more at the old man, the question coming unbidden to his mind.

"Poppy?"

"Yes kid?"

"Do you think that there'll be a place to go fishing in Heaven?"

Walker's eyes got thoughtful. And then he grinned, the grin that the boy knew so well.

"I sure hope so kid. I never really wanted to play the harp."

He got to his feet, moving respectfully aside as Mom and Dad and his aunts and uncles all came to bid Walker good night. Dad was there, with his hand on his shoulder while he put his boots on. Auntie Sal and Mom were hugging in the hallway when Dad and Danny helped Walker out to the car. He leaned in, to put the canes beside him on the seat and shake Poppy's hand.

"Well . . . so long Soldier. You remember what I taught you."

"I will Poppy."

He held Auntie Sal in his arms, smiling back at her when she kissed his cheek and let him go.

"You're a good boy Nels. I love you."

"Good night Auntie Sal. Goodbye Walker."

He held the door until she was inside and closed it behind her. Then he moved to the front of the car, to stand to full attention in the beam of the headlights, his right hand poised in the military salute as the old black Ford pulled away.

He spent the rest of the evening beside Mom, on the couch, with her arm around his shoulders. He made no protest when she said it was time to go home. But it seemed to him, saying goodbye to the family, that there was some soft sadness in the eyes of his aunts which mirrored the feeling inside of him.

On the way home he watched the streets flowing by, not seeing them really at all. Walker's last secret waited beneath the seat.

He lingered behind when they got to the house, going to look at the Manger. Mom and Dad were in the kitchen when he came in the back door. Mom turned, seeing the flat cardboard box cradled in his arms.

"What have you got there Nels?"

"It's a present. From Walker."

"What is it Honey?"

"I don't know Mom. He didn't tell me."

"Let's see."

The box was taped at either end. He laid it on the table and got a knife to cut the tape. Mom and Dad were on either side of him. He heard her gasp when he lifted the lid.

The rifle gleamed in its bed of crumpled newspaper. Its barrel had been freshly blued. The hardwood stock was polished to a fine gloss. The sling from a military carbine had been newly installed, so that a boy could carry it while he rode his bicycle.

"It's Walker's air rifle!"

Walker had bought the rifle to shoot the starlings which infested the city. They gathered in raucous flocks to feast in the mulberry tree and then soiled the clean wash on the line with their purple droppings. He had taught the boy how to shoot them, resting the rifle on the kitchen window sill when they were alone. Sighting in the vital spot on each bird; exhaling his breath until he was rock steady, never squeezing the trigger until he was certain that the phat! of the shot would bring a clean kill.

He lifted it out of the box, in awe at the gift, turning to look up into his father's eyes.

"He gave it to me Dad. Can I keep it?"

"May I see it son?"

He passed the precious weapon into his father's hands, suddenly tormented with the thought that Dad might say no.

John Sorenson held the rifle to examine it, marvelling at the craftsmanship and the care that it had been given. The feeling of it in his hands brought the memory of the .22 rifle with which he had hunted for rabbits at a similar age. He remembered then, the image of the scorched prairie of the Depression. Meat had been scarce and every shell was precious.

The image faded and went out. He passed the rifle back into his son's hands, smiling at him to relieve the anxiousness in his eyes.

"Yes son. You can keep it. But it stays in the house until I teach you how to use it."

The boy beamed in gratitude, anxious now to share with his father what he had learned.

"I already know how to use it Dad! Watch! You break the block and pull the barrel all the way down—like this. That cocks the spring, to arm it. You put the slug in the breech and pull the barrel back up until the block locks shut. Then it's ready to fire. If you want to disarm it, you pull the barrel all the way down and hold it tight and release the spring with the trigger. It's okay Mom—it's not loaded."

He closed the rifle, shifting it through 'Present Arms' with a practised skill and then resting it on its butt at his side; standing at ease, holding it by the barrel.

"I'm a really good shot Dad. I can snap a wooden match on the fence every time, the length of Auntie Sal's yard."

He watched their eyes, wide in shock, turning to stare at each other. It was Mom who said,

"That old devil!"

He stared up at his father, suddenly afraid.

"Dad?"

"Yes Nels?"

"Walker'll go to Heaven won't he?"

Dad smiled and put a hand on his shoulder.

"Of course he will son. He's a good man."

Mom smiled too, a funny little smile.

"Why don't you take Taffy upstairs and get ready for bed? I'll be up in a few minutes to tuck you in. Okay?"

"Sure. Thanks Mom and Dad. G'night Dad. Merry Christmas."

By the time she got upstairs he was fast asleep with the pup tucked in beside him. The bedside light was still on. The barrel of the rifle gleamed in the light, leaning up against the bedside table.

Margaret Sorenson stood for a moment, wondering at how innocent her son looked in his sleep. Then she switched the light off and went slowly back down the stairs.

On Sunday morning the church was packed for the Preacher's farewell service. The Sorensons sat in their usual place, in the front row of seats on the right hand wing of the balcony. It was the boy's favourite place. He could lean forward and put his hands on the rail and look out over the whole congregation.

Aunt Sally was there, for his award. Mom said it was okay when he asked if he could sit between them. He leaned forward to wave to Tommy, smiling up at him from the main floor. When he sat back there were butterflies inside him, fluttering around with the thought of going up to the stage in front of so many people.

Aunt Sally seemed to know that the butterflies were there. She turned to smile at him while they waited for the service to begin.

"Are you nervous Honey?"

"A little bit Auntie Sal."

She took his hand and gave it a squeeze.

"Don't you worry. You'll do just fine."

The lively hum of conversation began to fade as the two Pastors came out onto the stage to stand together. Auntie Sal leaned over and whispered to Mom how handsome the young Pastor was. Mom whispered back, that he looked no more than a boy.

The hall fell silent as the old Pastor stepped up to the simple wooden lectern. His grey eyes ranged out over the congregation, his quiet smile returning the smiles that greeted him there.

"Good morning. I would like to thank you all for coming out today. I know that many of you have family here, from out of town, who will be returning to their homes after visiting for the holiday. For those of you who are visiting, I trust that you will feel welcome. I have been advised that the roads outside of the city are drifting heavily. I will try to be as brief as possible. I pray that you will all have a safe journey home."

"As you know, this will be a special service this morning. This will be my final service to you as your pastor. There will be no sermon and no announcements this morning. Pastor Wilson will lead us all in the hymns of worship, after which I will share my thoughts with you on this occasion. Again, I will try to be brief, so that my wife and I will have the opportunity to speak to each of you personally after the close of the service."

"Before I ask Pastor Wilson to lead you in the singing, I would ask you all to bow your heads while I lead you in a moment of prayer."

The boy closed his eyes, savouring the warmth and quiet which surrounded him. The Preacher's words rose up over the congregation.

"Our Heavenly Father; we are gathered on this day in worship and in gratitude for Your Presence here among us. I pray that you will touch our hearts and bless them with that peace that passeth all understanding. We are all Thy children. In Jesus name we ask it. Amen."

There was the murmur of soft passionate "Amens" throughout the hall. The boy opened his eyes, leaning forward to look as the Preacher left the stage to join his wife in the front row. The young Pastor came forward to lead them in the singing.

The congregation rose to sing the favoured hymns. He found each hymn in the hymn book for Auntie Sal; holding the book open with her, looking past it himself, knowing all of the words by heart, letting his eyes rove out over the sea of smiling faces while he sang. They sang five hymns that morning, the sound of worship rising up to Heaven. When the singing was finished and they were seated again, he felt good.

The young Pastor left the stage to sit with his pretty young wife in the front row. The Preacher came to stand before the lectern once more. Every eye was upon him and he began to speak.

"Before we came to the service this morning, my wife and I were recalling a day more than twelve years ago now. I had just returned from a meeting with my superior in the Baptist congress. He had instructed me that I had been chosen to go and minister to a church in Canada. This church. Your church."

The Preacher paused, his smile quiet and thoughtful.

"As Americans, neither my wife nor I had ever been to your country before. I confess that our hearts were troubled by this new calling. Both of our families and all of our children lived in the United States. The prospect of leaving them to make a new home here, in Canada, was a burden to us."

"More than this, as we have come to realize over the years, it was the fear of coming to a foreign country, as strangers and as Americans, which was most unsettling. I know too, for some of you have confessed to me as our friendships developed, that it was unsettling for you, as Canadians, to have an American pastor come to minister to you in your church.

"Now my wife and I are about to take our leave of you. You have a new pastor and his wife whom God has called to minister to you. They are also Americans. I'm sure that they have similar fears to those which my wife and I shared when we first came to this great country called Canada."

The Preacher paused again, his smile broadening.

"The heart of the Christian faith, and the essence of what we call Democracy is the belief that we are all God's children. This is the great lesson that our Saviour came to teach us. Through that love of God and through the fellowship of the Christian family, my wife and I have had a home here. Both in your church and in your country."

"The Lord has opened our hearts to one another. Our years here, in His service, have been good ones. He has blessed us all for our faithfulness. I could speak for the rest of the day on the ways in which I have seen the love of God at work in this congregation."

The hall resounded with fervent "Amens." When the Preacher drew a white handkerchief from his pocket to clear the tears of his feeling from his eyes, others like it appeared throughout the hall. In the corner of one eye, the boy saw his father reach for his mother's hand. He leaned forward in his seat, memorizing the image of the Preacher with the forest and the stream behind him, moved by some remembered emotion from the day of his sister's birth.

The Preacher replaced the white handkerchief in his pocket, his smile undiminished.

"The Lord has blessed my wife and I with one last calling. We will be returning to our home state of Michigan, to a church in a small town close to where we were both born. Our families and our children all live nearby. It will be good to be reunited with them."

"The thought which I wish to leave you with is this. At times of change, it is always the fear of the unknown which troubles men's hearts and keeps them apart from one another. Our Saviour came to bring us the gifts of Faith and of Christian love, to heal those rifts which cause us to mistrust and to bring harm to one another."

"As it is with individuals, so it is with nations. We are all part of the family of God. Perhaps the day will come when the leaders of all nations will realize this truth, so that we may be able to say with the angels on the night of our Saviour's birth, 'Peace on earth and good will unto all men'. I pray that this will one day come to pass."

"I will ask you now to join me in a moment of quiet prayer. I would ask you to search your hearts, as I will, for anything which may have come between us, that the Lord may lift these burdens from us. I would ask of you that you thank the Lord for all of the blessings that he had bestowed upon us over the years that we have been together. I would ask of you, finally that you will pray for your new pastor, God's servant Pastor Wilson, that our Father in Heaven will guide his hand in his new ministry to you."

"Let us pray."

The boy closed his eyes, trying to think of a prayer. But his mind went whirling along, carrying him with it, wondering how it could be that the Preacher was from another country and he had never even guessed it! He opened his eyes, leaning forward to look down at the Preacher, wondering how you could tell. He wondered too what this new thing called 'Democracy' was. Just from the way the Preacher said it, he knew that it must be important.

He leaned back and shut his eyes again. Then the butterflies came flocking in, beating his thoughts away with their wings, flapping around inside him in the anxious fear that the service was over and the Preacher had forgotten about his award!

The silence went on forever; until the Preacher said 'Amen'. He opened his eyes to look down urgently as the Preacher began to speak again.

"I have one final responsibility to fulfil before I leave you. It is one that gives me a great deal of pleasure."

The Preacher turned, looking up into his eyes, smiling a smile that was only for him.

"Nels, would you come down here and stand with me?"

He froze, unable to move, until Mom touched his hand and whispered,

"You have to go down to the front now Honey."

The whole congregation was looking at him as he stood up. He moved fast, into the aisle, trying not to notice until he reached the safety of the corridor and went down the back stairs. He stopped at the bottom, trying to screw up his courage.

The image of Walker came to him. He pushed the door open and marched up onto the stage, coming to attention in front of the Preacher, not daring to take his eyes off him.

The Preacher put a hand on his shoulder and leaned forward to whisper,

"It's all right son. Don't be nervous.", in his ear.

He relaxed to at ease, looking around and smiling nervously at Mom and Dad smiling down at him from the balcony. The Preacher began to speak again.

"As you know, I have always encouraged learning in my ministry to you. Both for the adult members and for the children. In this respect as well, we are all children before the wisdom of God."

"Our Saviour tells us, in the tenth chapter of the Gospel of Saint Mark,

'Suffer the little children to come unto me, and forbid them not; for of such is the kingdom of God.

Verily, I say unto you; Whosoever shall not receive the Kingdom of God as a little child, he shall not enter therein'."

"I believe that what our Saviour meant was that we, as adults, must relearn our innocence when we approach Him in spirit."

"My young friend Nels has been studying the scriptures with me personally for almost a year now. In reward for his efforts, I promised him a copy of the Scofield Reference Bible, like my own. He has worked diligently, memorizing 300 verses of the scripture to earn this award. I would like to present it to him now."

The Preacher shook his hand. From the lectern he took the precious book with its gold edges and fine leather cover and put it into his hands.

"Congratulations Nels."

"Thank you Sir."

He started to leave but the Preacher put his hand on his shoulder.

"Stay a little longer son."

The Preacher's smile held him there, the grey eyes serene.

"Yes Sir."

The Preacher turned back to the congregation.

"Nels and I were discussing the Scriptures the last time we met. I asked my young friend what his favourite passage was. He replied that it was the 23rd Psalm."

The Preacher turned to smile at him again. Several voices were raised to say Amen.

"'Out of the mouths of babes . . .' At times of change, this Psalm of David is the one to which I have turned for comfort."

"Pastor Wilson, would you join us please?"

The young Pastor came to stand on the other side of him.

"As a benediction to this, my last sermon, I would ask my friend Nels to lead us in reciting this Psalm together. Go ahead son. We'll all say it with you."

The boy looked out at all of the smiling faces, the Preacher's hand on his shoulder, suddenly quiet inside.

"Now Sir?"

"Yes Nels. Go ahead."

He took a deep breath, focusing his mind, wanting to say it right, for the Preacher.

"The Lord is my shepherd; I shall not want."

"He maketh me to lie down in green pastures; He leadeth me beside the still waters. He restoreth my soul; He leadeth me in the paths of righteousness for His name sake.

"Yea, though I walk through the valley of the shadow of death, I will fear no evil; for Thou art with me; Thy rod and Thy staff, they comfort me.

He listened while he said the words, hearing his own high clear voice above the murmur of the congregation and the deeper voices of the Preachers on either side of him.

"Thou preparest a table before me in the presence of mine enemies; Thou annointest my head with oil; my cup runneth over."

"Surely goodness and mercy shall follow me all the days of my life; and I will dwell in the house of the Lord forever."

He finished the Psalm and looked over at the Preacher. The Preacher had closed his eyes and bowed his head. He closed his eyes too, knowing that the Preacher was about to say the final prayer. There were no words to describe how good he felt inside.

"Heavenly Father; we thank You for this blessing which You have given us. We ask of You that Your Presence will go with each and everyone as we leave here today, to keep us safe and to guide us. For Thine is the Kingdom and the Power and the Glory, for ever and ever. Amen."

The Preacher touched his shoulder. He opened his eyes.

"Thank you son. You can go sit down now."

The Preacher whispered the words. The congregation still sat with bowed heads and closed eyes. He smiled and slipped away, down the steps, grinning at Tommy who was watching him from several rows down. He crossed the wide space in front of the stage, reaching an empty place in the first row just as the Preacher began to speak again.

"I would ask you all to rise and sing my favourite hymn with me. Number 342 in your hymn books. 'Shall We Gather at the River'."

The people were all standing now. Mom and Dad and Ellen and Aunt Sally were smiling at him from the balcony. The organist played the introduction. He left the hymn book where it was, singing by heart, holding his Bible and raising his voice as they sang the final chorus.

"Yes we'll gather at the River,
That beautiful, that beautiful old River
Gather with Saints at the River
That flows 'neath the throne of God."

The Preacher was coming down the steps to stand with his wife in front of the stage. The hall was filled with laughter and the shuffle of people turning to talk with their neighbours. People began to flow in front of him, coming to smile and shake the Preacher's hand. He let his eyes range past them to the painting of the Forest, thinking about the River.

Then Tommy was there, beaming at him.

"You were great Nels!"

"Gee—thanks Tommy!"

"Can I see your Bible, Nels?"

"Sure."

He passed the precious book into Tommy's hands, both of them admiring the black leather cover and the fine onion skin paper with its gilt edges. Tommy looked wistful.

"Wow . . . it's beautiful Nels. I wish I could remember like you . . ."

"Yeah—but you can beat me at chess."

Tommy grinned and passed the Bible back to him.

"What are you doing on Monday?"

"I'm going to the library downtown. I have to take my books back and get some more."

"Mom said I could ask you if you wanted to stay over tomorrow at our house."

"Gee—that'd be great. I'll ask my Mom. I could meet you at the library. And we could go to Mr. Goldstein's store and look at the fish."

Tommy looked doubtful,

"I don't know—I guess we could. But you better not pick the lobsters up out the tank this time. I don't think he liked you doing that."

Nels Sorenson grinned at his friend.

"Aw—he didn't really mind."

"Hello Tommy."

"Hello Mrs. Sorenson. Hello Mr. Sorenson."

His family was there, emerging out of the crowd of people.

"Mom—can I stay at Tommy's overnight on Monday?"

"Sure you can. There's someone else here who wants to say hello to you Nels."

"Hello Aunt Mary! Hello Uncle Bill!"

Uncle Bill got a hold of his hand before he was ready. He braced himself, not letting it show how powerful the old farmer's grip was, his hand starting to hurt where he had punched David.

"We're proud of you son."

"Thanks Uncle Bill."

Aunt Mary said,

"When are you going to sit with us again for the service?"

"Next Sunday? Can I Mom?"

"Certainly you can Honey."

He lost himself in the realm of smiling adult conversations; until he found himself with his family moving to shake hands with the two Preachers and their wives.

Pastor Wilson was first. The handsome young pastor shook his outstretched hand.

"I'm very proud of you Bill."

He stalled, not sure what to say.

"Uh—it's Nels Sir."

"I'm sorry sonny. It'll take me a while to get used to the way you folks talk up here."

The thought came, that it was the new Pastor who said words that sounded funny. But he knew that it would be disrespectful to say anything. The Pastor had already turned to shake his father's hand.

The old Preacher smiled and held out his hand to him. They shook, the Preacher still holding his hand.

"I'm very pleased for you Nels. I hope you'll keep your studies up. The Lord gave you a good mind. Perhaps some day He'll have a calling for you."

The thought was too amazing to grasp. He blushed, wondering what he should say.

"Thank you Sir. Pastor—what's it like, where you're going?"

"It's very beautiful Nels. There are big old trees, and a river that flows through the town. There's a university there too. I earned my first degree there. Some day I hope you'll go to university too."

He had heard of university; but no one in his family had ever been there.

"I'll try Sir. Pastor?"

"Yes Nels?"

"What are the people like in America?"

"People are much the same wherever you go Nels. We're all God's children."

"Well . . . goodbye Sir,"
"Goodbye Nels. God bless you. I'll remember you in my prayers."

When they got home, Dad said,
"Come into the living room with me, son."
He followed his father into the room, looking at the angel on the Christmas tree, Bible in hand and Taffy following his feet. Dad sat down in the big green armchair where he read. The boy stood in front of him, waiting.
"Can I look at your Bible son?"
"Sure Dad."
He watched his father reverently turn the pages. The Bible was the only book that Dad ever read. Nels Sorenson loved books. It was from watching Dad's face while he read, as a child, that he had first sensed the wonder that books contained.
He turned to look at Dad's worn old Bible on the table. The covers were coming away from the pages. Here and there a sheet of the thick paper stuck out farther than the rest.
"Dad?"
Dad looked up at him.
"Yes Nels, what is it?"
"I want you to have my Bible. It's a present."
Dad smiled at him, a smile he had never seen before.
"That's very fine of you Nels. But it's your Bible. You'll have it now, for the rest of your life. If you let me read it, that be a gift enough. Someday, when you're an old man, you'll probably have a grandson to pass it on to, as a present."
"Gee Dad—you think so?"
"I'm sure you will."
Dad gave him the Bible back, and he felt better.
"Why don't you go take your suit off. We'll have some lunch and then maybe will drive out to the bush if the roads aren't too bad."

"Sure Dad."

He scooped up Taffy with his free hand and carried her up the stairs. He set the Bible on the bedside table and put the pup on the bed. He talked to her, watching how she tilted her head to listen while he changed his clothes. Then he went and sat beside her, to pet her.

"You're a good girl, aren't you. Yes. What a good girl . . ."

The thought came then, that Poppy and the Pastor were both gone. He rubbed at his eyes, looking at the talismans that they had given him—the Bible and the rifle. He curled up on the bed, folding his dog against his chest, suddenly exhausted by the whirl of thoughts and feelings that rose up inside him.

"They're gone girl."

He fell asleep, and into his sleep there came a dream. He dreamt that he and Poppy were together, and that they were fishing, at the River. The River was filled with light.

1960: PASTOR BILLY WILSON AND THE BOMB

*T*he first Sunday of the new year dawned in mottled yellows and grays. The Manger had been put away. The Santa Clauses were all gone from the snow covered lawns. The winter streets looked cold and bleak without their Christmas decorations.

By the time the family left for church the wind was up, hurling a screen of flying crystals against the windshield. Even with the heater on full blast it was still cold in the back seat of the Vauxhall.

When they reached the church Nels Sorenson saw the new sign. He turned to study it while his father parked the car. It was a lot bigger than the old sign. There were three shielded metal lamps across the top of it, just like the ones on the billboards which were all over the city.

"Look Mom—we've got a new sign!"

"Yes Nels. I saw it."

Mom didn't seem too interested. He turned back to it again, to read the words. At the top, in bold black letters was the name of their church and the new Preacher's name, Pastor William Wilson.

The words below that were very strange. The sign said,

MORNING SERVICE: 11:00 A.M.
"FOR ALL HAVE SINNED AND COME SHORT
OF THE GLORY OF GOD."
EVENING SERVICE: 7:00 P.M.
"REVELATION TODAY"
SUNDAY SCHOOL 10:00 A.M. YOUNG PEOPLES 6:15 P.M.
ALL WELCOME.

The old sign had read, "Morning Worship Service." He wondered why they had left out "Worship," and what "Revelation Today" meant. Strangest of all, the words had been painted right onto the sign. He wondered how they would change them before the service for next week.

Mom and Dad looked nervous as they hurried up the sidewalk to get in out of the wind. Deacon Brown and Mr. Hurley shook hands with them at the door. All of the adults who were taking their coats off in the lobby looked nervous too. The only adult who didn't look nervous was Mr. Hurley. He looked really happy. Mr. Hurley was weird anyhow.

He looked at Mom while he hung up his coat.

"Can I sit with Uncle Bill and Aunt Mary this morning, for the service?"

Mom frowned a little bit, the way she did when she was thinking.

"I don't know Nels. Maybe you'd better sit with us."

"But Mom! I promised!"

"Well . . . all right . . ."

"Thanks Mom."

He smiled and took off for his Sunday School class before she changed her mind.

The Sunday School teacher, Mr. Matthews, announced that since it was the first Sunday of the new year, they were going to leave where they had been studying in the Book of Proverbs and start over with the first chapter of the Book of Genesis.

Nels Sorenson didn't really mind. The story of Creation was his favourite. But Mr. Matthews seemed to be thinking about something else. Twice through the lesson he got lost.

By the time the lesson was over he had begun to wonder what was going on. He came up the stairs from the basement, along the corridor into the lobby, heading for the washroom beneath the main staircase. The services were two hours long. He always went to relieve himself before the service began. The feeling stayed with him, a sense of uneasiness while he emptied his bladder into the white porcelain urinal.

He washed his hands and paused to check his hair and his tie in the mirror, wanting to look nice for Aunt Mary. When he looked at his watch, he saw that it was almost eleven. He picked up his Bible and hurried out into the hall, scanning the rows of pews for Uncle Bill and Aunt Mary.

They were there, close to the back in the centre section where the old people sat. Uncle Bill was sitting next to the aisle with Aunt Mary beside him. Aunt Mary was looking up towards the front of the church. Uncle Bill was half turned with his back to the aisle, talking quietly with another old man who was leaning forward in the row behind him.

Neither of them noticed him there, standing politely in the aisle, not wanting to interrupt Uncle Bill's conversation. His uneasiness grew, looking at the old people's faces. The old man Uncle Bill was talking with looked as though he was angry about something. The old lady beside him looked upset. She turned and saw him there and leaned forward to touch Aunt Mary's shoulder.

Aunt Mary looked over and he smiled at her. She gave him a funny little smile, reaching to touch Uncle Bill's arm.

"Bill . . . Nels is here."

Uncle Bill turned to look at him.

"Good morning Uncle Bill."

"Morning son."

Uncle Bill seemed to hesitate for a moment before he shifted his legs so that the boy could squeeze in past him. He took his place between them, smiling up at Aunt Mary.

"Good morning Aunt Mary."

"Yes . . . good morning dear."

Behind him, the man who was talking to Uncle Bill leaned forward again, his gnarled hand grasping the back of the seat behind his shoulder. The voice behind his ear was an intense whisper.

"It's not good Bill. He didn't even consult the elders. He just went ahead and did all this without even telling anyone."

"Yes—I'd like to know who he thinks he is!"

Uncle Bill's whisper was just as intense. He felt suddenly strange and out of place, wishing that he could go and sit with Mom and Dad. But he knew it would be impolite to disturb Uncle Bill again. The service was almost ready to begin. The old man behind him sat back in his seat. He stole a sideways glance at Uncle Bill, who was staring straight ahead of him. Uncle Bill's jaw was clenched. His eyes were angry.

The boy shifted away from him across the bench, moving a little closer to Aunt Mary. He glanced up at her, but she was staring at the stage. There was something in her face that he couldn't read.

He followed her gaze to the front of the church. The shock was like a hand reaching inside him, squeezing his stomach.

The painting of the forest and the stream was gone! In its place, across the back of the stage there was just a plain white curtain. He closed his eyes and then looked again, not wanting to believe it. It was still gone. He turned instinctively to the old woman beside him.

"Aunt Mary?"

"Yes Nels?"

"Why is the painting gone?"

"I don't know dear."

She took his hand and tried to smile for him. But he could tell by her eyes that she felt the same way he did.

He stared back up to the front of the church, seeing all the other changes now. The simple lectern where the old Preacher had put the Bible while he spoke had been replaced by an elaborately carved wooden pulpit. There was a shiny metal microphone attached to it, like the one in the school auditorium.

Behind the pulpit, to one side of the platform stood an enormous red chair. It was beyond any chair that he had ever seen. With its carved wooden arms and high backpiece, it made him think of a picture of a throne that he had seen once, in a storybook. The old

Preacher always came down and sat with the rest of the congregation while the choir sang. The boy wondered why the old Preacher had never gotten a chair like that for himself.

He forgot the chair, his eyes drawn to the blank white curtain again, wondering if the painting was still there behind it. The thought that it might be gone altogether was too awful to contemplate.

He looked away, to the side of the stage. There were new hymn boards on the wall beside where the wings of the balcony ended. Then he forgot about everything else, staring at the statues that hung above the hymn boards, feeling his gut constrict into a knot.

Nels Sorenson had never seen a crucifix before. They were almost life size, carved from some dark wood. He stared at the one on the right, horror-struck, seeing the way the body hung from the spikes, the head lolling to one side. Even at a distance he could see the mantle of thorns and the appeal of helpless agony in Jesus' eyes.

He shut his eyes, unable to look at it. The image stayed with him, imprinted on his mind. There was a rustle in the hall. Someone coughed nervously somewhere behind him. He opened his eyes, trying to escape the image, seeing the handsome young Preacher smiling out at the congregation from behind the new pulpit.

There was an audible click as the Preacher reached out and switched on the new microphone.

"Good morn—"

His voice was cut off by a prolonged piercing scream. The Preacher's head and shoulders disappeared below the top of the pulpit. The boy swung around, looking for the scream. It was somewhere behind him. Aunt Mary had her fingers in her ears. The old lady behind him looked terrified. Then he saw the big new boxes mounted high up on the back wall. The screaming was coming out of them!

The scream changed pitch and died. The old lady behind him shut her eyes, one hand on her breast. The old man's face beside her was beet red with rage. He swung back around, staring up at the balcony, looking for Mom and Dad but he couldn't see them. He looked to the front, seeing that the Preacher was there again. If anything, his smile seemed even brighter!

The Preacher grasped the edges of the pulpit with his hands, leaning forward to put his mouth up close to the microphone. His voice boomed out of the boxes, startlingly loud, echoing in the hall.

"Good morning brothers and sisters! Ah! Isn't it good to know the Lord! I want to welcome you all to this first service in this year of our Lord, nineteen hundred and sixty, in which God has chosen me to lead you, His people. If there's anybody here who doesn't know me yet, I'm Pastor Billy Wilson!"

The Preacher's smile blazed up and then went out. His voice became suddenly serious.

"This is a very special service this morning. This is my first address to you as your new Pastor. These are troubled times, my friends. Satan and his followers are active in the world. Many are in sin. Many more are being persecuted for their faith, even as I speak to you now."

The Preacher bowed his head a little, sadly. Then he straightened up to his full height. When he spoke again, his manner and his voice were clear and determined.

"I feel the hand of God upon me as I stand before you today. I pray that He will open your hearts and minds to the message He has given me, so that you will hear His wisdom in my words and say with me, 'Not my will, Lord, but Thy will be done'."

"Let us pray."

The boy closed his eyes, waiting in the silence and the tension which buzzed inside of him.

"God—we thank You for bringing us together on this day, Thy chosen people, for we know that the time of Thy coming draws nigh, and that the time is short for our salvation. We pray that You will bless the faithful ones gathered to hear Thy words and to obey Thy Commandments."

"We pray that if there are any here among us who are in sin, You will touch their hearts and reveal to them their false pride. Humble them oh God! Be merciful and lead them away from the Evil One, the

Worm that dieth not, that they may yet come to know Thy love and Thy forgiveness."

"In Jesus' name we ask it. Amen."

The boy had never heard a prayer like it before. He was trying to understand what the Worm was when the Preacher's shout rang out so loud that he came right up off the seat.

"Stand up brothers and sisters! Stand up and sing! Hymn number 208! 'Are you washed in the blood of the Lamb!'"

He was on his feet before the old people around him began to rise. Many of them looked dazed, reaching forward for the hymn books in the racks on the back of the pews. He seized a hymn book and sped to the page and gave it to Aunt Mary. He grabbed another hymn book, hearing the opening chords of the organ as he found it the second time. Most of the old people around him were still looking for the page when the Preacher's voice rang out in song.

"Have you been to Jesus for the cleansing power?
Are you washed in the blood of the Lamb?
Are you fully trusting in His grace this hour?
Are you washed in the blood of the Lamb?"

It was a hymn that they had never sang before. The congregation stumbled over the unfamiliar lyrics. The Preacher drew them on, shouting out the words and beating out a fast tempo with his hand on the pulpit as they raced into the chorus.

"Are you washed—in the blood;
In the soul-cleansing blood of the Lamb?
Are your garments spotless—are they white as snow
Are you washed in the blood of the Lamb?"

He couldn't understand it at all. It made no sense—washing with blood to get clean! He looked over at Uncle Bill. Uncle Bill wasn't singing. He wasn't even looking at his hymn book. His eyes were locked on the Preacher. Aunt Mary was singing beside him, trying to follow the words. But he could tell by her eyes that she didn't understand it either.

The words to the second verse were even stranger. He'd mastered the simple melody on the first verse. He sang the words as he read them, singing in his high clear voice.

"When the Bridegroom cometh will your robes be white?
Are you washed in the blood of the Lamb?
Will your soul be ready for the mansions bright?
Are you washed in the blood of the Lamb?"

The choir sang the background harmonies. The flat amplified slap of the Preacher's hand on the pulpit thudded over their voices. They sang all four verses.

When the hymn was finished the Preacher was mopping his brow with a handkerchief and beaming down at the congregation. His voice swelled out in a shout of triumph.

"Isn't it great to know the Lord! Say Amen! out there if you love Jesus! Amen Pastor Billy! Say Amen!"

There was a faint scatter of "Amens", around the hall. The boy said,

"Amen Pastor Billy!" because the Preacher had told him to, but not very loud. An old man with a red face in the row in front of him turned around and scowled at him. Aunt Mary poked him gently in the ribs and held a finger to her lips. He hung his head, feeling the burn on his cheeks of hot ashamed embarrassment.

"Sit down brothers and sisters! Sit down!"

He sank into his seat. Aunt Mary took his hand as she sat down and whispered,

"It's all right Nels."

He raised his head and she smiled for him and he felt a little bit better. An old lady in the row ahead was still standing, looking confused. The lady beside her took her arm and guided her down to her seat. He looked up past her, looking right into the dark eyes of the Preacher.

The Preacher smiled at him in recognition. He smiled back timidly before the Preacher's eyes left him, ranging out over the congregation. The Preacher spoke softly now but his voice was still loud in the hall.

The boy watched him, seeing his lips move and wondering at how the Preacher's voice seemed to be somewhere behind him, coming out the speakers on the back wall.

"I know that, to some of you, it seems as though I'd going much faster than you're used to. I feel the power of God in me this morning. I ask you to bear with me."

"Brother James will come up now and read the announcements for the week while the collection plates are being passed. I ask you to open both your hearts and your wallets and give generously to the work of the Lord. If you have an extra dollar to give, God loves you for it. After the announcements the choir is going to sing my favourite hymn, 'The Old Rugged Cross'."

Brother James was a tall elderly man who always read the announcements. The boy watched him as he went up the aisle glad for the fact that there was at least one thing that hadn't changed.

The Preacher went and sat in the big red chair. Brother James climbed the steps and stood well away from the new pulpit. He began to read the announcements from the sheet of paper in his hand. His voice carried clearly in the natural acoustics of the hall.

Deacon Brown appeared at the end of the row beside Uncle Bill. The boy took the plain white envelope which held his tithe from Liberty magazine out of the pocket of his suit coat. It was only a dime. He wished now that he had put the whole dollar in.

Uncle Bill passed him the collection plate. It was new too. It was shiny silver, and there were patches of red velvet showing beneath the white envelopes. He placed his offering in it and passed it to Aunt Mary, wondering what had happened to the plain wicker collection baskets.

There were so many strange new things this morning. Some of the old people in the row in front of him had their heads together, whispering quietly. He couldn't hear what they were saying but he guessed that they were talking about all the new things too. He looked up at the crucifixes and looked away, repelled by them.

"Aunt Mary?"

He whispered to her. She turned and whispered back to him,
"Yes dear?"

"Why do they have the statues up there?"

Her smile faltered, her eyes nervous now. She whispered past him,
"Bill—"

"I know. I heard him. That's a good question."

Uncle Bill spoke gruffly, barely deigning to whisper. His eyes never
left the Preacher when he spoke.

He waited to hear if Uncle Bill or Aunt Mary would explain it
to him. Brother James had finished reading and he was leaving the
platform. He still didn't have an answer to his question. He turned to
Aunt Mary again, wanting to understand.

"Aunt Mary?"

"Ssh dear. They're going to sing the hymn."

The organist played a run of quiet chords. The deacons were still
in the aisles, taking the offering. He looked to the Preacher in profile
against the blank white curtain. The Preacher smiled and closed his
eyes as the choir began to sing.

It was another hymn that was new to him. It sounded very soft
and sad. He studied the Preacher's smiling face while he listened to the
words.

"On a hill far away, stood an old rugged cross
The emblem of suffering and shame;
And I love that old cross where the dearest and best
For a world of lost sinners was slain."

He realized that they were signing a song about the statues. He
listened closely, concentrating on the words as the choir began the
chorus.

"So I'll cherish the old rugged cross
'Till my trophies at last I lay down;
I will cling to the old rugged cross
And exchange it some day for a crown."

The soloist sang the second verse in a rich baritone voice. The choir
hummed the harmonies behind him.

"In the old rugged cross stained with blood so divine
A wondrous beauty I see;
For 'twas on that old cross Jesus suffered and died
To pardon and sanctify me."

His eyes drifted back to the statue against his will, no longer even listening as the choir began the chorus the second time. The eyes of Jesus haunted him, hanging in grotesque agony on the wall. He remembered how once he had stepped on a nail, the tactile image of searing pain coming back to him again. It was inconceivable that the adults who were singing could find beauty in such a thing!

He tore his eyes away from it, watching the deacons as they put the collection plates on the front of the platform and went back to their seats. It came to him then, that every hymn that morning so far had blood in it. He wished that they would sing a happy song, like they always did.

He looked up to the Preacher for reassurance. The Preacher's eyes were open and he was watching the congregation. As the last notes of the organ disappeared he saw the change that came over the Preacher's face. His smile died abruptly, his jawbone jutting out, his mouth drawing into a thin hard line. The dark eyes that stared out at him were as cold and empty as the eyes of a water snake.

The Preacher rose in one lithe angry movement and stalked to the microphone. The boy froze, the terrible thought flashing unbidden into his mind that someone must have stolen from the collection plate and the Preacher had seen them do it!

The Preacher raised his arms above his head, fingers spread, reaching towards Heaven. His voice came crashing down on the boy with the full force of his condemnation.

"For all have sinned and come short of the glory of God!"

The echo of his shout rang in the shocked silence of the hall. He stood for a moment, glaring balefully, the cold contemptuous eyes ranging out like gun-sights over the congregation. The boy saw his lips move and he cringed as the shout crashed down from behind him again.

"For all have sinned and come short of the glory of God!"

The Preacher's arms came down. He leaned into the microphone, grasping the corners of the pulpit in his hands. His voice, when it came was crisp and controlled. But the eyes that held the boy glittered, dark and dangerous.

"The Bible tells us, in the fourteenth chapter of the Book of Isaiah, about the first occurrence of sin."

The Preacher held a Bible up before the congregation. He opened it and placed it on the pulpit. His dark eyes flickered back and forth between the spread page and the people, his tone now scathing as he read aloud from the Scriptures.

"How art thou fallen from Heaven oh Lucifer, son of the morning!

For thou hast said in thin heart, I will ascend unto Heaven.

I will exalt my throne above the stars of God.

I will ascend above the heights of the clouds: I will be like the Most High."

The dark eyes softened; the lips curved into a gentle smile, seducing the boy. The voice, when it came again, was quiet and utterly calm.

"My friends: this was the very first occurrence of sin. Lucifer was the favourite of God. His beauty shone, even in Heaven, beyond that of all of the other angels. I believe that God loved him deeply, as He loves all of His creatures. But Lucifer was blinded by his own beauty. His sin was the greatest sin of all—the sin of Pride. He tried to place himself above the Most High. His punishment was just and righteous, as are all of the punishments meted out by Almighty God."

The Preacher swung his clenched fist through the air and brought it slamming down onto the pulpit.

"Yet thou shalt be brought down to Hell!—to the sides of the Pit! This is the punishment which God meted out to Lucifer—despite the fact that God loved him dearly! God cast him down, out of Heaven, to burn in the fires of Hell forever more!"

The Preacher's voice drove in on him, the words clipped and compressed, giving them a piston-like power. Their meaning was lost in the violence of the Preacher's assault. He wanted desperately to look away—to break and run! He fought with his sudden panic, whispering "I'm not scared" to himself, as the Preacher raged out at the congregation.

"But Satan—Lucifer—the Evil One—for they are all the same being—Satan was not cowed! Oh no friends! He swore revenge upon Almighty God. Upon Almighty God! He stole into the heart of God's Creation. With him, he brought sin into the world!"

The Preacher held the Bible up. He opened it and began to read again, certain words swelling above the rest.

"In Genesis, the Bible tells us, 'The Lord God commanded Adam, saying; Of every tree of the Garden thou mayest freely eat: but of the tree of the knowledge of good and evil, *thou shalt not eat of it*; for in the day that thou eatest thereof, *thou shalt surely die!*'"

"But Satan crept into the Garden, disguised as a beautiful serpent. The serpent said to the woman, 'Ye shall not surely die: *ye shall be as Gods!*'"

The Preacher's eyes changed again, became suddenly friendly. The boy sank back from the edge of the seat and closed his eyes when the Preacher smiled. The voice behind his head was quiet and conversational now. He felt Aunt Mary's arm slip across his shoulders.

"Now I know that some of you would say to me, 'But Pastor Billy; they were only children. They didn't mean to hurt God when they took that apple. Besides, it was the Devil that made them do it.'"

"Well friends—that's not the way God sees it. They chose to disobey God, friends. They chose to believe that lying serpent when he told them, 'Ye shall not surely die; ye shall be as Gods!'"

"My friends, their sin was the same sin as Lucifer's sin. It was the sin of Pride. God had to punish them for it, the same way that He had to punish Lucifer."

There was some soft sadness now in the Preacher's voice as he began to read from the Scriptures.

"The Bible says, God cursed the woman, saying, 'I will greatly multiply thy sorrow and thy conception; in sorrow thou shalt bring forth children. God cursed the man saying, 'Cursed is the ground for thy sake; in sorrow thou shalt eat of it all the days of thy life.

In the sweat of thy face shalt thou eat bread, 'till thou return unto the ground; for out of it wast thou taken. Dust thou art, and unto dust thou shalt return."

The Preacher stopped. The boy drifted in the quiet darkness behind his closed eyes. The familiarity of the Scripture had a calming effect on him. He sheltered beneath the safety of Aunt Mary's arm.

The voice slipped in on him again, gentle and insinuating.

"There might be some of you who would say 'But Pastor Billy; that's just a story. Even if it's true, it happened a long long time ago. What does this story have to do with me?'"

"I'll tell you what God says, in the Book of Romans. God says, 'Therefore, by the offence of one, judgement came unto all men to condemnation. For all have sinned and come short of the glory of God'."

The Preacher paused. The boy tensed squeezing his eyes tightly shut, waiting for the shout that did not come.

"These are not my words, my friends. This is the Word of God. 'Therefore, by the offence of one, judgement came unto all men to condemnation'."

There was another long silence. He hung from it, suspended, knowing that the violence was about to come again. But the voice, when it came, was soft and sympathetic.

"There are many kinds of pain in this world. There is the pain that comes to a body that labours long and hard to feed a family. There is the pain that comes in the labours of childbirth. Did you ever ask yourself why, friends?"

The question lingered in the silence. The voice began again.

"There are other kinds of pain that are harder still be bear. There is the pain that comes with injury, or the loss of a badly needed job. There is the heart-rending grief that comes to us with the death of a child, or of a member of a family who we have known and loved dearly. I'm sure that there are many of you here who have known these kinds of pain."

The Preacher was almost whispering now. The boy heard soft moans and sad "Amens" drifting in the pauses. He began to tremble, seeing Poppy's face, trapped in the web of massed emotion that the whisper spun in the air around him.

"Didn't you ever ask yourself why, brothers and sisters? Why God allows these things to happen?"

He shoved his eyes open, sitting up on the edge of his seat, staring up at the Preacher, wanting desperately to understand. The eyes that looked back out at him held no comfort. The voice was crisp and concise now, utterly devoid of any feeling.

"Brothers and sisters—I tell you now, with the authority of God's holy word, that the curses which the Almighty put on Adam and Eve are put equally on every one of us who are gathered here this morning. We are as guilty in the eyes of God of that sin of Pride as we would be if we had been there on that day in the Garden."

The Preacher paused, his features softening. He shook his head, his eyes holding out no hope to the boy staring up at him. His eyes drifted above the faces, as though he was reflecting, far away. The boy closed his eyes, unable to defend himself from the sadness which crept into the Preacher's voice.

"I remember discussing these truths with a man who came to my home one day. He was a good man in many ways. He was a kindly man—a learned man—respected by the members of his community. But he was not a Christian."

"He came to talk to me because his heart was troubled. He was an older man. His wife had just passed away. He said to me, 'Pastor Billy; all these things that you are saying seem to me to be true. The world of men is a harsh and cruel place. But the third curse—dying—does not seem to me to be a curse any longer. It is just the end of all this sorrow and pain.'"

"He passed away shortly after he spoke to me that day. I never saw him again. My heart still grieves for that man, my friends, for he died without coming to know the Lord. I believe that Jesus led him to my door that day. But he spurned God's offer of salvation. He went to his death believing that there was no God."

The voice behind the boy became stern and righteous.

"He was a learned man—a respected man in the community—a kind hearted man. But he was a fool! The fool sayeth in his heart, 'There is no God'. That man's sin was the same as the sin of Lucifer and Adam and every one of us who does not know the Lord Jesus Christ as our own personal Saviour. His sin was the sin of Pride. He put himself ahead of Almighty God! His fate on the Day of Judgement will be the same as the worst sinner, the foulest murderer!"

"Death is not just the death of the body. Oh no, friends! The third curse that God placed on Adam and all his seed is the cruellest curse of all. The suffering of the flesh and the mind are as naught compared to the torments of the soul who goes forth unto Judgement without first being cleansed by the blood of that sweet Lamb, Who suffered on the cross that we might be saved."

"You see friends, it says right at the beginning of the Book of Genesis, 'God created man in His own image.' That doesn't mean He looks like us. God can look like anything He wants—a burning bush or a pillar of fire."

"No friends—it means that we have an immortal soul. Those of us who are true Christians believe this. We who have accepted the Lord Jesus as our personal Saviour and have joined His Chosen Few know that when we leave this sinful wicked world, Jesus will be waiting for us in those mansions in the sky."

"The Bible says, 'In My Father's house are many mansions; if it were not so I would have told you.' But woe unto them who are smitten with Pride and who refuse to atone for their sin! Their fate is the curse of eternally dying, cast down into the Lake of Fire with the Evil One, whose greatest treasure is the scream of the lost soul!"

The boy's mind reeled under the impact, lost in some cloying blackness from which there was no escape. He squeezed his eyes shut, not daring to look up at the Preacher, pressing his Bible against his gut to try to ward off the ache of nerves.

"The Bible tells us, in the Book of John, 'For God so loved the world that He gave His only begotten Son, that whosoever believeth in Him should not perish but have everlasting life'. But the next verse says, 'He that believeth in Him is not condemned; but he that believeth not is condemned already'."

"If we turn our backs on God, His vengeance will be righteous and terrible. 'Vengeance is Mine, sayeth the Lord, I will repay!' These are not my words, my friends. This is the Word of God."

"In the Book of Isaiah, God gave us this warning; 'Hell from beneath is moved to meet thee at thy coming; it stirreth up the dead to meet thee, even all the chief ones of the earth'."

"How great was the torment that we caused to that sweet Lamb, the dearest and gentlest of all, who suffered unspeakable agonies for worthless sinners such as we are! It was men just like you and I who drove those cruel spikes through those innocent hands, my friends! How much greater will be the torment of those of us who spurn Him, for that suffering will last throughout eternity! I want you to think about it friends. Do you know where your soul is going when you leave this sinful wicked world?"

The blackness inside him was almost unendurable. The hush in the air around him was as silent as the grave. He began to pray that the sermon would be over. The voice began again, blocking his prayer, quietly at first and building to a fevered pitch of violent intensity.

"I know that some of you are thinking, 'Pastor Billy, I've been a Christian all my life. I go to church every Sunday. I'm a member of the church. I do my best to live the things that I believe in. I believe that when I die, I'm going to Heaven with the rest of the congregation'."

"My friends—beware of false Christianity! Jesus said, 'No man cometh unto the Father but by me'. There are many professing Christians who will tell you that if you go to church every Sunday and if you try to live right, you're Heaven-bound. But I tell you now, on the authority of the Scriptures, that these people are deceived! That's the Devil talking!"

"The Bible says, in the 64th chapter of Isaiah, 'We are all as an unclean thing, and all our righteousnesses are as filthy rags; our iniquities, like the wind, have taken us away'."

"My friends—unless you have gotten down on your knees and forsaken your pride before Almighty God—your fate is sealed! Unless you have pleaded 'God—have mercy upon me, a wretched sinner unworthy of Thy sight'—you have no hope of salvation! Unless your sin has been cleansed with Jesus' sacred blood—my friends—YOU ARE GOING TO HELL!!"

The crash of the clenched fist on the pulpit was a blow in the pit of his stomach. He doubled forward in pain, his courage shattered, barely aware of the presence of Aunt Mary's hand when she tried to draw him away from it.

The Preacher's voice was gentle now, filled with some strange compassion.

"Jesus doesn't want that to happen. He's here with us today, waiting for anyone who wants Him, to give us the Paradise that Adam spurned so long ago."

"The choir is going to sing now. I want you to close your eyes and search your hearts while I lead you in the altar call. Jesus is waiting to welcome you home and lift away your sin."

The boy huddled in the blackness, powerless to defend himself any longer. The choir began to sing, very slowly and very quietly,

"Just as I am without one plea,
But that thy blood wast shed for me
And that Thou bidst me come to Thee—
Oh Lamb of God, I come; I come."

There was a pause in the song. The Preacher began to whisper into his blackness,

"Just as I am, without one plea, but that Thy blood was shed for me . . . ah friends—what an offer Jesus has made to us, and at what a cost."

The choir slowly sang the second verse.

"Just as I am, and waiting not

To rid my soul of one dark blot;

To Thee whose blood can cleanse each spot—

Oh Lamb of God, I come; I come."

The whisper came again.

"Do you know where your souls are going friends? I want you to keep your eyes closed and search your hearts. If you're not sure I want you to get up from your seats and come down here and stand in front of the platform. Jesus is waiting for you here. No one else will see you."

The choir began the third verse. The voice behind him whispered the words along with them in the faint hiss of the microphone. Somewhere in the rows ahead of him a lady began to weep in jagged gasps. The boy felt the pain inside his head.

"Just as I am, tho tossed about

With many a conflict, many a doubt,

Fightings and fears, within, without—

Oh Lamb of God, I come; I come."

The lady was sobbing in the silence that followed the verse. The Preacher began to whisper to her,

"Yes Sister . . . your heart is troubled . . . Jesus loves the sound of your tears . . ."

Beside him, in his blackness, he heard Uncle Bill whisper to Aunt Mary. He sounded furious.

"Who is that he's tormenting Mary?"

"It's one of those poor ladies from the Home, Bill. He's frightened her half to death."

"That's it Mary. I've seen enough."

He opened his eyes to see Uncle Bill rise to his feet. The flush of outrage was there in the old farmer's face and in the way the vein stood out on his temple. He stood erect, glaring up at Pastor Billy. But the Preacher's eyes were closed. He was whispering intensely into the microphone.

"Come to Jesus Sister . . . he's waiting for you here, up at the front . . ."

Aunt Mary was standing now, on the other side of him. One by one, all of the old people rose to stand in silent protest. If the Preacher noticed them at all he gave no sign. The boy stood up too, not knowing what to do.

Uncle Bill stepped out into the aisle. He moved out behind him, so that Aunt Mary could get out of the pew. Aunt Mary took Uncle Bill's arm. The lady was still crying. The Preacher was still whispering to her.

Then, to Nels Sorenson's utter confusion, Uncle Bill and Aunt Mary turned their backs to the Preacher and walked down the aisle and out of the hall! He stood in the aisle, frozen, watching and listening as the five rows where the old people sat emptied out around him. The old men, including Deacon Brown and Brother James looked stern and angry. The old women looked sad and hurt.

The rest of the congregation sat, oblivious, with bowed heads and closed eyes, mesmerized by the spell of the Preacher's voice and the woman's weeping. He stared up at the front. The lady who was crying was on her feet too, pushing and stumbling over people's legs, trying to get to the end of the row. He looked behind him again. The last of the old people had almost reached the doors. He realized with a shock that he was all alone in the aisle!

He stared up at the balcony, at Mom and Dad, but they had their eyes closed. The Preacher's eyes were open. The Preacher was looking right at him! Then his legs took over, propelling him down the aisle after Uncle Bill and Aunt Mary, wanting desperately to know what had gone wrong.

They had their coats on when he got there. Uncle Bill was about to say something to Aunt Mary when she saw him there. He saw her place a restraining hand on Uncle Bill's arm.

"Where are you going?"

She tried to smile for him.

"We have to go home now dear. You'd better go and sit with your Mom and Dad."

Her voice was gentle but he felt the sadness in her eyes. The old people all seemed to become aware of him at once. He searched their faces, seeing the silent tears that were there in the eyes of some of the old ladies. He looked back at Uncle Bill. The old man held his hand out to him. He shook it one last time.

"Goodbye Nels. God bless you son."

The boy turned away them, unable to watch them leave. He went and stood at the entrance to the hall, unable to go any farther, looking towards the front at Pastor Billy.

The choir was singing the last verse of the hymn. The weeping woman was in the aisle, groping her way painfully along the ends of the wooden pews, half-blinded by her tears.

Pastor Billy's face was a fixed intense mask. His mouth was right up close to the microphone, his body straining forward to stare at the lady in the aisle. His voice was a sibilant whisper, coming out of the speaker box on the wall above the boy's head.

"Come on Sister . . . Jesus is waiting for you, to take your sin away . . . it's just a little further . . . Jesus is here . . ."

The woman reached the end of the front pew just as the choir finished the hymn. She took two staggering steps and collapsed to her knees, her arms outstretched to the Preacher. The only sound in the hall were the soft gasps of her exhausted weeping. The boy's legs were trembling violently. He pressed his Bible to the ache inside his chest, barely able to breathe.

Pastor Billy stretched his arms out towards her. The figures of Christ looked on, hanging with their arms stretched out on the crosses on either side of him. Pastor Billy raised his eyes to Heaven. His face shone with the glow of his triumph over the sin of Pride.

"Thank you Jesus! Thank you Lord!"

The Preacher switched off the microphone with a loud click and hurried down the steps to the lady on her knees. Nels Sorenson stared, stunned as he helped her up and led her to a door to one side of the stage. The sound of her sobbing faded and went out as the door closed behind them.

He turned away and staggered out the church sagging against a pillar, sucking in great lungfuls of clean Canadian wind.

After what seemed an endless time, the doors opened behind him. The people began to come out, looking dazed, hurrying away down the steps. No one spoke. In the shuffle from the lobby through the open door he heard the strains of 'Shall We Gather At The River'. It sounded as though someone else was playing it on the organ. The melody faltered, striking once or twice on a minor chord.

Then Mom and Dad and Ellen were there. Mom had his coat. He could tell by her eyes that she was worried about him.

"There you are Nels. We've been looking all over for you. My goodness—you must be freezing! Here—let me help you put on your coat."

He let her put his coat on him, looking back into her eyes while she did up the buttons.

"Where are Bill and Mary?"

"They had to go home early."

"Are you all right Honey?"

He tried to find a smile for her, not wanting her to be worried about him.

"I'm all right Mom."

"You're shivering all over. Are you sure you're all right?"

"Yeah. I'm just cold."

"Well . . . come on then. Let's go home."

It felt even colder in the back seat of the Vauxhall. He put his arm around his little sister to keep her warm until the heat came on. Ellen looked up at him with big startled brown eyes.

"He scared me Nelsy."

He drew her close to him, not wanting her to be afraid.

"It's okay Elly. He didn't mean to."

"Why are you shaking?"

"I'm just cold. That's all."

Ellen snuggled against him. No one spoke again until they pulled into the driveway. He waited until his father shut the motor off.

"Dad?"

"Yes Nels?"

"Why did Brother James and Deacon Brown and all the old people leave before the service was over?"

He caught the look that passed between Mom and Dad, knowing for sure then that they had not seen the old people go. Dad said,

"I don't know son."

"He said it all wrong, didn't he Dad."

His father stared out through the windshield, avoiding the blue eyes that sought his eyes in the rear-view mirror, wanting to know.

"Didn't he Dad?"

It was his mother who turned to look at him over the back of the seat.

"That's enough Honey. He's a Preacher. You're still a boy. You're not old enough to understand these things."

Her voice was gentle, a reprieve, but he could tell by her eyes and the trouble in his father's expression that they felt the same way he did.

"Okay Mom."

She gave him a funny little smile, turning to look at Dad now.

"Give me the keys John."

Mom took the keys and held them out to him over the back of the seat.

"Why don't you take Ellen and go and open up the house? Taffy's by herself—I'm sure she missed you. Your Dad and I will be in in a minute."

"Sure Mom. Come on Elly. Let's go see Taffy."

He took the keys, knowing that Mom and Dad wanted to have a talk. He took Ellen's hand, looking back at the car as they turned the corner of the house. Mom and Dad were just sitting there, staring at the windshield.

The thought came then, for the very first time, that something had happened that Mom and Dad didn't understand either. He felt his gut tighten up and he pushed the thought away from him, opening the door for his little sister and then bending down to scoop up Taffy, quivering with joy at the sight of him there.

It was quiet in the car for what felt like a very long time.

"I shouldn't have let him go this morning John. I should have told him that he had to sit with us."

John Sorenson heard what was there in her voice, turning to look at her sitting staring at the glass.

"Don't blame yourself Honey. It wasn't your fault. There was no way either of us could have known that was going to happen."

He clenched his hands on the steering wheel.

"I wish the old Preacher had of been there. He would of put a stop to it."

"Do you think they'll come back John?"

"I don't think so. I hope so. But I don't think so. You'd almost think he did some of those things—like covering up the painting— just to get rid of the elders.

"John! That's a terrible thing to say about a Preacher!"

He saw the shock in her green eyes, looking away from her now, looking down at his hands.

"I know. I shouldn't have said it. But all that preaching about pride—he split the congregation Marg! And then what he did to that poor woman—"

"That was a shameful thing John."

"Yes. It was. He's the one who should be on his knees, asking for forgiveness."

It was quiet again until she said,

"How are we going to explain it to Nels if they don't come back?"

He sighed in pent-up frustration.

"I don't know Marg. I've got no education. I didn't understand half of what he said. And he backed everything up with the Bible."

She turned in his defense.

"How could anybody be expected to understand him with all that yelling and banging going on? I don't think I even heard half of what he said. My stomach's still upset. Poor Ellen didn't know what was going on."

He sighed again.

"I wish I could call the old Preacher and talk to him about it. But I wouldn't even know how to explain to him what the sermon was about."

"The old Pastor's gone John. He can't help us with this one. It's Pastor Billy's church now."

He brought his open hand down hard on the top of the steering wheel.

"It's not his church Marg! It's God's church! And it's our church too!"

She reached across and put her hand on his, trying to comfort him.

"Don't let him make you angry John. It isn't going to help."

"No. I know. I'm sorry Honey . . ."

"What are we going to do John?"

"I don't know Marg . . . If everybody just leaves the church because of him, there won't be any church left at all. We made a promise to God when we joined that church. So did everyone else who became a member. They're good Christian people Marg. No matter what he says. And we're Christians too."

"It's more than that. I made a promise to God a long time ago, in the forest, that I would try to bring our children up to come to believe in Him. I can't break those promises to God Marg. I just can't. I won't."

"No John. Neither will I."

He thought for a moment, the image of the old Preacher slipping into his mind.

"You know, Marg—I think the old Pastor might have suspected that something like this was going to happen. I was just thinking about what he said last Sunday. Maybe that's why he asked us to pray for this new man."

"Maybe you're right John. I think we should pray for him. But I'll tell you this—I'll not be put through a performance like he put that poor woman through this morning. And I won't allow him to put our children through it either. I'll leave the church before I'll let that happen."

He saw the Irish in her green eyes. He felt something in his own eyes that matched it—not Irish, just simply Canadian.

"Listen Marg—I got down on my knees to God when my time came. When Nels is old enough to make that decision for himself, I hope and pray that he'll go off some place where he can be alone with God and do the same thing I did."

"But I won't be bullied into getting down on my knees by some pushy young American—whether he's a Preacher or not. And neither will our children."

"Fair enough John. We'd better go in the house now. Nels will be wondering what we're doing out here. I know that he's still a boy, but I sometimes think, just watching him, that there's more things going on in his mind than we can even guess at."

She paused, still holding his hand.

"And we'd better smile when we go inside. The kids have had a tough morning."

"You'd better give me a kiss first then Honey. I need something to smile about."

"Yes John. So do I."

He was on the kitchen floor with Ellen, playing paws with Taffy when Mom and Dad came in. They were both smiling and he began to feel better. Mom's eyes got wide, looking over at the clock.

"My goodness—is it only twenty after twelve? It can't be. I must have forgotten to wind the clock."

He checked his watch.

"No Mom—it's right."

"That was a short service. It seemed a lot longer than that."

"That's because we only got to sing one hymn Mom. And he only said one prayer. Hey Dad—if we had lunch early, we'd have lots of time to go for a walk in the bush."

Dad smiled.

"That sounds like a good idea to me son. Is that okay with you Marg?"

"Certainly—if everybody's hungry. Are you hungry Nels?"

"Well . . . not really. But I guess I could eat."

Mom bent down to give Elly a hug.

"What about you Honey?"

"Can I have a peanut butter sandwich with my dolly?"

"Oh, I guess your dolly could have lunch with us today."

"Goody."

The boy was already on his feet, holding his dog who was squirming around, trying to bite him. He looked over hopefully at Dad.

"Can I take my rifle?"

"No son. Not on Sunday."

"Oh—yeah."

Mom came over and ruffed his hair.

"You and that rifle—I'm surprised you don't take it to bed with you."

He grinned at her.

"I tried once Mom. But Taffy doesn't like it."

"Oh you—get upstairs and take off your suit. And you'd better bring it down with you so I can brush it before the service tonight. You've got dog hair all over you again."

But she was still smiling when she said it. He said,

"Sure Mom" and took off up the stairs. Behind him, he heard Dad call,

"Slow down son."

The strangeness of the morning returned to him, alone with his dog in his room. He sat down on the bed and put his Bible on the bedside table. Taffy was thrashing around in his lap. She sank her sharp little teeth into one of his fingers.

"Ow! Don't do that girl—"

He flipped her over on her back on the bed and rubbed her belly until she lay still, paws in the air, staring up at him with adoring eyes.

"Yeah—you like that, don't you girl? Oh yeah . . ."

His eyes drifted back to his Bible while he petted her. He thought about the old Preacher, remembering the time they had spent together while he learned the Scriptures. He felt sure that the old Preacher could explain Pastor Billy's sermon to him. But the old Preacher hadn't been there.

The thought came, that maybe he could call him on the phone. But he wasn't sure if you could phone to other countries. And he knew that he wouldn't be able to explain to him what the sermon was about.

Mom was right. He was too young. But the strangeness lingered, remembering the voice behind him in the blackness behind his closed eyes.

He shifted his eyes to the rifle, remembering what Walker had taught him. He felt suddenly ashamed that he had gotten scared. He reached over and lifted the rifle, holding it in both hands. The pup made little keening noises, wanting him to pet her some more.

He rested the butt of the stock on his knee, holding the rifle with one hand on the grip, the muzzle pointing up at the ceiling. He reached over with his free hand to pet Taffy again. The weapon felt good in his hand, looking at the pup, head cocked to watch him.

"I'm not scared of Pastor Billy, Taffy. No. I'm a soldier. He's not going to scare me any more."

He was still sitting there when Elly came in to tell him that lunch was almost ready. He realized then that he had forgotten to change out of his suit. When she left the room he changed his clothes and hung up his suit on a hanger.

Mom looked around at him when he came into the kitchen.

"Did you bring your suit downstairs for me Nels?"

"I'm sorry Mom. I forgot. I was thinking. Do you want me to go up and get it now?"

"You can bring it down later. What were you thinking about Honey?"

"Oh . . . nothing Mom . . ."

She was watching him closely. He looked away from her eyes.

"Where's Dad?"

"He's in the living room. Go in and tell him that lunch is ready."

"Sure Mom."

Dad was sitting in his armchair, reading his Bible. He was still wearing his church clothes. His forehead was creased in thought. The boy watched him, not wanting to interrupt him. After a moment Dad looked up and saw him there.

"Oh—hi Nels."

"Lunch is ready Dad. You've still got your suit on."

"Yes. I guess I forgot to change."

His father smiled, but his eyes were serious and thoughtful.

"Yeah Dad. I know what you mean."

Lunch was the same as it always was. It wasn't until he and Dad were alone in the silence of the snowy forest that the feeling came back to him. He looked over at his father, walking beside him.

"Dad?"

"Yes Nels?"

"It didn't feel right in church this morning."

"How do you mean son?"

He frowned, trying to express the feeling which was inside of him.

"I don't know Dad—it was like there was something missing. I mean—it feels more like Sunday out here, in the forest, than it did in the service this morning. Do you know what I mean?"

Dad nodded and put his arm around his shoulders.

"Yes Nels. I think I do."

There was a sudden beating of wings above his head in the treetops. He spun around, looking up, the service forgotten in sudden wonder.

"Look Dad! It's a hawk!"

The Sorenson family left early that evening to drive to the church for the service. When they arrived there were lots of other families who had gotten there early as well. There were no deacons at the doors to shake their hands as they came in. But there was Mr. Hurley.

The adults clustered in little groups in the lobby, talking quietly but with a certain intensity. Mom and Dad were talking with Mr. Matthews and his wife. Nels Sorenson stood politely to one side but he paid no attention to the conversation. He focused on the door through the shifting crowd in the lobby, watching Mr. Hurley who was smiling broadly, shaking hands, and waiting to see if any of the old people would come in.

None of them did. When Tommy and his family arrived, he touched Mom's arm to get her attention.

"What is it Nels?"

"Tommy's here Mom. I'm going to go and talk to him."

"All right. Just be sure you come and sit with us before the service starts."

Mom turned back to the conversation. He slipped away, gliding through the groups of adults clustered in the crowded lobby, looking up at their faces and seeing their intensity. None of them seemed to notice him there. The uneasiness began to build inside him again.

Tommy's parents were talking to the adults beside them at the coat rack. He came up behind them and touched Tommy on the shoulder. When Tommy turned around he saw that Tommy looked nervous too.

"Hi Tommy."

"Hi Nels."

"Let's go to the washroom. I want to have a pee before the service starts."

He waited for his friend to tell his mom where he was going. Then he turned and slipped back through the crowd towards the washroom under the staircase, with Tommy following behind him in Indian file.

There was no one else in the washroom. He gave his friend his Bible to hold while he stood in front of the urinal and relieved himself.

There was only the sound of his splashing against the clean white porcelain until Tommy said,

"I wish the old Pastor was still here."

He looked over at his friend, who was looking at his Bible.

"Yeah. Me too."

He finished peeing and zipped up his fly.

Tommy looked at him in the mirror as he moved to the sink to wash his hands.

"Everybody's acting really weird Nels."

"Yeah. I know. I sat with Uncle Bill and Aunt Mary this morning. All the old people left before the service was over. Uncle Bill got really mad when Pastor Billy made that lady cry. None of the old people came back tonight either."

He moved to the towel rack, to dry his hands. Behind him Tommy said,

"I didn't like the service this morning. He's scary."

"Ah—I'm not scared of Pastor Billy."

He didn't look at Tommy when he said it. He felt the uneasiness rise inside him.

"But I hope he doesn't start yelling again."

"Yeah—me too. Do you know what's going on with all the adults Nels?"

He moved to stand in front of the mirror, to button his suit coat and straighten his tie. He saw the question that was there in his friend's eyes.

"No. I asked my folks. Mom said I wasn't old enough to understand it."

"Yeah. My Mom said that to me too."

He turned to look at Tommy, reaching for his Bible.

"Listen Tommy—I'll tell you what—we'll both listen real good to the sermon tonight. I'll call you when I get home and we'll talk about it. Okay?"

"That's a good idea."

"We'd better get going. The service is going to start soon."

"Yeah."

Mom and Dad were gone when he came out of the washroom. The people left in the lobby were moving towards the hall. The staircase to the balcony was full.

"I'll call you later Tommy."

"Okay Nels. Don't forget."

He turned away, down a corridor, across the empty annex and then up the back stairs. He came up into another corridor which ran behind the balcony. He stopped in the doorway which led down a set of carpeted steps between the rows of tiered wooden pews.

His family were there, in their usual place, in the first row on the right hand side at the front of the hall. Mom was sitting close to the aisle, Dad was on the inside with Ellen in between them.

He stayed for a moment, looking out from his vantage point. In spite of the crowd in the lobby the church was only half full.

His stomach began to tingle. The people were all sitting down. He came gliding down the carpeted steps, suddenly wanting to be with his family.

Mom moved over to make room for him at the end of the wooden bench.

"Where have you been? I was getting worried about you."

She whispered to him. He whispered back,

"I'm okay. I've just been watching."

Then,

"Mom—there's nobody here!"

She started to say something. Somebody behind them said,

"Ssh . . ."

The hall went quiet. He looked down to see Pastor Billy coming out from the back of the stage. Mom took his hand and gave it a squeeze and let him go. He leaned forward to look down at the Preacher.

Pastor Billy went to the pulpit and switched on the microphone. He stood for a moment, holding his Bible, his handsome features curved into a gentle smile. Then he bowed his head and closed his eyes, leaning towards the microphone. The boy closed his eyes and bowed his head with everyone else.

"God—we are gathered here again, Your Chosen Few, to hear the words of Truth which you have prepared for us. We thank You for the soul of our dear sister who was brought to salvation this morning, and to who You have given the gift of Eternal Life. We ask of You that those whom we give offence will find it in their hearts to forgive us; so that they may be themselves forgiven and brought back into the fold. We ask that You will open our hearts and minds to the message which You have given me, so that many souls may be won from Satan in these last days before the Second Coming."

Pastor Billy's voice was gentle and comforting. He drifted in the pause, with Mom in the darkness beside him.

"In Jesus name we ask it. Amen."

He whispered "Amen" under his breath and opened his eyes.

Pastor Billy looked out at them, his smile broadening in welcome.

"Thank you all for coming. We will rise now and lift our voices in song. Hymn number three hundred and four. 'Stand up, stand up for Jesus'."

It was a hymn he knew well. The people rose. The Preacher smiled. He found the number in the hymn book and gave it to his mother. He was looking at the curtain while the organ played the refrain. Then the Preacher raised his hand up and they all began to sing.

"Stand up, stand up for Jesus,
Ye soldiers of the Cross,
Lift high his royal banner
It must not suffer loss . . ."

His eyes drifted out over the congregation, coming to rest on the five empty rows at the back of the hall.

"From victory unto victory
His banner shall he lead,
'Till every foe is vanquished
And Christ is Lord indeed."

He looked away from them, leaning forward to look at his father. The eyes of Jesus stared back at him, just past Dad, hanging there in agony on the wall.

The organ played the refrain again. He could see the drops of blood on Jesus' face from the thorns on His head. The spear wound was a ragged gash above the simple loin cloth. He felt a pain in his stomach. He tore his eyes away from the statue.

His mind went blank when they started the second verse. He stood stiff, not singing, until Mom nudged him and held out the hymn book. He sang the hymn, not listening, just keeping his eyes glued to the page. The eyes of Jesus haunted him, twenty feet away on the wall.

They finished the hymn. The Preacher asked them to sit down. He sat back, as far as he could, sliding down in his seat real close to Mom until Jesus couldn't look at him. Mom gave him a not-too-gentle nudge in the ribs.

"Sit up Nels. You're in church."

She whispered it out of the corner of her mouth. In the silence that followed when everyone was seated it sounded as loud as a shout.

He sat up straight, both of them looking back down at the Preacher. Pastor Billy was looking right at him!

"Thank you Sister."

Mom's face turned brick red. Every face in the balcony turned to stare at him. He stared out into open air, feeling the burn on his cheeks, knowing with the hollow ache in the pit of his stomach that he was going to get it when he got home.

"Ah—isn't it good to know the Lord!"

The faces all turned to look back to the Preacher. He pressed himself back as far as he could but he could still see him. He shut his eyes, miserable inside, wondering why Pastor Billy had to get him in trouble.

The voice pursued him behind his closed eyes.

"There will be no announcements this evening, except to inform those of you who came for the prayer meeting before the service tonight that it will be held on Tuesday nights from now on, at 7 o'clock, at my home. I will be leading the Young People's meeting, upstairs above the annexe, from 6:15 until 6:45 on Sunday evenings. I invite any of you who have teenaged children to ensure that they attend."

"There will be a special offering tonight, to help with the new improvements to the church. I know that you all gave generously this morning. If you have an extra dollar which you can give to the Lord's ministry, God loves you for it."

There was a pause. The thought came, unbidden, that the only times that they ever had a collection during the evening service was when they had a missionary who came to speak to them. The old Preacher always told them in the morning announcements, so that they could bring some money. All his money was at home.

Pastor Billy's voice sounded different when he spoke again.

"Some of our members are not here tonight. I would like to ask that four of you volunteer to do the Lord's work in taking up the collection."

The hall got very quiet. He felt Mom stiffen beside him. He kept his eyes closed, not wanting to even look down at the Preacher. The silence rang in the blackness behind his closed eyes. It lasted a long time.

"Thank you Jesus."

The voice murmured it softly into the microphone. He felt Mom relax a little bit. The tension lingered in nervous coughs. Pastor Billy waited until it was quiet again.

"Come forward, brothers. Your service will be rewarded. The choir is going to sing a hymn while the offering is being taken. I ask that you all give generously to the work of the Lord."

The organ played a run of quiet chords. To his surprise, it was one of his favourite hymns. The choir sang it sometimes during the worship service. He relaxed a bit and began to listen, wondering who had volunteered to take up the collection.

The choir sang the first verse in full harmony.

"Oh Lord my God; when I in awesome wonder

Consider all the worlds Thy hands have made

I see the stars; I hear the rolling thunder,

Thy works throughout the universe displayed—

Then sings my soul, my Saviour God to Thee,

How great Thou art, how great Thou art;

Then signs my soul my Saviour God to Thee,

How great Thou art, how Great Thou Art!"

They sang it softly and with reverence. He could almost see the painting of the Forest in his mind when Mom nudged him again. He sat bolt upright, eyes open, looking at her. She gestured towards the aisle behind him with her Irish eyes.

Mr. Hurley was standing there staring at him, holding the collection plate! He almost dropped it when it was passed to him. He handed it hastily to Mom and then stared straight out into open space, trapped between Mr. Hurley in the aisle beside him and Jesus, who was staring at him again. He didn't hear a word for the rest of the song.

When the hymn was over the Preacher sat, head bowed, a moment longer. Beside him, Mom whispered,

"Sit up straight and pay attention!" in a voice just loud enough for him to hear.

Pastor Billy rose and walked to the pulpit. Nels Sorenson stared down at him, not daring to look at anything else and wondering how much trouble he was in. The Preacher stood in silence for a moment, studying the congregation. The boy thought that at least he didn't look mad this time. He offered up a silent prayer that the Preacher wouldn't start yelling.

Pastor Billy leaned in to the microphone.

"Twenty years ago on this day the world was in grave peril. The German war machine was smashing its way across Europe. The Japanese were putting Asia to the sword. The spectre of fascism rose unchecked above the land."

The Preacher paused, looking out at the congregation. The boy leaned full forward, resting his hands on the railing, interested now in spite of himself. Pastor Billy was talking about the war! No one had ever explained about the war to him. Not even Poppy. The Preacher's features were quiet and composed. He waited for him to speak again.

"I know that there are many of you here tonight whose families still bear the scars of that great conflagration. I know that the pain of your losses is still there with you, even as I speak to you now."

"I know too that many of you would say to me, 'Pastor Billy—the war has been over for fifteen years. It's history. Why are you bringing this evil back now? And especially here, in the house of God?'"

The Preacher paused again. The boy darted a furtive glance at Tommy. Tommy was looking back up at him. He nodded his head at him—just enough—looking back at the preacher before he began to speak again.

"My friends—it is about history that I have been called to speak to you tonight. Not merely history as men see it, which is as through a glass darkly. I wish to speak of history as it is revealed in the Word of God."

"The Bible is the history of the Chosen People. In the first half of my message to you this morning, we examined the origin of that history in the story of Creation. The essence of those truths which God reveals to us in Genesis is best summed up in the first chapter of the Book of John."

Pastor Billy held the Bible up and then laid it on the pulpit. The boy frowned, lost now. The adults below him all looked confused too. The voice rang out, suddenly loud.

"In the beginning was the word, and the word was with God, and the word was God.

All things were made by Him, and without Him was not anything made that was made."

Pastor Billy smiled.

"We as Christians hold this to be true. We believe that Creation occurred exactly the way it is told in the Book of Genesis. We believe that the Bible is the authentic record of the history of the Chosen People."

Nels Sorenson knew this but he wondered what it had to do with the war. Then the Preacher's face changed. He saw the cold hard glitter in Pastor Billy's eyes.

"What men in their folly call history is no more than the chronicle of all the sin and wickedness that there is in this world." The eyes ranged out over the congregation, the voice becoming contemptuous now.

"There are some false prophets, like the followers of Darwin, who would have us believe that Creation itself is only a story—that it never really happened. My friends—beware of false prophets! They are deceived!"

He felt the tightening in his gut at the shout, darting a glance around at his family for support. Dad's jaw was clenched tight. Mom had her arm around Ellen. He looked back down at Pastor Billy as the voice began again.

"There are others, like Marx, who have taken that chronicle of sin and wickedness and twisted it around their own lies. Then they say to us, Look! The world is getting better! Men are becoming wiser through the lessons of history! We have no further need for God!"

Pastor Billy leaned in close into the microphone.

"I want you to take a look around you my friends, at the world we live in today. You don't have to look very hard to see what happens to people who put their trust in false prophets like Karl Marx."

The boy was thoroughly lost. He darted another glance at Tommy, wondering if his friend knew who Karl Marx was. The shout brought his eyes back to the Preacher and riveted them there.

"Beware my friends! That's not Karl Marx—that's the voice of Satan! The fool sayeth in his heart, There is no God!"

"If we wish to understand God's plan for us, we must look for it by coming to view the events of the world through the interpretation of the Scriptures. The Bible is more than just a history my friends. It is also a book of prophecy; of divine truths as they have been revealed to the faithful."

"It was no accident that I began the study of our history this morning with the fall of Lucifer, as it was revealed by God to the prophet Isaiah. The hand of God was there, guiding me in my message to you."

"We as Christians believe that the events of the Fall as they are told in Isaiah are real. They happened long before the time of Creation, while our first ancestor Adam was just a thought in the mind of our Creator."

The Preacher paused.

"The fundamental fact of human nature is revealed to us in the chronicle of Lucifer's fall from grace. It was the sin of Pride which brought him down. Lucifer's fall reveals to us the nature of our own fall in the Garden. We are all in sin."

"The history of the human race, as men know it, is no more than the illustration of our complicity in the vow of revenge which Satan swore against God on the day that he was cast down."

He paused again, staring out at them.

"I ask you to consider this; how else can we, as men, comprehend the magnitude of the atrocities wreaked upon the world by a man like Adolph Hitler—the death camps and the charnel houses—unless we recognize the hand of Satan behind him? The stench of death and the smoke of burnt bodies rose up in Hitler's obscene sacrifice to the power of the Evil One."

There were groans of protest in the rows behind him. He felt the hairs prickle on the back of his neck. The Preacher went quietly on.

"In the Book of Matthew, the nature of Satan's power over men is revealed to us in the eighth and ninth verses of the fourth chapter. It is a passage that I know you are all familiar with; the last temptation of our Lord."

Pastor Billy opened the Bible again. The boy listened, desperate to understand.

"The Devil taketh Jesus up into an exceedingly high mountain, and sheweth Him all of the kingdoms of the world, and the glory of them,

And the Devil sayeth unto Him, 'All these things will I give unto Thee, if Thou wilt fall down and worship me'." He closed the Bible and looked up at the balcony.

"My friends, here we see the Tempter at work. He made the same offer to Adolph Hitler. Hitler did not refuse him. Hitler was a slave of the Devil."

The boy stared back at him, horror-struck; seeing it clearly now. No wonder no one ever talked about the war!

"But Jesus was no ordinary man. Jesus was the Son of God. He refused the temptation that Satan offered Him. The Jewish people, who had been the Chosen People, spurned Jesus as the Messiah because He refused Satan's offer to establish their kingdom on earth. Satan hardened their hearts against God in their foolish pride. God turned His face away from them. Great has been their suffering at the hands of Satan ever since."

"My friends—God loves us. His love for us was so great that He sent His only begotten Son to hold out the offer of forgiveness from sin to Jew and Gentile alike. He sent His own Son, so that you and I could escape damnation and join the Chosen People. My friends—we still celebrate the day of our Saviour's birth as the brightest moment in the history of the human race."

"And yet, we killed Him. Our Lord became the blood sacrifice so that we might not have to suffer. Even in cruel death, Jesus pleaded to God for forgiveness for those who nailed Him to that cross."

"The choice is ours friends, just as it was with Pilate. Unless we ask Jesus to intercede on our behalf, we stand already condemned in the eyes of God. 'No man cometh unto the Father but by me.' If we wash our hands of Jesus, as Pilate did, God will wash his hands of us."

"In the weeks to come, in the morning service, we will examine the nature of sin and its redemption. Already, in this morning's service, one soul was saved. I pray that, through this humble ministry, many more souls will come to know God's forgiveness."

Pastor Billy bowed his head and closed his eyes. The boy did too, his mind still shocked, waiting for the closing prayer.

It wasn't the prayer. There was something else in the voice in the blackness, something that made him shiver.

"God will not always be so forgiving, my friends."

Mom poked him with her finger. He opened his eyes. The Preacher stared out beyond the congregation at things yet to come.

"The history of the Chosen People is contained in it's entirety between the beginning of the Book of Genesis and the end of the Book of Revelation."

"This world will come to an end some day. Some day soon. The wickedness of men will be extinguished. Satan will be cast down in that final conflict, chained in Hell for all eternity along with the souls of all those who spurned salvation."

"God will establish a Heavenly kingdom and gather unto Himself the souls of His Chosen Few. We as Christians hold this to be true."

Pastor Billy lifted the Bible from the pulpit and held it up for them to see. His voice rang out in the silence of the hall.

"I am Alpha and Omega, the Beginning and the Ending, which is, and which was, and which is to come; the Almighty!"

He paused again, laying the Bible down. Then he leaned in close to the microphone.

"These are the words of God, as He spoke them in the vision to His prophet John, nineteen centuries ago on the Isle of Patmos. He speaks to us just as clearly, through the prophecy of Revelation, here—tonight—in Canada, in the year nineteen hundred and sixty. He speaks to us about the end of History."

The boy stared down at the Preacher, unable to understand how History could end.

"My friends—God loves us. The prophecies of Revelation are His warning to us that the Day of Judgement is approaching. The final battle with the Evil One is at hand. God gave us the signs so that we, as Christians, will be able to prepare ourselves with clean robes before Christ's second coming."

"He that hath eyes, let him see; he that hath ears, let him hear!"

"These are not my words, my friends. These are the words of God. God has revealed His final plan for us. He has said, 'I am Alpha and Omega, the Beginning and the Ending'."

"This is the message He has given to me, and to all the true believers. This same message is going out tonight from countless pulpits across America. God has sent me here, to bring this message to you. The signs are there my friends. We as Christians have only to look at the events of the world that we live in to see them. In the time which remains, and in the Sunday evening services to come, we will examine their meaning as it is explained in the prophecy of Revelation."

"I began my message to you tonight by speaking of the Second World War. The signs were there then too my friends. Hitler had sworn a pact with Satan. Hitler wanted to rule the world. But men have always preferred the darkness of their own ignorance to the light of God's truth. The leaders of men chose not to see the hand of Satan in Nazi Germany. At Munich, they tried to appease Hitler. When Satan saw how easily they were deceived he loosed the evil of fascism in Europe. The forces of democracy were overwhelmed."

"In America there were many who were also deceived as to the true nature of this conflict. While the war raged on in Europe, Satan's deception kept America out of the fighting. Our Christian President, Franklin Delanore Roosevelt struggled for three years to make the American people aware of the danger. To America's shame, it wasn't until Satan and the Japanese attacked Pearl Harbour that the American people woke up from Satan's spell."

"But President Roosevelt was rewarded for his faithfulness. God chose America to liberate the world from the evil grip of fascism. God gave America a great victory. Hitler and his fiends were cast down."

"God gave America a prosperity unknown before that time as a reward. He gave America a mighty weapon, the atomic bomb, to safeguard the free world against any more of the abominations which Hitler had wreaked on the world. God entrusted America with the fire of His righteous fury."

"But Satan was not defeated. He caused the leaders of Soviet Russia to become jealous of America's prosperity and power. Satan held out the same temptation to Joseph Stalin that he had to Adolph Hitler. He caused Stalin to covet the earth. He caused him the curse God!"

Pastor Billy stopped, glaring balefully at the congregation. The boy sat, frozen, fingers locked on the railing, unable to take his eyes off him. The voice drove in on him again.

"When President Truman offered the hand of friendship to the Russian people, Stalin spurned it. Instead he brought down the Iron Curtain and took one third of the world hostage to godless Communism. The war which we call the Cold War had begun."

"Even then there were those who refused to see the hand of Satan controlling Stalin, just as the puppet master controls his puppet. There were those who wanted to make a Munich-style arrangement with the Communists. Just as Satan had blinded men to his pact with Hitler, he blinded men to the nature of Stalin's ambition."

"In America, men were blinded to the truth by their fascination with their new found prosperity. Just as it was with Aaron, as soon as the danger of oppression seemed past, men forgot God and made of their prosperity a golden calf. The evil of godless Communism crept into the heart of America itself. Satan sent his slaves to do his bidding. They stole the secret of God's righteous fire, the atomic bomb, and gave it to the Prince of Darkness!"

The fist came crashing down on the pulpit. The boy's heart was hammering in his chest.

"God's wrath was just and thorough, my friends. The souls of Satan's slaves, the Rosenbergs, were sent screaming to join their master. As with Moses when he came down from the mountain, God sent one good man to root out the corruption that Satan had sown in the highest offices of the land. America purged itself of Communism, as no other nation has been able to do, with the help of Almighty God."

"But it was too little and too late my friends. Without the help of God men everywhere have proven themselves unable to halt the advance of Satan. In the West the leaders of countries even such as this one show no sign of recognizing the evil that lies behind the Communist doctrines. Governments allow these false prophets to preach the words of Marx and his followers openly, both in the streets and in the universities."

"In the countries where Satan's evil empire reigns, millions have already been martyred for their faith. Whole families are tortured and killed, just for being found with a Bible in their homes. And all the while, Satan and his slaves are busy arming themselves with atomic weapons for the final onslaught on God-fearing America itself."

"The leaders of our nations steadfastly refuse to recognize the true nature of the Cold War. They seek to persuade us that we must learn to live in armed co-existence; that the arsenals of atomic weapons which are aimed at the God-fearing West will never be used against us; that war has been banished from the face of the earth by the fact that there can be no victory, only our mutually assured destruction."

"My friends—they are deceived. The signs are there. Him that hath eyes, let him see. War with Satan's evil empire is inevitable. The final battle between God and Satan which is prophesied in the Book of Revelation is at hand—the Battle of Armageddon!"

The silence in the hall which followed his shout was louder than any sound. The Preacher pressed his hands together, as if to contain the fervour he felt. His voice, when it came, was quiet again but tinged with a desperate earnestness.

"My friends—in the evening services in the weeks to come we will study the signs as they are revealed to us. I urge you all to watch the News and to study the events of the world so that you will understand them. This is your duty, as Christians. God calls to us, to heed His warnings, so that we may lead as many souls away from Satan as can be won to salvation before the fires of Armageddon come to consume the earth and all its wickedness."

"If any of you are in sin, I urge you now to come forward and seek redemption while there is still time. None of us knows when the thread of life will be cut off. Don't turn Jesus away my friends. If you say to him tonight, 'Lord—I'm not ready,' it could be too late. Your life could end tonight and you would be beyond forgiveness. Think about it friends, before you leave here tonight. Do you know where your soul is going?"

"I want you to close your eyes and bow your heads and search your hearts for the truth of what I have said. After a moment the choir is going to sing while I lead you in the altar call. If there are any of you here who would say with me 'Yes Pastor Billy. I know I am in sin', I want you to come down to the front. Jesus will be waiting for you here, to give you the gift of Eternal Life. Don't turn away from Him now."

The Preacher stepped back from the microphone. The congregation sat, silent, heads bowed and eyes pressed closed. The boy sat stunned, staring down at Pastor Billy from the balcony, struggling with the knowledge that the world was going to end.

Pastor Billy's eyes ranged out over the people, searching for some evidence of sin in the congregation. The handsome face turned up to the balcony, the dark eyes looking straight into the blue eyes of Nels Sorenson.

Pastor Billy smiled at him. He sank back against the seat and closed his eyes. The choir began to sing.

"Just as I am, without one plea,
But that Thy blood wast shed for me . . ."

And then a strange thing happened. He was stricken with the unbearable urge to pee. The sudden pressure inside of him was excruciating. He tried to fight down his panicked certainty that if he didn't go to the washroom right away he was going to wet his pants right there in church!

"Do you know where your soul is going friends? Jesus is waiting for you, down here at the front . . ."

The whisper slipped into the panic behind his closed eyes. He crossed his legs tight, squirming around on the hard wooden bench in an agony of fear that he was going to shame himself.

"Just as I am, and waiting not . . ."

Beside him Mom whispered sharply

"Sit still!"

He popped his eyes open, whispering back

"I've got to go to the bathroom Mom!"

"I said sit still! It's almost over!"

Mom wouldn't look at him. She kept her head bowed and her eyes closed, whispering to him out of the corner of her mouth. He pressed himself back hard against the seat and squeezed his eyes shut, fighting the sudden betrayal of his body with every ounce of his will.

"That's it Brother . . . no one's watching you. Jesus is waiting for you. Come on up to the front . . ."

He began to pray for help. Then the Preacher's shout of joy rang out.

"Thank you Jesus! Thank you Lord!"

He strained forward against the railing, staring down to see if the service was over and who had got saved this time.

It was Mr. Hurley, kneeling at the front. The thought flashed through his mind that Mr. Hurley didn't look like he was scared of the Devil and the Communists. Mr. Hurley was smiling!

He was up and gone in the click of the microphone, racing his panic past the bowed heads on either side of the carpeted stairway. He took the back stairs three at a time, sprinting flat out across the annex, bursting into the corridor and across the lobby, certain now that he would never make it. He hit the washroom door with his shoulder, his zipper already down, sagging with his free hand against the wall above the urinal at the very last second.

And then something even stranger happened. In spite of the aching pressure of his bladder, he couldn't pee a drop! He stood there, straining, in total confusion until he heard the music of the organ begin. But it wasn't 'Shall We Gather At The River'. It was 'Onward Christian Soldiers'.

The urge to pee began to fade. Into its place came the scary thought that Mom was going to be really mad at him now.

He zipped himself up and took a deep breath. Then he left the washroom, stepping back out into the lobby. His family were already there, waiting by the coat rack. He avoided his parents' eyes while he put his coat on. Mom handed him his Bible. No one spoke. The Sorensons were almost the first ones to leave the church that night.

It wasn't until they were all in the Vauxhall that Mom looked at him over the back of the seat.

"From now on you make sure you go to the bathroom before the service starts."

He started to say that he had and then thought better of it.

"Yes Mom."

He looked down at the floor, feeling Elly's eyes on him. Mom turned to look at Dad as the car pulled away from the curb.

"Stop at Sally's for a minute on the way home John."

"Okay Marg."

He poked his head up again.

"Are we going to see Auntie Sal?"

"No. I'm just going in to talk to her for a minute. You children can wait in the car with your father."

"Aw . . ."

"That's enough Nels."

He pushed himself back against the seat and turned to stare out the window. The urge to pee was completely gone. But the feeling of it had been so real . . . he wondered what had happened. Then he tried to forget it, glad for the fact that Mom wasn't mad at him after all.

They parked in front of Aunt Sally's house. Dad left the engine running while Mom went inside. Walker's old black Ford was still there in the driveway.

The images of Pastor Billy and Poppy grew in his mind while he sat in the warm car, waiting. He began to remember what the Preacher had said. He leaned forward, his hands on the back of the seat, his voice not much more than a whisper beside his father's ear, not wanting to scare his little sister.

"Dad?"

Dad was staring silently at the windshield. He turned towards him just a bit.

"Yes Nels?"

"Is there going to be a war?"

"I hope not son. I hope not."

There was something in his father's voice that he had only heard once before, on the day that they had found the forest wrecked. He sat back and closed his eyes, feeling the cold fingers crawling around in his stomach. Ellen sensed it in him.

"What's wrong Nelsy?"

He opened his eyes and put his arm around her.

"Nothing Elly."

Mom was inside for what seemed like a long time. At last the front door opened. Mom came out. Aunt Sally waved to them from the yellow rectangle of light in the doorway. He rolled the window down fast and called out,

"Hi Auntie Sal." hoping she was okay.

By the time they got home it was nine o'clock. He took off his shoes and bent down to pet Taffy for a minute. Then he headed straight for the phone. He hadn't even dialled Tommy's number before Mom was there beside him.

"What are you doing Nels?"

"I told Tommy I'd call him when we got home so we could talk about the sermon."

"Well it's too late tonight to call Tommy."

"But Mom! I promised!"

"Tommy will be getting ready for bed. And so will you, as soon as you put your shoes on and take Taffy outside so she can go to the bathroom."

She took the phone out of his hand and put it back on its cradle.

"But Mom—"

"Don't 'But Mom' me, young man. Tomorrow's your first day back to school. I want you in bed early tonight. We've had more than enough sermons for one day. Now go on and take Taffy outside."

"Oh—sure Mom."

"That's a good boy."

She ruffed his hair and turned to his sister.

"As soon as you've been to the bathroom Ellen I'll take you upstairs and tuck you into bed."

He went back to the door and put his shoes on and took his dog outside. When he came back in Mom and Ellen were already upstairs. Dad was back in his armchair, still in his suit, reading his Bible.

He called a soft,

"Goodnight Dad" from the doorway. Dad looked up and said,

"Yes. Goodnight son" like he wasn't really there and went back to his reading.

He stood in the doorway and watched him for a minute. Dad's forehead was wrinkled with concentration. It came to him then, that maybe Pastor Billy was wrong. But that didn't make sense. Pastor Billy was a Preacher.

He decided to just forget about church.

"C'mon girl. Let's go to bed."

He bent down and scooped Taffy up and headed up the stairs. Ellen and her dolly were already in bed. Mom was sitting on the edge of the bed, reading them a story. He slipped in just long enough to kiss his sister goodnight.

He was in bed when Mom came to tuck him in. Taffy was playing on top of the bed, growling and pouncing whenever he moved his fingers and trying to bite him through the blankets.

"Did you say your prayers Nels?"

"Yes Mom. Is it okay if I read for a while?"

"You can read until ten o'clock."

He looked at his watch.

"But Mom—that's only half an hour!"

"I want to see your light off at ten o'clock. You're not on holidays any more. Ten o'clock. Okay?"

"Oh okay . . ."

She bent down and gave him a kiss on the cheek. When she was gone he got out of bed and got one of his library books. He propped himself up on the pillows and tucked Taffy in so she was comfortable and rubbed her belly until she went to sleep. Then he opened the book and began to read.

His eyes kept drifting away from the page. He tried to concentrate on the words but it didn't do any good. His mind went racing along, taking him with it through all the strange things he had learned in church.

Hitler was the Devil's slave until the Americans got rid of him. The Devil's new slaves were the Communists and they had stolen a bomb from God. There was going to be a war. The world was going to end.

It was too strange. His mind raced, trying to find a way out. Nobody had ever said anything about it before. Poppy and the old Preacher must have known about it, if it was true. The thought came again, that Pastor Billy must have made a mistake.

It was hard to imagine Pastor Billy making a mistake. Even the old Preacher didn't quote Scripture like Pastor Billy did.

He sat there, staring into space, wishing he was old enough so that he could understand it. Then he remembered that Pastor Billy had told them to watch the News, so that they would know what he was talking about.

Dad sometimes watched the News at ten o'clock. He checked his watch. It was almost ten. He hesitated, knowing he was supposed to be in bed. But—

He slipped out of bed and went gliding across his room and out into the hall. The house was in blackness. Mom and Dad were still awake. He could hear their voices through their bedroom door but he couldn't make out the words.

He went back and turned off his light, hoping Mom wouldn't come out to check at all. He took a deep breath, his need to know more urgent than his fear of getting caught when he was supposed to be in bed.

He stole ahead into the blackness and crept silently down the stairs.

There was still a bar of light beneath his parent's bedroom door. He stopped, listening, ready to sprint back up the stairs if the door opened.

He heard Mom say something about Pastor Billy but he couldn't make out the words. She sounded upset.

It was dangerous to stay there and anyways it was wrong to eavesdrop. He stole forward into the living room. The television was at the far end of the room, in the middle of the wall. He felt his way along the front of the couch with his fingers so that he wouldn't bang his knees on the coffee table. When he got to the end of the couch he felt his way forward until his hands found the set. His fingers played over the front of it until they found the right button. He made sure that the sound was right down. Then he turned it on.

The TV set hummed softly to itself. There was a faint golden glow on the wall behind it. After a moment, the screen began to lighten. He crouched down, leaning forward, impatient to see what was there.

An image formed, crystal clear, of a shiny silver airplane flying in a cloudless sky. The sun gleamed on the fuselage and sparkled along its swept back wings. It was the most wonderful airplane that he had ever seen! He knelt down on the carpet, reaching for the button and turned the sound on just loud enough to hear.

A happy voice told him that the friendly bombers of the Strategic Air Command were in the skies twenty-four hours a day with their cargoes of atomic weapons ready to streak towards their targets inside Russia and deliver a devastating counter attack in the event of a Soviet first strike.

The screen went blank. The voice went away. The words, "THIS IS A TEST" appeared in block letters before he had a chance to think about it.

The screen cleared again. A new image formed, the image of a flat empty landscape stretching away to the horizon. There was nothing in it that he could see. He stared at it, puzzled, wondering what kind of a test it was. He leaned right in close, his nose almost touched the glass, trying to see if there was something he had missed.

The fireball formed in a blinding white incandescence of light that filled the screen as the firestorm swept out, consuming every atom of oxygen in its path. The edges of the screen cleared into a whorl of sparkling white dots that were sucked back into the vacuum that the firestorm had created. The crack! of thunder that rocked him back was the wrath of God.

Nels Sorenson stared in mindless awe at the pillar of fire raging up towards Heaven. Around it, near the summit like a sign, he saw the dazzling radiance of the halo cloud.

"What was that?"

Marg was out of the bed beside him before the words had left his mouth. He was right behind her at the bedroom door. The ominous rumble of the after shock reverberated in the hall. Then she froze in the living room doorway in front of him, one hand rising to her breast.

"Oh my God—"

He stepped around her and froze too, assaulted by some soul-numbing fear at what he saw there.

The living room flickered with a weird unholy light. Nels was kneeling in front of the television as if to some eldritch idol, silhouetted in the glare of the atomic bomb blast. John stared past his son, aware of his wife beside him, neither of them able to move as the flaming obscenity on the screen faded into the poisonous grey menace of the mushroom cloud. He closed his eyes and tried to think of a prayer.

Marg came out of it first. He felt the urgency of her touch on his arm.

"John—turn the lights on!"

He opened his eyes, reaching around for the light switch. The room lit up in its normal form. Marg was already reaching past Nels to shut the television off. The horror on the screen dwindled to a dot of light and went out.

"Nels . . ."

He crossed the room to stand beside her, nerves jangling at every step. Nels didn't move. He just stared blank-eyed at the empty screen.

Marg flashed him a look that was full of fear, moving to put herself between the set and her son. She knelt in her nightgown in front of him.

"Nels . . ."

She took his hands. The boy stared at her with strange eyes, aware of her for the first time.

"Oh . . . hi Mom . . ."

His voice was distant, far away.

"Are you all right Nels?"

He thought about it for a minute.

"I can't see very good. It was too bright. Everything's all shiny . . ."

"Close your eyes Honey. Let them rest for a while."

He closed his eyes. After a moment he said

"I can still see it Mom . . ."

"It'll go away. You'll be all right."

She flashed John a frightened glance. He stared back helplessly, bending down close to his son. The look in her green eyes mirrored what was inside of him. He tried to keep it out of his voice.

"Is that helping Nels?"

"I guess so Dad . . ."

Nels Sorenson was far away, in the desert, alone with the pillar of fire.

"What were you doing up Honey?"

Her voice in his desert was gentle, drawing him back. He opened his eyes and found himself in the living room. Mom was holding his hands. She looked scared. He wondered about it absently, blinking at the aura around her. He remembered why he was downstairs.

"Pastor Billy said we were supposed to watch the News."

Mom tried to smile. Her eyes were big and strange.

"I don't think he meant boys like you Honey."

"Are you mad at me?"

"No Honey. I'm not mad at you."

"Oh . . . that's good."

He felt his Dad's hand on his shoulder. His mind began to drift again, back into the desert.

"Dad?"

He turned his head, looking up at his father, still blinking at the glow on everything that didn't seem to want to go away.

"Yes son?"

"Was that the Bomb?"

"Yes son. That was the Bomb."

"Was it the Communists?"

John Sorenson clenched his jaw, avoiding his wife's eyes, wondering at how fast this boy was and how to make the world safe for him. The strange blue eyes blinked back up at him, wanting to know. He willed himself to smile.

"No son. It wasn't the Communists. It was the Americans. They were just letting us know that they've got the Bomb too, so that we don't have to worry."

"Oh . . . okay."

He looked at Mom again.

"Can I go back to bed now?"

"Sure you can Honey."

Mom stood up and helped him up to his feet.

"Would you like us to come upstairs with you?"

"No . . . it's all right."

Mom was still staring at him, holding tight to his hands.

"Are you sure Honey?"

He wondered absently why she looked scared.

"It's okay Mom. I'm okay. It's just too bright that's all."

She let go of his hands reluctantly.

"Well . . . goodnight Mom. Goodnight Dad."

"Yes . . . goodnight son."

He turned away and drifted across the shiny room to the quiet darkness of the staircase. The blackness at the top of the stairs sparkled with tiny flashes of coloured light. Somewhere in the distance behind him he heard his mother start to cry.

He got into bed, careful not to wake up Taffy. The coloured lights flickered like fireflies in the air. He sank back into the pillow, floating on a cushion of shock, devoid of any feeling. When he closed his eyes, the pillar of fire shone on brightly in his head.

Everything Pastor Billy said was true. He had seen it on the News, just like Pastor Billy said he would. The hollow shock inside his mind echoed with the knowing that the world was going to end.

High above the houses, a jet aircraft passed across the sky. The thunder of its wake reached out and touched him. It took him a long long time to go to sleep.

1962: JOHN F. KENNEDY AND THE CUBAN MISSILE CRISIS

*O*n the twenty-first day of the month of June, Nels Sorenson graduated from the yellow brick school on the banks of the polluted creek. The ceremony was held in the school auditorium. The families of all of the young graduates were there. The principal Mr. Edwards called out their names in alphabetical order. When his name was called, Nels Sorenson climbed the steps and walked numbly across the stage to the podium.

Mr. Edwards shook his hand and presented him with his diploma. He carried away to stand with his classmates, barely aware of their smiling faces around him. For the rest of the ceremony he stood staring out at the adults in the audience, overwhelmed by the awareness of what was happening to him.

The long awaited promotion possessed a significance for Nels Sorenson which no one in the auditorium could have guessed. Dad had told him, once, about how he had left the farm and the drought-ridden prairie of the Great Depression when he had finished the eighth grade, travelling alone in the box car of an east bound freight train to a logging camp in the forests of Ontario. Dad had become a man when he was fourteen years old!

It was this thought which filled his mind as he stood on the stage of the school auditorium. The rolled-up diploma in his hand was a tangible portent of the future. September meant high school and his fourteenth birthday. The thing which Nels Sorenson craved more than anything else was admittance into the mysteries of the adult world. There were so many things that he wanted to understand.

The last summer of his childhood raced by him with the urgency of his desire. It was there from the moment he opened his eyes in each new morning until his last thought chased itself past him on the pillow at night. Even on the days that he tried to outrun it, it echoed in everything he saw and in everything he did.

Margaret Sorenson saw the change which came over him although she did not understand it. At supper he was distant and pre-occupied. In the hot summer evenings which rang with shouts and laughter from the playing field, she would find him sitting on the backyard lawn with Taffy beside him, staring absently off into space. The concern which the change in him brought about in her led her to question her sisters whose sons were grown. They all agreed that there was no real need to worry; sons who were entering their adolescence were difficult beings to understand.

Often that summer she joined him on the lawn, trying to bridge the gap which she felt between them.

"A penny for your thoughts Nels . . ."

Always he would smile for her.

"It's nothing Mom. I'm just thinking."

He wanted sometimes to explain it to Mom.

But he could never figure out where to begin. The silence came down between them again, until Mom said,

"You think too much Honey. Why don't you go to the playing field with the other boys for a while?"

He didn't go to the playing field. The games and the conversation of his peers bored him into a nervous frenzy. All they knew how to talk about were the T.V. shows they watched and stupid things, like baseball.

The only boy he could talk to was his friend Tommy. He and Tommy talked about everything. On the days that they spent together they played chess or they went to the library. They talked about High School and the books they read. They talked a lot about the Bomb and the Communists and the end of the world. Both of them shared the same secret fear—that the world would end before they were old enough to understand it.

Tommy's family lived in a different part of the city. Aside from at church and on Saturday, which was library day, he didn't get to see his friend that often. Most days that summer Nels Sorenson spent by himself.

Mom packed him a lunch. He left right after breakfast, riding out of the subdivision on his bicycle with the rifle slung across his back and his fishing rod in one hand.

But Summer seemed to have lost its old magic. The good weather brought on a fresh invasion of subdivisions and shopping plazas and industrial parks. Little stands of bush which had been an easy ride after school disappeared beneath the blades of the bulldozers and the giant earthmovers. The creek where he had fished for two summers got dredged and a new cement bridge got put in. It felt like every time he found some place, the men with the machinery followed him there and wrecked it on him.

He began to range further out into the countryside than he had ever been before. It took him two weeks to find the old train bridge over the river. The trains didn't use it anymore. At least, he never saw any when he was there.

The river flowed through a hollow with the trestle bridging the tops of the land. There was hardwood bush on the slopes and sumach everywhere along the track. Below the bridge there was a deep hole and there were bass in it. Big ones. But he had to ride on the highway to get there. Even though he knew he wasn't allowed to. He couldn't go fast enough on the gravel roads. And it was a long ride too. Half the day got used up just getting to his spot and getting home again in time for supper.

Even when he caught a good bass he had to let it go. He couldn't take them home because Dad would want to go fishing there. He couldn't even tell Dad about the day's fishing at supper. If Mom and Dad found out that he was riding on the highway he knew they

LOOKING FOR GOD IN THE FOREST 215

wouldn't let him go to his spot anymore. Especially Mom. Mom was always worrying.

But it sure took a lot of the fun out of fishing, not being able to share it with them. It was scary too, riding on the highway. There were all kinds of cars, going faster and faster. More than once the thick gravel on the shoulder trapped the front wheel and sent him sprawling, legs tangled up in the frame and the riflebutt slamming into the small of his back when he pulled off too suddenly to get out of the path of a speeding car. He rode home bruised and shaken, only to ride out again the next morning telling himself that he wasn't scared, pedalling along on the edge of the smooth black asphalt.

The changes that summer imposed themselves everywhere in his life. When the woodlot where he and Dad went on Sunday afternoons got bulldozed again, the Sunday walks in the forest finally came to an end. Instead the entire family—still in their church clothes—got into the blue '57 Chevy which Dad had bought that spring. Then they all went for a Drive in the stifling heat.

It seemed to him that every car in the city followed them in mindless pursuit. They never seemed to get beyond the city limits. They joined the line of all the other cars, driving at five miles an hour through the tortured mazes of half-built subdivisions where there wasn't even any grass yet. All of the houses always looked the same.

Mom and Dad smiled a lot and said how nice it was to get out for a Drive together, as a family. He sat in the back seat, hot and sweaty and bored out of his mind, thinking that it wouldn't be so bad if all the subdivisions got blown up.

The only time that he and Dad had now to get out in the country together was on Saturdays. After an early supper they went fishing. Ever since Dad started fishing, they always went to the old fishing hole where Walker had taught him to fish bass.

The march of the subdivisions moved out in that direction as well. There were old tires and all kinds of bottles and even a shopping cart from a supermarket in the shallow water under the bridge. The river bottom trailed long streamers of slimy brown weed in the current. From the bridge they could see schools of suckerfish and the huge armoured carp which rooted like pigs with their snouts in the waterweed. But the black bass which had been so plentiful were few and far between.

One Saturday in midsummer there was something at the river which neither he nor Dad had ever seen before. At the far end of the deep pool where the river made its bend, a thick frothy blanket of brown and white scum covered the surface of the water.

He asked Dad what it was but Dad didn't know. It made them both uneasy, seeing it there.

He caught a good bass that night and they took it home. But when he cut it open to clean it, the stink that came out of its guts almost made him gag. Dad carried the carcass out to the garden, holding his nose with his other hand. They buried the bass under the rose bush.

The rose bush seemed to like it. But they never went back to the old fishing hole. It was just one of those things that he didn't understand.

There were a lot of things that Nels Sorenson didn't understand. No matter how hard he tried. After his graduation he badgered Mom and Dad until he was finally allowed to watch the News after supper with Dad. He knew from what Pastor Billy said that watching the News was important.

The world which he saw on the News bore no resemblance to the world of his day to day life. Even when Pastor Billy explained it in the Sunday night service, it still didn't make any sense. He had thought for a long time that Pastor Billy said that The Beast was somebody named Khrushchev. But when he saw him on the News, Mr. Khrushchev only had one head!

He was sure that Pastor Billy said that The Beast had seven heads. That night he decided that he would read the Book of Revelation for himself.

He told himself that he wasn't scared, reading in bed with Taffy and his rifle on the blanket beside him. After the first couple of pages he read fast, trying to find where it talked about the Communists.

The bleak psychotic imagery swarmed up inside his mind. He lasted until he got to the sixteenth chapter and the part where the angels pour dead men's blood into the waters and they all turn into blood and everything dies. He shut his Bible with a shudder of sane revulsion and hugged his dog.

It took him a long time to go to sleep, laying in bed with the light on.

He dreamed that night that he was a little kid again. In the dream, he was standing alone on the bridge at the old fishing hole, looking down onto the river.

Suddenly the water below him all turned into blood. Big pussy, yellow scabs began to grow and split along the banks. The snapping turtle shrivelled into a mummified horror on its boulder when he looked at it. Then the surface began to boil with struggling, dying fish. He woke up screaming.

He didn't tell Mom about his dream when she came running in to see what was wrong with him. It was too awful to think about. He didn't try to read the Book of Revelation again either. He slept with the light on every night for a week

The only adult who brought any relief to his mental struggle was the President of America, John F. Kennedy. He watched Mr. Kennedy with Dad whenever he was on T.V. Mr. Kennedy was on T.V. a lot. Even Mom—who didn't like to watch the News—would come into the living room and watch Mr. Kennedy. Mom said how handsome Mr. Kennedy was, and how young he looked to be the President.

Nels Sorenson liked Mr. Kennedy a lot. Everybody did. Even Pastor Billy said nice things about Mr. Kennedy in the services. If Pastor Billy liked Mr. Kennedy, Nels Sorenson knew that God liked Mr. Kennedy too.

Mr. Kennedy wasn't afraid of the Communists. He stood right up to them. But mostly he smiled all the time when he was on T.V. He talked about really interesting things.

Sometimes Mr. Kennedy talked about how his friends in the Peace Corps were volunteering their lives to go to places like Africa, where the people still all lived in mud huts, to teach them the American way to make their lives better. Nels Sorenson always thought that it would be great to be one of Mr. Kennedy's friends and go to Africa with the Peace Corps. It would be sort of like being a missionary. Except that you wouldn't have to do any preaching. It was just the Right thing to do.

But the thing that he liked the best was when Mr. Kennedy talked about the Space Program. Mr. Kennedy said that, someday soon, the Americans would put men on the Moon!

The thought of this cheered him up to no end. If there was enough time left for the Americans to put men on the Moon, then there had to be enough time left for him to grow up! And if anybody knew how much time there was left—besides God—it had to be the President of America!

The only thing that he didn't like about Mr. Kennedy was the way he talked. It wasn't like he yelled or anything. It was just that sometimes, if he shut his eyes and listened, Mr. Kennedy sounded a lot like Pastor Billy.

Of course, they were both Americans. Nels Sorenson thought that everyone in America probably talked like that. Although the old Preacher hadn't. At least, he didn't think he had. But Mr. Kennedy was a good speaker. Everybody said so.

Everybody said what a good speaker Pastor Billy was too. The church was full every Sunday now. Almost every Sunday somebody went up to the front to get saved.

Nels Sorenson developed the furtive habit of keeping one eye open during the altar call so that he could study the people who went up to the front to get saved. It always made him wonder what it was that they had done wrong.

Similar thoughts tormented him when he went out in the evenings for Liberty magazine. All of his customers liked him. But Pastor Billy said that everybody who wasn't saved was going to be on the Devil's side when Armageddon started. After God won and the world ended, they would all go to Hell for eternity.

It made him terribly uneasy, knocking on his neighbours' doors to collect the money. He tried to imagine them inside, worshipping

Satan behind the closed curtains. He studied their foreheads while they counted their change, looking for the mark of The Beast.

There was never anything there that he could see. He thought about it after, every time while he sat on the bed with Taffy and counted the money. It didn't make any sense. Especially the part that anyone who hadn't been saved by someone like Pastor Billy was going to Hell. It just didn't seem fair.

But Pastor Billy said it was prophesied in the Book of Revelation.

He began to dread having to do his job. The thought of Mrs. Gregg—who always gave him cookies—being tortured by the Devil—or any of them, for that matter—it was too awful to think about! He liked all of his customers. He lay awake long into the night, worrying about how he could tell them that they had to go and get saved. Especially Mrs. Gregg.

But he could never figure out how to explain it to her. He just didn't understand it at all. Each time, before he fell asleep, he told himself that as soon as he turned fourteen and became a man he would know how to explain about the communists to his customers. As long as the world didn't end before his birthday . . .

Mom and Dad never went up to the front to get saved. Neither did their friends—like Tommy's folks and the Matthews—who had belonged to their church before Pastor Billy came. But Mom and Dad were Christians if anybody was. That—and God—were about the only things in the world that he was sure about. And sometimes it seemed that even God had changed a lot, since he was a little kid.

The nature of that change was revealed to Nels Sorenson one Sunday morning lat in the month of July. Pastor Billy was thundering on about all of the terrible things that Satan would do to anyone who turned his back on God. At the peak of his rage Pastor Billy stopped dead and stared straight up into his eyes.

In the instant of that contact Nels Sorenson's mind was filled with the image of Pastor Billy's first service. He saw himself again, standing alone in the aisle with Pastor Billy watching him from the pulpit. And then he had turned his back on God and walked out of the hall!

The awful certainty swept through him with the force of revelation—he was going to go to Hell!

By the time the altar call came he was insane with fear. He reached over and tugged urgently on his father's sleeve.

"Dad—"

Dad opened one eye to look at him.

"Dad—I gotta go get saved! I've got to!"

He could hardly get the words to come out. Dad smiled and put a strong reassuring arm across his shoulders.

"It's okay Nels. You're all right son. When you're a man, your time will come. Then you can talk to God."

He sank back safe under his father's arm. Dad was a Christian. Dad knew. The fear slipped away and left him hollow and shaky. When the service was over and Dad asked him if he was all right he just said,

"Yeah Dad. I'm okay now."

All the way home in the car he felt ashamed for letting himself get scared. That night, when he said his prayers, he explained to God that he hadn't meant to turn his back on Him. He felt better about it when he got into bed and turned the lights off.

But as he lay there, trying to go to sleep, the nagging doubt crept into his mind about whether it counted to say you were sorry to God unless you went up to the front to do it. He tried to block it out but it wouldn't go away. He tried to imagine himself in the aisle going up to get saved. His guts turned into knots. The thought of going into the back room alone with Pastor Billy was scarier than the thought of going to Hell! At least in Hell there'd be other people.

And then another thought came racing in on him! He was almost a man! His birthday was less than two months away! If the world didn't end before his birthday he would have to go up and get saved!

After that night he began to dread going to church. All of the terrible punishments that Pastor Billy described in detail each successive Sunday seemed to be aimed at him.

And as if that wasn't bad enough, his bladder began to act up on him again. No matter how hard he tried to wring every last drop out of it before the service began, by the time Pastor Billy got to the altar call he would be sitting with his legs crossed, praying that someone would go up and get saved so he could get out of there.

He thought that he would go crazy sometimes, trying to figure it out. It never happened to him anywhere else. It was so real it was excruciating. He didn't even bother to run to the washroom after the service any more. If he did, nothing happened. The urge to pee vanished as mysteriously as it came as soon as he sprinted out of the church.

He didn't tell anyone about it. Not even Tommy. It was too embarrassing. It was just one more thing on the long list of things that Nels Sorenson didn't understand.

The month of August blew by him at speed, racing the rising sun out the highway to the river. At the end of each day he crossed it off on the calendar on the kitchen wall. As the number of unmarked squares declined his impatience grew out of all proportion. His thoughts were all of High School now. He and Tommy hardly talked about anything else.

August ended on the Friday of the Labour Day weekend. Saturday was a haircut and a whole day of being dragged, sullen and staring, down endless aisles jammed with sweaty shoppers at the annual Back To School sales. Sunday was church. Auntie Sal came out and had supper with them. Monday was the last day of summer.

He was gone before Mom and Dad were even awake, pedalling furiously to get to his spot before the sun crested the tops of the trees. It was a beauty of a morning, the sky clear blue and the air cool and sweet. The slanting rays of the early sun filled the surface of the river with light.

It took him no time at all to capture some bait. But he couldn't keep his mind on fishing. He had two good bites and he missed them both. After the second bite he tossed the bait into the river for the fish to eat and laid the rod aside. He spent the rest of the day just staring at everything, trying to memorize every detail of his last day of having to be a kid.

Before he left the river, he carved his initials and the date into the smooth bark of a beech tree. It seemed important somehow to leave a record. He made himself a promise that, next summer, when he was grown up, he would bring Dad to his spot. It wouldn't make any difference then. At least, if the world hadn't ended by next summer. And if it hadn't, if his spot was still there . . .

When he rode home in the glaring light of late afternoon and the heavy holiday traffic, he was ready to take his place in the adult world. He didn't pull off onto the shoulder once. Not even when the man in the red convertible shook his fist and swore at him.

At supper that evening Mom smiled at him across the table.

"How was fishing today Nels?"

He shrugged.

"It was okay I guess."

"Are you already to start High School?"

"Almost. I've got one more thing to do."

"What's that dear?"

"Oh . . . just something . . . Can I wear my good gray flannels and my new white shirt tomorrow?"

"Certainly. I'll press them up for you before I go to bed."

After supper he helped Mom with the dishes. He tried to watch the News with Dad but his mind just wasn't there. When Mom and Elly came in after the News to watch "Leave it to Beaver!" he got up from where he was sitting on the floor.

"I guess I'll go upstairs for a while."

Mom smiled at him from the couch and patted the seat beside her.

"Why don't you sit and watch the program with us Nels?"

"No thanks Mom. I've got some stuff to do. I'll come down later. Come on Taffy."

Alone with his dog in his room, Nels Sorenson performed the rites of passage. All of his favourite things lived on top of his dresser. There was the old lead soldier who had one arm shot off, wearing his Redcoat uniform. Beside him was the rubber monster with the bulgy eyes that Mom hated, which he had won from the claw machine at the fall fair. There was the rabbit's foot that Danny had given him and special rocks and strange Chinese coins and all kinds of good stuff.

He carried them all over and set them up in front of Taffy on the bed. The last thing was the wooden cigar box that Uncle Ernie had saved for him.

"Look at all this good stuff eh girl? Yeah!"

He admired each thing and showed it to Taffy before he put it reluctantly into the cigar box. He saved the Redcoat for last. It was way older than everything else. When the Redcoat was safely tucked inside he closed the box and reverently placed it in the back of his bottom drawer.

The top of his dresser looked lonely and bare. He flopped face down on the bed, feeling blue, almost wishing that he could just keep on being a kid. Taffy came over and licked his ear, trying to cheer him up. He rolled over on his back and looked up at her.

"It's okay girl. I'm all right. I just had to put away all my Childish Things."

When Mom came in to get his clothes to iron he was laying on the bed staring up into the ceiling. Mom smiled as soon as she walked in.

"Why Nels—you cleaned off your dresser! And without even being told! You must be growing up. I've been trying to get you to do that for years."

"Yeah . . . I know . . ."

He sighed.

"Well, I think it looks a lot better now. Don't you?"

He didn't want to look at it. He just stared into the ceiling.

"Yeah Mom. I guess I'm grown up now . . ."

He didn't sleep at all that night. He was afraid to go to sleep in case Jesus came. He sat beside the window staring across the sleeping street into the blackness of the playing field, wondering if he would understand everything all at once.

Sometime in the small hours the muted thunder of a passing jet reached down to him, eight miles high. He screwed his eyes shut and prayed with all his might that it wouldn't happen! Not now! Not when he was this close—

He didn't quit praying until the jet was safely gone. The silence of the hours closed in around him again.

By the time false dawn began to show beyond the window, he couldn't stay still any longer. He snuck down the basement and polished his good shoes until they shone.

Mom and Dad were just coming out of the bedroom when he came back up the stairs.

"Morning Mom! Morning Dad!"

Morning son."

"Good morning dear. How long have you been awake?"

"I couldn't go to sleep at all last night!"

Mom looked concerned.

"You'll be tired out by the time school's over."

"I'll be okay Mom. It's only half a day. I'm going to go and get dressed now. Did you iron my clothes?"

"Yes dear. I hung them right there, on the banister. You must have walked right past them."

"I guess I didn't see them. Thanks Mom."

"You must be all excited. Why don't you get dressed and have breakfast with your father?"

"I don't think I could eat any breakfast. My stomach's all full of butterflies."

"Well you'd better eat something anyways. Especially if you stayed up all night. How about some bacon and eggs?"

"I guess so . . ."

"That's better. Don't be too long—it will be ready in about ten minutes."

"Okay."

"Has Taffy been outside yet this morning?"

"No Mom. I forgot. Come on girl. I'm sorry. Did you have a good sleep last night?"

Taffy smiled up at him, heading for the door.

Dad was real quiet at breakfast. Mom teased him a little bit and told him how grown up he looked. He sat at the table, light years away, staring uncomprehendingly down at his bacon and eggs until Mom said that if he couldn't eat his breakfast he didn't have to.

Dad shook his hand before he left for work. Dad told him again how important school was. He spent a half an hour in the bathroom staring at himself in the mirror. He did look grown up. Although he couldn't figure out just how. He wished there was something he could use to make the scar from where Wolfgang had punched him go away. It was the only thing he could see that still made him look like a kid.

That and his stupid cowlick. No matter how many little dabs of Brylcream he used it just wouldn't stay down. Eventually he had to give up on it because Elly was outside banging on the bathroom door.

By a quarter after eight he couldn't wait any more. He kissed his mother and his sister goodbye and rode out into the bright blue morning.

There were hardly any other bicycles in the rack when he got to the High School. He parked his bike, feeling proud of the fact that he was one of the first ones there. The red brick building loomed up before him. It's steel and glass doors beckoned to him. He climbed the steps in a kind of awe and pushed his way inside.

Four bigger older guys were leaning against the wall in the lobby. They all turned to stare at him as he came in. They looked so grown up that he felt suddenly small and shy. He looked away from them, reading the cloth banner stretched across the lobby above their heads.

WELCOME GRADE NINE STUDENTS!
PLEASE GO TO THE GYMNASIUM

The biggest of the four guys pushed himself away from the wall and came over to stand in front of him.

"Hi! Can I help you with something?"

The big guy looked friendly. He smiled up at him and said, politely,

"Yes, please. Could you tell me where the gymnasium is?"

The big guy smiled back at him. All of the other guys came over and stood around him. They were all smiling too. The big guy said,

"Sure. Are you a Greeny?"

He thought about it for a minute.

"I don't know—what's a Greeny?"

One of the guys started to snicker. The big guy turned and gave him a dirty look. The guy quit snickering. The big guy turned back to him, serious now.

"You must be new so I'll explain it to you. Our school colours are green and white, see? When you start here on your first day in Grade Nine, you're a Greeny. So—are you a Greeny?"

It seemed pretty strange. But the big guy seemed to like him.

"I guess I must be."

The guy who had started the snicker was behind him now. So was one of the other guys. He heard them both snicker this time. He started to turn, to look at them but the big guy reached out and laid a hand on his shoulder. He looked back up at him. The big guy smiled.

"That's not quite the right answer. See—we're in Grade Twelve. Today, if somebody like me asks you if you're a Greeny, you're supposed to say 'Yes Sir. I am a Greeny Sir!' Go ahead—give it a try. Are you a Greeny?"

"Yes Sir. I am a Greeny Sir,"

The big guy beamed at him.

"That's really good! Isn't it guys?"

"Oh yeah!"

"For sure!"

He turned to look around at them. They were all grinning at him and he felt better. He grinned back up at the big guy.

"So what's your name Greeny?"

"It's Nels—Nels Sorenson."

He stuck out his hand. The big guy looked past it at his friends.

"What do you say we take Nels here to the gym guys?"

"Yeah!"

The two guys behind him grabbed his arms before he knew what was happening!

"Get his legs!"

"Lemme go!"

"Got 'em!"

"Hey! Put me down!!"

They had him up in the air! They took off running with him down a hallway lined with green lockers and they were laughing at him! He bucked and squirmed with all of his might but he couldn't get free!

"Lemme go!!"

"Hang onto him!"

"Jesus—he's strong!"

"Okay—okay! Drop him!"

He hit the floor and he was back up in a rage, fists clenched, facing his tormentors. The big jerk gave him a mocking grin.

"So—are you a Greeny?"

"You go to Hell!"

It wasn't a curse. It was a prediction.

A door swing open beside him. A teacher stuck his head out into the hall.

"What's going on here Briggs?"

The other jerks looked down at the floor. The big jerk smiled innocently at the teacher.

"Just a little orienteering Sir."

"Well knock it off! Leave the little kids alone!"

The teacher disappeared. The door banged shut behind him. The big jerk grinned at him again.

"Welcome to High School kid."

He watched them walk away, squashed flat as a bug. He couldn't decide which one he hated most—the jerk named Briggs or the teacher.

Margaret Sorenson didn't know that he was home until Taffy went scrambling across the kitchen floor.

"Is that you Nels?"

The house was silent. She dried her hands and went to the back door to see what the dog was all excited about.

He was there, just inside the door, staring down at the floor with his fists clenched at his sides. She put on a smile, wondering what in the world had happened now.

"Oh—hello Nels! I didn't hear you come in."

He wouldn't look up at her at all.

"Aren't you even going to say hello?"

"Hello."

"That's better. How was your first day of High School?"

"It was stupid! I hate it!"

His eyes never left the floor. Taffy looked up hopefully, wagging her tail. The fact that he hadn't even bent down to pet his dog was an indication to her of how upset he was.

"What happened Honey? You were all excited when you left this morning—"

"I don't want to talk about it."

"I can't help you with it if you won't tell me about it . . ."

"You can't help anyhow!"

He stared up at her then. She saw the rage and frustration in his fierce blue eyes.

"They treated me like a little kid! I'm not going back!"

She reached out automatically to smooth his hair. He ducked out sideways from under her hand.

"Don't Mom!"

"My goodness! You are in a bad mood aren't you?"

"I don't care! I'm not going back! I'm not a little kid anymore!"

Her heart went out to him. For an instant she wished that she could change him back into a child and just hold him.

"Oh Nels—Why are you in such a hurry to grow up?"

"Aw Mom—you don't understand!"

Margaret Simpson sighed.

"No. I guess I don't."

The silence came down between them again until she said,

"You haven't even said hello to Taffy yet. You don't want to hurt Taffy's feelings do you Honey? She doesn't understand either . . ."

"I guess not . . ."

"Why don't you take her outside and play with her until your sister comes home? I'll have lunch ready by then. Okay?"

"Yeah, sure. But I'm still not going back. Come on dog. Let's go outside."

He didn't come in for lunch when Ellen came home. She went to the back door to call him twice but he wouldn't budge. He was still sitting on the lawn when she heard the car pull into the driveway.

She went to give John a kiss at the door as he came in.

"Hi Honey. I'm home."

"How was your day today dear?"

"Pretty good."

She reached to take his lunch pail. He hesitated at the door, turning to glance back out into the yard.

"What's the matter with Nels? I said hello to him and I asked him how school was. He didn't even answer me."

"Something happened at school. He wouldn't tell me what it was. He came home all upset. All he said was that they made him feel like a little kid, and that he wasn't going back."

"Well he is going back—"

"Of course he is John."

She smiled at the frown that creased his forehead.

"He'll get over it. He likes school. Just be easy with him if he talks about quitting at supper."

"Yes. I will. I wonder what happened?"

"I think his expectations were a little too high, that's all. By tomorrow he'll have forgotten all about it. Go and wash up John. Supper's almost ready. I'll go and tell him to come in."

At the supper table, he waited just long enough for the blessing to be said. As soon as Dad was done he looked over at him.

"Dad?"

"Yes Nels?"

"Can I quit school and get a job?"

Dad looked at Mom. He turned to look at Mom too. Mom smiled at him.

"You already have a job dear. Have some potatoes."

He looked back at Dad.

"I don't mean that kind of a job. I mean a real job. Can I Dad?"

Dad looked away from him, reaching for the meat.

"No son."

"Why not?"

Dad put the meat platter down and looked right at him.

"Listen Nels—when you're my age and you've got a good education and a good job you'll understand why not. Now I don't want to hear any more about it."

Dad went back to filling his plate. He looked down at his own plate, feeling something even worse than the hunger pains in his stomach.

"I'm never gonna get to be that old!"

"Nels! What kind of a thing is that to say to your father?"

"Aw gee Dad—I didn't mean it like that—"

It was all mixed up. They were both giving him The Look.

"Just what did you mean?"

He looked around at Mom again, powerless to explain it.

"Aw . . . I don't know . . ."

"Maybe you should think about what you say before you say it. Now have some potatoes and pass them along to your father."

He stared holes in the bowl of mashed potatoes, feeling like he was going to explode!"

"May I be excused? I'm not hungry."

Mom gave him The Look again. He could feel it.

"No. You may not. You didn't eat any breakfast or any lunch. Now you're going to sit there and eat your supper."

He snapped his eyes up.

"Now you're treating me like a kid!"

"Just eat your supper. You've got lots of time to grow up."

"No! I don't! And I don't want any supper!"

He shoved back his chair and boiled up the stairs and slammed into his room. John Sorenson started to get up to go after his son. Margaret Sorenson gave him The Look and he sat down again.

"Eat your supper John. He'll come back down. I know he's starving."

Ellen looked around confused.

"What's wrong with Nels Mommy?"

Margaret Sorenson smiled at her daughter.

"He's all right Honey. He just didn't have a very good day at school."

The rest of the week the house was in a turmoil. In the mornings Margaret Sorenson had to practically chase him out of the house to get him to go to school. He came home at the end of each day in a foul mood. When she suggested to him that he take his bike and go for a ride before supper he just stared sullenly at the floor and said there wasn't any place left to go.

On Thursday night, which was Liberty night, there was a big row at the table when he announced that he wasn't going to do his stupid job any more! By Friday after school her patience was at an end. She ordered him to go to the playing field until supper was ready. He came home with his shirt torn and his nose bloodied.

John Sorenson took his belt off and took his son upstairs. He came back down alone. The silence at the table that night was as loud as the rolling thunder.

On Saturday morning Nels Sorenson was back on his best behaviour. He said "Good morning" to everyone when he came to the breakfast table. Mom put a fragrant plate of ham and eggs in front of him. He looked up cautiously.

"Thanks Mom"

"You're welcome dear. Are you hungry this morning?"

"I'm starving."

"Well that's what happens when you don't eat your supper. Right?"

"Yes Mom."

He looked down, avoiding all three sets of eyes, busy putting lots of pepper on his eggs. The ham and eggs were gone and he was filling up on toast when Mom said,

"We don't have a lot of time this morning Nels. Your father has a doctor's appointment at 9:30. I have a lot of shopping to do. We'll drop you off at the library when we go downtown."

"Are we going downtown first?"

"No. The doctor's office is in the other direction. We're shopping at the plaza there."

"Do I have to go shopping Mom?"

"Yes. You do. You're not staying home by yourself."

"I was thinking . . ."

He turned to look to Dad for support. Dad never said it but he knew Dad hated shopping too.

"Now that I'm in High School, instead of me going shopping, couldn't I just ride my bike to Tommy's and go to the library with him? I rode my bike to school all week. It isn't that much longer ride to Tommy's. Can I Dad?"

"I don't know son. Your mother doesn't like you riding in the traffic."

He turned to give Mom his most winning smile.

"Can I Mom? I'll be careful. I'll ride on the sidewalk. I've just got to talk to Tommy!"

"What are you in such a hurry to talk to Tommy about?"

"Oh . . . school and stuff. Please Mom?"

Mom smiled—just a little bit.

"Well . . . what do you think John?"

"I think he'll be all right Marg. Just be careful Nels. Do you know how to get there by yourself?

Sure! Thanks Dad! Thanks Mom!"

"Sit down and finish your toast Nels."

"Oh yeah—"

He was halfway to Tommy's house, riding along up the sidewalk on Hamilton Street when a sign in the storefront window stopped his eye. He stood up on the brakes and skidded the back tire around and came cruising in for a closer look. It was just a little sign, block printed on a plain white piece of paper.

DELIVERY BOY WANTED
FOR AFTER SCHOOL

He turned, staring up at the weathered blue and white sign hung out over the sidewalk about his head.

REALE'S PHARMACY
EST. 1928

And there it was! The answer to his prayers! He propped the bike against the faded gray building and hurried inside, barely daring to believe it! Over the threshold into the soft gloom and silence and he stalled, breathing strange fragrances, reaching automatically for the comb in his back pocket. His heart beat anxiously, combing his hair down and peering into the murky light. There didn't seem to be anyone else there . . .

The afterglow of bright morning sun faded, resolving into detail. It was an old store; an adult temple, one of the gates to the Mystery! The board floor stretched away long and narrow into the dimness at the back, the wood almost black from passage of countless footsteps. The shelves and the display case and the ceiling were all carved out of ancient dark wood.

He turned to let his eyes range out, looking for an adult, searching along the length of the wall on his left all the way to the back. The entire wall was filled from floor to ceiling with row upon row of brightly labelled bottles and boxes and jars. But there was no one there.

He scanned the back of the store, seeing the dark panelling and the raised dais of the druggist's counter. There was no one there either. A green glass globe on the counter caught his eye. It seemed to glow in the twilight. He stared down the length of the store at it, trying to evade the uneasiness which was mounting inside of him, wondering what it was that made it glow the colour of a cat's eye.

There was still no one else there.

He looked again, shifting his search to the glass and wood display case which ran the length of the right hand side. The black steel cash register beckoned unguarded on the top of the case at the very back. There was a narrow passage between the end of the druggist's counter and the display case. An aisle behind the case was revealed by the distance between it and the wall. He searched the aisle for an adult, running his eyes along the glass counter top, across the row of medicine bottles on the wall behind it and coming up again.

There was a sudden spasm of self-consciousness, shoving away his comb and staring anxiously down at his wristwatch. It was already three minutes after nine! They had to be open—"

He took a deep breath and followed the glass display case towards the back, staring in covetously at cameras and transistor radios and all kinds of good stuff going by.

"May I help you?"

"I need to see Mr. Reale!"

He stared up caught, bleating it out.

The lady who had materialized behind the cash register smiled at him. She turned to call through an open doorway beside her into the back.

"Jack? There's a young man here to see you."

He felt himself flush at the compliment. The lady was young and she had bobbed red hair the colour of Aunt Sally's. She was really pretty. She turned back to smile at him again.

"He'll be right with you."

"Thank you."

He smiled shyly, looking past her to watch the doorway under a full attack of the butterflies.

"What can I do for you young fellow?"

It was a cheerful voice, somewhere above and behind him. He swung around startled again staring up at the man in the short—sleeved white tunic who was leaning out over the high druggist's counter looking down at him.

"Are you Mr. Reale?"

"That's me son."

The first thing that struck him about Mr. Reale was how old he was! Mr. Reale had white hair and bushy white eyebrows behind round gold-rimmed spectacles. His eyes behind the lenses were bright blue. The second thing that struck him about Mr. Reale was his grin.

He stalled again, staring up at him, trying to think of what to say next.

"Please Sir—I need a job!"

Mr. Reale exchanged looks over his head with the pretty red-headed lady. He could tell just by the way that he was smiling at her that Mr. Reale liked him already! The bright blue eyes sought him out again.

"Do you mean the delivery boy's position?"

"Yes Sir! That's the one!"

"How old are you son?"

He swelled his chest out proudly.

"I'm fourteen Sir. In two weeks. I'm in High School already. I'm a real good rider!"

He gave Mr. Reale his very best smile. The old man looked down at him thoughtfully.

"Do you have your bicycle here?"

"Yes Sir! It's right outside!"

"Let's go and have a look at it shall we?"

"Yes Sir!"

Mr. Reale disappeared into the back. He turned around to look at the red-headed lady again, struggling to keep his eyes from straying to the front of her blouse. Mr. Reale came out of the back and saved him. When he saw the way that they smiled at each other again he knew for sure that Mr. Reale was going to give him the job!

He led the way to the front of the store, turning and smiling at once as they stepped out into the warm September sunshine.

"That's it there Sir!"

The old balloon-tired bicycle leaned against the brickwork, the battle scarred veteran of a thousand campaigns. Bright sun shone on bent spokes and bald rubber. The fenders were scratched and dented in. Here and there along the frame the flat gleam of metal showed where his impacts with the gravel had chipped the red paint away.

He looked on proudly as Mr. Reale bent forward to examine it. But when the old man straightened up and turned around to look at him again he saw the change which had happened in the way that he smiled.

"I'm sorry son. I'd like to give you a job. But I'm afraid this old bike of yours just wouldn't be safe enough. Or fast enough."

He looked away, staring down at the sidewalk, not wanting the old man to see how bad he felt inside.

Mr. Reale patted him on the shoulder, trying to cheer him up. It didn't help.

"Thank you for coming in son."

"Yes Sir. You're welcome."

He didn't look up, even knowing that it wasn't polite. He couldn't. Mr. Reale said goodbye to him and went back inside. He stood alone on the sidewalk, staring bleakly at his bicycle, squashed flat as a bug for the second time in a week.

And then it hit him—Mr. Reale hadn't said anything about him not being old enough! It was just his bike!

He was on it and gone, pedalling madly for home before Mom and Dad left to go shopping. The bike had never been so slow before! He hit the subdivision several minutes and an eternity later flat out, chest heaving. The car was gone when he came careening around the curve.

"Aw no!"

He skidded the bike out sideways and dropped it and sprinted to try the doors. The house was locked. He rattled both doorknobs and it was so stupid! He took off, circling the house, seething with frustration at the certain knowledge that some other guy was getting his job while he was locked out of his own house!

And then he saw the T.V. tower . . . as if he had never seen it before . . . He stared at it open-mouthed, seeing the way that the steel cross-bracing looked just like the rungs of a ladder! His eyes followed it up, measuring the gap of empty space which yawned between the closest rung and his windowsill, accepting it. He moved in close and tested the first two rungs with his weight, praying that it wouldn't come crashing down on top of him.

"Please God—"

God heard him. He went up the tower like a spider. The amazement at his discovery was already eclipsed by a vision of his money jar waiting for him on the top shelf of his closet. Taffy was thumping up the stairs barking furiously as he swung his legs out over the two-foot gap and onto the windowsill.

There was an instant of gut churning fear changing his grip and turning over to slide in backwards, arms stretched and feet searching frantically for a foothold. His fingers locked onto the steel strut, suspended above the abyss, staring down at the raised edge of the cement tower pad directly beneath him—

His feet touched the floor. He forced his fingers to let go and then he was inside!—in his room!

He stared out the window at the tower, knees wobbling with relief, lost in its implications.

Taffy attacked in a rush, growling happily with his pant leg in her mouth.

"Not now girl! I gotta hurry!"

He bent down hastily to free himself, hurrying past her to the closet. She caught his excitement, prancing behind him, nipping at his ankles.

"Ow! Cut it out!"

He reached up lifting the heavy green two quart Mason jar down off the shelf with both hands. Inside it was all of the money he had saved from Liberty magazine in quarters and half-dollars and big round silver dollars with a few crumpled paper dollars stuffed in on top. All that he ever needed money for was for fish hooks and slugs for the rifle and for presents at Christmas and birthdays. And Cokes.

He forced his sudden craving for an ice cold Coke aside, trying to remember how much money he had spent since the last time he had counted it. It took too long. There had to be enough to buy a bicycle!

And he had to hurry!

There was no time even to savour the sweet sensation of being alone in his own house for the very first time in his life! He took the stairs two at a time with Taffy right on his heels. The kitchen clock said it was already 9:30!

He put on a fresh burst of speed to the basement going for his knapsack. The weight of all that money dug the strap into his neck when he stuffed the jar into the knapsack and slung it on. He ignored it, bounding back up the basement stairs.

"Bye Taffy!"

The back door slammed behind him and he was gone again.

He took the fastest way to the old neighbourhood, riding hard on the road beneath the tunnel of the trees, straining forward towards O'Malley's Bicycles and Repairs. He couldn't ride on the sidewalk any more. The weight of all that money almost yanked his head off when he tried to jump the curb. Left at the light into the traffic on Main Street praying that Mom wouldn't see him, pedalled right out on the long downhill stretch with the wind in his ears and the cars sliding by inches away from his handlebars.

Past the factories—past the fairgrounds—standing up on the pedals pumping speed until he saw the sign and darted across Main Street through a gap in the oncoming traffic. He took the curb and came down hard and let the bike fall away in a clatter. There was a stabbing pain in the side of his neck but there was no time to think about it.

He stepped clear of the frame and swung the knapsack around, holding the weight of all that money out in front of him with both hands.

The O'Malleys had been their neighbours at their old house. Mr. O'Malley wasn't there. It was Timmy's big brother Pat who looked around at him from the workbench as he burst in.

"Hi Nels. Come to buy a bicycle?"

He nodded urgently, wondering if his chest was going to explode.

"Please—Pat—I want—to see—the fastest—bike—you've got!"

He panted the words out. Pat grinned at him, like he was kidding. He shook his head hard, wincing at the pain in his neck.

"Hurry—got to hurry—"

"Oh sure Nels."

Pat was used to his speed. He waited anxiously while Pat wiped his hands on a rag, working hard to slow his breathing.

"It's right over here. This one. It's a Raleigh Racer, made in England. Isn't she the finest looking bike you've ever seen?"

He fell in love at the sight of her, gold paint and bright chrome shining in the yellow light through the grimy shop window.

"She's beautiful!"

"Take a look at her Nels. I bought one just like her. I'll tell you, she's a dream to ride. Three speeds forward, Sturmy-Archer changer, ball bearing sprocket. Hand brakes. The generator that runs the head and tail lights is built into the front hub here. See?"

He didn't look down at it. He looked at Pat.

"Is she fast?"

"Is she fast?"

Pat's eyebrows climbed right up onto his forehead.

"Are you kidding? She's a racer! Listen—I put a speedometer on mine. I had it up to 37 miles an hour wound out coming down the overpass!"

"37 miles an hour!"

He felt his eyes go wide at the thought of it.

"That's as fast as cars! Oh yeah—I want her!!"

Pat appraised him realistically.

"I doubt it. I'll be working mine off until next year. They cost a hundred and four dollars."

"I've got tons of money. See?"

He reached into his knapsack and pulled his money jar.

Pat's eyes almost bugged out of his head.

"Holy Cow Nels! What'd you do? Rob a bank?"

"I saved it! It's all the money I've got! Do you think it's enough?"

Pat grinned at him; a real Irish grin.

"Dump her out on the counter and we'll see!"

It took forever to count it, stacking quarters and half-dollars out of the mound of coins. When it was done there was ninety-eight dollars and fifty cents.

He counted it all again, out loud, praying silently that they'd made a mistake. Pat watched him count it. Pat wasn't grinning any more. There wasn't any more money either.

"I've got a really nice three speed for seventy five bucks—"

"No! I want the Racer!"

He stared down bitterly at all that money. It was all of the money that he had in the world and it wasn't enough. He felt like he had been betrayed—felt like smashing something!

"You could come back with the rest of the money. Maybe your Dad would lend you the seven bucks—"

"That's too late!"

"You're really in a hurry. Aren't you Nels?"

He snapped his eyes up at Pat. Pat was grinning at him! Pat's grin vanished when he locked the sights on him.

"You don't understand!! I need it!! I need it right now!!"

"Okay—okay—Take it easy Nels—Maybe I can help you out. How did you get here? On your bike?"

"Yeah, it's outside."

"Go get it. Bring it in."

He went, not knowing why, just hearing hope. Pat winced at the sight of it when he wheeled it in.

"That's it? Oh brother . . . Dad'll kill me for this . . . To Hell with it! If you need it that bad I'll give you the difference for your old bike. You can have The Racer. Deal?"

"Oh yeah!! It's a deal!!"

He fidgeted at the edge of his control while Pat adjusted the seat and showed him how to work the gears. He didn't hear a word he said about the brakes, seeing racks of bicycles parked in front of the drugstore. He looked at his watch. It was quarter after ten!

"I gotta go Pat!"

The knapsack and the money jar were still on the counter. He didn't even see them there. Pat called after him,

"How come you're in such a big hurry?

"I gotta go get a job! See you!"

He was out of the doorway and up onto the pedals already figuring out the fastest way back to the drugstore.

The next cross street was Central Avenue. He turned left at the corner, away from the church, still on the sidewalk. The overpass loomed up in front of him, spanning the railway yard. Hamilton Street was at the bottom of the hill on the other side. He powered up the slope in first gear like it wasn't even there!

He paused at the summit, feet still on the pedals, holding himself upright with one hand on the railing. The Racer was a dream. The city spread out before him was his beatific vision.

South, the familiar streets of his childhood nestled beneath the deep green of the maple trees.

To the east, the prosperous columns of white factory smoke hung like the banners of the adult world in the clear blue sky.

Ahead of him in old dark wood and cat's eye light the Mystery waited—

He turned right round, looking back at the church gleaming white, rising out of the trees.

"Thank you God!"

He smiled to himself, his secret smile, his thoughts all welling up in God and the adult world and 37 miles an hour!

There were no cars coming up the slope behind him. Ahead of him, at the bottom of the hill, a half a dozen cars waited for the light to turn green on Central Avenue.

The drugstore was east. He had to turn left. He pushed off the sidewalk and dropped lightly down onto the road. He crossed the flat summit at 90° to take up position on the centre line, heart hammering. He had just enough time to point the nose downhill.

The light turned orange on Hamilton Street. He let the Racer go, swooping like a hawk on his adversaries the cars in pure adolescent joy! He was pedalled out in first and already through second before the light turned green. He hit third, pedalling like a demon, eyes streaming with the wind and grinning madly, flashing along past the line of startled drivers. The intersection was a blur of speed. He took the turn leaned right down on the frame, rocketing across the bow of a bus and racing away up Hamilton Street with the blare of angry car horns clashing behind him!

The adrenalin rush carried him breathless for a block and a half, thinking 37 miles an hour!! The Racer coasted almost to a stop before he even knew where he was. He came back, looking round. There, beside him, a full part of his vision was the red Coke sign on a Variety Store.

He reached for the brake levers and squeezed them both tight. The Racer stopped dead and bucked him off on to the road.

He hit hard, stunned, and got back up, bending to pick up the Racer. She wasn't hurt. He checked himself over and he wasn't hurt either. But he had to sit down on the curb until his legs quit shaking.

He got up again lightheaded and went in to get a Coke. His quarter was where it always was, in the watchpocket of his jeans. He paid for his Coke and the ritual red licorice at the counter. He was back outside before he realized that the quarter he had just spent was the very last one out of all that money!

It didn't feel good at all! He wolfed down his licorice and guzzled his Coke, terrified now that somebody would beat him to all that money at the drugstore!

The drugstore was only a few more blocks. He scanned it up ahead, closing the distance. There weren't any bicycles parked out front. He let the Racer coast the rest of the way, his need for speed countered by his nervousness about the brakes, belching gratefully with Coke when he saw that the sign was still in the window.

He circled twice, bringing his speed right down before he swung off onto the sidewalk and stopped her with his feet. He put the Racer up onto the chromed kickstand, staring at her lovingly while he combed his hair down flat. Then he hurried inside, knowing nothing could go wrong this time!

Mr. Reale beamed down at him from the dais, a prelate of work welcoming an eager probationer.

"Back again young fellow?"

"Yes sir!"

"What can I do for you this time?"

He looked up hopefully into the bright blue eyes.

"Well Sir . . . you remember what you said about how you'd give me a job if I had a faster bicycle?"

The old man looked down at him thoughtfully.

"I suppose I must have . . ."

"Yes Sir. It's right outside. My new bicycle. Would you come and have a look at it?"

"You've got a new bicycle?"

"Yes Sir! I just got it! I had to get it, so you could give me the job! Please Sir?"

"I guess I'd better, if you've gone to all that trouble—"

"Oh—it was no trouble Sir! No trouble at all!"

He looked around for the red headed lady while he waited for Mr. Reale to come out of the back. She was leaning on her elbows on the display case showing a camera to a customer and she had big ones!

"Let's go have a look son."

"Oh—yes Sir—"

He flushed, caught, heading for the front, hoping Mr. Reale hadn't seen him looking. They stepped out into the sunshine again.

"Here she is Sir! She's a Racer!"

He watched the old man anxiously while he studied the Racer. When he turned back to look at him his smile was still there.

"That's a beautiful bicycle son. English made, isn't it?"

"Yes Sir!"

"What's your name son?"

"It's Nels Sir. Nels Sorenson."

I'm pleased to meet you Nels."

"Thank you Sir."

He stuck out his hand. Mr. Reale shook it. Mr. Reale had a good grip for somebody that old. He knew for sure that Mr. Reale liked him now. The old man gave him another thoughtful smile.

"Why don't you tell me what you've been doing since you were here—what—an hour and a half ago?"

He checked his watch.

"Yes Sir. It's 10:30 now. I was here at 9 o'clock."

"Yes. Go on . . ."

"Well Sir—after I talked to you and you said—you know—what you said—"

"Yes?"

"Well—I rode home and got my money. Then I rode down to Mr. O'Malley's store and bought the Racer. Mr. O'Malley used to be our neighbour. But he wasn't there. Patty sold it to me. He's their son. Then I came here."

He saw the bus again, hoping that now Mr. Reale wasn't going to ask him which street he'd come on.

"Where do you live son?"

"On Thornberry Drive Sir."

"I know where it is. That's quite a ride. And then you went to O'Malley's store. Is that over by Main and Central?"

"Yes Sir."

"And then you bought your new bicycle and rode it back here. All inside of an hour and a half. Is that correct?"

"Yes Sir."

Mr. Reale grinned at him.

"You're certainly fast enough. Tell me—how much does a bicycle like this cost Nels?"

"It cost a hundred and four dollars Sir."

"A hundred and four dollars?"

Mr. Reale looked suitably impressed.

"That's a lot of money son."

"Yes Sir. It took me four years to get it."

"And where did you get all of that money from in the first place? From your allowance?"

"Oh no Sir. I don't get an allowance. I've got a job working for Liberty magazine. I've had it since I was ten."

"Really? Why do you need another job then?"

He frowned, trying to figure out how to explain it.

"Well—I'm in High School now. It's kind of a little kid's job. And—"

He couldn't explain about Armageddon.

"I don't know Sir—I just need a better job."

"I think I understand."

"You do?"

"Mm-hmm. I was your age once too you know."

He looked at the old man, who was grinning at him again. It was kind of hard to imagine. But Mr. Reale understood. He grinned back up at him.

"So can I have the job Sir?"

"Tell me—what do your parents think of this?"

He felt his grin go out.

"I don't know Sir. They weren't home. I had to go in through the window to get my money—"

"So your folks don't know about any of this?"

"No Sir . . ."

He stared up desperately at Mr. Reale.

"Please Sir! I really need a job! I know how to ride with cars! I've been going fishing on the highway all summer!"

"I'll bet your folks don't know about that either. Do they?"

Mr. Reale was smiling but his blue eyes were serious now. He wanted to lie like he'd never wanted to lie before in his life. Something about the old man's eyes made him sure he would know that he was lying. He looked down miserably at the sidewalk.

"No Sir. They don't."

"You like to fish do you?"

"Yes Sir. I've been fishing every day all summer. Except Sunday 'cause we're Baptists. Fishing's the best!"

"Yes. I like to fish myself. But tell me—why do you have to ride on the highway to go fishing?"

He frowned, wishing he understood it so that he could explain it to Mr. Reale.

"They wrecked all the places where I used to go when I was a kid. Even the place that was the very best. It's full of garbage or something."

Mr. Reale frowned, like he understood that too. Then he smiled again.

"You must be a good rider if you've managed all summer without having an accident. I'll tell you what. We'll just keep that between us. Unless of course you decide to tell your folks yourself. Is that all right with you?"

"Oh yes Sir! Thank you Sir!"

"Thank you Nels. For telling the truth. Now about this job . . ."

He held his breath, praying silently again. The bright blue eyes seemed to look right inside him.

"If I gave you the job would you promise me that you would ride as safely as you can?"

"Yes Sir."

I need someone who is dependable too. You'd have to promise to come after school every day—except Wednesday—and on Saturday afternoon as well. It's a lot of work Nels. And it's important work too."

I promise Sir. I'm a good worker."

"Yes. I imagine that you are. The pay is three dollars a week."

"Three dollars? Wow!"

"There's just one more thing."

"Yes Sir?"

"You'll have to have permission from your folks if you want the job. I'd like you to call your Dad and ask him to come and see me."

"They're at shopping right now Sir. They won't be home until lunch time."

"Very well. I'll tell you what I'll do. I'll take the sign out of the window for now. You go home and explain it to your folks. If it's still okay, bring your Dad in to see me this afternoon. If it's not, I'd like you to call me. Can you do that?"

"Oh yes Sir! I can explain it to them!"

He beamed up at him. Mr. Reale grinned back at him again.

"I have no doubt that you can. I have to go back to work now. I'll be hearing from you this afternoon. And be careful riding your new bicycle home. I imagine that it's quite a bit faster than what you are accustomed to."

"Yes Sir! I will Sir! Thank you Sir! Goodbye Sir!"

"Goodbye Nels."

He started off slowly, on the sidewalk, practising with the brakes every time that he came to the curb. By the time he got to the subdivision he was up into third gear again.

The car still wasn't back. He made one circuit around the playing field, not deigning to notice Billy and David and all the other kids staring enviously at his gleaming golden machine. He rode out majestically across the street and up the driveway and around behind the house out of sight. He wasn't about to let David and Billy see him if he fell off her again.

The brakes worked fine. He put the Racer up on her stand right beside the back door. Then he went to look at the T.V. tower again.

He went up the tower and then in through the window a different way this time. It was easier to lean out with his feet still on the bracing and then pull himself in over the windowsill head first. It was quieter too. He stood up in his room. Taffy hadn't heard him this time.

"Come and get me Taffy! I'm up here!"

Getting back out onto the tower from inside was a lot harder. He had to sit on the windowsill with his legs outside and then fall forward without losing his seat until his hands caught the steel strut. Taffy looked on anxiously from the foot of the bed while he practised. He went in and out through the window until he was satisfied. Then he went downstairs and abandoned himself to this newly won solitude.

He was sitting in Dad's armchair flying down the overpass when he heard the Chevy pull into the driveway. He leaned forward to put his hand on Taffy to keep her from running to the door.

"Ssh girl—stay here—"

Taffy looked up at him like she didn't understand. He leaned a little farther so he could whisper in her ear.

"Mom and Dad will see the Racer but they won't know whose it is! Then we'll really surprise them!"

He grinned at Taffy, letting her know that it was a game. Taffy grinned back at him. The engine died. He sat dead still, hearing the car doors close, counting the seconds from the driveway to the back door.

The lock clicked in the silence. The back door squealed ever so slightly. Dad's voice at the back of the house said,

"Hello?"

The silence closed in again. He strained his ears to make out the words when Mom started whispering.

"There's someone in the house John! Ellen—you wait outside—"

"Calm down Marg—there's no one here—Hello?"

He was grinning so hard that his face was starting to hurt! Even Dad sounded nervous! The whispers were even more urgent this time.

"There is someone here!—I can feel them—"

"There's no one here Marg—the house was locked—"

"Then where's the dog? Whose bicycle is that? Come outside John! I'm going next door and call the police!"

"Get 'em girl!"

He whipped around the corner into the kitchen with Taffy in full clamour!

"Hi Mom! Hi Dad! Hi Elly!"

Mom dropped her purse and went up about a foot in the air! Dad's eyes were bugging out of his head! The only one he didn't get was Elly. Elly was behind Mom and Dad, grinning right back at him.

Mom touched down and was she ever mad!

"How did you get in here?! Who's bicycle is that?! What are you doing home in the first place?! Don't you ever do that to me again!!"

"Aw gee Mom—it was just a little joke!"

He looked to Dad. Dad's face was beet red.

"What do you think is so funny about scaring your mother and your sister like that?!"

Dad was really mad too. Elly wasn't scared. But it didn't seem like a good time to mention it.

"Aw gee Dad—I didn't mean to!"

Mom moved in front of Dad, battle formation.

"You'd better have a good explanation young man!"

He grinned again. He just couldn't help it.

"I can explain everything! See—there's this man named Mr. Reale. He's got a drugstore. He wants Dad to come and see him so he can give me a job. I had to get in through the window to get my money to buy the Racer so he'd hire me. Can we go and see him now Dad?"

Mom's eyes were green bonfires! Dad's jaw was sticking out a mile!

"We'll all go and see this Mr. Reale! Right now! Won't we John!"

"Oh yes! We sure will! Go get in the car!"

"Sure Dad!"

Back at the lunch table three quarters of an hour later Mom said,

"I'm still not sure that Nels is mature enough for something like this John . . ."

He looked over at Dad. Dad smiled at him. Dad was proud of him. They both turned to smile at Mom.

"He'll be just fine Honey. You met Jack. He's a fine man. He wouldn't have given Nels the job if he thought that he was too young to handle it. Did you hear what he said about Nels? He said that in all his years in business he'd never met a boy who wanted to work as bad as Nels. I'm not going to discourage that in my son."

"I suppose not John. But—"

"I'll be okay Mom. You heard what Mr. Reale said. It's just delivering to the old people who don't have cars. I don't have to ride on the busy streets. I can ride on the side streets. Some days Mr. Reale said there aren't any deliveries. Then I'll just be in the store. Please Mom?"

Mom smiled. Just a little bit. Then she gave him The Look again.

"I want your promise that you won't go off the sidewalk on that bicycle. And another thing young man—I don't want you climbing on that antennae tower ever again! I want your window locked from now on when we're not home. If you could get in someone else could too! From now on if we go out and you're not with us, I'll leave a key outside where you'll know where it is."

He floated on a cloud of grace. Mom wasn't nearly done yet.

"My Heavens!—I thought you had more sense than that! If you'd have fallen on the cement you would have broken your neck! How do you thank that would have made us feel?"

"I guess I didn't think about that . . ."

"Well you'd better start thinking before you do things like that again! Now you stay off that tower! And you'll not ride that bicycle unless you're riding it on the sidewalk! Do you hear me?"

He looked as sincere as he possibly could.

"Sure Mom. Don't worry—"

"I do worry. And that's not good enough. I want to hear you say it."

"I promise."

"Good! Now eat your lunch."

He uncrossed his fingers under the table and started cramming a sandwich into his mouth.

Dad said

"Don't eat like a dog Nels!"

"I gonna gem to ne mibrary!"

Mom said

"And don't talk with your mouth full!"

He looked over at his sister. Elly was grinning at him again. He opened his mouth and showed her half of a chewed baloney sandwich.

After supper that night he helped Mom with the dishes. When the dishes were done he went to watch the News. It was already started. The News man was saying that they had special footage tonight of the latest Atomic Bomb test when he walked in to the living room. Dad got up from his armchair and said they didn't need to look at that and shut the News off.

Dad was right. He could still see every detail of his first test, inside his head, whenever he shut his eyes and thought about the Bomb. It didn't seem strange to him any more, that he could do that. Everybody had seen the Bomb go off on T.V. He figured that everybody could probably do it too. If they tried.

Dad talked to him for a while about how important school was. He listened politely but it didn't make much sense. Not if the world was going to end. When Mom and Elly came in to watch 'Leave it to Beaver!' he went upstairs and got his homework for the weekend and brought it down to do it on the kitchen table.

There was more homework than he'd ever seen before! He hadn't heard a word in class so he had to figure it all out. From time to time his family laughed on the other side of the wall. He found himself listening to Beaver's dopey voice. He was glad when it was finally over. He wondered while the last of the music played if all of the kids in America were as dumb as Beaver Cleaver.

He just got done his homework when Mom came in and told him to get ready for bed. It was only 9:30! He tried to protest but Mom said he'd been so hard to get up ever since school started that he was going to go to bed early.

He went upstairs glowering. He took some solace in wrestling the dog on the bed. He skipped his prayers, telling himself he'd do it when he was done reading. He took his library book and went to bed. It was a good one, about these guys who went to Venus on a rocketship.

He couldn't read. He kept getting lost. Something was wrong. He put the book down and went chasing after his thoughts, trying to figure out what it was.

It wasn't the Racer. Or even the thought that he'd spent all that money. The Racer was worth it.

He thought about High School but that wasn't it either. School seemed pretty pointless now. But other than that it was just school again. Except that they made you do way more homework in High School.

It wasn't his job either. But he still didn't feel any more like an adult. That was it. He refused to admit to himself that he was still a kid. But his birthday still wasn't until a week from this coming Sunday.

He shut his eyes. The Bomb went off inside his head. He watched the pillar of the fire rage upwards into the phallus of the mushroom cloud, charging his nervous brain with its weird energy. Pastor Billy said it could come any time.

If Jesus came right away he'd never get to have his birthday. If He didn't come by then he'd have to get saved right away before He did. He didn't want to get caught like one of the Foolish Virgins. But he had to do something right now before he went crazy!

He snapped his eyes open, escaping from his vision. The hall light was off. He switched his lamp off and lay still, listening to the silence until he was sure Mom and Dad were asleep. Taffy was asleep on the foot of the bed. He slipped out of bed and ghosted to the window and eased it all the way open without waking her up.

The rain had stopped. The houses slept. Here and there the yellow light of a bedroom lamp still glowed on a curtained window. He braced his elbows on the windowsill and leaned way out, staring around at the night.

The night was alive! He resonated in time to it. The blackness of the playing field sang him a siren's song. Wraiths of mist shone in coloured auras around the shielded bulbs. Every curtained window concealed a mystery!

He glanced up staring as the Moon appeared, a pale silver promise behind a veil of cloud. But even Mr. Kennedy couldn't help him now . . .

The T.V. tower beckoned, Jacob's Ladder glistening with dewdrops. He tasted the first tang of Autumn in the chill night air. He filled his lungs and it was like rocket fuel igniting in the sudden wild yearning to just run!

Then he looked down, at the raised edge of the cement tower pad—

If he fell and broke his neck he'd never get to be fourteen either! If Jesus was going to come tonight it wouldn't make any difference. But—

One by one all of the bedroom lights went out. The adult world slept on oblivious while he dressed and went out the window.

On the Sunday morning which was his birthday, Nels Sorenson awoke behind closed eyelids. He couldn't open them. He could barely breath, feeling around in the sheets with his fingers.

It had to be real this time—he'd go crazy if it was just another dream—

He shoved his eyes open and sat up into the pale early light.

"I made it girl! I'm still here! I'm fourteen!"

Taffy opened one eye and regarded him dubiously. She stretched and sighed in dog's disdain and went right back to sleep.

Reality closed in on him. He stared around at his room, frantically trying to escape bleak shipwrecked certainty—

It was all still the same.

He groaned aloud, closing his eyes on the world as he sank back into his pillow. His hands reach down with a will of their own and drew the blanket up over his head.

He was still there when Mom lifted the blanket back and smiled at him.

"Good morning Honey. Happy birthday."

His anguish was bottomless when she bent to kiss his forehead. He didn't have the will to resist. Mom straightened up and smiled at him again.

"What are you doing still in bed? Did you forget that it's your birthday?"

He looked up pale on the pillow.

"My stomach hurts Mom. I feel real sick."

Mom reached down and put a cool hand on his fevered brow.

"You're not even warm Honey. You don't have a temperature. You'll feel better when you get up and move around. It's time to get dressed for church."

The thought of church was like getting a spear in his guts!

"It really hurts Mom! I don't think I should go to church this morning . . ."

He didn't have to try to look sick. Mom looked concerned.

"Did you go to the bathroom yesterday?"

Just for a second he almost lost it. He fought to keep his brain from exploding coming bolt upright in bed.

"It's not that! I'm sick! I don't want to be sick! It's my birthday! If I have to go to church I'll be sick all day!"

He sank back, exhausted again.

"Please Mom—it's only once! And it's my birthday—"

"Well, I suppose I could stay home with you while your father and your sister go to the service . . ."

Mom was starting to look like she almost liked the idea. He sat up frantically again.

"Oh no Mom! I don't want you to have to miss church!—"

"Well I can't just leave you here by yourself if you're sick—"

"I'll be okay Mom! I mean—I'm old enough to stay home by myself—you can lock the door—I'm just gonna sleep—Please Mom!—"

Mom was looking at him funny. He laid back down and looked sick again.

"Well . . . I suppose if you just want to sleep . . ."

"Yeah Mom! I'm just gonna sleep! Right Now! Can you take Taffy outside?"

He looked around for Taffy. Taffy looked really worried about him. He wanted to let her know he was okay but he wasn't sure if he was.

"All right Honey. You go back to sleep."

"Thanks Mom."

He rolled over and buried his face in the pillow. Mom stroked his hair.

"You'll be all right Nels. I'll look in on you before we leave. Come on Taffy. Let's go outside."

Taffy keened at him anxiously once and hopped off the bed to the floor. He lay still trying not to listen to the familiar sounds of morning. The winds of change were gusting up inside his head.

He knew he was different!—he had to be! He shoved his face into the pillow, trying to shut the house out—

"How come you get to stay home from church?"

He groaned into the pillow.

"Go away Elly. I'm sick."

"I don't believe you! I think you're just making it up so you can stay home! I'm telling Dad!"

Elly hated church. He shoved himself up on one elbow and faced his accuser. Elly was scowling at him beside the bed.

"I am sick. And it's my birthday."

"So what? I didn't get to stay home on my birthday!"

"Just go away! You're not old enough to understand!"

"Well I'm telling Dad anyhow!"

Elly pulled a face at him and flounced out of his room. He shoved his face back into the pillow and thought about church until his stomach really hurt, just making sure.

When Mom came up to tell him they were leaving he pretended he was asleep. He held himself still at the edge of his control until he heard the Chevy pull out of the driveway.

He shot out of bed, the eyes of a blond hurricane blowing frantically through the house searching for something—anything!—that was different! Through Elly's room and down the stairs—scouring the kitchen—staring out through the living room window at the street and it was the same!

He flew down the basement stairs and came face to face with the furnace. They'd lied to him! He stared around in desperation

"Oh shit!"

He fled back up the stairs to the calendar. It had to be a mistake!

It was Sunday, the twenty-third of September. The day he was born. He stumbled into the living room into Dad's armchair and pressed his hands to his head. He wasn't a kid—he couldn't be—

He was 14 years old! He'd been in High School for 3 whole weeks! He had a job and a Racer! He was home alone and not in church for the very first time in his life!

But he wasn't an adult either! The thought of going up to the front and getting saved scared him spitless. He ran the Bomb one more time through his head. It still didn't make sense! No matter what Pastor Billy said!

Mr. Kennedy wouldn't let it happen! They still had to go to the Moon! And besides, how could he do something as important as getting saved when he didn't even know what he'd done wrong?

Nels Sorenson struggled to make sense out of it until his head hurt too much to think about it any more. The silence of the house oppressed him. He was lonely, even with Taffy there at his side. His thoughts took him back to the Sunday mornings of his childhood, remembering how good it used to feel to be in the Worship service . . .

He pushed it away, looking down at his watch. It was eleven o'clock. He got up, restless, burdened with a heavy load. The radio offered a respite. He switched it on, moving across the band, past Elvis Presley and Patsy Cline and coming to rest on the American station.

A deep melodious voice said, "This is Brother Jones, welcoming you all out there this Sunday morning to the radio ministry of the First Black Baptist Church."

The radio swelled into song and it was, "Shall We Gather at the River?"

The black people sounded so happy singing that he wished to God that he would make Pastor Billy black! He turned the volume up loud.

He sang all the hymns while he did a little dance with the dog. When the hymns were over he felt good. He felt even better when he switched off the sermon. Taffy was grinning, spring-loaded to play.

The thought came out of the blue.

"I'm not a kid any more Taffy—I'm an adult! But I'm new at it, so I don't known much about it yet! It's sort of like 'getting a job—'"

Taffy wagged her tail in canine consensus. He chased the thought.

"But if I don't understand it yet then it's too soon to go get saved. Nothing's gonna happen before next Sunday. It didn't happen all summer. I'll figure it out this week and do it next Sunday. But not today! It's my birthday! Come on dog—I'll race you around the yard!"

The rest of his birthday was swell. Mom made blueberry pancakes—his favourite—for lunch. Then he got his presents. There was a knapsack with shoulder straps to carry his homework in and a new pair of gloves for riding the Racer.

But the best present was a book. It was a collection of science fiction stories. Inside the front cover there was a certificate. The

certificate said that he, Nels Sorenson was now a member of the
Doubleday Science Fiction Book of the Month Club and that he would
receive a new book for each month for a whole year!

He was still staring at it when Mom said,

"Do you like your present, Nels?"

He looked up staring at Mom and Dad, still trying to comprehend
it. Mom and Dad were smiling at him.

"It means that I get a new book every month for a whole year?"

"That's right dear."

"Honest?"

Well of course, Nels."

"That's great!"

Mom and Dad knew! He went upstairs in a happy daze wondering
how he could have been in such a panic about the end of the world.
The only answer that he could come up with was it was because he had
still been a kid.

He was unpacking the cigar box onto the top of his dresser when
Mom came in to tell him it was time to go to Aunt Sally's house. Mom
gave him a funny little smile.

"What are you doing, Nels?"

"Oh . . . I thought I'd put my stuff out again. Just for a while. Is it
okay Mom?"

"Yes Honey. It's just fine."

Auntie Sal made fried chicken and corn on the cob and an angel-
food cake for his birthday supper.

That evening in the service he didn't hear a word the Preacher said.
He sat up high in the back of the balcony and studied all the adults in
the rows below him.

If Mom and Dad knew how much time was left . . . .

Pastor Billy raged and thundered in the pulpit. For the first time
he saw how many of the adults weren't listening either. There was some
new awareness tugging at his brain all through the sermon. If the
world was going to end as soon as Pastor Billy said, nobody seemed too
worried about it . . .

He had to have a leak again when the altar call came. He stared across the balcony at Susie Brown until he couldn't have peed with it if he'd wanted to.

He was even more certain that the adults all knew something, standing on the steps with Tommy, seeing them all smiling and talking. It didn't make sense any other way. Even if they were all saved, they had to have friends who weren't saved yet . . .

On the way home in the Chevy, he decided that he would have to think about getting saved for a while before he did it. If it looked like something was going to happen, Mom and Dad would know about it. If it happened before he had figured out what he'd done wrong, he'd get saved anyhow. As long as he watched the older adults carefully, he'd be okay. But other than that, he decided he would do the adult thing and just quit thinking about the Bomb.

There was one uneasy moment, saying his prayers. The thought came unwanted that, maybe by not going and getting saved on his birthday, he was committing the sin of Pride. But that didn't make sense either. Whatever the sin of Pride was, it had to be way more serious than just trying to understand.

As soon as the house was asleep, he dressed silently in his darkest jeans and sweater. He climbed out the window and went down the T.V. tower to the street.

No one in the whole world even knew that he was there! He ghosted invisible from shadow to shadow, drawn to the last lit windows, stalking the Mystery. He didn't see anyone worshipping Satan through the gaps in the curtains. But he saw some things through Mrs. Gregg's bedroom window that made his adolescent blood pound in his head!

When the last light went out he decided he would be Tom Sawyer. It took him a while to find an apple tree to raid, ranging through dark yards and vaulting the fences.

It was two o'clock in the morning when he climbed back through the window, sated with apples and his newly won freedom. He fell asleep with an untroubled mind for the first time since he couldn't remember when.

In the days that followed his birthday Margaret Sorenson smiled at the change which had come to her son. Whatever crisis which had visited him between the beginning of High School and his birthday had passed. If anything he was busier and happier than he had ever been.

In the morning when she went upstairs to waken him his door was always closed. She respected his newly discovered need for privacy. A single knock was sufficient to bring a cheerful if sleepy,

"I'm coming Mom . . ."

His appetite was insatiable. He teased his sister while he devoured his breakfast. There was time for a romp with Taffy each morning before he sped off up the street on his precious Racer.

There were other more subtle signs which only a boy's mother could read. When he went upstairs with Taffy at her heels to make his bed the sheets and the blankets were no longer in their familiar tangle. There was only a single indentation on the pillow to show where he had laid his head down before sleep had claimed him.

The Bible and the rifle disappeared from the bedside. His rifle resided in the closet now for the first time since Walker had given it to him. His Bible found a resting place in the drawer of his bedside table. On the first morning after his birthday, when they were not in their places, she wondered at its significance.

Where his Bible had been, there was always a library book under the lamp. The names of the authors—Asimov, Bradbury, Clarke— meant nothing to her. But her brief maternal perusals brought her a smile, some secret sharing of his lurid imagination. Men in rockets . . . men on Mars . . .

She closed the books each time and wondered if he was getting enough sleep.

He came home ravenous and happy at the end of each day. No matter what the weather was. At the supper table there was some new closeness between father and son which warmed her heart. They were like two men—her men—sharing the weather and the day's work with their meal.

Nels chattered like a magpie between mouthfuls. Mr. Reale who had a whole room filled with books. Miss Johnson, who he thought was beautiful. The new old lady way out on Waterloo Street who had a piranha fish and a cat with two toes missing, from a fishing accident. Each day he brought new stories to the supper table. The only disconcerting thing was the feeling she had that he was as much watching them as she was him.

When supper was over, he didn't watch the News any more. Unless his hero, the handsome young President came on. He seemed to have lost interest. He settled as soon as the dishes were done with his homework spread out on the kitchen table.

Mr. Reale had been to university. Nels Sorenson had decided that he wanted to go to university too. But Mr. Reale said that you had to have really good marks to go there. The mid-term exams began on October 15 and it was almost October already!

The benign influence of the old man at the drugstore seemed to Margaret Sorenson to have filled some void in her son's life which had been there since Walker had passed on. But it was the intensity with which he pursued his new ambition that most surprised her. She thought that a Bomb could have gone off in the kitchen while he was doing his homework and he wouldn't have noticed it at all.

When his homework was done he joined his family for half an hour before bed. He wrestled with Taffy on the living room carpet, oblivious to the television programs. Again the feeling came, turning to find him watching her or John.

"What is it Nels?"

Always he would smile for her.

"It's nothing Mom. I'm just thinking."

He went off to bed early, to read. When she went upstairs to say goodnight his door was always closed. She knocked again.

"Nels? Can I come in?"

"Just a minute Mom . . . okay."

It was a ritual. He was propped up on his pillow with his book laid upside down on his lap and Taffy on top of the blanket beside him, still a boy.

"Goodnight dear."

She leaned forward to brush his proffered cheek with her lips.

"Goodnight Mom."

"Remember—lights out by 11:00."

"Sure Mom."

She went out, closing his door behind her. On her way down the stairs Margaret Sorenson shivered, wondering how he could sleep in a room with the window open.

September vanished into the past, the time flying through the first three weeks of October. He burst into the kitchen out of a rainy Monday afternoon with the marks for his mid-term exam in his hand.

"Mom! I got all A's!"

He babbled happily all through supper. After supper Mom even said that he didn't have to help with the dishes. He was half-way to the back door with his dog when Dad called out to him from the living room.

"Nels—Mr. Kennedy is coming on—"

"Wait girl—I'll be right back—"

He cut a fast U-turn, hoping that it was new news about the space program. Dad was in his armchair. The President appeared on the television screen. He stalled on the carpet halfway across the livingroom, knowing that it wasn't going to be about the space program.

Mr. Kennedy didn't look right. There was something wrong with Mr. Kennedy's eyes. Nels' courage began to crumble as the President started to speak.

"Good evening, my fellow citizens. This government, as promised, has maintained the closest surveillance of the Soviet military build-up on the island of Cuba. Within the past week, unmistakeable evidence has established the fact that a series of offensive missile sites is now in preparation on that imprisoned island. The purpose of these bases can be none other than to provide a nuclear strike capability against the Western hemisphere."

He turned to look at Dad. Dad was leaning forward in his armchair, his eyes nailed to the T.V. screen. The fear came swarming up and he couldn't look at Dad anymore. The stern and righteous voice compelled him back to the dark eyes staring out at him.

"This urgent transformation of Cuba into an important strategic base—by the presence of these large long range and clearly offensive weapons of mass destruction—constitutes an explicit threat to the peace and security of all the Americas."

"We no longer live in a world where only the actual firing of weapons constitutes a sufficient challenge to a nation's security to constitute a maximum peril. Nuclear weapons are so destructive and ballistic missiles are so swift, that any substantially increased possibility of their use or any sudden change in their deployment may well be regarded as a definite threat to peace."

The President paused. The thought struck him a numbing blow—the Communists had tried a sneak attack!

"Our own strategic missiles have never been transferred to the territory of any other nation under a cloak of secrecy and deception; and our history—unlike that of the Soviets since World War II—demonstrates that we have no desire to dominate or conquer any other nation or impose our system upon the people. Nevertheless, American citizens have become adjusted to living daily in the bull's eye of Soviet missiles located in the U.S.S.R. and in submarines. This sudden clandestine decision to station strategic weapons for the first time outside of Soviet soil is a deliberately provocative and unjustified change in the status quo which cannot be accepted by this country, if our courage and our commitments are ever to be trusted again by friend or foe."

"Our unswerving objective, therefore, must be to prevent the use of these missiles against this or any country and to secure their withdrawal or elimination from the Western hemisphere."

"Our policy has been one of patience and restraint, as benefits a peaceful and powerful nation which leads a worldwide alliance. We have been determined not to be diverted from our central concerns by mere irritants or fanatics. But now further action is required—and it is underway; and these actions may only be the beginning."

"We will not prematurely or unnecessarily risk the costs of worldwide nuclear war, in which even the fruits of victory would be ashes in our mouth—but neither will we shrink from the risk at any time it must be faced."

Mom stepped in front of him, blocking Mr. Kennedy.

"I want you to go upstairs and stay with your sister until this is over."

But Mom!—"

"Do as I ask you!"

He stalled, still trying to listen. Mom's eyes were big and scared. Dad was staring with his mouth hanging open.

". . . a strict quarantine on all offensive military equipment under shipment to Cuba.—"

"Go on! Now!"

He turned and sprinted to the top of the stairs and stopped to listen again. Mom turned the sound down. Mr. Kennedy was still speaking but he couldn't hear the words. He sprinted the rest of the way to Elly's room in an agony of indecision. Elly looked over at him from the bed.

"What's the matter Nelsy?"

"Nothing Elly—I'll be right back—"

He stalked down the staircase and flattened his back to the wall beside the living room door.

". . . I call upon Chairman Khrushchev to halt and eliminate this clandestine, reckless and provocative threat to world peace and to stable relations between our two nations. I call upon him further to abandon this course of world domination and to join in an historic effort to end the perilous arms race and transform the history of man. He has an opportunity now to move the world back from the abyss of destruction by returning to his government's own words that it had no need to station missiles outside its own territory and withdrawing these weapons from Cuba—by refraining from any action which will widen or deepen the present crisis—and then by participating in a search for peaceful and permanent solutions."

"My fellow citizens: let no one doubt that this is a difficult and dangerous effort on which we have set out. No one can foresee precisely what course it will take, or what costs and casualties will be incurred. The path we have chosen for the present is full of hazards, as all paths are—but it is the one most consistent with our character and courage as a nation and our commitments around the world."

Mr. Kennedy paused again. He snuck a look around the corner. Mom had her back to him so he couldn't see her face. Dad was praying on his knees on the carpet in front of the pushiest American of them all.

"The cost of freedom is always high—but Americans have always paid it. One path we shall never choose is the path of surrender or submission. Our goal is not the victory of might, but the vindication of right—not peace at the expense of freedom, but both to peace and freedom, here in this hemisphere and we hope, around the world."

"God willing, that goal will be accomplished."

The President disappeared. Nels Sorenson ducked back behind the wall. He squeezed his eyes shut and fought to keep from puking. The voices of the News people were a barely controlled panic saying that the Strategic Air Command was on full alert—

Mom switched the News off. He darted around the wall into the living room, desperate to know. Dad was still praying. Mom turned and saw him there.

"Is everything okay Mom?"

"Yes Honey—everything's fine—it was just a false alarm. Why don't you take Taffy and go outside for a run? Your Dad and I have to have a talk."

Mom was smiling. Mom's voice was the same. Mom's eyes were glassy pools of green terror. She didn't seem to know that the tears streaming down her face were even there.

"Sure Mom . . ."

He turned away, fear freezing into certainty that left him powerless. Taffy was still waiting for him by the back door. He tried to blank his mind out—to pretend it hadn't happened—

"Let's go outside girl."

He opened the door for her and stepped out into the rain, looking up at once at the night sky. The spasm choked him. He staggered across the patio and dropped to his knees, vomiting all over the wet grass.

He gagged and wretched until all that was left was the jagged edge of fear. Taffy cried in the darkness beside him. The night sky menaced him behind his closed eyes. The Rider on the Pale Horse waited on his righteous challenge, just over the southern horizon.

He shoved his eyes open and staggered up, into the house. The silence roared around him. The sickness in his guts hit him again. He stumbled into the bathroom and stalled, face to face with his reflection in the mirror.

His hair was plastered down with rain. His chin was messy with vomit. His eyes—

He had to look away. He couldn't look at what was in his eyes. He wiped his hand across his chin thinking he couldn't let Mom see him like this—he had to get to his room—

He fled from the mirror across the kitchen, peering around the wall. The living room was silent. The television was off. He couldn't look at the television. He heard Mom crying and Dad talking softly to her behind the bedroom door.

He slipped around the corner and ghosted up the stairs, flattening his back to the wall beside Elly's door. He couldn't let Elly see him this scared either. He snuck a look around the door frame. Elly was playing with one of her dolls on the bed. Her back was towards him. He started to shiver.

Elly'd be okay—Elly was still a kid—Taffy came thumping up the stairs behind him. He shot past Elly's door before she knew that he was there.

He stalled, tasting bile, one hand on his door handle, turning to look down at his dog. Taffy stared up anxiously at him from the floor.

Elly was all alone. He stared into the luminous brown eyes of his dog. It hurt worse than anything.

"Elly—call Taffy—"

"Taffy! Come here Taffy!"

"Go see Elly girl. Elly wants to see you."

He opened his door and ducked inside, closing the door on her until it was just the last crack. Taffy cowered, not understanding, alone outside in the hall.

"Go see Elly girl . . . she's all by herself . . ."

"Come here Taffy! Come on!"

He shut the door and sagged against it. He was shivering violently and he couldn't seem to stop. The smell of vomit choked in his nostrils from the front of his shirt. Through the door his little sister's voice came to him from a lost world.

"Oh Taffy—you're all wet! You're shivering too! Didn't Nelsy dry you off? You wait right here. I'll go get your towel and dry you all up nice!"

He waited for an answer. There was only the ringing silence in his head. He stumbled into bed and hugged his knees to his chest. He couldn't close his eyes. The pillar of fire would be waiting for him.

His mind went whirling on out of control until he ran it into the Wall. When Mom and Dad came upstairs to comfort him, he had surrendered consciousness.

And then he was running, heart hammering, searching frantically through a maze of hostile rooms with green walls and gray metal chairs.

"Pastor Billy!"

The hostile rooms reverberated with mocking echoes.

"Pastor Billy!—Pastor Billy!—Pastor Billy!—"

"Oh no!—Oh no!—Oh no!—"

He tried to shut his ears to his own panicked voice. There was only one door left.

He raced to the door and threw it open, staring around at the stage. The balconies and the rows of pews were all abandoned. Pastor Billy was gone—

Then he stared in awe, Pastor Billy forgotten. The Forest shimmered with electric blue fire. He tried to get in. The heat drove him back. He stared in through the flames. The Forest burned with crackling blue incandescence. An Angel watched him from beside the cool saving waters . . .

He felt his mouth form his silent plea. The Angel tried to smile. Big golden tears began to flow down her cheeks. The Angel turned her face away from him.

The flames leaped out at him, sent him staggering backwards. He looked up staring to the twinned crucifixes. The horror struck its talons into his brain.

The holy old suffering Christs were gone! The flames reached the old rugged crosses stained with blood. He watched them smoulder into lurid red smoke, gagging on the good Christian stench of blood, burning—

He leaped clear of the stage and landed running. It was too late. When he burst out through the double oak doors the Bomb went off.

Some benevolent hand reached down from above and switched off the madness in his head. The firestorm dwindled into a tiny dot of white light and went out. He tumbled headlong into the blackness.

For the next four days the world hovered at the edge of a nuclear conflagration. It was consistently there in the catchwords, like a catechism.

"Missile Criis . . . Nuclear War . . . Strategic Air Command . . . Total Retaliation . . ."

He could never clearly remember those days. They were a blur of jagged images.

Mom, trying to smile for him when he came downstairs in the morning. Taffy and Elly watching him, not wanting them to see that he was afraid. Hugging them all at the back door before he left for school, not wanting them to ever let him go. Riding off th school on the Racer, staring anxiously back over his shoulder—

The same strained smiles and frightened eyes on the faces of his teachers. The shocked numbness of the kids in the rows around him shattered in the nightmare wail of a recorded air-raid siren over the P.A. system. Staring out from under his desk at the cruel stupidity of the Duck and Cover drills.

Girls crying in quiet terror on the floor. The big feet of the Principal and the Civil Defense people walking by in the aisle. Boys whispering urgently across the aisles from under the desks until the teacher cracked.

"You boys stop talking! This is serious!"

And they all knew, then, that they were dead.

The brief respite riding to work under the blue sky until the vapour trail of a jet made him block that too. The drugstore, full of adults with haunted eyes, lining up for prescriptions, muttering the catechisms. Mr. Reale, filling vial after vial with little yellow pills counted out from a big glass jar. Mr. Reale didn't look like he was afraid. Mr. Reale looked old and tired and sad somehow. He slung on the satchel, and rode out on the racer, hoping that Mr. Reale and Miss Johnson were saved.

The whispers were everywhere. They were all around him, threading his way through the adults on his way out to the Racer. They were there again in a snatch of conservation passing by—in the frozen faces of a dozen people up the street staring in at the black Russian freighters at sea carrying death on the screens in the appliance store window. They were there in the haunted eyes and silent mouths seen moving as the cars slid inexorably past him. He cowered down onto the handlebars in the thunder of a jet.

Dad prayed for peace in the blessing. He added his fervent Amen in his head but he couldn't look at his supper. When Mom asked him how his day had been he said,

"Okay, I guess."

After that it got awful quiet. Elly kept staring at him. He asked if he could be excused and went out to the lawn with his dog.

Mom came out and asked him if he would keep Elly company for a while. He sat on the bed with Taffy between them, hearing the whisper of News from the bottom of the stairwell. Elly and Taffy were both staring at him.

"What's wrong Nelsy? Why is everybody so scared?"

He forced his gorge down, almost gagging on it.

"It's nothing Elly. It's like church."

He lay awake long into the night with the issue of his salvation looming leviathan-like on the ceiling. His mind searched frantically for a way out while the catechism went on in his head. Nuclear war . . . Armageddon . . . He awoke in the morning with his guts tied in knots. It started all over again.

The breakdown of the Missile Crisis came on the Friday night of that week.

On Friday morning at school there were posters put up with masking tape in the halls. The posters said that a famous American evangelist and Bible scholar would be making a special appearance that night at the High School.

Each poster bore a blown-up photograph of the Good Man, the handsome face with wavy hair and bright penetrating eyes that shone with some inner truth. His lips described a benevolent smile like the mouth of a muscular cherub.

The posters said that the purpose of the Good Man's visit was to explain to all Christian young people the true meaning of the Cuban Missile Crisis. For the first time since Mr. Kennedy's speech, Nels Sorenson saw a glimmer of hope.

He clung to that hope under his desk while the siren wailed. He clung on even tighter after school, riding the Racer in the paranoid traffic. At supper he asked if he could go to a Young People's meeting at the High School. Mom and Dad agreed that it might to him some good, to get out with people his own age for an evening.

He fiddled with his homework for half an hour but he couldn't concentrate. After four days of the whispers and the haunted eyes of the adult world he was more than ready for any adult who could make sense of it. Because it had to make sense—he just didn't know how yet. And if he understood it—He went upstairs and put his homework away and put on his good gray flannels.

Mom said it was going to be cold tonight and to put on a sweater. He said goodbye to his family and his dog and stepped out the front door, into the eye of the hurricane.

Outside, it was a crisp October night. He stopped, looking around, the thought coming that he had not been out through the window since Sunday night. He drew in his breath, filling his lungs with charged oxygen. It was like he'd forgotten to breathe. He stared up into the black pool of diamond stars above the playing field, knowing now that it was the end of the week and it was all a misunderstanding—

Hope swelled into a sheer flood of relief. God wasn't going to destroy the world! Mom and Dad and Elly and Taffy were right there safe on the other side of the door! Just for a moment he turned and stood with his hand on the door handle, wondering how he could have doubted God.

But he had to know. He turned away, still in a state of grace, determined as he walked up the street to find out the truth about the Cold War.

He sat up front with the driver in the empty bus, staring out through the windshield at the flow of Main Street passing by. The familiar landscapes shone surreal, lit up in the bright beam of the headlights.

The driver let him off right in front of the High School steps. There were other kids going in. He followed their backs to the auditorium through the silent halls. It was a big auditorium, slanted forward towards the front like the motion picture theatre he had snuck into once. He stopped in the doorway, watchful and quiet inside, staring up the aisle at the stage.

There was no one on the stage yet. All there was on the stage was a grand piano and a microphone stand. In the subdued light he saw that the hall was more than half full. The strangeness of it touched him, the hushed brooding silence of two hundred teenagers, no one even whispering, all with eyes straight ahead.—

He looked down at his watch. It was two minutes to seven. There was a sudden spasm in his gut and he wondered if he was going to be sick. Someone tapped him on the shoulder.

He turned, looking up into the ravaged face of the gangly red headed man who towered over him. The red headed man's face was horribly scarred with big flaming red pustules of chronic acne. There was something in the yellow eyes that told him he was staring.

"Go inside and find a seat. I'm closing the doors now."

He took off up the aisle to get away from the acne-faced man. He found an empty seat half-way down, on the aisle, in case he had to get up and go to the washroom. He turned to sneak a look towards the back. The acne-faced man was standing with his arms folded in front of the closed doors.

He looked around, at the kids in the row beside him. He felt it then, that they were all scared, all silent, all staring straight ahead. He pressed his back into the seat and sucked in his breath and closed his eyes.

"I'm not scared—"

The piano played a terrifying run of chords. He shoved his eyes open staring up at the four pretty blond ladies in long white gowns on the stage. They parted their red lips and sweetly sang,

"On a hill far away
Stood an old rugged cross—"

He clapped his hands to his head and doubled forward, protecting his gut, trying to block them out. They sang the words to the first verse. A new voice came, over the microphone. It was a lunatic voice from a children's program.

"Hello there, boys and girls!"

The piano played the melody softly in the background. The angelic quartet hummed the harmonies. He snapped his eyes up, staring at the Evangelist smiling out at them from the stage.

"I know that you are all afraid. You don't have to be afraid. Jesus doesn't want you to be afraid. He's coming soon, to put an end to all this trouble. I'm not afraid. I know that if He comes tonight, my soul is washed in the blood that He shed for all of us. I know that He will take me to those mansions in the sky."

"The True Christian has nothing to fear. But if any one of you here tonight is still afraid, then you're not saved. You're not walking hand in hand with the Saviour. Your soul has not been truly cleansed with Jesus' sacred blood."

"Boys and girls—I plead with you—Jesus is knocking at your hearts' door. Oh—won't you open up and let Jesus come in?"

The pain in his guts made him grind his teeth together. The music went on like a dirge for the human race. The Evangelist radiated love on the stage. His voice came again, infinitely caring and concerned.

"The hour of final reckoning is at hand. Jesus is going to come like a thief in the night. You may never have another chance to decide for Salvation. Those missiles may already be up in the sky, bringing the fires of Armageddon—"

The music stopped. The Evangelist raised his eyes to the projection room, looking for a sign. It wasn't God who threw that fucking braker!

The auditorium was plunged into total blackness. A girl screamed hysterically somewhere behind him. He rocked back, clapping his hands to his ears as a mass of screams erupted into bedlam all around him. The boy beside him was clawing and falling over his legs, trying to get out. The Evangelist was suddenly illuminated by a shaft of silver light from the projection room.

He stared up at him past the black silhouette of the boy half splayed across his legs. The screaming died away into the crying of terrified children in the night. The Evangelist was still smiling!

"I'm here boys and girls. Jesus is up here with me. He's waiting for you to come to Him and ask Him to take all your fear away. Don't turn your back on him tonight. Think of how Jesus will feel when He comes back and you are not saved. Think about how your Mom and Dad will feel when they are taken and you are left behind . . .

The ladies' quartet began to sing 'Just as I am—'. Something snapped inside his head.

"Oh—won't you come up to the front?"

He kicked out blindly at the boy sprawled across his legs. There was a sharp cry of pain and his legs were free. The screaming rose up all around him.

His legs were like rubber when he tried to stand up. His mind was one featureless terrified purpose. He stumbled out into the aisle, colliding off the black shapes streaming into the aisle fighting to stay on his feet. The strains of the hymn flickered in and out of his mind, distant and remote from the screaming shoving mass of young sinners all around him. He surrendered himself to it, swept along inexorably to his salvation.

There were dim lights ahead and adults cutting into the panicked herd. He was sheared off into a knot of other boys and they were going away from the stage and they surged out through double doors into the antiseptic light of an empty hallway. The doors banged shut behind them. They stopped as one.

The face of the boy beside him was pasty white and streaked with tears in the sudden silence. He wheeled around looking for the smiling Evangelist to save him. It was the acne-faced man!

The acne-faced man opened the door into a classroom.

"Who wants to get saved first?"

He was inside the doorway before anyone else could move. He heard the door click shut. He kept his eyes on the floor when the big man clamped one hand on his shoulder and steered him up the aisle to the front. The terror roared in his head!

"Get on your knees boy."

The acne-faced man shoved him down to his knees, standing right in front of him beside the teacher's desk. He squeezed his eyes shut, horror struck.

"Say after me boy—Jesus I am a wretched sinner unworthy of thy love. Come into my heart and make it yours and cleanse me of my sin."

The words went gibbering off inside his head. He still didn't know what his sin was.

"I didn't mean it—"

His throat locked tight. He couldn't speak. He let it all go and opened it up to Jesus.

"That's it boy. You're saved now."

A hand intruded under his armpit and pulled him roughly up onto his feet. Another hand clamped his arm and held him upright when he staggered. He kept his eyes squeezed shut, loathing the touch of hands half-dragging him towards the door in a newly rising panic. He snapped his eyes open in the click of the lock, staring up into the horrific face in the open doorway and it was too soon!—Jesus hadn't come yet! He was still afraid!—

The acne-faced man looked past him with dreamy yellow eyes.

"Next . . ."

The boy who was crying came forward in a rush. The acne-faced man caught his shoulder and drew him inside. The door closed in his face.

The shock wave reached him. He turned to look at the other boys, unable to make sense of it.

"He didn't come! It didn't work!"

They were all staring at him. The nearest boy began to back away from him. Some nameless terror leapt out at him, reflected in their eyes.—

He whirled away and took off running, the slap of his feet echoing out off the lockers. There was a fire door ahead at the far end of the corridor. He hit it flat out, taking the bar with his hip, crashing the steel door against the outside wall and racing off up the street with the fire alarm pealing danger through the school in his wake.

He shoved it away from him, chasing the bus up the street to the bus stop. The driver looked at him funny but he didn't know why until he asked him for his ticket and he'd forgotten. The bus was warm and empty and safe. It was hard to walk when the bus pulled away. He went lurching down the length of it. He let himself fall into the last row of seats, sliding over until he was pressed against the wall below the window.

He'd be okay. He'd be home soon. Main Street soothed him. The bus ride home was a blur. He walked home from the bus stop feeling incredibly light, drifting along past the houses that were all the same. He came up the driveway past the Chevy and stopped under the light at the back door.

The lawn sparkled with frost at the edge of the patio. He drew in his breath, filling his lungs with the chilled night air. His mind was clear as glass. He opened the back door and walked in through the kitchen and stopped, staring up at the clock but it didn't make sense. The clock said that it was only twenty-five after seven—

He remembered somehow that he had been somewhere else at two minutes to seven. But he didn't know where he'd been . . .

The television was chattering away happily in the living room. Mom and Elly and Dad were all sitting on the couch watching a family program. Taffy was there on the floor. They all turned to stare at him when he stopped in the doorway.

"Hi Mom. Hi Dad. Hi Elly."

His words felt incredibly light. Mom was getting up and coming towards him and he wondered if he had to go get stitches.

"Are you all right Nels?"

"I don't know . . ."

"What happened to you Honey?"

Mom was talking to him gently now, like she did when he had to get stitches. He searched his mind. It was clear as glass.

"I don't remember . . ."

"Didn't you go to the Young People's meeting?"

There was a distant alarm ringing somewhere but that was all.

"I got scared and I came home. I'm going to go and lay down now."

"Do you want me to come upstairs with you?"

"It doesn't matter."

They were all there in the room with him. He wondered why he felt like he was all alone.

He turned away and drifted up the stairs. He remembered to take off his shoes. He lay down on top of the bedspread with his clothes on and pulled the spare blanket up over his head. It was warm and dark and safe under the blanket. He'd be okay. He'd just go to sleep. Everything would be okay again when he woke up in the morning. His last thought was that if he could get back to the Forest, God would be waiting for him there.

He awoke, suspended, eyes opening in the blackness under the blanket. He pulled the blanket away from him and sat up in the darkness, wondering why he was still dressed and why he was sleeping on top of the bedspread. The house was silent. He knew it was late. Taffy wasn't on the bed but she sometimes slept with Elly.

The silence made him restless. There was some strange energy coursing through him. He slipped out of bed and opened the window. There was something outside in the night. It drew him out onto the windowsill in his stockinged feet—

He let himself go, falling forward onto the antenna tower, feeling the cold of the metal in his fingers and his toes. He climbed half-way down and dropped clear, suddenly wary, landing on all fours on the brittle grass like a crab and scuttling sideways into the shadow of the house. He stared around the corner.

The adults from all of the houses were all standing out on their lawns. They all had rifles. They were all frozen, fixed and staring like zombies with bleak unseeing eyes. They were all facing towards the playing field.

He turned to look for Mom and Dad but they weren't there. Some distant alarm began to ring, very faint and far away in his head. He stared back at the neighbours' faces, lit up in the glow of the streetlights. They all had the same livid red welt from the bridge of the nose to the top of the forehead. His eyes followed the direction of their bodies into the playing field.

He felt it then, the cold stare of intelligence. There was something watching him—something in the playing field—

He sprinted across the street, flattening against the front corner of the house which flanked the entrance. He peered around the corner and It was there again, waiting for him and It could still see him—

He ducked back into cover. The ringing in his head was louder now and there was danger. He whipped around the house and sprinted flat out down the length of the yard into the playing field, throwing himself prone in the blackness and rolling over and over until he stopped, knowing that It could not know where he was now. The blackness rang in the silence around him, knowing he should run for his life.

He slipped to his feet, feeling the hair prickle on the back of his neck. He couldn't run away—he had to know—he crept forward, trembling, stalking it to Its hiding place in the middle of the field—

And then It was there, waiting for him in the blackness, something so incredibly old and evil that the scream froze in his throat!

He turned and ran, fleeing for his sanity from the gibbering horror at his heels, frantically trying to cry out to Mom and Dad!—to God!—to anyone who could save him!—

He was almost to the entrance when the streetlights all went out. Something caught his ankle and he was falling—

The Russian missile ships went home. The News people said that President Kennedy had made the world safe again for Democracy. Pastor Billy said that God had made John F. Kennedy His Chosen Warrior, to give the world one last chance to come to salvation. The adult world forgot the Cuban Missile Crisis as quickly as possible, as though it had been a very bad dream.

Nels Sorenson tried to forget about it too. There was still the News and Pastor Billy and the thunder of jets passing in the night. It still didn't make any sense.

But he didn't go out the window anymore. He slept at night with the window locked and the lamp turned on on the bedside table.

Some nights he awoke to the thunder of jets, listening to the silence of the house when they had passed, knowing Jesus had come, too rigid with fear to go down the stairs and discover Mom and Dad's empty bed.

Most nights, the Demon that lived in the playing field pursued him through his dreams.

1963: TRADITIONAL VALUES REVISITED

*T*he final period on Tuesday afternoon was History, with Miss Pendergrast. The clock on the classroom wall said ten past three. The teacher's back was turned to the class as she covered the blackboard with fine spidery handwriting. Miss Pendergrast was a drab old woman with a head full of dried up facts, like dead flies. She had a talent for making them even less interesting.

Nels Sorenson edged his desk a little closer to the wall. He turned away from the Spanish conquest of the New World, staring out through the second storey window beside him into the brooding November sky.

A mass of cloud lowered down over the city, leaden gray and swollen with the promise of the first snowfall. Below, in the street, the cars had their headlights on. The tips of the bare branches of the maple trees seemed to melt into the watery twilight.

He stared out past the trees, gauging the sullen density of the cloud, restless with a rising anticipation. It was going to be a beauty of a storm! If it would just hold off until he got off work at the drugstore.

"Nels!"

He swung around, caught, staring up at the old spider glaring at him from in front of the blackboard.

"Yes Ma'am?"

"I asked you a question!"

"Yes Ma'am. Uh . . . could you repeat the question, please?"

There were snickers and giggles in the rows beside him. Miss Pendergrast's face got even longer.

"I asked you to tell the class how many Conquistadores were with Cortes when he landed in the New World!"

His mind went blank. Every face in the classroom turned to stare at him. The Principal's voice over the Public Address system saved him.

"May I have your attention please?"

He broke eye contact with Miss Pendergrast, grateful for the diversion. Every face in the class turned to stare obediently at the intercom. The metal grilled speaker was silent. He ignored it, ransacking his memory for the answer before the announcement was over. He almost had it when the Principal said,

"I have just been informed that the President of the United States of America has been shot and killed by an unknown assassin. I repeat—President John F. Kennedy is dead."

The words snagged in his brain, sharp talons dragging him up through the surface into bright shiny terror. His heart began to hammer in his chest.

"President Kennedy was shot earlier today as his motorcade proceeded through Dallas Texas. He was pronounced officially dead at 1:36 p.m., Dallas time. The forces of the Strategic Air Command have been placed on full alert—"

The voice broke and left him hanging above the abyss. Until the Principal said,

"God help us. We will observe a moment of silence for the fallen President."

He closed his eyes and bowed his head and tried to think of a prayer. The thought came racing in on him instead, that God's Chosen Warrior was dead—that God had done nothing to save him—

Mary Brown began to whimper softly in the seat behind him,

"Oh please no . . . oh please no . . ." over and over again. He squeezed the heels of his hands into his head and fought to keep the madness from taking him.

Then the awe-filled truth swept everything else away with the power of Revelation.

Satan had killed President Kennedy! The final battle with the Evil Empire had begun! There was no one left to save them!

The knowledge made him numb. He opened his eyes to the final act of the Mystery, knowing that he was damned. His schoolmates' stricken faces imprinted themselves in his memory.

The disembodied voice over the loudspeaker began again, the Principal's words mingling in eerie counterpoint to the whimpering in the seat behind him. He fought to shut Mary out, clinging to what the Principal said in the last desperate hope of sanity.

"Classes will be dismissed at the end of this announcement. All activities scheduled for after school hours are cancelled. I ask all of you to leave the building in an orderly manner. Please don't panic. Go directly home to your families and wait for further developments. That is all."

The speaker went dead. No one moved. An air raid siren began to wail. It was inside his head.

The school bell rang and shattered him. The adrenalin rush sent him surging across the front of the classroom past Miss Pendergrast, a broken gray doll propped against the desk, throwing the door open out in to the hallway with the classroom erupting behind him.

The front staircase opened beside him. He took the stairs three at a time sprinting flat out across the lobby, bursting open the steel and glass doors. He stalled on the steps, staring up into the sky, searching for the trails of fire that were the banners of Armageddon.

Big white snowflakes came tumbling down around him. He stared at them, mesmerized, knowing that they were not the same. Then the terror leaped out at him as the doors burst open behind him.

He fled into the suddenness of the storm with the darkness closing in around him. The Racer appeared in front of him. He yanked it clear and swung up onto it, spinning the back tire with his first lunge. The treads slipped, balancing on a fine edge when it hit him—he had to warn Mr. Reale!

He shot out of the parking lot into the slow traffic, the snowflakes blurring by him like white tracers in the sudden glare of headlights, oblivious to the cold clinging wetness through his thin cotton shirt and on his face and his hands.

His terror was a live thing, waiting in ambush in every fleeting shadow. He fled through the traffic with the adrenalin ringing in his brain, whipping himself past the cars spinning helplessly in the intersections. Around him the sky was falling.

The drugstore loomed up out of the wall of snow. He took the curb feeling the wheels going out from under him, leaping clear and landing running with the Racer skidding away on the snowy sidewalk. He hurled himself through the door almost knocking Miss Johnson down.

"Watch out Nels!—"

"Where's Mr. Reale?"

"He's in his office. What's happened?"

"They killed Mr. Kennedy!"

Then he was running flat out again down the length of the store with the knowledge exploding in his brain that Jesus had already been there and taken Mr. Reale—

He caromed off the counter racing his panic up the corridor across the back of the store.

"Mr. Reale!"

He burst through the office door into the front of the desk, unable to go any farther. Mr. Reale looked up at him from his chair on the opposite side. He sagged against the desk panting with in terror.

"Mr. Reale—"

"Yes Nels? What is it?"

"They've killed him—they've killed Mr. Kennedy—"

"Yes son. I know."

The bright blue eyes regarded him calmly. Across the desk, the terror peaked inside of his head.

"You don't understand! The Devil killed him! It's Armageddon! I gotta get home before Jesus comes! I gotta say goodbye to my Mom and Dad—"

"Jesus isn't coming today Nels. There isn't going to be a nuclear war. Not now. Not ever. Armageddon is just a story they made up to frighten you. Your folks are safe. The telephone is right here. Would you like to call them?"

Mr. Reale lifted the telephone from where it sat, leaning across the desk to place it in front of him.

"You're safe Nels. Believe me. The world isn't going to end."

He stalled, stunned, caught by the old man's stillness. The terror swirled around him, urging him to run!

"But—Mr. Kennedy saved us last year when they tried to attack us! I saw him on T.V.! And Pastor Billy said Mr. Kennedy saved us too! He said that Mr. Kennedy was God's Chosen Warrior! And now he's dead!

"I'll bet Pastor Billy told you that the Russians were all devils too."

"Yes Sir—that's what he said!"

"Tell me Son . . . do you believe everything that Pastor Billy says?"

"But he's a Preacher! And the people on the News said it too!"

"What did they say?"

"They said that Mr. Kennedy saved the world for Democracy!"

He saw the flicker of something in the old man's eyes, like winter lightning. Then it was gone. The clear blue eyes looked inside of him.

"Do you know what democracy means, Nels?"

"Well . . . no Sir . . ."

"It means that you have to think for yourself. Do you think that God would destroy His own Creation?"

"Well no Sir—but—I don't know what to believe any more—"

Mr. Reale leaned forward towards him across the desk.

"Listen to me carefully son. If you really believe that God would allow one man to destroy his creation just to prove that he was right, then God is dead. Either that or God really is the monster that your Pastor Billy and every other fanatic since that madman who wrote those letters on the Isle of Patmos have made him out to be."

Mr. Reale sat back and smiled at him.

"God isn't a monster, Nels. It's only men who become monsters. And God isn't dead, son. It's Jack Kennedy that's dead."

His frustration peaked.

"But I don't understand! Why would they say all of those things if they weren't true?"

"It's a game, Nels. They were trying to trick you."

"A game?"

Mr. Reale nodded his head. His incredulity ignited into a flash of white, hot rage.

"A game? I've been having nightmares for a whole year! What kind of a game is that?!"

Mr. Reale got up from his chair and came around the desk towards him. Nels swung his body around to face him, fists clenched, every fibre of his being demanding to know.

The old man stopped in front of him, the blue eyes that looked inside of him acknowledging what he saw there.

"It's the oldest game in the world, son. The game of one man trying to impose his will on everyone else. It's been going on ever since Cain slew Abel."

"Jack Kennedy wasn't God's Chosen Warrior. He was just a man. The devil didn't kill him either. His own people did, because he was dangerous. In any case, it's over. You're safe now."

The rage fell away and left him shivering in the presence of the Mystery.

"It's so cold . . . so cold . . ."

Yes son. I know. That's why they call it the Cold War. Here . . . Come and sit in my chair by the heater and get warm. Let me help you . . . You're safe now. You've had a bad scare, that's all . . ."

Gentle hands guided him to the chair. He sank down into it, leaning forward towards the heat. He pressed the palms of his hands over his eyes. The bomb wasn't there any more.

"I'll be right back son. I'm just going to get my coat and put it around you."

From the doorway he heard Miss Johnson's voice, quiet and concerned.

"Is he all right Jack?"

"Yes, I think so."

"His eyes, when he came in—can I do anything to help?"

"He just needs to sit quietly for a bit and get warm. He's in shock I think, but he's made of good stuff. I'm going to stay with him for a while, until I'm sure that he's all right. The bastards!—I'm sorry Evelyn. Is there anyone out front?"

"No. I don't think there will be now. It's snowing so heavily I can barely see the street."

"Would you go out and bring his bicycle in? If anyone comes in for a prescription, ask them to wait until I'm free. Perhaps I could borrow your coat to take him home. I'll do his deliveries after we close the store."

"Of course Jack. I can look after the store until you get back. I'll go and bring his bike inside."

He heard the click of the door closing, felt the weight of the coat draped over his shoulders. He sheltered in the quiet darkness behind his closed eyes.

"Are you all right son?"

"I—I can't stop shaking—"

"Just relax and let it go. There's no hurry. You've got all the time in the world now."

Gradually the tremors began to recede. He took his hands away from his face and sat back slowly, his sentence of eternal damnation lifted by the rifle shot in the distance. He opened his eyes.

The world returned in the soft glow of the desk lamp. He stared into the tangible colours of the bindings of the books piled up in the pool of lamplight, coming to land in the wake of a life threatening storm, knowing that he was changed.

"Are you all right Nels?"

He raised his head, bringing his eyes to bear on the white haired old man watching him from the other side of the desk.

"Are you all right son?"

He thought about it for another minute.

"Yes Sir. I'd like to go home now."

"Evelyn said that she'd lend you her coat. I'll put your bike in the trunk of my car. We can go by the school. There should be someone there. You can get your coat. Are you sure that you're all right?"

He stood up, testing his legs, feeling some strange new energy coursing through him.

"Yes Sir. I think I'm okay now."

"Good."

He came around the desk and stopped, at attention, staring deep into the old man's eyes.

"Mr. Reale?"

"Yes Nels?"

"How will I know if they're lying to me again?"

The old man looked thoughtful for a moment.

"I can't tell you that, son. You'll have to learn to decide that for yourself. That's the responsibility you have to assume when you live in a democracy. We all do."

"But I will tell you this—if any man threatens you with violence in the name of God, God has nothing to do with it. Whether it's a preacher or a President or a mad man in the street. Have you got that Nels?"

"Yes Sir. I won't forget."

"Good."

"There's one more thing . . ."

Mr. Reale paused. There was a far away look in his eyes, as if he was remembering. He smiled and laid a friendly hand on the shoulder of the young man standing in front of him.

"If anyone ever promises to give you the moon . . . Well . . . it's like my Dad used to say; 'Don't put it in your mouth, son. It's horse shit!'"

"Yes Sir. I'll remember that too."

"Good. Let's go then, shall we?"

The snow had begun to change to rain by the time they reached the High School. Mr. Reale waited for him in the parking lot. He climbed the steps, wearing Miss Johnson's red coat.

The front doors were unlocked. The clock in the lobby said it was ten past four. Nels Sorenson stared at it for a moment, the image coming clear in his mind's eye of his classmates' stricken faces, an hour and an eternity ago. They stayed with him through the empty echoing corridor to his locker, smouldering in his brain.

He came back out carrying the red coat on his arm, feeling like the ancient Inca in the story, who held one of the white foreign gods under water and discovered that he drowned.

Mr. Reale dropped him off in the driveway. He wheeled the Racer around to the back door and carried it down to the basement. Mom was waiting for him when he came back up the stairs.

"Hi Nels."

"Oh hi Mom."

"You're home early. Didn't you go to work today?"

"Mr. Reale drove me home, because of the storm."

Mom smiled at him.

"He's an awfully nice man."

She hesitated, watching him closely.

"I guess you've heard about President Kennedy."

"Yeah Mom. They told us at school. I think I'll take a hot bath before supper. I've got a bit of a chill."

That was all he said.

At supper that night, Dad said a prayer for the soul of John F. Kennedy. He kept his eyes down on his plate, not closing them.

When the blessing was over, Dad looked around the table.

"Would anyone mind if I took my plate into the living room and watched the News?"

The hurt and anger in his mother's voice took them all off guard.

"For Heaven's sake John—leave it off! It's bad enough that they have to shoot their own President without them having to make a spectacle out of it for the whole world to see!"

Mom shoved her chair out and went to stand by the stove with her back to them. He could tell by the way that her shoulders were shaking that she was crying. He got up from the table and went to her, to comfort her.

"Are you okay Mom?"

Mom turned to face him, the sorrow of Irish mothers for all their sons in her green eyes behind her tears.

"I don't know why you men have to keep killing each other . . ."

Then Dad was there, holding her. Nels went to the table and sat back down with his sister, who was still a kid.

"It's okay, Elly. It's going to be all right. He can't scare us any more."

When supper was over and the dishes were done, he took Taffy outside and then he took her upstairs. He undressed quickly and climbed into bed. He was asleep as soon as his head touched the pillow.

He awoke in the small hours, instantly clear. There was no sound of the heavy rain that had been falling when he went to bed. The luminous dial of his wristwatch told him it was 3 o'clock. He lay still for a moment, listening to the hum of the furnace through the hot air register, knowing that his family were all safely asleep.

He sat up in bed and looked out the window. The rain had washed all the snow away. The houses slept, window eyes closed tightly shut. There were haloes of mist under the helmets of the streetlights.

His eyes ranged into the blackness of the playing field. His gut constricted into a knot. He turned away from the window and slipped out of bed.

He went to the closet and dressed in his night clothes. He lifted the rifle from the place where it waited, caressing the barrel and the polished wood of the stock. He took the box of ammunition from the dresser and slipped it into his pocket, intent on murder. He carried the rifle to the window.

Taffy woke up at the foot of the bed to the sound of the window opening. He stopped to pet her, to let her know that it was all right. He whispered to her,

"It's okay, girl. Yeah, you're a good girl . . ."

She watched him anxiously as he climbed out onto the T.V. tower. He looked back into her big brown eyes, stretching to lift the rifle out after him. He paused for a moment, wanting to explain it to her.

"Well dog—I guess if God had of wanted it to be light all the time, He wouldn't have made it get dark. Would He."

He lifted the rifle clear and slung the strap across his shoulder. Then he went down the tower to the ground.

He shot the streetlight out in front of the house. The flash of electric blue fire mirrored the cold blue flame of his determination.

Nothing moved in the wake of his first shot. He loaded the rifle again and dumped the rest of the ammunition into his hand. He raised his hand to his mouth, tasting the flat metal taste of the slugs on his tongue.

He turned away from the playing field, looking up the brightly lit street at the crescent curving away ahead of him. He began to run.

The next streetlight came up fast. He sighted it in, firing from almost directly beneath it. He was already reloading before the tinkle of glass sounded on the concrete behind him.

He went racing around the crescent, hurling his challenge at the Demon in the darkness. One by one the streetlights all went out.

And then he was back in front of the neighbour's house. There was only one streetlight left. He stopped, sighting it in, aiming his body at the entrance to the playing field.

The last light bulb exploded into blue fire. The image of it imprinted itself on his retinas. He loaded another round in the total blackness while he waited for his eyes to adjust. The blue flame that burned in his mind was as cold as the glaciers.

The Demon was waiting for him. His last thought was to wonder if Walker could see him from Up There.

"YAAAAH!!!"

He charged into the blackness, fuelled with a killing rage. He raged up and down the playing field with the rifle at the ready, quartering back and forth, completely intent on finding his Demon and slaying it.

Until his sudden epiphany—that he had vanquished it—even if it had never really been there at all—

He sank to his knees and laid the rifle down, trembling with a wild exultant joy. Then he looked up and he saw how beautiful the stars were.

In the morning he awoke reborn. The sun was well up into the sky. He looked at his watch. It was 10 o'clock. He rose and dressed, savouring the change.

He came down the stairs, wondering if the images in his mind of his run in the night were the fabric of a dream. Mom was talking on the telephone.

"Morning Mom."

"Oh hi Nels. Look Sal, I'll call you back. Nels is up."

He smiled at Mom on his way to the bathroom.

"Hi Auntie Sal."

"Nels says 'Hi'. What? No, I let him sleep in—"

He closed the bathroom door on their conversation, moving to stand in front of the mirror, studying the change in the blue eyes looking back at him.

"Yeah . . ."

When he came into the kitchen Mom was layering bacon into the cast iron frying pan. He went to stand beside her in front of the stove.

Mom looked different somehow too, although he wasn't sure how. But the smile in her green eyes was the same as it had always been.

"Good morning Honey. Are you hungry?"

"Yeah Mom. I'm starving. How come you didn't call me for school?"

"I did once, but I couldn't wake you. I thought it might be best just to let you sleep. This business of Mr. Kennedy getting killed has got everybody all upset. How about you?"

"No Mom, I'm fine. I had the best sleep last night that I've had for a long time."

"Well that's good. You look fine this morning. I guess you should. You were asleep by 7 o'clock. Did you sleep right through?"

"I woke up once, about 3 o'clock. But I went right back to sleep."

Mom frowned, the way she did when she was thinking about something.

"You didn't hear anything outside when you woke up, did you?"

"No Mom. Why?"

She turned to check on the bacon.

"There was a policeman at the door, first thing this morning. Someone shot out all the streetlights in the middle of the night. He was going to all the houses, asking if anybody had seen anything. The neighbours are all upset. Especially after—you know . . ."

He slipped his arm around Mom's waist and leaned in close to give her a big Walker kind of a wink.

"I think it was the Russians!"

2012:
NOTE FROM THE AUTHOR

Looking for God in the Forest is a novel in 70,000 words. It is a coming of age novel written for and about the baby boom generation. It is the story of Nels Sorenson, a Baptist kid from a blue collar family growing up in Canada in the years between 1952 and 1963.

It is a book about the nature of God. It is a book about the nature of violence. It is about the blending of these two in Nel's hyperactive imagination, in his escalating awareness of the Cold War and the apocalyptic fervour of the Evangelical movement. It is historically accurate.

Nels Sorenson's adolescent crisis, like that of his generation, is the anxious dread that the world is going to end before he is old enough to understand it.

R.D. Burkholder
April 21, 2012

Edwards Brothers Malloy
Oxnard, CA USA
June 20, 2013